The Heir

to the

North

Steven Poore

www.kristell-ink.com

Paperback ISBN 978-1-909845-89-3

Cover art by Jorge Luis Torres
Cover design by Ken Dawson
Typesetting by Book Polishers

Kristell Ink

An Imprint of Grimbold Books

4 Woodhall Drive
Banbury
Oxon
OX16 9TY
United Kingdom

www.kristell-ink.com

For Harriet & Oliver

and

Holly & Jack

Prologue

ORCERY TORE THE castle to pieces around him.

Baum had no time to dodge the stones falling from above. They thumped onto his back and his shoulders, unbalancing him as he took the steps two at a time. They rattled off his helm and he staggered and slipped, bracing himself against a wall he knew could give way at any moment. The low, primal roar that shook the stones and clawed through his bones underpinned everything.

It could not overcome the raw screams of terror that echoed from below.

Thin streams of energy trailed around him, seeking him blindly as he climbed. Translucent tendrils burned as they touched him, searing his skin and scorching his clothing, raising sparks from his armour.

If this was the very edge of the warlock's rage, then Baum dared not imagine what it was doing to those left below in the Great Hall. The screaming told enough of a tale.

His entire world jerked, dragged a few degrees awry, and he fell onto the spiralling stairs, calloused palms broken open on the edges of the stones, his breath torn away.

A high-pitched cry of agony. He would not have recognized it, if the sound of her voice had been less precious to him.

Aliciana.

Not even the Queen, he realised, numbed by the scale of Malessar's wrath. Not even she would be spared. A vision rose into his mind: the first time he set eyes on her, a beauty blazing in the morning on the ramparts above Caenthell's gates. He had carried that moment in his thoughts ever since. Now it was overlaid, horribly, with what he knew would be the last time he would ever see her. Rising slowly from her throne, her smile frozen and cracking into terror, the colour drained from her skin, one arm outstretched as if to ward off the approaching danger.

This is how I am repaid? Malessar's fury assailed the senses of all present, driving many to their knees. *With treachery?*

Baum fled the Great Hall then. And the warlock had unleashed a vicious torrent of magic upon the castle.

He didn't understand. What had the High King done to provoke Malessar's wrath? The warlock had been their ally for a decade – had helped Jedrell in his plans, advised him in his steady conquest of the Northern territories. Baum had been there when the two men – the two most powerful men in all of Hellea, they were called – when they stood on the high peaks above Caenthell, surveying the kingdom below, discussing how to move against the ancient, impregnable fortress. They had shared hot wine; they had laughed and jested, and divided the world between them.

With treachery?

But Jedrell was an honourable man. An ambitious man surely, even a brutal man at times, but treacherous? Baum could not think it of him.

The top of the stairs, at last. Baum staggered as the tower shook. He didn't have long, he was certain Malessar's fury would topple the structure soon. He might have to find a different way back down, if he survived that long.

The door hung ajar in its twisted frame. He heard two voices in the room beyond, one sobbing, the other the frightened wail of a child. He barged through the door and cast about quickly for the infant.

The wet nurse huddled on the floor by the crib, her eyes wide with terror, pleading with him to save her. But his attention was focused on the bundle in her arms – the most important person in the castle now. The most important person in his life. His sworn duty. He had failed to protect his liege, down there in the Great Hall. Now there was only one part of his oath to fulfil.

Even as he ripped the child – the High King now – from the nurse's arms he was looking desperately around the room for something, anything, that he could use to speed his flight from the awful rage below. But the nursery was sparely furnished: only the crib and the nurse's own pallet lined the walls, while the table and two chairs in the middle of the room were useless to him. That left the thick woollen curtain that had been pulled across to prevent the night's chill touching the room.

It was as insane a thought as he had ever had, and he could only pray the tower would fall in the right way, but there was nothing else to work with . . .

Hands tugged his shirt, pulling him back. He tore away, backing towards the curtain, and the wet nurse fell to her knees.

"Please, sir! Save me! For Pyraete's sake, save us both!"

She was young, a distant cousin of the Queen, he understood. Their resemblance usually tugged at his heart. But even so, he already had little chance of living through the night.

A resounding crack, then a rumble from deep underneath. There was no more time.

"I cannot," he said simply. Pushing her away, he leapt through the curtain to the small balcony outside. The world tilted madly to one side as he moved.

The tower was coming down – the warlock's fury had ripped the foundations, from the ground. Baum was assaulted by tiles sliding from the roof. They smashed into his head and back as he shielded the child in his arms. His stomach lurched as his field of vision wheeled and the castle's curtain walls surged upward to collide with the tower.

He had only one chance, but judging the right moment was impossible with the stones flying apart around him. There was no time even for a prayer.

He hurled himself into the air, away from the crumbling balcony, twisting his body in mid-leap. He landed hard on the rampart, skidding along on the backplate of his armour until he hit the wall under the crenelations, the infant clutched tight to his chest. His helmet flew off and disappeared over the edge of the rampart, lost forever.

Baum gasped for breath that would not come and turned once more, keeping the child under his body as the ancient tower collapsed in on itself with a long series of shuddering roars, spraying him with stones and thick, lung-clogging dust.

This was what a castle sounded like when it died, and he knew he would never forget it.

He could not stay where he was – he was not yet safe. He clambered to his feet and staggered along the wall in the direction of the postern gate, furthest from the chaotic wreckage of the Great Hall. It was hard to tell – his eyes streamed as he blinked away the thick clouds of stone particles – but he thought the gatehouse still stood.

He cast a glance behind him. The curtain wall was beginning to yaw outwards dangerously. It would not last long.

One man could do all this? It seemed Jedrell had seriously underestimated the warlock's powers. The High King had at last encountered a foe deadlier than himself.

Baum summoned the last of his strength and sprinted along the wall as fast as he dared, skipping over stone blocks that had fallen onto the ramparts as the tower fell. The roaring of destruction was behind him now, and Baum thought it had lessened a little. Malessar must be tiring. Or running out of people to kill. He had to keep moving. The warlock's curse already felt heavy upon his shoulders.

Flashes of unearthly light illuminated the gatehouse through the swirling stone dust. It was indeed intact. Malessar's maelstrom had focused tightly on the keep and the towers so far, though Baum guessed even these outer buildings would not be left standing by dawn. He pushed the heavy door open with his boot, wincing at the squeal of protesting hinges, and descended hurriedly, past the abandoned guardrooms with their toppled pallets and chairs. The tower was deserted: the watch had already fled, the gates flung wide open. He followed, taking the road north out of the kingdom.

There were others on the road, crying, angry, afraid, wounded. He overtook them, paying them no heed. Already he felt a sucking at his flesh, his bones, and the steel core of his strength. It had to be the effects of the warlock's curse, trying to pull him back into the devastation. The other survivors must feel it too, and they would succumb to it. They would return to the castle, and they would die there. Baum was pragmatic enough to know he could not stop them.

Malessar would be true to his word. He would extinguish the people of Caenthell forever.

It took hours to force himself away from the castle, step by step. At last exhaustion took its toll on his muscles and he subsided into a weary limp as he passed the waystones marking the border of the northernmost passes. The edge of the civilized world, it was said. He no longer felt the warlock's compulsion in his body. There was nobody else left on the road. The child had long since stopped crying and now slept peacefully in his arms. Baum lowered himself into the thin grass by the side of the road and gazed down at the boy for a while, waiting for morning to come.

"You will never come into your inheritance," he told Jedrell's son softly. "Malessar has made certain of that. Your life will be miserable and incomplete. But I swear this, and I swear it to Pyraete: I will not rest until I have broken the curse Malessar has set upon Caenthell. Whether it takes one year, ten, or ten *hundreds* of years, I swear I will revenge the High King of Caenthell."

A soft breeze swept over them, and Baum thought he heard a single word carried upon the air.

Sworn.

Chapter One

JUST MAKE SURE you feed that bloody mule!"

Cassia's father hurled his leather purse at her with painful precision. It smacked into her cheek before she could raise her free hand to catch it, and spun away over her shoulder.

Her cheek smarted, but she knew better than to protest. Norrow's rages were like the thunderstorms that swept through the upper valleys – torrential and violent, but also often random and short-lived. If she stayed quiet, did as he said, and kept from his sight until the end of the evening, her father would have forgotten that he had even lost his temper.

Cassia sighed under her breath as she watched him cross the muddy street and shove his way past a pair of ale-soaked old men who propped each other up outside a narrow, curtained doorway just inside the alley. With that mood hanging over him, he would likely be in the middle of a brawl within the hour. And who would have to pay for the damages?

She twisted, reaching down for the purse, and the mule chose that moment to tug in entirely the wrong direction, pulling her feet from under her so she collapsed in a heap.

She lost her grip on the tattered rope, and the mule trotted purposefully down the street towards the market square while Cassia sprawled in the dirt, to the amusement of passers-by.

"Come back here, you mangy beast!" she shouted, clambering back to her feet and pausing only to pick up the purse before chasing after the mule, her ears burning. The mule paid her no mind, intent on the aromas wafting from Keskor's market square.

She caught up with it as it entered the square, impeded at the last by a gaggle of children who poked both the beast and the roughly-tied bundles that hung over its back with sticks. Cassia had to snatch up the bridle rope and fend off the inquisitive children at the same time. She vented her frustration by landing a few satisfying slaps until the brats ran off. A couple of the more daring ones flung curses and pebbles at her, but she'd had enough now, and she wasn't about to let the stupid mule get away again.

She wrapped the rope around her wrist, and checked the purse to see what her father had left her. Two silver bits, to her dismay. Not enough to buy oats for both herself and the mule. The rest was probably already in the grubby apron of one of the backstreet barkeeps.

One of us will be going hungry tonight, she thought. *And if I had my way, it wouldn't be me. It's not like you can tell him I didn't feed you.*

But Norrow had a way of knowing these things. Cassia couldn't hide the truth from him for very long. So the mule would have a bag of fresh oats while Cassia would have to improvise, take a few risks.

Again.

She tucked the purse into the pocket inside her sleeve and ran her free hand through her hair, wincing as her fingers snagged on knots. Too long now, and too wavy. If she could find a mirror, or even a still pool, she'd take her knife to it and hack a good hand's worth off. Perhaps there would be time later, once her father had finished his performance, if the sky stayed clear and the moon was bright enough.

Cassia tugged the mule – suddenly recalcitrant and contrary – around the edge of the market and headed for a clear area on the far side of the square where the stallholders rarely pitched up. The reason for that was clear. A high brick wall, pitted and scarred enough to provide an easy climb to the flat stones at the top, formed the backdrop to the town's gibbet. Currently unoccupied, the stained wooden frame loomed over the north-western corner of the market, waiting, watching, and warning . . .

It helped to keep the traders honest, Cassia supposed. A man was unlikely to play games with weights while Keskor's gibbet sat at the edge of his vision. She imagined profits were on the low side whenever a corpse swung gently against this wall.

The sun was beginning to descend from its midday heights, and though the rest of the market baked in the heat, this corner collected some welcome shade. An old man, one-armed and gaunt, sat hunched over on the corner of the gibbet's wooden platform. He held out an upturned soldier's helmet, occasionally shaking it and calling for alms. Cassia was certain he'd occupied the exact same spot the last time they passed through Keskor.

She nodded courteously to him and led the mule to the back of the platform, tying the rope to a post there. The old soldier scowled at her. Perhaps he remembered her, or perhaps he thought Cassia meant to move in on his territory.

One side of a nearby stall was piled with wicker baskets of oats. Her two coins bought a scoop large enough to keep the mule happy, though her own stomach had started to rumble by the time she hooked the feed bag over the beast's head. She kept a handful of feed back and passed it to the beggar to keep him quiet and friendly. As before, there was an unspoken agreement that he would keep an eye on the mule if she slipped into the market for a while.

Though she was hungry she didn't fancy chancing the stalls right now, so she climbed the wall behind the gibbet instead. It was a fast ascent for somebody used to scrambling around, and she would have an excellent view of the square from the top. She imagined herself to be Pelicos, scaling the legendary cliffs of Kalakhadze. Pelicos had not made his ascent in broad daylight, however, and Cassia was not hampered by the weight of the virginal princess the old stories said he brought with him.

Beyond the wall was Keskor's school. One of the town's most impressive buildings, it sat on the site of the old temple to Pyraete, the God of the North, which had been demolished by Imperial decree over two hundred years ago. It was built in a modern Hellean style that Cassia had seen elsewhere in the North. Students sat in lines flanked by slender stone columns and ornamental pools. The space between the building and the boundary walls was used as a practice ground for sports such as archery and wrestling, and also for the military drills that the Emperor's Factor supervised twice a week.

This was one part of coming to Keskor that Cassia always enjoyed. The schools in other towns were less accessible, and there was rarely such a vantage point available to her. As long as she didn't make any noise or interrupt the lessons, the tutor here tolerated her occasional presence atop the wall. Apart from the time she had got bored watching the boys shuffle in formation under their heavy rectangular shields, and started throwing stones at them for the fun of it. She'd had to take to her heels rather quickly that day.

Today the boys in the school were quiet, bent over their tablets while the tutor recited in dry tones. Cassia strained to catch his words, but the bustle of the market behind her was a little too loud. She had a few years' advantage on them. She probably knew just as much as they did, thanks to her natural curiosity and the upbringing – of sorts – that her father had begrudgingly given her, but the boys would quickly overtake her. It wasn't fair that she wasn't allowed into a school. Think of all the tales and histories she could both tell and learn . . . and, she thought proudly, she already knew how to read. That was one thing Norrow had done properly, even if it was only because he wanted to enliven the sheer boredom of traveling between villages and towns.

"Cassia!" The shout came from below her, in the market square. She twisted around to see who called her.

Not all the town's boys attended the Factor's school. Many men could or would not pay the additional fees. They saw no sense in depriving their workshops, flocks, orchards and stalls of able-bodied help, believing their boys would learn everything they needed through hard work alone.

Hetch's father fell soundly into that camp. It did not take more than a single glass of wine for Rann Almoul to start expounding his theories on why too much learning was a Bad Thing. A Bad Thing for Keskor, a Bad Thing for the Empire in general, and a Bad Thing most specifically for Hetch himself. The pursuit of knowledge was second only to the worship of the foreign god of the Eastern Hordes in Hetch's father's pantheon of Bad Things, Cassia had quickly discovered.

So Hetch ran free, apparently not caring one way or the other on the matter of his schooling. He apprenticed for his father, who had started life as a soldier's son before founding a small bakery in the town. Rann Almoul had become involved in Guild matters and lent money to other traders, putting on airs that clashed colourfully with his drab and mean features. These days he walked in the same circles as Attis the money-lender and even the Factor himself.

Hetch stood at the foot of the wall, hands balled against his sides. Since Cassia had last visited the town a few months ago he had filled out, his chest broader and his biceps more prominent than before. The only thing he had inherited from his father was the thatch of wispy brown hair that threatened to blow away in the slightest breeze.

"Ma said she saw your father stomping around this morning," Hetch said. "I guessed you'd be here."

Cassia shrugged. It wasn't as if she had many other places to go. "That thing wanted to come here, not me." She pointed to the mule, which chewed on the contents of its feed bag.

Hetch grinned, an expression he had definitely *not* acquired from his father. "You here for long?"

She shrugged again. "Maybe. Maybe not. It depends."

One of Norrow's greatest skills lay in his ability to wear out any welcome given to him. With the best will in the world, any man generous enough to open his door to Cassia's father would find his hospitality sorely tested by the third day. Norrow could be charming enough when he *really* tried, but there was a petty, vicious streak in his nature that sat too close to the surface to be contained for long. Catty comments, deliberate slights, outright insults; all would come pouring forth, aimed with the studied accuracy of a master knife-thrower.

Hetch's grin widened. "Ma spoke to Norrow, too."

"What about?"

"She offered your Pa dinner tonight, and a floor too," Hetch explained. "I think it were my father's idea."

Cassia stifled a groan, her heart sinking. If Hetch was right then his father was plotting something. Rann Almoul didn't make such invitations lightly.

"Are you going to sit up there all afternoon?" Hetch asked, still staring up at her. His gaze was starting to make her feel uncomfortable, even though they had known each other since Hetch was old enough to run his father's errands on his own. He was a little younger than Cassia, but he was fast becoming a grown man. And he should have more important things to do than wait around for her. Suddenly she felt quite exposed.

"Maybe," she hedged.

"We could go for a walk around the market," Hetch suggested. "There's a fellow on the far side who'll let you take some chicken stew if I'm there with you."

Cassia sighed. "I'm not that hungry right now," she lied. "But thank you anyway, Hetch. I'll see you when we come up to the house this evening, won't I?"

For a moment he looked hurt, frustrated by her refusal, but then the easy smile returned and he nodded. "Of course. Look, I've got to do something for Pa, so I'll see you tonight, yes?"

She waved as he jogged off towards the crowds. Her stomach growled rebelliously and she almost regretted turning down his offer, but not quite enough to climb down and follow him.

Cassia sat there for the remainder of the afternoon. She watched the gentle rhythm of Keskor's markets and tried not to think too hard about what might lie in wait that evening. She felt saddened by the sudden change in her relationship with Hetch, but with hindsight she thought she should have seen it coming. These days, every time she led the mule through the gates of a town or down the main street of an outlying village she felt eyes upon her, weighing her up, judging her. A week ago there had been a few whistles aimed in her direction, and her father had alternated between narrow-eyed calculation and glaring balefully at everybody who dared come near for a full day after that.

There had been something just as speculative in Hetch's eyes, she decided, and she wasn't sure she liked it. She drew her feet up, tucking them under the frayed hem of her dress and wondered if she *should* feel flattered by the attention.

The sun sank towards the rolling foothills, silhouetting shepherds as they guided their flocks back towards the farms on the outskirts of the town. Cassia desperately wanted to head down between the stalls to see what she could filch as the markets slowed down for the evening, but now she feared running into Hetch again, so she didn't move.

At last she spied her father entering the square and she almost sighed with relief. Almost.

He walked slowly along the edge of the square, another

passer-by, peering at the stalls of nuts and drying herbs, eyeing chickens that stared beadily back at him, oblivious to their fates. He weaved back and forth with no discernible aim, almost certainly drunk. Every so often he would clap his hands once, loudly, and Cassia knew he was humming and chanting under his breath. Just enough to attract attention to himself.

And people *were* taking notice: a small group slowly gathered around Norrow, following him as he threaded between the stalls. As the crowd grew larger Cassia thought she saw Rann Almoul's sour features, which meant Hetch and his older brothers would also be there.

Dear Ceresel, she prayed silently to the goddess of fortune, *please don't let him make them angry this time. Please let it go well.*

It hadn't gone well in Varro. Fortunately for Norrow Varro was too far to the east of Keskor for rumour to have reached here so soon. There, he had told tales guaranteed to antagonise the locals, alluding to their complicity in the last wars against the Hordes. Cassia watched with mounting horror as the crowd began to shout to drown him out. Yet Norrow had continued loudly and remorselessly – until someone at the back of the audience cast the first stone.

At that point Norrow screamed, calling a curse on all of Varro's sons and daughters. Quite how he escaped both the lynch mob and the resultant riot in the town square Cassia would never know. Norrow claimed he remembered nothing of the night, but Cassia would never forget their panicked flight over the town's walls, leaving their packs and all of their possessions behind. And their mule, too – Cassia missed that animal. This replacement Norrow had bought cheaply a couple of days later was good for nothing but skinning and roasting.

Norrow led the crowd of men and boys – *his* crowd, now – into the space before the gibbet, where the starved old soldier still sat, helmet outstretched in his trembling hand. Nobody paid him any mind. They were hooked, one and all, by the low, ululating chant of the storyteller.

An answering chant rose from somewhere in the crowd. Even from her elevated position Cassia could not tell where it emanated from. It was taken up by the rest of the crowd, and Norrow's voice soared above it, calling out the ritual prayer to Movalli, the patron of all storytellers. Cassia echoed the prayer silently, careful not to let her lips move, lest her father see her speaking it. It had been bad enough when he overheard her singing it while she washed her clothes one day, and the bruises had taken a week to fade. The prayer wasn't hers to call, and the stories weren't hers to tell.

Norrow raised his arms high above his head, and the crowd hushed. Now he was not a selfish, malicious drunkard with no home and no sons. He was transformed and refreshed, a king amongst men.

That would not last long, Cassia thought darkly.

"Who remembers the days of old?" Norrow spoke in a deep tenor that reached easily across the crowd to Cassia's ears, but she still found herself straining to hear every word.

"Who remembers the great and the good? Their deeds and their trials? Who remembers the battles of times long past, when the heroes and generals have gone to dust once more? Who will remember *our* times, when we too are gone from the world, when our lives are done and our last breaths escape to rise past the tallest peaks of the mountains?

"One may only wonder if such were the thoughts of the great Lords of Stromondor as they gazed down for the last time from their towers of gold and silver at the mighty host besieging the gates of the glittering city that once – it is said – took tribute from no less than five of the Nine Talons!"

So, Stromondor it was. Cassia let herself relax. Her father was on solid ground tonight. As far as she knew Keskor had not sent any men to help lift the siege, over three centuries ago, but the town always rose to the aid of Brael when Stromondorian galleys harried there, and so tales of Stromondor's fall always went down well here.

"Was there ever a sight to rival the dawn over Stromondor?" Norrow asked his audience. "The rising of the sun caused such shimmering and blinding reflections to be seen as far west as the isle of Kalakhadze. The people of this great city walked on streets lined with gems of every hue, their wonderful gowns woven by young girls of such beauty that the Lords kept them locked away behind strong walls, in lush gardens of boundless tranquillity."

Cassia had only to look around at the muddy lanes of Keskor, at the rough linen and woollen shirts and gowns of the crowd, to understand the magic Norrow weaved. She yearned to travel there herself every time she heard these tales told, to see the fabled towers and gardens of the wonderful city of Stromondor.

But it could never be so.

"As the sun rose this day, the great Lords met in their council, in the highest of the glittering towers." The crowd was silent, entranced by his descriptions and eager to hear the tale. "They looked out upon the host camped beyond their gates, and they knew *fear*. A vast forest of spears and shields stood firm upon the plain before their walls. The Lords turned to the sea, which they had always commanded in the past, and saw to their dismay that to the west was another fiery sunrise – their great fleet of galleys and dromonds set ablaze and destroyed, and the Hordes owned the harbour. Thus were the invincible hulls of Stromondor burned down to their waterlines."

Cassia shifted her legs from underneath her and began to climb down the wall, moving slowly to avoid breaking her father's concentration. It wouldn't do to distract him in full flow, especially since this sounded like it would be one of his better tellings.

"Jathar Leon Learth was the eldest and richest of the Lords of Stromondor; a famous warrior of tremendous wisdom and courage, yet he trembled and fell to his knees as he beheld the carnage deep in the bay, exclaiming that there was nothing to be done! On that day he wore a cloak of the finest silvercloth, the sigils of his house emblazoned in scarlet upon it. He unfastened the delicate clasp and let the cloak slip, along with his steely resolve, to the floor of the tower. And he said to the Lords, *I am not fit to lead men on this day.*"

Cassia made her way to the mule and pulled her own cloak and hat from one of the bags. The cloak had belonged to her father's father and was poorly patched and faded. Once it had been decorated with a fine embroidered depiction of Movalli's First Tale, but the stitching was torn in many places and obscured the design. Now the ragged old thing helped identify her as the storyteller's assistant, while at the same time hiding her shape and her curves. She scraped her hair up under the ill-fitting cap, and her transformation was complete. She dug into the bag again to find her bowl, and then walked to the edge of the crowd.

"The Lords looked around to the last of their number," Norrow was saying, having described the cowardice of several of the councillors by now. "This was a man of the North, wreathed always in black. His voice was cold, his eyes stone and ice. He carried himself with the bearing of a king, yet he had no title save those whispered by men in the dead of night, in dark corners where they could not be overheard. This was Malessar the warlock, the destroyer of ancient Caenthell."

The mood of his audience shifted; indrawn breaths, murmured prayers to Pyraete. The Fall of the High King of Caenthell was a tale known in all the towns under the mountains, though the old kingdom of the North had not existed for more than six centuries. The high ranges of the mountains, where Caenthell had once been, were said to be cursed and were avoided by all. Cassia held back for a moment, waiting for the right moment to enter the crowd.

"Jathar was the first to speak to him. *Malessar, will you not lead us to safety and salvation?* the old hero implored him. He held out his fine, rich cloak. *Will you not take up the mantle of Champion of Stromondor?*"

Cassia spotted Rann Almoul near the edge of the crowd. Hetch and his brothers would be near him. She circled further around the fringes until she judged she was far enough from them to not be seen, then edged forward past the first onlookers, ducking her head and holding up her bowl.

"*Why should I do anything for you, Jathar Leon Learth, when you have never thought to lift a hand to aid me?* the warlock asked in a voice so low the Lords strained to hear his words. *Why should I do anything to save Stromondor at all?*"

Cassia passed slowly through the crowd, and the first coin clinked against the lacquered wood. Many of the men ignored her, their arms folded across their chests, their purses unopened. More than once she was pushed aside, and she kept her wits about her for the callous type that would try to trip her or grab the bowl. That had happened before, and she had come away with nothing. Norrow's beatings on those nights had been especially vicious.

It would have been different had she been born a boy, as her father had wanted. A boy to be taught the storyteller's trade and to carry on the proud tradition. A boy to be a true and proper companion for her father; to grow into a man who could earn him money and support him in his old age. A boy, rather than a weak, unwanted, useless girl. Norrow had never forgiven her for being born first. There would have been a boy – a brother for her – but her mother had never been strong. The two bodies, one inside the other, were marked by a crude shrine on a plain hillside. And there were never any stories told of Cassia's mother. Norrow would tolerate no mention of her. Cassia could not even remember her.

Given the chance, Norrow would gladly abandon her, but he needed *somebody* to work his audience and drag the mule between towns, and his reputation was so poor that no man would apprentice a son to him. Who would want to be apprenticed to a man who had no home, who had no prospects?

Sometimes Cassia wished she *had* been born a boy. Perhaps then she could try her hand at storytelling – at the very least she could shake this damned bowl without needing to disguise herself.

And maybe, just maybe, her father might actually like her.

He was done describing the fall-out of the Council of Lords now, moving on to Jathar's desperate search through the terrified streets of Stromondor for a hero to lead the city's armies against the besieging Horde. This gave him plenty of opportunity to digress into scenes of comedy or romance, inserting new, transitory characters as he wished; rehashing jokes or giving blow-by-blow accounts of gutter brawls. There could be a mysterious, doom-laden encounter with a disguised god, foretelling Jathar's eventual end, or even a chance meeting with a fair maiden who would seek to woo him from his purpose. This was the meat of Norrow's tales – the setting might change, the characters may differ, but if he really wanted to he could keep a story going for hours using his incidental scenes, never once losing the narrative thread, or his audience.

Cassia hoped he wouldn't stretch his tale too much tonight – she was hungry, and even though the invitation had to be double-edged she had started to look forward to Ma Almoul's dinner.

One circuit of the crowd brought five small bits. Not an encouraging haul. People tended to be freer with their money towards the climax of a tale, perhaps because they thought they'd had value by then, but this was disappointing by Keskor's usual standards. She pushed her way between a pair of men, deeper into the audience, working her way back around in the opposite direction.

"A man sat in the darkest corner of the inn, at a small table crowded with emptied tankards." Norrow hunched his shoulders, drew himself in. "At the other stools sat huddled, miserable men, asleep in their reek, hiding behind their fears and cowardice. But this one man stood, and he cried, *I shall lead your armies!*" And Norrow strode around the cleared space at the centre of the crowd, his uncertain gait only half an act as he took on this new character.

Cassia was surprised by how quickly he had progressed his tale – a lot faster than usual, even given the promised meal. She wasn't unhappy, though she would now have to work with more speed.

"Jathar Leon Learth was amused by the man's words, for the man was unkempt and ragged, clearly no hero. *You?* he exclaimed. *But sir, what is your quality? You are a vagabond, sir. How will you lead even a latrine detail beyond these gates, let alone an army?*

"The decrepit old man rose from his seat and flung back his holed cloak, and now Jathar saw he wore armour underneath. Battered and plain it was, with gouges and dents and scored lines that spoke loudly of the man's long experience on the field of battle. And now he looked more closely at this man, as he came into the light to make clear his challenge, Jathar saw too the scars upon his flesh. And there, deep within his eyes, were older, more ancient wounds, that Jathar judged had never healed."

Norrow stared fiercely into the crowd, daring each man to meet his gaze. "*Look upon me, Jathar Leon Learth*, this grizzled warrior said quietly. *I will not recite my pedigree to you, for this city would fall ere I finish. I can see the demons that war within your soul, that demand you surrender your courage to them. I can lead your army, sir; I can lead them into places where you will not tread. Look upon me, and tell me that this is not truth.*"

Cassia had not paid attention to her wanderings. She was close to where Rann Almoul and Hetch stood, and she ducked her head even further, hoping to avoid being seen. But both were hooked too deep within the tale and did not notice as she passed behind them.

Her eyes came to rest on a fine pair of leather boots, almost new by their look. Low-heeled and rising high up their owner's legs, they bore the dust of the road but very little mud. She lifted her gaze, surprised to see such good workmanship here. Why would anybody so obviously wealthy stop in Keskor's town square to hear a storyteller?

A narrow, emotionless pair of brown eyes stared back down at her. They were set into a strong, chiselled face, with high cheekbones and an aquiline nose. The man's mouth and chin made her think of carved images of Pyraete she had seen at the few roadside shrines still dedicated to the god of the North. His shoulder-length brown hair was tied back in a tight tail to emphasise his noble features.

His clothing reinforced that impression: a clean white cotton shirt under his leather jerkin, and breeches tucked neatly into the tops of his boots, with a thick woollen cloak over his broad shoulders. The hilt of a greatsword stuck out from beneath the cloak.

Cassia blinked and shook herself, suddenly aware that she was staring directly at the young lordling. She did the first thing that came to mind, and presented her bowl, lowering her head again.

After a long moment in which nothing happened, she peeked back up. The man's eyes were still on her, with that unnerving, slightly blank look.

A faint chuckle came from the old man next to him – his companion, it seemed, but an odd pair they made if that was so.

A full head shorter than the young lordling, the old man was weather-beaten and lined, his hair thin and fading from grey to white. His nose was crooked, and looked like it had been broken more than once, and a thick scar cut down his left cheek and through his lips, twisting his smile. His cloak was wrapped tight around him and he leaned on a thick staff, but something about the way he carried himself gave Cassia the impression he had once been a soldier.

"The girl seeks a coin, Meredith," he whispered, in faintly mocking tones.

Meredith turned his head to regard the old man. "Why?" he asked, not bothering to lower his voice. Several men nearby half-turned at the interruption. Cassia winced, expecting to hear her father's tale falter into one of his terrible tempers.

The old man opened his mouth to reply, then changed his mind with an exasperated sigh. He dug into his own purse, dropping two small coins into the bowl. Cassia bowed, relieved, and turned to hold the bowl out before the man on Meredith's far side.

"And they always get it so wrong . . ." she heard the old man mutter as she hurried away.

When she glanced over her shoulder a few seconds later, the pair of strange travellers had gone.

Chapter Two

RANN ALMOUL'S HOUSE was on the road that led to the Western Gate; they had passed it on their way into town. The mule balked at being led up the hill and Cassia found herself alternately hauling on the rope and smacking the beast from behind to drive it forward.

As usual, she had no help from her father: Norrow strode ahead, oblivious to her travails, basking in the glory of a tale well told. Men halted him to clasp his hand and pat his shoulder; a few women sought to attract his attention from a curtained doorway off to one side. They were no better than they should be, Cassia thought sourly, eyeing their low-cut dresses with distaste.

Norrow's purse was full again. Tonight, at least, they would not have to pay for food. The money might last slightly longer than usual.

She paused, turning to look back down the darkening road. Lights flickered in the windows of the houses. The early moon was luminescent; it would be a clear, cool evening. The streets emptied slowly as Keskor wound down for the night, but there were still plenty of people about, making their way to their homes or to taverns.

All perfectly normal, yet there was a prickling sensation at the base of her spine – something she couldn't put a name to. If not for the clear skies overhead, she might have believed a storm was brewing close by.

She returned her attention to coaxing the mule forward, aware she was falling behind even her father's languid pace. It was probably nothing. Nothing other than still feeling unsettled by the encounter with the strange young lordling earlier.

Cassia had risked looking for the strangers again while she worked her father's audience, wondering what had drawn them into the square to listen to the tale, and puzzling over the old man's last comments. Perhaps they were storytellers, like her father? But she abandoned that line of reasoning quickly – she had never known any storyteller carry a sword, or own such finery as the lordling wore. It would make more sense if the strangers belonged to a troupe of traveling players, but again the young man – Meredith – looked clothed rather than costumed. And what troupe would come into the hills, when the vast plains of the Empire offered far richer pickings?

The pair had vanished completely however; not merely withdrawn to the fringes of the audience. Cassia continued her task, distracted, hardly listening as Norrow's tale gathered pace, as it tumbled to its tragic and bloody conclusion. The great spires of Stromondor fell, as they always did; the terrible warlock Malessar deserted the Lords of the City to their violent ends, as he always did; and the drunken old soldier, the unnamed hero of the hour who had humbled and shamed the once-great Jathar Leon Learth, stood against the massed armies of the Eastern Hordes like a sharpened rock against thunderous tides, just as *he* always did.

Norrow's audience cheered the soldier's strength and nobility, just as they cheered the ruin of Stromondor itself. The hypocrisy of these positions always amused Norrow. He never missed the opportunity to point out that only the very best storytellers could sway a man's support from one side to the other with just a few words.

The evening thus far was a triumph, then, but the closer they came to Rann Almoul's house the more troubled Cassia became, both by what might lie ahead and by her sharp memory of Meredith's cool, piercing gaze. Her imagination was getting the better of her, she decided.

They came to a small square where the road split into two. The right fork would take them through a lesser gate onto the ancient road that wound into the mountains, while the left fork, broader and well-used, left Keskor through Pyraete's Arch to join the Emperor's March, curving down into the plains. Standing proud in the angle of this intersection, a blade upon which the road was cut in two, was the house of Rann Almoul.

Almoul displayed his aspirations for all to see. Every year brought some new feature or decoration to his house. This year, he'd added stone pillars and a portico on either side of the squared gate, and completely replastered and whitewashed the outside of the building. Cassia supposed she should be impressed, but she thought the house looked vulgar and intrusive next to its more common neighbours. None would say it to his face, but Almoul had imitated the style of the Factor's residence.

The gate was open but Norrow did not go through it: he was a guest, but not as esteemed as those Almoul welcomed in for business during the day. Instead he took the left fork and headed to the far end of the house, turning down an alley that linked the two diverging roads. Cassia followed, her stomach grumbling.

There was another, plainer gate at the rear of the house, set into a high wall that had not been there several years ago when this space had been occupied by pens of chickens. Cassia remembered playing with Hetch in the dust and mud, once accidentally letting the chickens loose. She grinned at the memory of the chaos they caused that day, feathers flying everywhere while Ma Almoul raged and cursed.

There was still a yard beyond the gate, but now it was cleaner and tidier, and the hens were confined to a large wooden shed against the wall. The two forked wings of the house enclosed an area paved with stone slabs, with a table set up in the middle. Two young girls ferried trays from the kitchen to the table, watched vigilantly by Ma Almoul herself.

Cassia led the mule off to her right, where Almoul's two horses were tethered under a sloping thatched roof. The shelter was small and quite crowded; Almoul's steeds had been joined by several much larger horses, with old blankets laid over their backs. Just as her mule was dwarfed by Rann's well-bred colts, so they in turn were lessened by these great beasts. She managed to find space to tie the mule to a metal ring at the far end, struggling with the knots in the tight confines of the shelter. One of the big chestnut horses watched her with mild disinterest.

She wondered who these other guests were. Trading partners of Rann Almoul, most likely, or at the very least men he thought he could make a profit from. She began to understand the reason for her father's invitation to the meal. He was the evening's entertainment, of course. There was nothing sinister about it, no reason for her to feel uncomfortable.

But telling herself that did not help, she found, as she stepped from the lean-to and walked across the paved yard to join her father.

Norrow had paused near the table to gaze at the feast that the two girls had set down. But not too close. Ma Almoul stood nearby, hands braced against her broad hips, scowling at him as though he was a beggar. Norrow had affected not to see her, but he turned away quickly as Cassia approached.

"Don't make a fool of me here," he hissed between his teeth. "Rann has important dinner guests. This will be worth a lot of money to me. Stay out of my way."

Cassia felt her cheeks burn, but she kept her mouth closed, biting back the retort that sprang to her lips.

Her father nodded to a bench that sat underneath the house's overhanging roof, some distance from the table. "Go and sit there. And *stay* there. I'll not need you this night."

Humiliated, she turned her back on him without a word and slumped on the bench, watching as Norrow attempted to smooth his clothing and tidy his wiry hair, radiating an air of self-importance that he thought made him more than he truly was. Ma Almoul, she could tell, was not impressed by his appearance, and would not trust him further than she could spit.

A wise woman, she thought.

Hetch slithered onto the bench beside her, an eager grin splitting his face. He had changed into a clean shirt and wore knee-high riding boots with a small heel, rather than the tattered sandals he habitually went about Keskor in.

"Your Da's tale was brilliant!" he told her in a low whisper. "Nobody does the old wars like he does. How much did you take?"

Cassia shrugged. She had no chance to count the money once the story had ended. Norrow had snatched the bowl from her and emptied it into his purse. It had been a reasonable take, for the bowl was two-thirds full. Of course, the Factor would want his share of that before Norrow left town again. As would Rann Almoul, who had loaned money to Norrow in the past, when old Attis refused him. The payments on those loans were what drove them back onto the roads, time after time.

"Enough for a room," she said shortly. Again, even though Hetch was one of her oldest friends – one of her only friends – she didn't much feel like talking.

Hetch clearly did. "I wish I could tell those stories like he does."

She grunted, familiar emotions rising to do battle inside her, as they always did when she heard somebody praise her father. Pride, anger, jealousy; everything she knew she shouldn't feel.

I bet I can tell them just as well as he can. Not that I'll ever have that chance.

"Want an apple?"

She blinked, her mind pulled away from that well-worn path by the question. Hetch held a bowl of fruit, stacked with rosy apples and clusters of grapes pilfered from the table. Cassia reached for it hungrily and they sat in silence for a few moments while she worked her way through the first of the apples.

"Those horses," she said at last, picking at the skin stuck between her teeth. "Do you know who they belong to?"

Hetch shook his head, swallowing before answering. "Da's got company tonight. Old Attis is here, but there's two men I never saw before too. Well-spoken, I think, or at least one of them is. Might be they're from Trenis, or Hellea." He paused, rolling a grape in his fingers. "He could be a prince!"

Cassia shivered a little. Could they be the two strangers she had come across in the crowd? The younger of the pair had looked noble enough. But why would they be visiting Rann Almoul's house? Anybody so highly born would surely choose to dine at the Factor's much grander house in town.

"You've heard far too many of my Da's tales. Prince, indeed!"

"Well, I don't know," Hetch said. "My Da's been running about for them all afternoon."

That piqued her interest. Rann Almoul didn't bow and scrape for many people. No wonder her father was pacing nervously in front of the tables.

Hetch's voice dropped to a whisper. "I heard they had business with Attis – and he won't say a word about it."

Attis was Keskor's most influential moneylender. Cassia had heard it said the old miser could make or break a man's business on a whim. There was no love lost between him and Norrow, thanks to a long-standing and never-to-be-mentioned quarrel that, over the years, had turned into bitter dislike.

But Attis was also Almoul's closest ally, and they had built their personal fortunes together, the moneylender funding many of Almoul's successful enterprises. In some ways the two men had more influence in Keskor than even the Emperor's Factor.

Cassia sat back thoughtfully. If nothing else, the sparks between Attis and her father would make the evening interesting.

"Anybody else?" she asked Hetch.

He frowned and shook his head. "I don't think so," he said.

Cassia turned back to the bowl of fruit, plucking a handful of grapes before Hetch could get there. She crushed the first few between her teeth, revelling in the juices that burst onto her tongue.

"These are good," she said, licking her fingers clean.

"I'm glad you're enjoying them." Hetch grinned, shifting on the bench next to her.

It took her a moment to realise that he'd shuffled closer, that his arm had crept up and behind her shoulder. The discomfort she had felt during the afternoon flooded back and she wasn't sure whether she should be shocked and angry, or grateful for the sudden attention.

She was wondering if she could get away with pretending that nothing had happened when the curtains inside the doorway to Rann's day chambers parted. Hetch stiffened and pulled his arm back, scrambling to his feet as his father stepped into the yard. With a small bow and a precise flick of his hand, Rann Almoul invited his guests to follow him. All thoughts of her changing relationship with Hetch fled from Cassia's mind as the first figure brushed through the curtains. It was the young lord, Meredith, from the market square. Of course, she thought. Rann's guests could hardly have been anyone else.

The lordling paused, and his impassive gaze flitted across the yard, coming to rest on Ma Almoul who stood proudly before the tables. He performed a low and perfectly measured bow of his own, bending smoothly from the waist, and even from where she sat Cassia could tell Ma Almoul was flattered. A rare occasion.

His companion, however, was just as plainly unimpressive. While Meredith was sharp and clean, the old man still wore his tattered cloak and came into the yard absently picking at something stuck in his teeth. He greeted Ma Almoul with effusive charm, but that only made her draw back a step in suspicion.

Next came old Attis, who was greeted as though he was a member of the family. He embraced Ma Almoul with genuine warmth before making his way to the table and lowering himself into a chair at one end.

Last through the curtain was Rann's eldest son, Tarves. While Hetch took after his father, Tarves bore a heavier resemblance to his mother, right down to her perpetual frown. He had always held himself above the other children of Keskor, and Rann had moulded him firmly in his own image, with the clear intent of passing his business on to him.

"Please, be seated," Rann Almoul said as his wife withdrew to supervise the serving girls. "Tonight my table is yours."

The lordling looked to his companion and the older man dipped his head courteously. "Your hospitality is most generous, sir," he replied.

It was odd that the old man took the lead – it wasn't what Cassia had expected. Perhaps there was more to their relationship than she had first supposed.

They took their places along one side of the table, with Meredith sat at Attis's left hand. The moneylender looked uncomfortable with the arrangement. His smile was thin and forced, and his eyes flicked repeatedly from Rann to Meredith. Cassia watched as Hetch and Tarves took seats on the opposite side of the table, then turned to look for her father. Norrow hung back, near the door to the kitchens, waiting to be summoned to tell his tales. Ma Almoul's serving girls had to duck and edge past him to bring covered plates and bowls to the table, but Norrow looked too nervous to take any notice of them. It was rare he was invited to recite at a private party – indeed, Cassia could remember only one other occasion – and he much preferred to play to a larger crowd. This intimate setting seemed to have unnerved him as much as Attis, if for different reasons.

She plucked another grape and settled back on her darkened bench, glad to be away from the glare of attention at the table. It would be interesting enough to witness the dinner from here.

Rann paused on the way to his place at the head of the table, resting one hand briefly on Hetch's shoulder.

"My son and heir, Tarves, you have already met," he told his guests. "His brother Vescar serves as an officer in the Factor's legion, where he does great credit both to his name and to that of his family. This is my youngest son, Hetch, who is also learning my business affairs."

Hetch adopted a suitably serious expression and bowed his head. "My lords, we are honoured by your presence," he said, sounding much like his father.

Again it was the older man who spoke, while Meredith sat in silence. "Then we are well met and alike, sir, for we are both men of learning," he said to Hetch with a smile. "I am Baum. I was reckoned a great commander of men in the legions when I was younger, but I have spent the last few decades on my own quest for knowledge."

He nodded to his companion. "And this is Meredith. A man cannot safely travel alone in the world these days, it seems, but Meredith has his own interest in the North. One might say he seeks his inheritance," he added with a slight smile.

So Meredith wasn't a prince after all, but he certainly had to be the younger son of some noble family, to judge by the cut and quality of his clothes.

She glanced across at Attis. The moneylender had absented himself from the conversation completely, his head bent over his plate as he deliberately tore his bread into smaller chunks.

Rann Almoul watched everything from the other end of the table, his composed features hiding his thoughts. His attempt to impress his guests was not going according to plan, Cassia thought. Something troubled him, that much was obvious. Something about Meredith and Baum, although it was impossible to see what that might be.

"Attis recommended you to me, sir, and I hope you have found my services to be beyond compare," Rann Almoul said, leaning forward. "He also said that you wished to be entertained by a storyteller. I pride myself on my reputation as a good and decent host, but I confess I am intrigued by the nature of your requests. Now you are my guest, and you are eating at my table, perhaps you will explain what you wish of us."

Rann Almoul's cold tone appeared to have no effect on Baum's demeanour. The old man only smiled and tilted one shoulder in a small shrug. Cassia sat very still, just as she would have done if her father had been raging before her, deep in his cups. It was the best way to remain unnoticed.

"I come to free you from the Hellean yoke," Baum said, as though it was the most natural thing in the world. "To send the Factor and his tax collectors reeling back to the low plains. To bring power, wealth and independence to these lands once more. The North *will* rise again, Rann Almoul – and it will do so in your lifetime."

There was silence. Cassia hardly dared to breathe.

"Well?" Baum said at last. "Isn't that what you want?"

Almoul's ruddy complexion had paled into a death-mask. He stared intently at the old man, while his bread hung limp and unheeded from his fingers. His sons took their cue from their father, though Hetch could not hide his clear-eyed shock. Only Meredith and Baum himself seemed unconcerned by the tone of the conversation.

"You dare to sit at my table and talk of sedition? Of *rebellion?*" Cassia had never heard Almoul so astounded. Or so angry. "And you dare to presume upon my desires! I will not be spoken to in such a manner!"

Not just anger, Cassia thought. Something else too. Rann Almoul's list of Bad Things did not end with schools and foreign gods; he was also intolerant of dishonest traders, purse-snatchers, the indigent and the lazy, beggars, and workers who did not pull their own weight, amongst many other things that could affect his capacity to make a profit. The very idea of rebellion against the Empire that now called the North a province was guaranteed to bring his temper boiling forth.

Yet it was Hellea that leaned upon him continually as a source of revenue. Taxation. Subscriptions. Supplies for the legion, and coin for the festivals. Almoul had lost a son to the legion. He was still proud of Vescar and his achievements, Hetch had told Cassia once, but he resented the Empire for taking him in the first place.

No, not just anger. Agitation, and denial. Rann Almoul was like a child caught in a lie. She recognised it well. The man was caught on a stake between Hellea and the old North.

Baum dispelled the oncoming storm with a nonchalant gesture. "As you wish," he said. "I was under the impression that you were your father's son."

"My father joined the legions," Rann Almoul bit down upon every word. "He defended the Empire."

"Against the Berdellan uprisings." Baum nodded. "As did I, sir. And I knew your father. Oh, no need to look so surprised. I had my reasons then, as I have them now. In fact, although you have your storyteller here, let me give you a tale of my own."

He chewed upon a crust of bread for a moment and the yard was silent. Even Cassia's father could not have silenced an audience so effectively.

"I was a full commander of five hundred swords and spears," Baum said at last. "It was a terrible land for infantry, with rolling, sandy plains, and soil barely worthy of the name. Nothing grew well, so we had to rely on our wagons, and the

Berdellans wasted no opportunity to make life harder for us. They abandoned their towns and fired their fields, and drove their herds deep into the plains, where we could not reach them. They harried us from horseback, picking away at our flanks and raiding in force by night. They sought to wear us down and thin us out; for they would not meet us in the field."

Cassia tried to recall her history. The Berdellan campaigns had been at least fifty years ago and, even if Baum had been young for his rank – say, thirty years old – it meant he must be over *eighty* now. He would certainly have been older than Rann Almoul's father. She regarded him carefully as he paused to sip his wine, and wondered if he really could be that old.

"Now then," Baum continued, gazing down into his cup, apparently oblivious to his host's growing impatience. "Factor Grosculi, who was meant to be collecting these taxes that the Berdellans didn't want to pay, was good at counting coins. But tactically he was clueless. He wanted to react to every attack, every provocation, despite the fact that we'd end up getting pulled out of position and one of our units would be left behind or trapped beyond the flanks. Easy pickings. The mood in the camp grew sour and mutinous. I needed some way to regain the initiative.

"I sent my best scouts deep into Berdellan territory, while we dug in and fortified our encampment as best we could. We had sent messengers to the other divisions of Grosculi's legion, but we had no way of knowing whether they had been received safely. Eventually we were relieved, of course, but before that happened one of my scouts struck gold." Baum gave Hetch a dazzling smile. "Quite literally, in fact."

Hetch had forgotten his meal. "Gold?"

Of them all, only old Attis did not respond to the mention of riches. He had barely said a word since taking his seat. It was most unlike him, Cassia thought. She wondered if he was feeling ill.

"About six miles from our camp was an old, fortified mound

occupied by a somewhat reclusive Berdellan force. We had not even known it was there. It was a good, defensible position that, if we could take it, would turn the fight in our favour and ease the pressure on the other divisions. My officers argued for moving in to besiege the hill, but I had a far more ambitious plan.

"As night fell, we moved camp, taking the wagons as close as we could to the hill without alerting their guards, and no doubt frustrating the raiders who had planned to attack us in the early hours. We pulled the wagons around in a circle and set fire to them. I left a third of my men there to raise a clamour with their swords and shields, and the defenders could not have missed it. Meanwhile, I approached the hill with the rest of my force, circling around to the far side. As the Berdellans watched the blaze and wondered at the sounds of battle, we scaled the walls and took them by surprise.

"At last they had no choice but to stand and fight. I will give them their due; they fought well. But they were unprepared, and they had sent a party out to investigate the burning wagons, weakening their own strength. The fighting was at close quarters, brutal and murderous. We had no objective other than to decisively beat them.

"They put up their most determined resistance in the great hall. Several of my best officers fell to knives and spears. The stones were treacherously slippery, coated with blood. My half-captain stumbled, hard pressed by one opponent, and he would have ended his days right there had I not engaged the man myself and cut his legs from under him.

"Only when this man fell did the Berdellans finally lose heart, for he was Gyre Carnus, the eldest son of their rebellious king. And now we realised, my half-captain and I, why this fort had been hidden away. This was the secret heart of the rebellion. While King Carnus had been forced to abandon his cities, he had enough foresight to build a network of small forts deep in the wild – forts that Grosculi knew nothing about. And secreted in this fort were the golden tributes and gemstones that Carnus had gone to such great pains to deny to Grosculi."

Baum sat back, eyes half-lidded, looking around the table.

"This is all very well," Rann Almoul observed. "But a long-dead prince and a chest of riches do not answer any of my questions."

His tone was not threatening, but Meredith turned his head to watch him. Tarves, in turn, frowned at the young lordling and shifted on his seat. Cassia's skin prickled with goosebumps, from nerves and fear as much as from the rapidly cooling evening.

Baum shrugged. "Indulge me a moment more," he said, his own voice not quite as courteous as it had been. He turned and called over his shoulder. "Storyteller – do you know the tales of Berdella?"

For perhaps the first time ever, Norrow looked genuinely lost for words. He blinked and tugged at his tattered robe, glanced quickly across at Cassia, and took a hesitant step forward.

"A little, sir. But they are not well-known in these parts."

"Understandably so." Baum smiled. He must have caught Norrow's sideward look, for he turned his gaze upon Cassia next. "And your apprentice?"

She shook her head, barely trusting her throat, which felt dry and constricted. "No – but—"

"She knows nothing—" Norrow started, but Baum raised one hand to silence him.

"But?" he prompted.

Cassia licked her lips. "But he didn't. Grosculi. The gold – I mean." She took a deep breath. "He brought back the taxes, but the treasures of King Carnus were lost. That's what they said. At the school. I heard that once."

"And they were right." Baum nodded, and gestured to the table. "I would feel more comfortable if the pair of you weren't hiding in the corners of the yard like that. Sit down."

Rann glowered, but said nothing as Cassia timidly perched next to Hetch and Norrow settled for a cramped seat on the other side of Tarves. Meredith watched them with the same dry expression he had worn all evening.

"Now sir," Rann said, his words dangerously clipped. "Explain yourself. Without these games. I will not be toyed with in this manner."

"Gold and gems," Baum said. "Perhaps enough to pay a whole legion until the end of the world. Grosculi did not need to know about it. It was ours to take. We left the fort burning, the Berdellan corpses heaped outside the gates. My men – those who lived – were paid well from the spoils, but there was still more than enough to make my half-captain and myself exceedingly rich. More than enough for us to implement our own secret ambitions.

"My half-captain was a radical-minded man, much like myself. He did not love the Empire. He viewed his position as a means to an end, and now he had that means, and much sooner than he had anticipated. He also owed me his life, and for that I asked him for a few small favours."

The smile dropped from Baum's lips. "Keskor can be at the heart of a great new Northern kingdom, just as you wish it to be. Just as Caenthell used to be. I can make that a reality. Make no mistake, the North *will* rise again. But you will need your own legions, to dissuade Hellea's certain retaliation. Half-captain Attis still possesses the means to pay for them."

Cassia gasped, staring at the moneylender in disbelief. Attis still hunched over his plate, his eyes haunted and distant.

It was hard enough to imagine the old man in the uniform of the Imperial legions, let alone picture him wielding a sword, struggling for his life in battle. But this had all taken place half a century ago. She could only see Attis as he was now.

She looked back up at Baum. He had returned his attention to his food, apparently oblivious to the waves of shock rippling across the table. There was no doubt that he, at least, was exactly what he claimed to be. And that only added more weight to what he had said of Attis.

"This is ridiculous," Rann said, breaking the silence, but some of the conviction had left his voice.

Because it wasn't all that far-fetched after all, Cassia thought. Everything was moving into place, like the pieces of a shattered plate. What better way to make quick money than to join the legions, even for a man opposed to Imperial rule? An officer's wage, along with the pillage and robbery that was frequently shown a blind eye – a man could make a fortune. And Attis had.

"Is it?" Attis said, so softly even Cassia, sat next to him, scarcely heard him. He raised his head, straightened his back, a faint echo of a soldier's posture. "Is it so ridiculous, Rann? Did you think my money grew on trees? And your father's business too – why do you think he was so successful?"

Rann's lips tightened. "My father never mentioned any of this—"

Attis shook his head. "Your father held a spear. He wasn't paid to think. He marched and he fought as he was ordered. He set a torch to the wagons to help distract the Berdellans, and he was paid in gold to keep quiet about the things Grosculi did not need to know. He was a small man, Rann. He joined the legion to build his future. As did I."

Attis sat back and folded his arms wearily. "And so you return again, for the oath you made me swear. I am too old for such games now, and Ceron Almoul is long dead."

Baum shook his head. "I have lost track of the years. They are not so important. But the *North* is important, as are its people. Think of what you learned while you held your commission. Battlefield tactics, leadership skills, arms drills, teaching all those young men how to obey orders – how to fight."

"How to die," Attis muttered.

Baum ignored his remark and spoke to Rann instead. "With both Attis and your sons at your side, you will raise and train small companies of soldiers right across the region, right under the Factor's nose. He has no reason to suspect any trouble here. Then all you have to do is wait for my word, or my signal."

Rann frowned, sceptical as always, but Cassia could tell the idea had taken root in his mind. He and Tarves shared a silent look.

"What signal?" Rann asked. "Where will you be? Will you be using us as crude puppets?"

"My own part is just that, mine and mine alone," Baum said curtly, before softening his tone. "It is safer – for you as well as for me – that you know nothing but your own part. But rest assured you will not mistake my signal when it comes. *Nobody* will miss it."

Almoul's barked laughter was unpleasant. "Will you resurrect Caenthell for us so we can rally at the High King's feet? Do you think you are a sorcerer, or even a god?"

The hush that followed was tense and uncomfortable. Cassia stared down at the surface of the table to avoid drawing attention to herself. She should not be hearing this. She wished she had been able to stay out of the way, on the other side of the yard.

When she looked up, it was to find that none of the men at the table could meet Baum's stern, determined gaze. There was stone in his eyes. They were as disconcerting as the half-twist upon his lips that might have passed – in full light – for a smile. And the lordling, Meredith – he chewed some morsel placidly, as though nothing was amiss. That was worse than Baum's glare, somehow.

"I will require the locked casket that was left with Ceron Almoul," Baum said, as the silence was threatening to become unbearable. "I trust you still possess it."

Rann hesitated, and then nodded.

"Good. I will also require the sum of seventy-four silver bells. That was the amount promised, if I recall. And then there is the small matter of the storyteller."

Cassia saw her father's head jerk up. "What?"

"What of him?" Rann Almoul said.

"He will be traveling with Meredith and myself," Baum said. "He will have his own part to play."

Norrow's eyes were wide with surprise and horror. "Me?"

"Hah! You're welcome to him," Rann said. "His tongue is glib enough, but he's a sot and a fool. We'll not miss him."

"No, wait," Norrow said quickly. "I don't understand any of this. You say you have a part for me in this scheme?"

Baum nodded.

"As a storyteller?"

Another nod, and now a smile spread across Norrow's face. Cassia caught her breath. She knew that smile. Her father was casting his own plots, seeking out ways to take advantage of the situation. Baum had mentioned a sum of money, and Norrow would inevitably angle for a share of that.

"If you need a storyteller, I'm your man," he said. "My tales are famed across the entire North. Did you hear my recital tonight, back at the market? Of course, I have no love for the Empire either—"

Attis snorted. "No love to spare for any but yourself, you idiot. Perhaps Hellea will appreciate you. But what of Cassia? You will not need her."

All eyes turned upon her. It was as if they had only just remembered her presence. She shrunk back.

Norrow's smile widened further. "No," he said. "I don't suppose I will. Just another mouth to be fed. A dead weight. You may go, girl. I dismiss you."

Cassia could not find words for what she felt. Just like that? Abandoned and dismissed in so few words? She felt bile rising in her throat – the sweetness of the fruit, lying unsettled in her stomach.

"Go? But . . . where?"

Norrow shrugged. He seemed unable to conceal his delight at being able to leave her behind at last. Then she saw him glance across at Attis, and there was a fresh glint of calculation behind his eyes. Calculation that turned to malice. "Never let it be said I do not pay my debts," he said. "Rann?"

Rann Almoul regarded him with distaste before turning his attention to her. After a long moment, during which she felt she was weighed and prodded like a bird bound for the pot, he nodded and extended his hand down the table. Norrow reached up to clasp it.

"Done, and done," Almoul said.

It had all happened too quickly for Cassia to comprehend. Realisation dawned as her father sat back with a self-satisfied smile. Anger burned through the numbing shock.

"You . . . *sold* me?"

She looked around the table at them all. Meredith, as disinterested as his companion was attentive; Attis, flat-faced and disgusted; Tarves, merely amused; her own father, raising a cup of wine in triumph. And Hetch, his expression mirroring that of Rann Almoul.

"Look, it's all for the best, Cassia," Hetch said, leaning forward. He touched the back of her hand. A firm, warm touch. "Don't you see? We'll look after you. You can work for Ma as a maid."

Cassia felt his other hand drop onto her hip. He had reached around her, she realised, to prevent her from standing up. To stop her from fleeing. She stared into his eyes and at last she recognised what she saw there. Hunger. Hetch was, after all, his father's son.

Attis protested, but Cassia did not hear the words. She could see the days stretch out before her. She would be as much a slave to the Almouls as she had been to her father, but now confined to Keskor . . . and expected to be grateful for it. This was not how friends ought to treat each other. But perhaps Hetch had never truly been her friend.

"*You*, Attis? Buy the girl from us in turn?" Tarves barked with laughter, richly amused by what the moneylender had said. "Oh, but this is hilarious!"

Hetch no longer paid any attention to her, though his hand was firm upon her hip. "No, sir, she is not for sale."

"Not until you've had your use of her, anyway." Tarves grinned.

Cassia clenched her fists. Blood pumped through her veins with the rhythm of festival drums.

"This is no way to treat the poor girl!" Attis said.

Rann Almoul shrugged. "It came of your suggestion."

"But it was not what I meant!" Attis snapped back at him.

Cassia pulled her hand free of Hetch's grip. "I will not stay here," she said. Her voice was close to cracking. "I'll run. You can't keep me here."

Tarves grinned over her head at his brother. "A length of chain will solve that issue."

She looked to Baum and Meredith, pleading silently with them. *Please. You can see this is wrong. You can't let them do this. Don't leave me in Keskor!*

"No," Baum said at last, and it was as though he had heard her thoughts. "I will not countenance that. The North has been shackled long enough. Keep the promised amount of seventy-four bells, Rann Almoul. I will take the girl instead."

The party erupted into noise. Meredith stood, his hands braced firm against the table. He cast a great shadow across them all, and the protests died as suddenly as they began.

"So," Baum said. "I believe that settles everything."

Her emotions were coiled too tight for her to remain at the table. She decided it might be best to get out of the way.

"I'll see to the mule," she muttered aloud to nobody in particular, and walked as calmly as she could toward the lean-to. Her legs trembled with every step and her vision was blurred by tears welling up in her eyes. When she reached the lean-to she could not hold them off any longer, and she buried her face in the mule's foul-smelling hair, hugging the beast's neck.

It wasn't fair, she thought. It just wasn't fair. How could the day have turned so ill, so quickly? Even their escape from Varro's mob had not been so awful, not compared to this.

The mule tried to pull away. She was holding it too tight. She wiped away her tears and stared at the bags hanging from the beast's back. The sum total of their lives, she thought miserably as she began to untie them, a task made harder by her quivering fingers.

"Girl," a voice whispered quietly from the yard, making her drop one of the bags in fright. She peered around to see Attis at the gates leading from the yard, making good his intent to go home. Cassia was not certain she wanted to speak to him. After all, he had tried to purchase her too.

He glanced back in the direction of the table, making sure he was not observed. "Listen well, girl," he told her. "The gods know your father for a damned fool. Normally I'd not waste my time helping him, but now he's got you involved too."

Attis paused and took a deep breath. "Baum is a dangerous man." His voice lowered even further. "If you think that young swordsman of his is trouble enough, think again. I knew Baum fifty years ago. He hasn't changed, girl. Not a bit. He's more than he says he is. Tell your idiot father to keep his head down if he wants to keep it on his shoulders. And you – be careful, and stay away from Keskor. Rann Almoul will not forget this night."

Cassia felt the trembling return, the muscles in her arms and legs threatening to betray her. She held tight to the bags on the mule's back.

"Thank you, sir," she said, her voice cracking. "I'll tell him."

Attis opened the gate. Halfway through he stopped, looking back over his shoulder. "If I thought you had even half a chance, I'd tell you to take that mule and run now."

There were so many questions, but there wasn't enough

time. "Why?" she heard herself say. She wasn't even sure which question she had meant to ask.

The old moneylender stared at her, and he seemed to shrink a little, bowed by an unseen weight on his shoulders.

"Because I had a daughter too. Once."

The gate closed.

Chapter Three

IN THE END Cassia avoided her father completely, spending the night on the bench in Rann Almoul's yard, huddled under her threadbare blanket. It was no worse than sleeping on the ground, as she normally did. The bench was so secluded that she felt safer there than she might have in the servants' rooms.

Sleep was a different matter. She was too tense to rest, waking at the slightest sound. Several times she thought she heard somebody come into the yard, and she stayed as silent and still as she could. It could be Meredith, or Tarves, checking that she had not run off.

As though she had anywhere to run.

Panic eventually subsided into exhaustion, and she must have finally fallen into a deeper sleep, because suddenly the sky was lightening and Almoul's ancient cockerel hoarsely called in the dawn. Her hands and feet were cold, and her blanket was damp with dew, but at least it hadn't rained.

It was only when she peeled back the blanket from over her head that she realised she was not alone. Meredith stood perfectly still in the centre of the yard, his back to her, in the space the tables had occupied last night. He was bare-chested and barefoot, wearing only woollen breeches, his greatsword in its scabbard at his side. His arms were flung out wide, as though he had been crucified. Cassia could see the ridges and curves of the muscles across his back and shoulders, delineated as perfectly as any sculpture. The old man had picked his bodyguard wisely.

As she decided to swing her legs from under the blanket, the young lordling moved, with such alarming speed that she froze once more. He fell backwards, turning the fall into an effortless roll, and came back to his feet with sword drawn, held two-handed against some invisible enemy. He maintained that position for perhaps two heartbeats, and then the blade dipped, whirled and sliced through the air in a complex sequence of moves, his body following behind the weapon, twisting, crouching and jumping in counterpoint to every thrust and looping cut. Cassia could only watch, spellbound by his grace and athleticism. There were acrobats who performed these moves, perhaps, but surely not wielding such a blade at the same time.

He did not appear to have noticed her. As far as Cassia could tell, his attention was fixed on the air a mere pace in front of him. His muscles rippled as he drove the sword silently through arc after arc, lashing out to each side, both high and low. Whenever her father described swordfights in his tales, this was exactly how she imagined them.

After a minute or so, she became aware of the patterns and the rhythms within his movement. Meredith performed a dance of sorts, weaving seamlessly between long-practiced forms. She tried to imagine how anyone could stand against him, but she could only see bodies falling to the ground, life hacked and shorn away by the lordling's sword.

Meredith did not tire, nor did he stumble. That amazed her more than anything else. How in the world could he be so constant? The heroes of her father's tales were as nothing compared to this man.

And then at last, just as she began to wonder if he was truly human at all, Meredith stopped. He brought his sword around and down in a great two-handed chop that was clearly intended to decapitate a man, and dropped to one knee, the blade halting mere inches from the ground as though the weight behind the swing was of no consequence. He laid the sword on the ground in front of him and bowed his head reverently. Several hairs had worked loose from his ponytail, and they fell forward over his face as he prayed. Now Cassia felt awkward. This was a private moment, she knew, and she didn't dare move or make any sound.

His head still bowed, Meredith stretched out one hand, palm raised. "Girl, bring me water."

She blinked, startled. Had he known she was awake all along? She pushed to her feet, too disturbed to even wince at the complaining twinge of her legs, and edged around the yard. An earthenware jug sat by the wall nearby. She guessed Meredith had filled it and brought it out with him. With her heart thudding – it wouldn't be a great effort for him to pick up that sword and run her through – she tried to stop her hands trembling as she held out the jug to him.

Meredith took a long draught, water streaming from his lips down onto his chest. Then he solemnly upended the jug over his head, and Cassia had to step back quickly to avoid being soaked.

He rose, dripping, and handed her the empty jug before sheathing his sword. "Baum expects you to be ready to leave within the hour," he said, looking at her for the first time. Just as before, his gaze was devoid of all but an odd hint of curiosity.

"I – I'll tell my father," Cassia forced the words out, clutching the jug tight. Meredith's proximity was unnerving, intimidating, even.

"Good." Meredith gave a curt nod, and turned abruptly

away. He walked back into Almoul's house, leaving her alone once more.

Cassia stood for a moment, listening to Keskor awaken beyond the walls of the yard, before shaking herself loose with a relieved curse. There was too much to do, and too little time to do it all. At least that meant she'd have no time to waste in thinking and worrying.

She found her father unusually subdued and withdrawn. He was also quite sober, as far as she could tell. Perhaps he'd had second thoughts about his hasty agreement to join Baum's plot. After passing on Meredith's message she fled back into the yard and set about repacking their bags. Better to stay out of his way than risk touching off one of his tempers.

The mule tried to bite her, treading on her toes and pulling hard against its tether, but there wasn't enough room for it to manoeuvre under the cramped shelter. She got her own back by giving it a few sound whacks on its rump, as a small down payment on what she figured she owed the beast.

"It won't respect you for that."

Her hands stiffened in the mule's fur and it brayed another complaint. She had been so focused on her own tasks that she hadn't seen Baum come to the shelter.

The older man prepared his own mounts with the brisk, economical movements born of long years of practice, his strength undiminished by age. His bedroll was as tightly folded as that of a soldier, as were the leather-wrapped packs that he hung across the stallion's haunches.

"Have you eaten?" Baum asked casually, as though nothing untoward had occurred the previous night. As though she was an equal, rather than a possession. Cassia found herself unable to answer, only shaking her head dumbly in response, one hand pressed hard against the mule's flank.

"We have a long journey ahead," he continued, "so make sure you have something to break your fast before we leave. Travel on an empty stomach is never pleasant."

Cassia nodded and ducked her head as she backed out of the shelter, uncomfortable under his piercing gaze. There was something about his smile, she thought: it was hard and cold. Superficial. Attis' warning echoed through her mind. *He's more than he says he is.*

They made an uneven bunch, Cassia thought, as they waited for Hetch to drag the gates wide open. Meredith and Baum – her master and owner, now – with their great mounts and spares, clothed and prepared for a long journey, weapons covered but visible under their cloaks. Norrow shifted restlessly behind them, his boots worn bare by the years and the miles, a small pack containing his robes and purse slung uncomfortably over his shoulder. And his daughter of course, unwanted and sold away, leading the mule that carried the rest of their worldly possessions. An uneven and mismatched company.

Rann Almoul had come out to bid them farewell. He looked to have spent a long night deep in thought. He seemed older and more lined than he had the previous evening; strange, she thought, that such a change could be effected in only a few hours. But it was one thing to dream of escaping Hellea's yoke. It was another matter entirely to actually attempt to raise the Northern lands against the Empire.

He passed a small, locked chest to the old man, and Almoul and Baum spoke in low tones for a minute or two, the words unclear but their meaning unmistakable. *Build quietly, take your time. Watch and wait. Be ready. Word will come.*

And then, a single whispered word: *Caenthell.*

A chill breath swept across the yard, like the curse itself, so quietly Cassia thought she had imagined it. But Almoul took a step back, the colour draining from his face before he managed to regain his self-control. At the gate Hetch twitched, glancing over his shoulder at the darkened shapes of the mountains to the north, his guileless face suddenly edged with fear.

Caenthell. Of all the tales her father knew, those of the

ancient mountain kingdom were most rousing and inspiring. They were also the darkest and most dreadful. The Age of Talons was coming to an end, and the dragons retreated slowly from the world. With the blessing of the god Pyraete, or so it was told, Caenthell rose in place of the dragons. The High Kings of the North dominated the lands for hundreds of miles around, ruling from an impenetrable fortress filled with countless riches and treasures. The earlier stories were filled with impetuous heroism, incredible creatures and sorcery, and powerful and wise kings and queens.

But all that changed as the cycle of tales carried on. The golden optimism that suffused the stories became tarnished, the resolutions darker, the actions of the heroes no longer selfless or justifiable. Over time the High Kings lost their nobility, and the lands they ruled fell under Caenthell's savage tyranny. Pyraete turned away from the mountains in shame, and at last Caenthell was broken, stone from stone, when the warlock Malessar cursed the entire kingdom as he savagely murdered the last High King.

Rann Almoul recovered his composure, and he stepped back, gesturing toward the open gate. "May you go with Pyraete's blessing," he said, "and may the road take you swiftly and surely home."

"And may Pyraete send favour to your house and your family," Baum replied, touching his forehead lightly with two fingers. It sounded more like a curse than a blessing to Cassia's ears. Then Baum turned to Meredith, who watched the exchange indifferently. "To the road, my friend."

Meredith nodded and led the way through the gate, turning left immediately to follow the alley onto the broad road on that side of the house. Baum and Norrow followed quickly, and then it was Cassia's turn. She steadfastly refused to look at Hetch as she passed him.

For once the mule decided against pulling awkwardly away from her at every opportunity. Perhaps it had taken heed of the far more refined examples provided by the grand horses a few yards in front. Or maybe she had finally managed to beat the obstreperous attitude out of it.

Or it might just be that it saw no point in rebelling any further. *Like me*, she thought.

Even this early the streets of Keskor were bustling. This was one of the town's busiest roads, even before it met the Emperor's March. Traders pushed handcarts and larger wagons toward the market square, while bakers, blacksmiths, wood-workers and other craftsmen stoked ovens and furnaces or hung goods on rails over their shop fronts. Small gangs of men overtook the travellers, or crossed the street in front of them, some headed for fields and pastures beyond the town walls, others for quarries in the hills beyond that.

Baum and Meredith had already drawn ahead, even though they too were walking alongside their mounts. The mule wasn't the fastest beast at the best of times, and Norrow tired quickly. Cassia wondered how long her new master would accept such a slow pace. And that led her to wonder what he would do once he decided that she and her father were altogether *too* slow.

Her thoughts drifted back to the whispered mention of Caenthell. Although the kingdom had long since faded into history, its lands swallowed up by vengeful neighbours and, after that, Hellea, its name still had a double-edged potency. Mothers hushed their children with the threat of a visit from the spirit of the last, cursed High King, or from the warlock Malessar, who was said to steal infants from the crib. Cassia had heard that further south men thought of Caenthell when they spoke of the savage, treacherous north.

At the same time, however, Caenthell was a symbol of the independence and dominance that the North had once enjoyed. Such a powerful symbol could not fail to draw the hearts of men, as her father's tales proved over and over again. The stories of the end of Caenthell always looked to revenge and to the breaking of the curse.

The North will rise again, long-dead men and women promised through Norrow's words. Prophecies like that gave people something to live for. And they made the Helleans nervous. Baum had to know that.

The old man paused at the edge of the square that lay just inside Artrevia's Arch, waiting for them to catch up. The legion had a guard post here, watching over the Emperor's March as it descended into the hills, and collecting tolls from those who wished to travel the road. Norrow tended not to use the Imperial roads if he could help it, preferring to take the long, rough paths across the country. He claimed his purse could not stretch to such extravagances.

But there's always enough for another drink, she thought bitterly.

Meredith crossed to meet them, leaving his horse with the old man. He was dressed as he had been the previous night, once more looking the part of a young noble lord, but this morning he also wore a thick shirt of hardened leather under his cloak, with a pair of gauntlets tucked into his belt. He ignored Cassia and made directly for her father.

"Do you have coins?" he asked bluntly.

"Almoul never paid me," Norrow replied, ducking his head to avoid Meredith's gaze. He was evading the question as well, Cassia realised.

"But you have coins," Meredith said. "You collected from the crowd last night."

Her father exhaled slowly, as though the air in his lungs was too precious to release. "I doubt there's enough to pay the tolls for *four* of us," he said. The cutting edge of his words made it plain who he blamed for this.

Meredith's expression finally changed, as he tilted his head to one side and raised his brows in something that might be amusement. He turned his head smoothly to look across at Cassia for a moment. She felt herself flush, uncomfortable under his attention, and uncertain how she could possibly help with or resolve the situation. Her father was about to get them into a terrible fight again, and this time he might have taken on much more than he could handle.

Just as the tension was becoming so unbearable she thought the guards must have to step in, Meredith turned back to her father and made a throwaway motion with one hand, a movement that looked as awkward as his swordplay had been fluid.

"You have coins. You will earn more in other towns. You will pay our way today. Come with me; we must pay our tolls."

He waited until Norrow moved ahead of him, as if he was herding a stubborn animal to its pen. Cassia exhaled slowly, coaxing the mule back into motion behind them. *That was . . . odd*, she thought. There was no other word to describe it. Meredith might be a master swordsman, but he was a strange and unnerving man.

Baum fell in alongside her and watched the two men head toward the guard post. A smile quirked the corner of his mouth.

"Your father doesn't travel well," he observed.

"No," Cassia agreed, before she could stop herself. She cursed herself silently for speaking out of turn, then sighed and shook her head. What did it matter, after all? "No, sir, he does not."

"He'll be all the more upset before the end of the day, I'll wager," the historian continued.

Cassia watched her father shrug his pack to the ground and delve deep into it for his purse. She didn't like the sound of this, though it clearly amused Baum. The more foul-tempered Norrow became, the more likely it was that he would lash out at her.

"Why, sir?" she asked, dreading the answer.

But Baum only smiled at her. "Oh, the reason will come soon enough. More to the point, how are you this morning?"

She wasn't sure how she should answer this question. She was tired and afraid, worried by her forced involvement in a treasonous plan against the Emperor, and the muscles in her shoulders and her neck ached from a tension she could not dispel. Layer upon layer of betrayal and abandonment. First by her father, then Hetch. And even old Attis had sought to buy her, though she could not understand why. Several times she had wanted to cry, but somehow the tears would not flow.

It was all this man's fault, this strange old man who plotted the revival of the North. Now he seemed concerned for Cassia's welfare, the morning after he had bought her like a sack of winter roots.

"I don't know," she said cautiously. It was the truth, after all.

Baum seemed pleased with that answer, nodding as though it had confirmed what he already thought. "An unsettling night," he remarked. "But if it reassures you at all, we are not the monsters you may believe us to be. There are still men in this world who are infinitely more treacherous and murderous than either of us."

But they are not here, right now, Cassia thought. *Small comfort indeed.*

By the side of the road, just outside the gates, a squared-off stone marker indicated the distance to Escalia and beyond that, to Devrilinum. Cassia had been to Escalia several times over the last few years, but Norrow had rarely ventured further south than that, and Devrilinum was completely unknown to her. She thought it must look much like its near-neighbour, and not much different to Keskor itself, with low buildings huddled together on undulating countryside, their roofs sloped to counter the snows of winter.

She occupied herself for a time by picturing herself in the market square at Devrilinum, reciting the story Baum had recounted last night. She was surrounded by a crowd that thronged six or seven deep, and they laughed and gasped, just as they would have if Norrow had told the tale. The soft clink of coins came frequently from a bowl that passed, unseen, around the circle.

But her mind could not maintain the illusion. Tarves and Rann Almoul were in the crowd somewhere, and she could almost hear Hetch's voice, interrupting her as she tried to remember the name of the Berdellan king. After that her concentration crumbled and she imagined the circle of men shouting to outbid each other as she was led around the perimeter in shackles.

She sighed and paused for a moment to look around, kneading one fist in the small of her back to relieve the aches that had accrued over the morning. The Emperor's March rose and fell with the terrain, rather than cutting through it as it did elsewhere. Coaxing the mule up the slopes and then being dragged down the other side was uncomfortable to say the least.

But she was faring better than her father, who was weighed down by his pack – and his purse. Norrow had fallen behind soon after leaving Keskor. As she looked back she saw him struggling along the road. His muttered curses were barely in-telligible at this distance. Meredith rode his horse beside him, the great beast kept to an impatiently slow walk.

A fine company we make, so strung out along the road. Earlier there had been the best part of half a mile between the two riders and her father, and Baum had been forced to wait while Norrow caught them up. Cassia sensed her new master's growing frustration. Clearly he had not banked on her father being so slow.

The sound of hooves approached from further up the road. Baum had given up waiting. Cassia tightened her grip on the mule's rope.

"Can you move any faster than this?" the old soldier asked, in the tones of a man who was genuinely interested in the answer.

The day wasn't remarkably warm, but Norrow's face was ruddy and beaded with sweat. He looked angry, afraid, and ill. And old, she realised. It was as though the last day had aged him by more than a decade.

"Perhaps you should leave me behind," Norrow said, pushing each word out breathlessly.

Baum laughed, but there was little humour in the sound. "Oh no, I don't think so. Attis has no faith in your character, I'm afraid, and I trust his judgement now as much as I did when we fought side by side in Berdella. No, we'll keep you with us yet."

Cassia breathed out. The mule tugged at her hand experimentally, eager to carry on toward Escalia.

That gave her a thought.

"The mule can carry him," she said. "It's used to that."

Norrow glared at her, his mouth thinning to a hard line, but he said nothing.

Baum grunted. "That ragged beast?"

"It's stronger than it looks," she said, smiling at the irony of having to defend the obnoxious thing against criticism. "When he's too drunk to walk it's the only way we can move on."

Baum considered her for a moment, rubbing his lips with one hand. The mule tugged again, threatening to unbalance her, and as she turned to smack it with her free hand she caught her father's eye. Her heart sank. He would not forgive her quickly for this.

"Will it be any faster this way?" Meredith asked.

"That, of course, is the real question," Baum agreed.

Cassia took a breath before answering. *I don't think anything I say now could make the beatings any worse than they will be already.* "Well," she said slowly, "it could hardly be any slower."

Meredith made a short, barking noise. It took her a few moments to realise that the lordling was laughing.

The packs she carried were heavy, once the weight had been redistributed. The mule bore Norrow and little more than that. But Cassia was used to carrying extra weight, even if the load was uncomfortable and fatiguing, and she had no intention of falling behind. Just as she had always done, she sang under her breath and kept her eyes on the road a few feet ahead. She had long ago discovered that it helped her make reasonably good time.

And they *were* moving faster than they had done earlier that morning, even though the road now ran downhill more often than not. Keskor and its outlying fields had been left far behind, and the influx of farmers and traders from the small roadside villages had slowed to a trickle. They might not reach Escalia before nightfall, but they would surely be better than halfway there. There was an inn outside the town's gates, one where Norrow was still tolerated, and they might be able to spend the night there.

Thoughts of the evening to come made her lose her rhythm, and she cursed silently while she regained her step, rolling her shoulders to shift the weight on her back. She wondered how long her father would wait before seeking her out. With the best of luck he would be in his cups quickly, too drunk to vent his anger on her. But her luck could not even charitably be described as good these past few days. Just as long as the bruising did not make walking too difficult, and she could still keep up with the others . . .

She forced her mind onto another track and glanced to her left, where Meredith's silhouette blocked out the sun, which shone infrequently through the slow-moving clouds. The lordling had taken up station alongside her and had not moved away once. Was he there to make sure she could keep up with the others, she wondered, or to protect her from her father?

It was a curious thought. If she had breath to spare, and if she could summon the courage, she might have asked him outright. Either way, his presence kept her father at bay for the time being. He rode the mule in an uncomfortable silence, just behind Baum's horse, responding to questions with grunts or reluctant one-word answers.

By her reckoning it was just past midday when Baum halted and looked back over his shoulder, smiling. He waited for them all to reach his position at the side of the road.

"How well do you know this land, sir?" he asked Norrow.

Norrow shrugged. When the words came, it was clear he didn't like to say them. "As well as many. I was born outside Devrilinum."

"So you'll know what lies east from here?"

"Not much," Norrow replied, venturing a foul glance in Meredith's direction. The lordling's blank stare quickly defeated him. "Old quarries, mined out."

"The stone that made the North," Baum said, nodding agreement. "Shipped as far afield as Trenis and even Hellea itself, I believe. But this is also where the ancient stones of Caenthell itself were quarried. Pyraete himself guided the first High King to this land and told him to take the stone from here. *The rocks of the mountains are strong enough, but these are the stones on which the mountains rest,* he said to Gallemas, when Gallemas thought to question him."

"So say the stories," Norrow grunted. "Shouldn't we move faster for Escalia?"

Baum flashed a conspiratorial smile at Cassia. "Oh, so the stories say, indeed. Perhaps one day we shall find out for certain. But as for Escalia, we go no further on that road, I'm afraid. We head eastward from here, out into the country."

He heeled his horse about and set off into the grasses. Norrow stared around, his mouth and eyes wide open in confusion, apparently lost for words. Cassia looked up at Meredith in disbelief – surely this wasn't what Baum had meant, back in Keskor? There was nothing out there – no roads, no houses, nothing. The lordling only lifted one hand to point eastwards, his expression as impassive as usual.

"This day just keeps getting better and better," she muttered to herself, shaking her head.

The going wasn't as bad as she had feared, to her surprise. For the most part the ground was hard beneath her feet, and the path Baum chose seemed raised above the rest of the land, which rolled in waves as far as she could see. Untouched and unfarmed, low bushes and stands of trees fought for their place amidst the long grasses. The only signs of life were the pellets left by rabbits and sheep. At least they might be able to catch something to eat out here, she thought, allowing her hopes to rise a little.

They travelled in single file. The ridge that Baum followed was too narrow for Meredith to ride alongside either Cassia or her father any longer. Instead the lordling took up his position at the rear, making certain they did not lag behind.

As the afternoon wore on, and the ridge did not deviate either south or north, Cassia was struck by a thought. Emboldened by Baum's current good mood, she picked up her pace to draw closer to his horse.

"Sir, is this a trail that Gallemas had laid down?"

Baum tugged at his reins, forcing her to stop too. Behind her, Norrow muttered curses at the mule.

Baum nodded, a smile half-formed upon his face again. "What makes you think that, girl?"

Cassia felt heat rise into her cheeks and looked away quickly. At the ground, at the horse's hooves, and at a thin tree that contrived to grow at an angle from the slope below. There was no reason to be embarrassed, she told herself angrily. Every small thing she learned could be used to help her, just as Hestella the Maiden had learned founding those tragedies that bore her name.

"This ridge – it's too flat," she said. "And too hard. And too long – it can't be natural. But that means it must be really old."

"And?" Baum prompted.

Cassia thought for a moment. "And . . . it had to be built to carry the stone from the quarries to the Emperor's March?"

"And from there into the mountains," Baum said. "Of course the March was known by other names in those days, and it ran by another route, passing by Keskor entirely. Keskor was a village, little more than a dozen herders' cottages in all."

He flicked his reins, and his horse resumed its steady walk. Cassia forced her tired muscles into motion, listening intently all the while. She hadn't known any of this. The Factor's school in Keskor taught Imperial history, and Norrow's own tales rarely touched on anything so mundane as a quarry.

"Small towns grew up around the quarries," Baum called back over his shoulder. "Towns like Kennetta, Gethista and Aelior. Thriving places; heralds of a new dawn in the North. The buildings sprung up as fast as the stone could be hewn from the ground. The townsfolk grew rich and hung golden tapestries from their walls. They lived in such finery and luxury that even the great lords of Stromondor were jealous of them; even the meanest of those labourers had servants to wait upon them."

He pointed with his left hand. "Aelior stood over the horizon – the smallest of the quarry towns. Eventually this road will turn to find it, but that is not the road we follow. We seek the way between Kennetta and Gethista."

Norrow snorted. "If these towns were so rich and famous, then why have I never heard a single tale of them, eh? Where are they now? There are no fabulous houses outside Escalia, I can tell you that now."

Cassia winced at his abrasive tone – it was as though he wanted to annoy the man – but she had to admit he had a valid point. If Gethista had ever been a real place, it was one she knew nothing about. It certainly didn't sound all that real.

Baum shook his head and Cassia thought she heard him

sigh. "Just because it is no longer there, that does not mean Gethista never existed at all – nor Kennetta or Aelior for that matter, storyteller."

Norrow hawked and spat loudly into the grass. As the day wore on he had become more difficult and bitter. Cassia knew this meant he had no wine in his pack. In this mood he was wholly capable of provoking a fight. She drew in a breath as Baum's shoulders stiffened.

When he spoke, his voice sounded quite natural, almost conversational, but Cassia found herself slowing to allow his horse to pull ahead. "Perhaps you will allow me to enlighten you," he said, without looking back. "Here is a tale you can add to your own stock, and it may be as you say – that none in the North now know it. When Pyraete had come to Gallemas and told him of these lands, where the rock was the foundations of the mountains themselves, the High King called for his sons, his lords and his banners, and he led them down to conquer and hold this new, god-given place.

"Gallemas' scouts found three places where Pyraete's stone was close to the surface of the earth. He named his eldest son, Gethis, as the overseer of the quarries, and it was Gethis who founded all three towns that stood in this region. He drafted the local farmers and herders to build for him, and employed them as slave labour in the quarries. Gethis was a hard, practical man who thought and planned for the future. When he set his mind to a task, it would be done – and done well. He planned these roads, you know? How else to move such massive loads of stone back up into the mountains?"

Cassia risked a glance back at her father, only to see scepticism plainly written across his face. For her own part, she had already wondered why such fabulously wealthy towns had vanished from history so completely that not even their names remained. And, as Norrow had already pointed out, how did the old man know all of this?

"And so the great work progressed," Baum continued. "The

earth was gutted in Pyraete's name, and Gallemas saw the walls and towers of Caenthell raised high in the mountains. All along the way, throughout the project, prayers and sacrifices were made to Pyraete; thanksgiving for his blessings, and for the growing might of the North. In fact, if you look hard, you can still see the remains of some of the roadside shrines."

He halted again and drew Cassia's attention to a brush-covered mound at the bottom of the ridge. At first she took it for an overgrown shrub atop earth that had tumbled from the side of the slope, but after a moment she perceived the regular stone lines hidden under the branches and leaves, and recognised it for what it was.

"How did all this become lost, if it really was as you say?" she asked, marvelling at how much could be hidden in plain sight.

"Ah," Baum said sadly. "What is history but an overlong tragedy? You wonder why the North was not always so great right from the very beginning? Or why those towns were never resettled?"

"What point, if the quarries were worked out?" Norrow said, sounding somewhat defensive. "The land is dry – not worth having. And dangerous too, for all the old workings."

"Exactly so," Baum nodded. He started moving again, and Cassia wished he would make his mind up. All this stop-and-start was tiring her faster than any amount of walking. "What happens when men over-reach themselves? They fall. And as with men, so with the towns of Gethista, Kennetta and Aelior. They were not content to have the glory that would come with Caenthell. They saw how others envied and desired the stone from their quarries, and they saw opportunities. Markets. They were taken in by avarice, and they began to sell the stone that was meant for Caenthell to places such as Trenis and Hellea, just as I have already said."

He shrugged and made a throwaway gesture. "For a while that was not noticed. There was enough stone to satisfy everybody's needs. But in time Gallemas found cause for concern over his son's behaviour. Some said afterwards that Pyraete appeared to him and warned him that Caenthell would surely fall if he did not act. Others reckoned Gallemas had already seen the danger and that he tried to forestall the god's wrath. In any event, he arrived in Gethista unannounced and in force. After publicly denouncing Gethis he forced the inhabitants of all three towns – man, woman and slave alike – to haul one last massive shipment of stone into the mountains. The exodus from the plains must have been incredible to witness."

Cassia looked around and tried to imagine the lines of people that would have wound along the length of the road, all hauling at ropes, pushing at the rear of slowed wagons; their fine clothes ripped, their hands and feet torn and bleeding. Surrounded all the while by soldiers from their own homeland. It sounded all too believable.

"What happened to them?" she asked hesitantly, fearing she already knew the answer. "And what happened to the towns they left behind?"

"There even the ancient histories fail," Baum said. "Gallemas returned to the mountains, and sealed Caenthell from the world while he finished his fortifications and built an army to conquer the North. *Those* tales are told even now. But of Gethis and his lords and merchants, and all those who were seized from the towns of Gethista, Aelior and Kennetta, nothing more is known."

He reached out to an overhanging tree and snapped off the end of a branch as the horse carried him underneath. "One tale I have heard, regarding the fate of the towns themselves, is that Pyraete had grown angry that Gethis abused the god's gifts of stone. After the town was emptied, Pyraete withdrew his blessings from the land, and the quarries became unworkable. The grand houses, pillars, colonnades and statues of the new towns cracked, crumbled and returned to the ground. Gone, as if they had never been raised at all, with not even memories to survive them."

"Phah," Norrow scoffed. "Rubbish. That's just plain poor storytelling. If none escaped then who remained to pass on the stories, eh?"

Cassia ducked her head as Baum shifted in his saddle to give her father a sharp glare. *Oh Ceresel,* she prayed silently, *strike my father silent, please!*

Norrow said nothing more after that, but Meredith's looming presence behind him surely had more to do with that than the goddess of fortune.

"Do you think the lords of Caenthell would be proud of such a story?" Baum said at length, his tone much darker than before. "Would they wish it spread throughout the North that they displeased Pyraete and enslaved their own people? Perhaps, perhaps not. Suffice it to say that when Caenthell died, all of its history was brought down and scattered with it."

He smiled at Norrow for a brief moment. Cassia saw no humour in that smile, and she felt a chill run through her limbs. "Perhaps, my good friend, you are the first man of the North to hear this tale since Caenthell fell. Wouldn't that be an occasion to celebrate?"

To Cassia's immense relief, Norrow did not reply.

Thick clouds turned the late afternoon grey and cold, and the landscape was now rugged and stark. Cassia began to doubt there was any living beast out here. All this land, untouched by men for centuries, and yet they were less than a day from Keskor. Before today she would not have believed a land could be so empty.

The road had turned south again early in the afternoon, heading down to where Baum said Aelior had lain. The old soldier had paused to survey the eastern horizon for several minutes, before leading them down from the ridge and across a field of knee high grasses that whipped in the wind and stung Cassia's legs as she struggled through them. She stumbled on loose chunks of earth and stone that were hidden underfoot, and she fell behind the others, tiring rapidly. Not once did her father look back or offer to ease her load.

"I'm afraid we've missed the southbound road," the historian called back at one point. "But not by too much, I believe – we should still pick it up before nightfall."

"Shouldn't we have stayed upon the March?" Norrow asked, his voice almost a whine. "If you'd intended to go south—"

"And if I'd intended to let the Factor know exactly where to find me, I'd have done just that," Baum interrupted. "Now, stay silent and let me find our road, storyteller."

Cassia allowed herself a weary private smile, despite her fear of the old soldier and his silent, formidable companion. At least her father was being given the level of respect that he really deserved.

As daylight drained from the world and she began to think that she might have to pick her way across the treacherous slopes in darkness, Baum called out again. "Ah, better than I thought! Girl, lift your feet, we are here at last!"

She gritted her teeth and pushed forward as fast as she dared, until she joined the other three, who had dismounted at the bottom of a gentle but overgrown upward climb. Even in the gloom she saw the historian's smile of satisfaction. Her father's sullen scowl looked to have been set in clay and fired, while Meredith merely glanced about with the same detached curiosity with which he approached everything.

"Is this the road, sir?" she asked breathlessly. Even the climb up to it couldn't be worse than those endless swathes of awful grass.

Baum shook his head. "Much better than that," he said, stooping to sweep away the dirt at his feet. "Take a look, girl."

She leaned forward and squinted, focusing on the dark

patch he had cleared. Beneath the topsoil the ground was smooth and flat. It looked like stone, but somehow patterned. She realised, with a drawn-in gasp, that the pattern had to be man-made.

"Tiles," Baum confirmed. "The remnants of a mosaic, if I am correct. We have come to Gethista."

Chapter Four

As tired as Cassia was already, there was still much to do before she could rest. The familiar routines of setting a camp helped distract her from the strange truths of her surroundings.

Her first task, as always, was to secure the mule to a low branch and gather the packs together at the site Baum had picked as their camp. She heard him pointing out landmarks and long-buried features of the dead town to her father. Norrow grunted and muttered as he was drawn reluctantly along. She kept her head down, working fast despite her weariness, glad Baum was keeping him occupied. She was certain he had not forgotten his earlier anger toward her.

Next came the shelter, pegged out against the prevailing winds, the stretched hides propped up at their open end with a branch snapped from a nearby alder. She piled the packs around the shelter to act as a further windbreak.

Her stomach growled all the while, reminding her she had not eaten since early morning. One of the packs held three bundles, each of three stakes bound with twine. All the stakes were carved and notched, to fit together and make a series of small frames. Cassia took her stakes and walked away from the camp, peering at the ground intently.

She counted about fifty paces before she found the droppings she was looking for. Now she only had to build the traps. The rest would come with patience, and Ceresel's grace.

Her skin prickled, as if touched by a cold breeze, and she glanced nervously over her shoulder. If this town was dead, it might still have ghosts. She was suddenly aware that in the gathering gloom, she could no longer clearly see the camp.

She turned back – and Meredith was before her. She had no time to cry out before she lost her balance and fell backward, the breath knocked from her by the shock of his unexpected appearance.

He took a step closer and she shrunk back against the ground, her hands grasping for the bundle of stakes she had dropped. The darkening sky lent stone grey tones to his skin, and her mind raced away from all the horrors she could imagine. Her eyes fixed upon his arms as he bent and reached down -

Oh Ceresel, please, no -

A strong hand closed firmly on her arm and pulled her upright as though she weighed nothing at all. Cassia blinked and stared straight at Meredith's chest. The fine golden chain looped around his neck, falling into the folds of his shirt. The links of the chain mesmerised her.

"Why have you left the camp?" Meredith's voice broke into her scattered thoughts, dragging her back.

She ducked her head, anger battling with relief and embarrassment. Her limbs had started to shake, as they had done the previous night once the immediate danger was past. But this time it felt different. The lordling was uncomfortably close to her . . .

Cassia pulled her arm from his grasp and backed away. He seemed content to let her do that, but his passivity only served to unbalance her further.

"Sir, I need to set these snares." Her voice sounded as unsteady as she felt.

Meredith glanced down at the bundles that lay behind her. "Why? There is no danger here."

She swallowed, and stared up at him. Was he serious? There was no humour in his face, only the same guileless expression he had worn all day.

He really has no idea what these are for!

She took a slow, deliberate breath, rubbing her arm where he had gripped too tight. Shock was giving way to anger, and indignation.

"Do you have enough food back there to feed all four of us, sir?"

Meredith frowned and shook his head. "No, I do not think so."

She snatched up the nearest bundle of stakes. "Then why don't you let me get on with setting these snares, so we can all eat tonight?" She punctuated her words with angry jabs with the stakes. "Or do you want to starve us now?"

Meredith stepped back. His eyes widened and his hands rose in a defensive gesture, which served to inflame Cassia's temper even further. She pressed home her attack before she considered the wisdom of doing so.

"Why are you following me, anyway? Don't you know it's rude to sneak up on people? Why don't you lump off and make yourself useful somewhere else? Go on, go and . . . go and gather some firewood, will you? Make my life a bit easier!"

She paused to take a breath, and her gaze lit upon the short sword sheathed at his side. The realisation of what she was saying fell on her like the sea had fallen on Destrill, the great Galliarcan hero.

Oh, you stupid girl! She cursed herself as her anger was quenched by cold reason. What use was a bundle of sticks against a blade? The muscles of her outstretched arm trembled, betraying her nerves, and she lowered the stakes quickly. She bent to collect the other bundles to hide the rush of crimson she knew had burst into her cheeks.

Meredith had not moved, other than to lower his arms again. His expression was one of mystified amusement, as though he did not quite believe what he had heard.

Cassia's embarrassed anger flared once more. "What are you waiting for?" she snapped, though the same aggression was much harder to maintain. "Firewood!"

Meredith's head dipped in a slight bow, a movement that took her aback. "As you say," he said, and turned away. Her embarrassment turned to open-mouthed disbelief as she watched him begin to collect the deadfall branches that lay under the nearby trees.

"Not here," she told him, with an exasperated sigh. "I'm setting the snares here. You'll scare off the game. Go over to the other side of the camp."

The lordling bowed again and stepped back into the colourless evening without another word. Cassia stared after him for a moment, the bundled stakes still clutched tight in her hands, while her temper bubbled and drained away. Then, at last, she sank back to the ground with a ragged exhalation.

The knots that tied her snare stakes together were too tight for her trembling fingers to manage, so she had to sit there until she felt calm enough to continue. While she waited her gaze roamed over the rough ground, seeking suitable spots for her traps. All she needed were a few good-sized rocks and somewhere that looked like a run between warrens. Once she had these it was simple enough to prop up each rock with a set of snare-stakes so it would fall on any small beast that passed underneath.

She felt a sudden empathy with the unsuspecting rabbits. In many ways, she was walking underneath rocks herself. She hoped that if she triggered her own trap one day she would be lucky enough to never know it. Some rabbits she had caught in the past were not so lucky, and the squeals of pain had been distressing, at first.

She made her way back to camp slowly, alert for any sound of her father arguing with Baum. But there was nothing other than the deep, low tones of the old man, humming a song she did not recognise as he erected his own shelter. He looked up as she came closer, and were it not for the poor light she would have sworn he smiled at her.

"You've set traps, I hear? Good, though it may be rather late in the day to start cooking."

She shrugged a reply. Her father's wild temper and varying levels of sobriety made meals unpredictable at the best of times. It was something she thought Baum, as a former soldier, would have been used to. If her snares worked tonight they would have food to carry in the morning.

In the meantime there was little to do but wait. Wait for something to trigger one of those traps, wait for Meredith to return with fuel for the fire. Force of habit drove her back to where the mule was tethered, to check the knots held firm.

She passed her father's shelter, wondering if he had retreated inside to nurse his sour mood. It was an easy decision not to duck her head inside to find out. Until a fire was lit and something – anything – was cooking over it, Norrow would not be pleasant company for anyone.

Not even with dinner served, she thought. In fact, not even a full roasted haunch served on silver plates, with the Factor's own wines -

She sensed him behind her, much too late. He pulled her around, twisting her arm with a savage jerk. She had time to glimpse his face, sharp and ugly, lips curled into a snarl, before the back of his other hand connected with her cheek.

White pain bloomed behind her eyes as her head snapped to the side. Norrow shoved her to the ground with a push that took her breath away. She landed as she had learned to, without a single cry or whimper, curling instinctively into a ball to protect her stomach.

Eyes screwed tight against the pain, she could not tell exactly where he was until he hissed venomously into her ear, his spittle moist against her cheek.

"What do you think you're doing? Making me look a damned fool? Trying to get us both killed? Idiot girl!"

He gripped her chin and dragged her face toward his. She didn't want to look at him, but she knew if she did not the beating would be far worse.

"If he *wants* you," her father ground out the words, "he *has* you. Whatever he says, you do. You don't argue, you don't refuse. Understood?"

She nodded, the only movement he would allow her to make. *Yes, I understand. I am a shield for your safety. My body to be traded for your life.*

She felt sick. This was the second successive night Norrow had shown how he intended to use her to save himself. Yet it was he who had spent the whole day needling and picking arguments with Baum, not her.

Norrow released her and withdrew, as suddenly as he had caught her. Back to the shelter to await his meal. She would not be released from that duty.

She rolled onto her stomach and pushed herself up onto her knees. She was brushing dirt from her dress when she realised she was being watched. Meredith stood a short distance away, branches piled in his arms. She wondered how long he had been there. Had her father spotted him and made his retreat? If the lordling had seen anything, what must he have thought? Had he thought to intervene?

As ever, Meredith's face held no indication of his thoughts. She held his gaze a long moment as she raised one hand to massage her jaw, and then drew herself unsteadily upright with a muttered curse.

He strode down into camp as though nothing had happened. "This wood will suffice for now," he said as he passed.

"Thank you, sir." She fell in behind him, making sure she

gave her father's lean-to a wide berth. Baum seemed to have settled into his own shelter – at any rate, he was nowhere to be seen. How much of her father's attack had *he* witnessed?

Meredith dropped his load with a clatter, midway between the two shelters. "Light the fire," he said to her, as a lord might order a slave. "I have my own tent to erect."

He paused for a moment, and Cassia wondered if he was waiting for her to reply. "I will stand watch on this camp tonight," he added, at last.

It may have been for her father's benefit as much as her own, but she appreciated it all the same.

"Thank you," she said again, turning away quickly as she heard the catch in her voice. She sat with her back to Norrow's shelter and began sorting through the firewood.

Cassia snapped awake at the faint sound of leather scuffed on loose stone. Her hand closed on one of the fist-sized rocks she had gathered and laid out by her bedroll, and she tensed her legs to spring out from her blanket. The sound came again. Behind her, on the other side of the fire. Where she had set her father's lean-to.

With one swift motion she rolled, flung the blanket aside, and landed in a crouch with her hand drawn back to make the throw.

Meredith stood on the far side of the makeshift hearth, frozen in place, staring unblinkingly down at her. He held his great sword over his head as though he was about to leap at her and run her through.

Very slowly, very carefully, she lowered the stone to the ground and kicked it away, never taking her gaze from the lordling who stood poised to strike only a few feet away. Meredith's eyes followed her movements intently, but he did not relax, even when she spread her hands wide to prove they were empty.

"Continue," Baum's voice whispered, away to her left. Meredith spun in place and the blade whistled down in a smooth arc, lifting into another dizzying sequence of forms, just as he had the previous morning.

Cassia edged backwards as quickly as she dared. She felt for her blanket and wrapped it over her shoulders. First light had come, but the night had been cold and damp, and even the thin blanket was better protection than nothing. Joining her father in his mean shelter had been completely out of the question.

The fire she had built and tended, until she was too exhausted to keep her eyes open, was still alight. Someone must have nursed it through the night while she slept beside it. Once Meredith stopped swinging that great sword of his around she might feel able to sit a little closer to it.

She glanced sidewards and saw Baum sat cross-legged at the mouth of his shelter, busy with a covered clay pot that steamed in the cold morning air.

"Sir, does he do this every morning?" she asked hesitantly.

Baum nodded. "Without fail. And thus, without failure. I think you surprised him. Not many people manage that much."

"And if I had thrown that stone at him?"

He smiled and dipped into his pack for two smaller bowls that looked to have been fired from the same clay. "It would not have been a good idea, girl."

Meredith spun and dipped, working his way across the space step by step. Cassia thought she recognised a few of the moves from the previous morning. Her stomach protested the lack of food last night, and she suppressed a miserable sigh. It was past time to check the snares. She hadn't dared venture beyond the small camp after setting the fire for fearing of being ambushed by her father again. Or worse. With luck, at least one of the three would have been triggered, but she had left them so long that scavengers would almost certainly have snatched anything that had been caught.

Baum looked up as she moved, and raised one of the smaller bowls to her. "Here. It's been cooking most of the night, I think. Plain, but more than fair."

She took the bowl cautiously, realising the contents were hot. Steam brought the aroma of cooked meat to her nose and she breathed it in deeply, not caring that the clay came close to scalding her hands.

It's rabbit? But . . . She looked up sharply. Baum returned an innocent smile and a shrug.

"It seemed a shame to let your catch go to waste, girl," he said. He spooned up a mouthful of the stew with one hand and nodded with satisfaction as he chewed, pausing to wag an admonitory finger in her direction. "Eat up. It'll be less fair when it cools down. Cold rabbit – bah . . ."

She didn't need telling more than once. The bowl was empty too quickly, but she had not eaten so well in several days. She cast surreptitious glances at Baum while she ate, surprised and wrong-footed once again by his actions. He did not *appear* to be a man seeking to destroy the influence of the Empire in the North. Nor did he seem to be the hard military campaigner he had apparently once been. There was still a lean edge to him, an impression of capability, of something held back. But that was almost intangible – it came and went like a shadow on a cloudy day.

It was just enough to keep her from relaxing too much. And when her father finally crawled from his shelter, cursing under his breath and glaring across the hearth at her, she decided it was time to retrieve her spent snares and search for a source of water. If they had built a town here, there must be water nearby.

Baum passed her his bowl wordlessly. A part of her bridled – *I am a bought slave now* – but she bit down her temper as she realised she had even better reason to search for water now. She hurried away from the camp, aware of voices behind her. Baum had diverted her father by offering him some stew, she guessed. That was a blessing unasked for, and yet another act that countered her impression of him.

By daylight the land that had once been Gethista looked as though it still possessed some vestige of its past life. The overpowering grey skies gave way to lighter, wispy clouds that allowed the sun to filter through, and the ground was bursting with fresh growth. Cassia found a trickling stream that ran behind their camp, emptying into a small pool further down the hill. It was just large enough to fill all their waterskins comfortably. After that she plunged her head into the water and scrubbed hard at her face and arms. The water was so cold that it helped draw away the sharp aches of her new bruises, but it was still difficult to turn her head very far to one side.

She briefly considered running, finding a hiding-place somewhere deep in the long grasses that surrounded the rubble of Gethista. She had enough craft to live off the land, at least for a while, and she did not think that Baum would waste much time searching for her, especially since he had tasks awaiting him elsewhere. She was quite certain her father would not miss her. But Meredith – she told herself in vain it was the cold water that caused her to shiver – Meredith would not halt until he had found her. He might not be able to hold an intelligent conversation, but she could not doubt his determined nature.

Despite the meal she had eaten, her stomach roiled; an empty, queasy sensation as she saw the day stretch out before her. Another uncomfortable march through the untended country, with her father's black moods continuing to threaten their safety. She wondered if she would have been better off remaining at the Almoul house – whether as a prisoner, servant, or slave, surely her future would have been more certain.

But then perhaps not. Neither Meredith nor Baum had yet threatened her, had they?

No, the fatalistic voice in her mind said. No, they had not. Not directly.

Not yet.

The day played out much as she had expected. Once she dismantled the shelters and repacked as much as she could onto the mule's back, she discovered her own pack felt a little lighter than the previous day. She had no time to wonder at the difference, however, as Baum and Meredith had already cleared the remainder of the camp and the old man was impatient to set off.

Only Norrow delayed their departure: he insisted he be allowed to find a stout, straight branch to use as a walking staff, and by the time they finally left Gethista the sun had fully cleared the hills to the east and Baum's face was set in a frustrated grimace. Cassia did not have the courage to go a near him while he was in such a poorly-checked temper and so, since travelling alongside her father was also out, she dropped back until she was walking just ahead of Meredith's mare.

Around mid-afternoon the path Baum had picked out began to slope steeply downhill, following the stream into a gulley lined with sharp, spray-dampened rocks. They were forced to slow, leading the animals carefully and frequently deviating from the path to search for more gentle gradients.

Norrow's constant grumbling counterpointed the lively gurgles of the stream as it fell beside them and gathered into small pools. Cassia slipped a few times and skinned her palms, but the pain soon receded as the need to concentrate on her surroundings took over. Even Baum cursed under his breath when he thought no-one else was in earshot. When he caught Cassia grinning at him he clamped his mouth firmly shut and glared at her, although the effect was spoiled by another loose stone underfoot.

Only the mule seemed content in any way; despite having to cope with the heavy packs hung over its back and, when the path allowed it, the weight of her father, the beast had never looked happier. Perhaps it enjoyed the change of view. All it had ever seen were dusty, winding roads and tracks between the towns of the province. Back and forth, back and forth, plodding slowly and endlessly from gate to gate. Now, for the first time since Norrow had acquired it, the stubborn old mule had left its contrary streak behind. If only the same could be said for Norrow himself.

Remembering her father's angry words the night before, Cassia tried to stay close to Meredith as they wound their way down into a valley that opened gradually before them. The lordling matched the mule's calm temperament, as well as the beast's intractable silence. She tried several times to engage him in conversation, but Meredith apparently too wrapped in his own thoughts to bother with talking.

He raised his head occasionally to gaze around at the walls of the valley, as though searching for some approaching threat, but even then he would only give monosyllabic replies to the questions she asked. How had Baum come so far in his company without wanting to scream at his unresponsiveness? Cassia could not have imagined a less likely partnership than these two men.

After a while boredom and frustration set in. They were dangerous companions when she travelled with only her father for company, but the events of the past day emboldened her. Why should it prove so difficult to draw a straight conversation from either of them?

"Can you teach me how to use a sword?" she asked.

Meredith blinked, frowning down at her.

"I've seen boys learning their formations and drills in the Factor's school in Keskor. It looks easy enough for them, so it can't be all that difficult, can it?"

Now Meredith's face set into that familiar expression of dry amusement. "You wish to learn a weapon? You already have a knife. If you cut a staff for yourself tonight, you will have a most suitable weapon. You have no need of a sword. What would you do with one – attack rabbits?"

She squared her shoulders. "Why shouldn't I learn anyway? *All true Northerners should bare steel to their enemies* – that's what Pyraete said when he raised the great mountains, you know."

It was part of a children's story, not one Norrow told often, for fear of drawing unwanted attention from the Factor's men, but it was one of the first Cassia had learned by heart. Norrow wasn't beyond using his stories as a means to get what he wanted, so why shouldn't she do the same?

Meredith smiled down at her. "Cut yourself a staff," he repeated. "First we must see if there is steel within you."

"Oh, there is," Cassia said fiercely, her embarrassment gone as fast as it had risen. She and Hetch had practised with staves several times, and she was proud of her skill with them. Five times from six it was Hetch who would end up stunned on the ground or cursing as he clutched a fresh bruise and hopped from foot to foot in pain. To her mind this sounded like a challenge.

"We shall see," Meredith replied.

It *was* a challenge, Cassia decided. Suddenly she looked forward to making camp that evening. And, now she'd had some luck in getting the lordling to open up, she pressed on with more questions.

"Do you practise like that every morning?"

"Without fail."

"I've never seen any of the Factor's soldiers do those moves. Is it something they do in other parts of the Empire? Or Galliarca?"

Meredith shook his head, his eyes on the hillsides once more. "It is not from the battlefield. It is a dance . . ."

He stared into the distance, lost in his own thoughts again, and Cassia realised there was little chance of him answering any more questions for the moment. She sighed and pulled at the straps of her pack to tighten them before turning her attention back to the winding pathway down through the valley, which had closed in around them once more.

After a minute or two she became aware that she was catching up to Baum, at the head of their small party. She hadn't realised she was walking as fast as that, and she wondered if he had deliberately slowed his pace to meet her.

He turned in his saddle to nod a greeting as she came alongside. "The path becomes easier in another mile, if my memory does not fail me," he said. "This was once a clear and fast route from the south to Gethista."

Cassia nodded, though it was as hard to imagine anybody using this path as it was to visualise Gethista at the height of its glory, when all that remained was the collection of crumbled mounds where they had made their camp.

Baum changed the subject without warning. "Was that Pyraete's *Call To The North* I heard you quote back there?"

Cassia nodded again, and he smiled. "I thought so. An old favourite of mine. I haven't heard it in quite some time – is it still told up here?"

She had to think before replying. When was the last time she had heard her father recite it? "Not very often, sir," she said. "The Factor does not like most of the older histories or legends being told in public – he calls them inflammatory."

"I thought as much," Baum said. "But they are still told in private?"

"Sometimes, sir. Rann Almoul has a written copy of the *Call To The North* locked in a chest in his study. Hetch showed it to me once when we were children."

It was after that she had started the long battle with her father to be taught her letters. Rann Almoul's treasured copy of the *Call To The North* was a delicate long parchment rolled into a leather case. The margins were decorated with elegant illuminations that depicted Pyraete and the other gods of the pantheon as they played and fought amongst each other, while in one corner the men of the North came from their strongholds to conquer the plains below the mountains.

The text was a wonderful collection of beautifully painted symbols that she could not understand, but Hetch read it out to her in hushed tones, frowning with concentration when he stumbled on an unfamiliar word. Meanwhile she dared to touch the parchment with the tips of her fingers, finding pinpricks on the slightly rougher underside where a scribe had used this sheet to lay out and copy another. She had seen the boys in the Factor's school learning their letters by tracing texts in the same manner, and it occurred to her that this single sheet must be valuable indeed for it to be used to create other, lesser copies.

That knowledge was scant comfort when Rann Almoul caught them and beat them both, his face purple with rage as he punctuated his imprecations against the curiosity of meddling children with heavy, full-handed slaps that left the pair bruised for weeks. Norrow had no sympathy for her, and even thrashed her himself, as though Cassia had offended him rather than his sometime friend. But Cassia's curiosity was already alight; she had to learn to read those beautiful words.

"That's what made me want to be a storyteller," she added. "All these stories my father knows – they're all written down somewhere, aren't they? And there must be even more written down that he doesn't know. I want to learn them all."

Baum regarded her with something bordering on amusement. She hoped he wasn't about to make fun of her ambition, like Hetch had – until she poked him in the eye to silence him.

"An admirable desire," he said, and it sounded like he meant it. "One can never have too much learning, girl. Even a little knowledge can be used as a lever to gain what you want. The god of knowledge lives in us all. Have you memorised the entire *Call To The North*?"

She shook her head. "No, sir. I never saw it after that. We weren't allowed near Rann Almoul's study again. My father knows some of it, but the rest he has to spin out. I think that might be part of why he doesn't tell it often."

"I see." Baum nodded. "Ah – see if you recognise where we are now, girl."

While they talked, the path had curved back on itself once or twice, winding down past a pair of high-sided hills. Now it veered sharply to the left to take a gentle way across a slope that would have otherwise been too steep to take the horses down. At the bottom of the slope, it met up with a road that she knew well.

"This is the South Road? We merely bypassed Escalia?" Norrow called from his position at the rear of the party. He sounded disgusted.

"Of course," Baum replied.

"But . . . we've been along this road so many times," Cassia said. "I would never have thought Gethista was so close to us."

Baum's expression was unreadable. "When Gethista fell, it fell absolutely. I think Pyraete hid even the ruins of the cities Gethis founded. Perhaps some of his magic lingers in the hills, turning people away from those cursed lands."

"So how did we pass through?" Norrow asked. "It can't be all that cursed."

Cassia looked back over her shoulder. The path into the hills already seemed harder to follow, disappearing from view long before it should have done. Was it a trick of the eye, or was it caused by the will of the god of the North? With everything Baum had said over the last couple of days, she was no longer certain.

"This was all a waste of time and effort then," Norrow grumbled. He spat loudly into the undergrowth.

Baum stared at him until Norrow was forced to look away. "I don't care to make public my travel arrangements," he said bluntly. "I have my own reasons for coming this way, storyteller."

Norrow's mouth was a thin line of barely suppressed anger.

"So where are we going? You employed me, but you still have not told me what for. Am I to tell stories to the mountains?"

Cassia held her breath.

For a moment it seemed Baum would lose his temper. Then he shook his head. "No, Norrow, I have ambitions far greater than that. But you will know more when we come to Hellea."

Norrow stared after him. "Hellea? *Hellea?*" He slapped the mule and urged it forward onto the slope, forcing Cassia to step quickly out of the way before the beast could knock her over.

Cassia closed her eyes. Hellea was a land so far beyond her reality that it might as well be another story. And Baum had work there for her father. Would he be grateful for that? No, of course not. She sighed and muttered a quick prayer to Ceresel again, then adjusted her straps and followed the mule down the trail.

Chapter Five

THE NEXT DAY passed in a haze of rain, the clouds so heavy and low that sometimes Cassia could barely see the road ahead. Not that she paid much attention to her surroundings. Her thoughts were darker and more miserable than the weather. Even the distant promise of Hellea could not lift her mood.

After passing by Ecsalia entirely, she had hoped they would stop at Devrilinum for a night. Anything other than open fields. But Baum pressed onwards deep into the evening, and Cassia and her father were forced to follow.

Neither Baum nor Meredith seemed to notice that their new companions travelled in sullen silence, as though they were prisoners chained at the wrists marching behind their captors. Cassia's feet caught in every rut in the road, and the wind gusted the cold drizzle through her bedraggled hair, which whipped around constantly into her face. Malicious spirits of the sky that bore some arcane grudge against her, spitting and laughing at her misfortune. Just like when Gelis got lost in the mountains after she was cast out from her village.

But that was only a story. This was her life. There were other parallels with Gelis, although they did not match in every way. The young heroine of the romantic tales had lived with a father who did not love her and, just like Cassia herself, she had fallen in with strange companions on the road. But while Gelis's tale had a happy ending, with justice served by the prince who had saved her, Cassia was not so optimistic. Meredith was most likely the only noble she would ever meet, and she doubted he would have any interest in a poor storyteller's daughter.

This morning the silent young lordling was as aloof as usual, hardly noticing that she or her father even existed. Cassia's bold request to learn how to use a sword was not even alluded to. She had sat by the dead embers of the campfire with heat rising in her cheeks, all too aware of Norrow laughing silently at her from the shelter of his rough lean-to.

Baum seemed oblivious to the change of mood. He whistled snatches of tunes Cassia did not recognise, cursed the state of the March, pointed out overgrown shrines by the road, and chatted to both her and Norrow apparently without realising that they replied only in hesitant, subdued tones.

Cassia found her thoughts wandering again to dreams of escape and freedom. It was strange how her world had changed so much over the course of a few days. Before, she and her father had been free – in a sense – to wander between the villages and towns of this region, never tied to the land or to a contract. Farmers stared enviously at them from their fields; smiths and other craftsmen looked out from under their sheltered workshops and sighed as they passed by. They may have been hungry more often than not, but they could go where they wished.

But her father's recent actions had disabused her of that notion. She was a property, to be bought and sold at her owner's whim. Perhaps she had not been chained and tied like the slaves she had seen in the coastal towns to the east, but she was a captive nonetheless. There was scant consolation in the thought that though her father seemed free, his future was also ruled by Meredith and Baum.

Surely, she thought as she drew her sodden blanket closer around her shoulders, chilled to the bone by the endless drizzle, surely things could get no worse than this.

The clouds lifted in the early afternoon and, if nothing else, the welcome sensation of sunlight on her shoulders improved her mood. Her father, still astride the tireless mule, remained dark and foul, and Cassia avoided him as much as possible.

"Perhaps we should have stayed a while in Devrilinum," Baum mused, almost to himself, when Cassia came alongside him. The March had crested a hill and they now faced a winding road into a vale of green orchards, surrounded by the wilder pastures common to the region. The rain had brought fresh colour to the fields, the sun reflected from glistening leaves that swayed in the breeze. The hillsides still loomed away to the west and north, but they seemed less threatening. Dormant, perhaps, was the right word.

Cassia waited for Baum to say something else, to attempt to draw conversation from her, but he remained silent as she passed him, allowing the downslope to speed her way.

Meredith caught up with her as the road levelled out, approaching at a trot. "Hold and wait a few minutes, girl. Did you not hear us call?"

She frowned and looked back. Baum had dismounted some way back, and now strode off the road toward a low, grass-covered mound. Even Norrow had stopped, stretching to relieve the aches in his limbs and his back, directing curses at the old mule.

"No, sir. I must have been lost in thought," she said. "I'm sorry. Should I go back?"

Meredith shook his head. "No need. Baum goes to pray for success." He stared directly down at her. "Do you also pray to Pyraete?"

"Not very often." Cassia didn't want to risk offending them by telling the truth. She'd heard men mutter curses and beg Pyraete to save them from the Factor's taxes, but she never had any reason to thank the old god of the North for anything. There were enough Hellean gods to go around. It was little wonder that any remaining shrines to Pyraete were lost, hidden at the edges of fields or walled away and left to gather dust.

The old man knelt at the mound and bowed his head. Cassia saw his jaw working as he prayed aloud, but at this distance she heard nothing. He stayed there for several minutes, and she shifted uncomfortably from foot to foot, aware of the aches creeping into her muscles. They had halted a little too long now, and it would be hard to coax her tired limbs back into the rhythm she had found during the morning.

Had Baum fallen asleep? She was about to start toward him when he finally raised his head and climbed back to his feet. He strode briskly to his horse, remounting with such ease and energy that Cassia thought he had lost a full score of years from his age. She told herself it was a trick of the afternoon light that Baum appeared straighter and younger than he had just a few minutes before. But as he brought his horse level with her once more, she realised she wasn't so certain.

Baum smiled down at her. "Come along, girl. We have plenty of ground to cover before the day is over."

The sunlight was no longer as warm or as welcoming as it had been. Cassia pulled her packs tight against her shoulders and pushed herself into motion, reluctantly following the horses down the road before her father managed to catch her up.

The road wound gently south and east, through lands that Cassia no longer knew well. Newer shrines, to Hellean gods, sat by the road next to the half-buried remains of camps left by the legions that had passed through the area.

She snagged fruit from untended orchards, watching carefully for the farmhands before she left the road. Baum looked amused by the theft, though he said nothing to her about it. Meredith, on the other hand, told her that theft was morally wrong, in such a loud voice that several heads popped up in the nearest field and they had to increase their pace to leave that area behind before anybody came to demand recompense.

"Why did you do that?" Cassia snapped at the lordling.

"Because you were in the wrong," Meredith replied.

"It's not like we have a choice," she told him. "You might be able to afford to buy your food, but we can't."

"So you steal it? That does not make it right."

"You try going hungry every night for a whole week. See if you can still lift that bloody sword after that. Sir."

And that, she realised, was the problem: Meredith was a noble. He had been born and raised with all sorts of benefits and privileges. He'd never had to fend for himself, everything had been handed to him on a polished tray. He couldn't possibly understand how hard and unfair her life really was, even if she told him.

Meredith's gaze shifted away from her. He stared fixedly past, his eyes narrowed in sudden concentration.

"We are watched," he announced.

Cassia turned, alarmed at his tone. A group of some half-dozen riders had crested the hills behind them and stood silhouetted by the afternoon light. She could see the rectangular shapes of their shields, along with the spikes of the javelins that rose from behind their helmeted heads, giving them the appearance of sinister amalgams of man and horse.

Baum did not seem surprised to see them. He squinted

against the light, turning his horse on the spot, and nodded slowly. "Yes. Yes, we are. Scout riders, unless I am mistaken. We shall have company soon."

Cassia bit her lip, her thoughts racing. Scout riders – from the Factor's legion? Had Rann Almoul betrayed Baum to the Factor?

She had no chance to ask. Baum motioned them onwards, and she had to hurry to keep up with the faster pace he set. She glanced back over her shoulder several times; the riders followed them down into the vale but kept well back, as if they had orders to remain at a distance. Norrow watched them too, she saw him twisting on the mule's back to keep them in sight. She recognised the speculative cast of his expression and her heart fell. She hoped he would not do anything rash or selfish, but the odds were set against her.

And whatever you do, father, you make me answerable for.

Baum led them westward, away from the stream and doubling back up a sheep trail. The Factor's scouts followed them still, and Cassia felt her nerves tighten with every step she took. Meredith rode out on the party's flank, placing himself between them and the scouts. He directed his horse with one hand, his other resting at all times on the hilt of his sword, and he watched the slopes both ahead and behind as intently as he watched the riders.

As Cassia rounded a small rise, tugging the straps of her packs in a vain effort to ease the strain on her shoulders, she heard an unfamiliar voice bark an order and she stumbled to a halt, her breath catching in her throat.

Baum and Norrow had already pulled up, and Meredith was returning swiftly from the far side of the trail. Before them, arrayed in a perfect line, stood six more armed riders, each with a pair of javelins slung over their back and a squared-off cavalry shield held out before them.

A snorting from behind her announced the arrival of the other squad of scouts. They were surrounded. Whatever Baum had planned, it would never be allowed to come to fruition.

One of the soldiers looked familiar. Cassia frowned as she realised who he was. Vescar, Rann Almoul's other son. She hadn't seen him for several years, and he had grown into a sharp-faced, serious man, as tightly coiled and contained as Hetch was blithe and energetic.

The two soldiers dismounted and came face to face in the open.

"Baum," Vescar said. "You've led us a merry dance, old man."

The historian nodded. "Good. Your men look like they could use the exercise, sergeant."

Vescar's mouth thinned. "Half-captain."

Baum shrugged. "As you wish. A bone for the native. But I don't have time to bandy ranks with you, sir. Let us pass."

"I don't think so. For one thing, you have something that belongs to us." Vescar nodded at Cassia without looking at her, as if she was a piece of baggage.

I belong to him? She clenched her fists, and only a sharp gesture from Baum kept her back.

"Ah, I see. You would be Vescar Almoul, then? I see the resemblance." Baum smiled disarmingly at him. "Tell me, half-captain, has the Factor sanctioned this little pursuit? Does he know of your father's agreement with me? Or is this a private enterprise?" He glanced around and raised his voice. "Do your men know the real purpose of this mission?"

Vescar's jaw worked silently and he lifted one gloved fist into the air. The soldiers beside him drew their swords, steel rasping harshly against the scabbards. Cassia saw the other squad, javelins to hand, move in the corner of her vision, working around the small party to surround it completely. Meredith sat passively in his saddle, turning his head from side to side to watch their deployment, but he did not draw his own weapon.

Oh Ceresel, Cassia thought. *Please let it be fast. I can't go back there. I can't.* Hetch's face flashed into her mind. No longer bright and naive, his eyes were cold and calculating, and he resembled his father more than he had ever done before. She gripped her staff tight against her chest, desperately trying to think of a way that she could avoid the volley of javelins that now seemed inevitable.

"Did your father tell you what power I represent?" Baum asked, his voice as hard as the land they stood upon.

"I know what you represent," Vescar replied scornfully. "Sedition, unrest and revolt. The North will rise again as a power, old man, but it will do so without your warmongering."

"Hah. You think you can fawn your way to eminence? Hellea has used you, drained you and spat you out as a dried-up husk – a small, insignificant province, where you *could* be as powerful as the High Kings once were." Baum waved a dismissive hand. "No matter. It is your choice, cowards and slaves to the Empire's coin that you are."

Cassia flinched at the words. Surely he had sealed their fates with those insults. She felt Meredith nudge his mount away from her, and realised he had already anticipated the start of the fight.

Vescar's face flooded with scarlet anger, and he drew the long, flat blade that hung at his side. "I'll hear no more of this slander and cant. Let's see if you can handle that sword as well as you throw your words, old man. The Empire and the North!"

He gestured savagely and the men behind him bucked their horses forward, their swords raised high. The contest was so uneven it could only end one way, but Cassia could not watch. She had to defend herself. She dropped to her knees and rolled away into the longer grasses at the base of the slope, hoping desperately to avoid the first flight of javelins that would have been aimed at her by the other squad.

"*Caenthell* and the North!" Baum gave a fearsome roar as the battle was joined.

Horses screamed, men cursed and shouted warnings and

incoherent orders, and the sound of steel upon steel shook Cassia's bones. Abruptly she realised that she was not safe here, especially if she could not see what was happening. She levered herself into a crouch with her staff, muscles tensed to run or fight, and stared in horror at the carnage before her.

The lead squad had dispersed, no longer a tight and well-drilled formation. Two soldiers slumped in their saddles, clutching wounds that bled freely over their hands. A third struggled on the ground, one leg pinned under his fallen horse. The remaining scouts had galloped clear and wheeled about, tugging free their javelins instead. Baum stood firm in the centre of the field, his blade stained dark red and his cloak and sleeves torn, his left shoulder dipped as he faced Vescar. Rann's son had halted his charge, and now he looked less sure of himself.

Several yards away Meredith easily held his own against the second squad. Broken javelins littered the ground around him and as Cassia watched he swung his weapon in a precise arc to batter another javelin from the air. Having seen Baum's success against their companions, the scouts had clearly decided against attempting to charge Meredith, even though he was only one man, but they were fast running out of javelins.

Not a single weapon had landed near her, and she realised that Vescar wanted her alive. She wondered if that was Hetch's idea. It certainly wasn't what Rann Almoul would want.

"Yield," Meredith barked. He sounded so authoritative that some of the scouts hesitated before drawing their swords, but that moment of hesitation was all the lordling needed. He spurred his horse forward, smashing one rider to the ground with a backhanded stroke that echoed across the small vale. He hauled his weapon around to chop down a second before the man could react. The next nearest scout managed to aim his last javelin at the lordling, but he was too close to throw with any force. Meredith plucked the javelin from mid-air with his free hand and returned it to him, thrusting it into the man's stomach and driving him from his saddle.

Another charged at him, sword and shield at the ready, and this time Meredith had to defend himself with a flurry of blows so quick Cassia could hardly follow. The other two members of the squad edged around the fight, searching for a weakness in Meredith's defence. But, as she watched, Cassia recognised one or two of the moves the lordling made. These were movements she had seen for the last three mornings. When his blade arced over his left shoulder and then down as Meredith ducked to dodge a wild slash from his right, Cassia knew exactly where he would strike next.

Sure enough, one of the flanking scouts had got too close. Meredith hacked down at his arm so hard the crack of bone was audible even over the nearby fighting. The man fell from his horse with a scream of raw pain, blood spraying from the severed arteries of his forearm.

The last two men threw down their weapons and disengaged, hunched low over their reins as they fled. Meredith held his own horse in check and watched them, unsmiling. He was not at all out of breath, in fact, he wasn't even breathing hard.

A shout of alarm and frustration brought her attention back to Baum's duel with Vescar Almoul. Vescar was also retreating, but he was cut off from his men by Baum's relentless attacks. Vescar had clearly underestimated his opponent, too confident of his own skills. As Cassia was learning, there was much more to Baum than first met the eye.

Vescar made a desperate lunge at Baum, and his blade met thin air. The older man had seen it coming and side-stepped easily, hacking into Vescar's unprotected leg. The half-captain collapsed with a howl, and Baum kicked him into unconscious silence before turning to calmly survey the rest of the field.

Of the dozen Imperial scouts that had set upon them, only three were still on their feet or mounted, and all three were fleeing back towards Devrilinum. Cassia wondered how long it would be before they brought reinforcements to try once more.

Baum frowned after the men, muttering under his breath. Curses, most likely. He had been a soldier, after all, so he must know plenty of curses. Cassia struggled to her feet to watch the retreating scouts, her limbs wobbly and disobedient, as though they belonged to somebody else.

Blood. There's so much blood . . .

Baum gestured sharply at the scouts. A flash of light seared Cassia's vision and she dropped to the ground with a squeal of terror, echoed from further away by agonised screams.

Silence flooded back over the field. Cassia realised the sobbing breaths she heard were her own, and she peeled her hands away from her head, raising herself on tremulous arms to see what had happened.

What *was* that? It had looked like a bright line of molten fire, just like she had seen in smithies in winter when they were the only places she could go to keep warm. But true fire did not look like that. Nor did it fly through the air in straight lines. Yet the bright after-images burned behind her eyelids told a different tale.

Baum, calm and business-like, as if he had not just killed several of the Factor's legionaries, stooped to wipe his blade clean on the grass before sheathing it. Meredith still held his sword in one hand, using it to prod the bodies of the fallen scouts. Neither man seemed to have noticed she was still there.

I could steal the horses and leave them stranded. I could ride away and be back in Keskor by tomorrow night. But she didn't want to return to Keskor, and now Vescar had been defeated she knew she could never return there again. A huge weight lifted from her shoulders as that road was closed to her. *I could make for the coast road, and try to buy a passage to . . . to anywhere. I can go* anywhere.

She reached for her staff, and came back to her feet again, more warily this time. It was then she saw the three scouts who had fled . . . or, rather, what remained of them. They lay by the trail, limbs twisted and scorched, tendrils of smoke curling from their wrecked corpses. Cassia stood rooted to the spot, unable to force herself any closer to the horribly burned men.

"Oh, mercy," she prayed with a sob, disbelief warring with the evidence before her.

It was magic. That was the only thing it could be. Magic, straight from the tales of the Age of Talons, or of the High Kings, or of the spiteful, petty wars of the gods themselves and their pet spellcasters. There was no other way to explain how three men could be healthy and whole one moment, and burning husks the next. But this wasn't the work of the gods, was it? She turned slowly, to stare at Baum.

Was it?

Baum looked up and met her gaze. His eyes were hard, but they held no threat that Cassia could see. Now he was an old soldier, long-retired from campaigning, just as he had been before.

Vescar broke the spell, moaning and rolling onto his side. "Bastard sorcerer – finish me off then."

Baum strode over to him, and Cassia found herself headed there too, without having made any conscious decision to move.

"No," the old man said, standing over the fallen half-captain. "You'll carry a message for me, boy. Whose idea was this farce of an ambush?"

Vescar grimaced and clutched his leg with one hand while tearing at his sleeve with the other. "He said you were dangerous – insane. But you're an old man . . ."

Baum folded his arms and watched the man struggle to dress his wound. Cassia approached quietly, trying to keep out of Vescar's sight.

"Older than you know, boy. And I carry Pyraete's blessing with me. The God of the North is on *my* side, not the Empire's. Remember that, and tell your father that too, if this was his idea. And here's the message. The North *will* rise again, with or without his help. There is far more at stake here than petty power-brokering with some minor Imperial functionary who was raised soft and moneyed in the south. Far better men than you have tried to stop me in the past, and all have failed. When the High King's armies return to the mountains, you had better know which side you are on."

Vescar stared up at him in disbelief. "The High King? You mean *Caenthell*? You really are insane, old man. It'll never happen."

Baum shrugged. "Perhaps. Perhaps not. But I advise you to leave me well alone. If he sends anybody else to silence me, I will not be merciful. Look to your squads here, *half-captain*, and think yourself lucky."

Vescar levered himself onto one knee. Cassia moved aside quickly, but the half-captain was not interested in her anymore. His attention was fixed on the bodies spread over the field. "And how do I explain this slaughter? How do I explain magic?"

"That's not my concern. One more thing, boy. The girl and her father stay with me."

"Fine," Vescar growled. "I did not want them anyway."

Cassia could not stay silent. "Then who did? Hetch?"

His contemptuous expression was enough to make her back off. "It speaks. My brother thinks with his cock. But you're plain enough that I'll wager he'd have tired of you inside a week. Good riddance."

Baum coughed. "My patience is wearing thin. Go and bury your men. On foot, mind, leave the horses."

Vescar rose unsteadily and took a javelin from one the fallen scouts to use as a staff. With one last glare at Baum and Meredith, as if committing their faces to memory, he limped toward the trail.

Cassia watched him, her heart empty and cold. That was what they thought of her? Then they could rot in the ground for all she cared. Hetch could take his false friendship and stick it up his backside. The damned mule was a better friend to her than Hetch ever would be.

She paused, mid-thought, and looked around again. Where *was* the mule? Come to that, where had her father gone?

She turned a full circle, unable to see either of them, and she felt her breath race again, panic surging into her muscles. Had they been caught by the scouts? By the first flight of javelins?

"Father?" she called out. "Father?"

Baum heard her and looked up, then motioned to Meredith. The lordling jogged up the nearest rise, gaining higher ground for a better view. After a long moment he shook his head.

"Nothing. He has gone," he called down.

Baum kicked at one of the corpses and cursed vehemently. "Behia take me for a damned fool! That must be the fastest he has moved in the last three days! If I didn't know better I'd say he planned this all along."

Cassia dropped to the ground once more, her legs unable to take the weight of the world that had crashed onto her shoulders. *Gone. Abandoned.* Her thoughts buzzed around those words like moths to a flame, never settling long enough in one place for reality to take hold. She raised one hand to the straps that cut into her shoulders: the pack was all she had now. All that was left of her world.

Abruptly she shrugged it from her back and tore at the knots that sealed it, pulling ragged cloths and dented pans onto the grass, scrabbling through the meagre collection in a desperate search for the one thing that should have been there . . .

. . . and was not.

Norrow had swapped the purse into another bag. He had never intended to do more than save his own skin.

She rolled onto her side with a sob, tears flooding into her eyes. *Gone. Abandoned. Set free.*

She didn't know whether she was laughing or crying.

Baum led them away from the Emperor's March, into the rolling hills of the lower Antiachas. The trail passed several empty sheepfolds before petering out altogether, but the old man did not appear to notice; he was so wrapped up in a foul, darkened mood.

Cassia was absorbed in her own thoughts. At least now she did not have to walk. Meredith had lifted her, unresisting, onto one of the horses that had not fled the field of battle, enlisting another to carry their baggage. Left to her own devices for a few moments while the two men saw to their own mounts, she could easily have followed her father's example and made a bid for freedom. After all, a small voice in her head said to her, if he could make it clean away on that damned mule, why couldn't she, with a warhorse to her credit?

But the effort was beyond her. *Why?* she asked. *Where would I go? What would I do?* The voice did not seem able to tell her, so she sat on the horse, skirt rucked up above her knees, her staff held across her lap, and waited.

She looked back once, and saw that Vescar's scouts still lay where they had fallen. Vescar had abandoned them, just as her father had abandoned her. And Baum had not spared time to see to their burials, or any of the proprieties that all the tales of great battles stressed were so important. These men weren't part of any story of the golden campaigns of the past. And they were dead, after all, so why would they care how they lay?

An uncomfortable thought kept circling her mind, like the birds and four-legged scavengers that would soon find the dead scouts. Where was Baum taking her? Why were they travelling so deep into the hills? Did he mean to murder her too, and leave her body in the wastes of the Antiachas, never to be seen again?

She was painfully aware of Meredith's looming presence, only a yard or so to her left. He had not been so much as lightly winded by the fight, let alone taken a single scratch. The exercises he rigorously performed every morning were as nothing compared to the speed and vicious skill with which he had despatched Vescar's men.

If he cut her down without warning at least it would be a quick end. Nobody would miss her.

The tears came upon her so suddenly she could not hold them back. Her vision blurred, and her shoulders shook with wracking sobs as the staff fell from her unresisting hands.

She felt, rather than saw, someone take the reins to keep her horse walking uphill, but it hardly registered. It seemed all she could do was cry to prevent her heart from bursting, and she surrendered herself to the misery.

At last, when she wiped her eyes on her sleeve and let her breathing slow to normal, her horse had halted. In fact, the whole party had stopped on the crest of a hill, and Baum and Meredith both watched her, waiting for her to recover. She met Baum's intent frown with a guilty flush.

"I – I'm sorry," she began. "I don't mean to hold you up—"

Baum shook his head in an impatient gesture, but his words were more conciliatory. "Not to worry, girl. It is only to be expected. We can move faster now we have you on horseback, but I think it best if we do not travel much further today. We can always make up the time elsewhere."

Meredith looked unhappy at the prospect – as much as he ever seemed to look unhappy. "The half-captain will raise the alarm, and we will find ourselves surrounded by daybreak."

Baum made a gesture of denial. "Unlikely. Vescar has far too much to lose. He will have to spend some time coming up with a plausible reason why he has lost a dozen of the Factor's scouts for no gain. Without mentioning us or Caenthell, of course."

Cassia shivered at the name. It slipped through the air like a curse, and even the wind stuttered in its passage for a moment.

"And the storyteller?" Meredith asked.

Now Baum swore softly. "A far greater loss. Who could know the North could breed such a damned coward? It seems plain he would be of little use in Hellea, so perhaps we are better off without him." He glanced at Cassia. "Yes, in fact. Far better off. Pyraete strengthens our hand . . ."

"Sir, I don't understand," Cassia said. There were so many questions. Which would he answer? Which would make him angry? How could she know which to ask? "I – I just don't understand . . ."

That brought an unexpected, wry smile. "I'm not surprised, girl. This must be quite a shock to you. It usually is."

The comment made no sense to her. She rubbed her eyes again and then stared down at her hands. Where had the staff gone? She remembered holding it across her lap earlier as she rode . . .

Meredith passed it to her. He must have picked it up when she dropped it. "Never lose control of your weapons," he told her, in the manner of a teacher passing on wisdom to a slow-learning pupil.

"Can you ride a little longer?" Baum asked. He looked satisfied with Cassia's hurried nod. She had no wish to spoil his sudden good temper, even though she wanted to do nothing more than curl up on the ground under her blanket. "Good. There is – was, at least – a small copse on the far side of that hill. It will give us shelter for the night, and our fire will not be visible from the road. Once we are settled, I will see if I can lift the clouds of your confusion somewhat. Quite a long story – you may even know a little of it," he added, his lips quirking into that familiar wry smile.

If his last words were a bait, then Cassia was hooked, despite her fear of these men and the strange powers they appeared to possess. It wasn't as if there was anywhere else she could go anyway, and so she urged her horse after Meredith and Baum as they started down the hillside.

"Now . . . where to begin? *When?*" Baum's expression was quizzical, as if Cassia was the one with the answers. She wrapped her arms around her knees and inched closer to the fire, waiting for him to continue.

The copse had turned out to be larger than Baum had described it, and he had joked that he had spent too much time out of the North, before leading them under the branches of the weather-twisted trees. Their camp was completely obscured from view, and Cassia glanced up at the overhanging branches nervously, half-expecting them to start moving of their own accord, reaching down menacingly . . .

She shivered. This was not a night for dark tales, but she had an inkling Baum's story would not be a happy one.

"The High Kings of the North," Baum said. "That's where we'll begin. Do you know the High Kings?"

"Gallemas," she said hesitantly. Her father hadn't favoured many tales that old, so her knowledge was sketchy. Once the old myths of the North entered the Age of Talons, she was on much firmer ground. "You said he was the first. And Jedrell was the last. I know that much."

Baum nodded. "Go on."

She paused. What did he want? "Jedrell?"

The quizzical look had been replaced by a more solemn expression. He was remembering something, Cassia thought, as she tried to put the stories back together in her own mind. Everybody enjoyed tales from the Age of Talons, although many of them were set in the plains and on the high seas to the south and east, and yet more took place in far-off Galliarca or Stromondor. When they touched on the North they were dark and tragic, lined heavily with feuds carried from father to son. The High Kings walked through them with all the arrogance and impunity of the true nobility, handing out justice and vengeance in equal measures. They were rarely the heroic focus of the tales – more often they were obstacles to be overcome or avoided. In some of the more bloodthirsty stories, they could be found as invincible warriors on the battlefield, or commanding great armies that pillaged and burned their way across the land.

Jedrell had done all that, and more besides. The stories of his life portrayed him as a man driven by greed and ambition, a child of one of the lesser branches of the royal line who bitterly resented the lowly position he had inherited.

"Jedrell was the son of Cathos," Cassia began slowly. "The youngest son. And Cathos was a . . . a captain of the High King's armies. He was satisfied with his lot, and he never raised his gaze to the skies, but Jedrell was not content to live out his life taking orders from other, lesser men. And when he looked into the night skies he saw his name written there in the stars."

She looked up, saw Baum smiling, and felt the colour rise in her cheeks. "Am I wrong?"

He tilted one hand in a non-committal gesture. "Who can truly say, so many hundreds of years after the fact?"

"It *is* wrong, isn't it?" Suddenly she was certain of that, and she felt the need to defend herself. "But this is how I learned the story. I can't tell it any other way."

"Then carry on," Baum told her. "I will not interrupt."

Cassia gathered her thoughts for a moment. Behind the old man Meredith constructed their shelters with methodical economy, paying no attention to the conversation at the fire.

"Cathos was an experienced campaigner when he fathered Jedrell," she said. "And when the boy came to his majority and joined the army himself, Cathos was an old man who had lost much of his prowess and strength, but kept all of his mighty reputation. He won a position for his son, and the High King gave him a full legion to command, but Jedrell was angered by this. He said that he wanted to be known and feared for who *he* was, not for who his father was.

"His father was dismayed by his words, and the High King took them as a grave insult. He vowed to make an example of Jedrell and make him swing from the walls of Caenthell. When he heard this, Jedrell sent a reply saying the next time he saw the great halls of Caenthell, he would call himself the true High King of the North, and all would kneel before him."

She paused again. Was this too much detail? How much of the story did he want her to tell?

Baum poked at the fire, his mind clearly elsewhere. Despite his earlier promise, he did speak to fill the uneasy silence. "And so they did. Jedrell left the North as a brash, hot-headed young man, his temper as wild as the dogs of Galliarca, his legion untested, his reputation in tatters, and his heart broken. But when he returned, years later, he stood above the Hamiardin Pass and raised his standard in challenge, and his vast army lined every peak that could be seen from the great castle. The High King – Rosmer the Black, an ineffectual man," he added in a scholarly aside, "sat safe behind his walls, secure in the knowledge that Caenthell had never fallen. He knew that while the castle held, Jedrell's campaign against him would fail. Winter was coming, and Jedrell's army could not maintain a siege through the inhospitable weather that Pyraete would throw at the mountains. Jedrell was no fool, though. He had been raised in the shadow of Caenthell, after all, and he knew the turning of the seasons. He did not intend to let Rosmer wait him out. Do you know how he took the castle?"

Cassia nodded, tongue-tied for the moment. Baum talked as though these events had occurred only yesterday. And where was the Hamiardin Pass? In all of the tellings of this history, she had never once heard of such a place.

"Sorcery," she managed at last. It was an answer that reminded her of the slaughter on the hillsides only a few hours ago, and she shivered.

Baum gave her a thin smile. "Exactly. Sorcery. So great was his ambition that Jedrell enlisted the help of one of the most notorious warlocks of that age – Malessar."

Even though she knew this part of the history she still felt her stomach roll queasily at the mention of the name. "The Man of Stone," she said quietly. The warlock passed through many ages and tales, up to and beyond the Fall of Stromondor. How ironic it was that her father had narrated that very tale the other evening in Keskor. Malessar was as harsh and frightening a presence as any of the greatest High Kings.

"The Betrayer." Meredith's voice was flat and cold. Cassia flinched. At that moment, if she could have willed her legs to carry her, she would have fled the warmth of the fire in favour of the darkened hillsides, just to escape from the violence behind those words. But she was far more terrified by what might happen to her if she ran, and so she ducked her head to avoid his gaze, her limbs quivering and chilled.

"Amongst other names," Baum agreed. "So, they do at least still tell *these* stories in the North. Carry on, girl, and cut to the core of it."

She took a breath and forced herself to hold it for a moment, so that she could speak again without her voice breaking. "Malessar used his sorcery to bring Jedrell into the castle unseen. Then Jedrell confronted the High King. He struck him down and took his crown, his castle, and his lands, and took Rosmer's daughter Aliciana as hostage to bring Rosmer's nobles under his command. After that he became the greatest High King in all of Caenthell's history, inspiring loyalty in his allies and fear in his enemies. He conquered all the lands as far south as the waters of the Castaria, and even the mighty Lords of Stromondor sent tribute to the North. And after his last campaign in the lowlands, he returned to Caenthell and married Aliciana."

"And then?"

She moistened her lips. "And then Malessar returned to Caenthell and destroyed it."

Baum looked away into the darkness. "He did much more than that, girl. Oh, much more indeed. He murdered every single man, woman and child inside the castle's walls – burned them or tore them to shreds with his sorcery. His rage consumed the very stones themselves. He pulled Caenthell to the ground and left it as a grave, fit only for rats, weeds and revenants. When dawn broke, bleeding into the valley, it was as though the kingdom had never existed at all."

He jabbed angrily at the fire, and embers spilled out over Cassia. She swatted them away before they could settle and burn through her skirts.

"But that was not all. He cursed the very land itself, cursed it so harshly that even the gods, appalled and aghast, could not undo his work. And they *feared* him. The gods themselves feared Malessar the warlock and what he might do to them if they opposed him!" Baum snorted bitterly. "Do you know the curse he laid upon Caenthell, girl? Do they still whisper it in dark places, or is it long forgotten, just like the glories of the North?"

Cassia shrank back in alarm, frightened by the turn of the conversation. Just as it had earlier, it seemed to her that Baum must have seen all this happen, but that was impossible. Caenthell had fallen hundreds of years ago. Only the gods would remember it now . . .

Her mind revolted. "Please, I don't understand," she gasped. "Who are you?"

Apparently Baum did not hear her. "*Caenthell will stay buried, and never again will the North arise, until I freely offer my sword to a true descendant of the High Kings, or one takes it from my dying hands!* Those were his words. They echoed over the whole kingdom, even over the roar of the castle's death, and they sunk into the earth and pinned Caenthell's soul into the stones of the mountains."

His voice subsided, though his eyes still blazed with elemental anger. "And I still hear them. They are as much a part of me as my arms, or my heart, or my mind. They course through my blood and stir my dreams. Even the blessings of the God of the North can only dampen them to whispers for a time."

"But . . ." Cassia breathed. "But you can't have been there.

You – you were a captain in the legions – I don't . . ."

"A soldier, and a storyteller too, in my own way. In my time I have been almost everywhere, and I have been everything a man can possibly be. But I *was* there, Cassia. I stood watch above the Hamiardin Pass while Jedrell and Malessar discussed their attack plans. I sat within arm's reach of the High King's table, at the feast to celebrate our victory over Rosmer. I watched Caenthell die, and I barely escaped with my life. Since that day I have taken employment with every army ever raised; I fought with the Eastern Hordes and against them, both defended the Empire and attacked it. I learned every discipline and craft known to man – and many others more secret and arcane. Kings, emperors, cities and countries have gone to dust, and all the long years have blended into one and become indistinguishable to me, yet I have aged little more than a score of years in the meantime."

This time his smile was bittersweet. "Truly, Pyraete has smiled upon me, eh?"

Cassia had covered her mouth with one hand. Everything she had thought to say had been smashed from her mind. Before her, she realised, was a man who had seen what only the gods were privileged to see. He was as close to immortality as any of the greatest heroes.

"You really mean to raise Jedrell from the dead?" she managed to ask.

"That cannot be done. Death is still death, a shore from which none may return." For a moment a shadow passed before his eyes, and then he leaned forward into the firelight once more. "But if the old High King is dead, his line still survives. I did not escape Caenthell alone, Cassia. I carried Jedrell's heir safe, in my arms, over the northern borders and into the wild countries beyond. Out of sight, out of danger, and out of history. Until now."

She blinked, uncomprehendingly, trying to make sense of what he was telling her. He was pointing her towards some secret conclusion, she realised, but she felt stupid. She could not see the end of the story.

Meredith emerged silently from the gloom, crouched down by the fire, and laid a pair of dead rabbits before her. "Yours to prepare," he said.

She stared at the animals, her thoughts turned about once more. *Last night he knew nothing! How could he have caught those?* "I – you laid snares?"

Meredith returned her stare. "No," he replied bluntly.

Something cried out for her attention, as if from a great distance, and she struggled to hear that voice. Meredith shifted and leaned forward, and the pendant that hung around his neck slipped into view, glimmering in the firelight. Small and golden – a mountain that rested on a closed fist. Cassia had seen that image before, and it didn't take long for her to remember where, and when.

Pyraete's *Call to the North*. It decorated the sides of the scroll; a recurring motif that had been worked into the illuminations. It was the ancient symbol of the High Kings.

The air punched from her chest as Baum's hints made sense at last. *Out of history. Until now.*

"*Meredith?*" she gasped, and the lordling raised his head to look at her. "You . . . you're the heir to Caenthell?"

"My flesh and blood is of the mountains," he replied gravely.

Baum tossed another stick onto the fire. "Which is to say, *yes*," he told her. "Do you find it so hard to believe?"

Cassia's gaze flicked back to the pendant as it swung gently from its chain and reflected the firelight in several different directions, giving it the appearance of being forge-heated. "Sir, I don't know what to believe any more. I've never heard any of this story told."

Baum grunted. "Of course not," he said. "That's because I've never told it, and everybody else is long dead. Malessar intended to kill every single man, woman and child in that castle when he tore it down. Why should I risk the chance he would learn that I still live, and that Jedrell's line was *not* cut short?"

She shook her head, cursing her woollen thoughts. It was obvious – what else would happen if the warlock had found out? In all the tragedies she knew, grudges were held across generations, and vengeance was always bloody.

She could not take her gaze from Meredith's face. His skin was unlined, unworn, chiselled with sharp lines, while it was easy to see the passage of centuries written on Baum's features. "But surely you were not both there, at Caenthell?"

The old soldier laughed, although the sound was not light-hearted. "Of course not, girl. Pyraete only saw fit to extend my own life. Jedrell's boy lived a natural span. He took a wife, grew old, and was buried far from his rightful home."

"As did his son," Meredith said quietly. "And his children after that."

"All through those long years, I remained true to my promise," Baum said. "I kept Jedrell's descendants safe from harm, nursed them through their lives, until they had forgotten where their origins lay. Then I left them alone. I sought training and knowledge, to arm myself for the battle I knew would one day come. Every ten years or so, I made sure to pass through and check on the families, but I never revealed myself or let them realise who they were."

It was an incredible story. Nothing Cassia could think of, not even the tales from the Age of Talons, could match the power of Baum's history.

"But – where . . . ?"

"Beyond the sight of the Empire that rose up to take Caenthell's place," Baum said, and a note of disgust entered his voice. A long-held and deep-seated emotion, Cassia guessed, from the way that it sounded so natural. Like Rann Almoul's contempt for her father. "There are lands far to the north of the mountains, where even the steel will of the High Kings could not reach. Civilised lands now, but very different to our own.

Sometimes their ships find the docks at Kalakhadze and they trade stones and warm furs for spices or dried meats that they call exotic and rare. It was easy to settle there. Unless you wished to undertake the same arduous journey as their seafarers, the safest route to these countries was through Caenthell and the Hamiardin Pass. But the pass was blocked by the same curse that felled the castle, and I was the last man to travel that way."

He clapped his hands and Cassia jumped at the sharp noise, her nerves shattered. "So! Now you know who we are and why we are here. What do you say?"

She hesitated, her hands slippery with blood and one of the rabbits only half-skinned. What could she say? Did he look for her approval? Surely not. Why would such a man need the approval of a mere girl? But the way he had despatched Vescar's men made her wary of saying anything that might anger him.

"But . . . I still don't understand. Why did you need us, sir? You have the Lord Meredith, and the blessings of a *god,* so why did you need my father?"

Meredith frowned. "I am no lord, girl."

Cassia ducked her head. "Yes, sir, but if you are heir to the High King's throne . . ."

Baum smiled. "For now, *Meredith* will suffice. But why do *you* think I decided to bring a storyteller on this quest?"

For a long moment she was uncertain, and she shied away from the more unpleasant reasons that came to mind. *Who knows how or why the gods work? And why would we know how their agents work?* She bit her lip and forced herself to think more positively. *Think like my father does: he puts himself into his characters and acts how he believes they would. But how can I make myself into a man who is nearly a thousand years old?*

She thought back, gathering up everything she had heard him say, sifting through the words for any kind of clue. One phrase – an overheard quip – circled and repeated itself, jostling for her attention.

And they always get it so wrong . . .

"Stromondor . . ." she breathed.

Baum leaned forward again. "Ah. So you heard me."

The pieces were falling into place. "You were at Stromondor. You were the man who challenged Jathar Leon Learth!" She paused; it wasn't quite right. "But the man in the story has no name."

"I never *gave* my name," Baum said. "You forget, the damned warlock was there too."

She *had* forgotten. But still, now she thought about it, she realised she knew what Baum wanted. Just like the illuminations that decorated Rann Almoul's copy of Pyraete's *Call to the North*, he had curled sinuously around the history of Hellea for several hundred years. But there the likeness faltered. The illuminations were in the margins, true, but they were visible. Baum's journey, if his presence at Stromondor was to be believed, had been either invisible, or undocumented.

Now he wanted that to change. He wanted to be a part of history again, part of the tales that would be told down the years about this quest to resurrect the ancient power of the North. To be acknowledged by the world once more.

"You want somebody to tell this story," she said. "And you thought that my father would accompany you . . ."

Baum spat into the fire. "So much for that idea," he muttered. "All this time and still I make such simple errors of judgement."

A strange prickle crept up from the base of Cassia's spine. *There's an opening – a chance. Even half a chance must be better than none . . .*

"So now you have no storyteller?" She tried to keep her voice as flat as possible. *Show no interest. None at all.*

"It appears not," Baum agreed. "A hitch, but not insurmountable."

She drew in a deep breath and straightened her shoulders. "Sir, *I* can be your storyteller."

The old man stared across the fire at her, the deep lines

creasing his skin highlighted even further by his raised brows. To one side Meredith looked on with little more than amused interest.

"You? But you are just a girl." Cassia clenched her fists at her sides. *But he hasn't yet refused me . . .*

She took another deep breath. What she said next could either sway him, or fall horribly flat. "And I am *just* a girl who can tell all her father's stories much better than he ever could."

Now the old man laughed, but, Cassia realised, it was not a derisive sound. He rocked back and clapped his hands together in delight. "Well fought, and well done! You have a deal, Cassia of Keskor!"

Chapter Six

CASSIA WOKE WITH a start as somebody nudged her ribs with the toe of their boot. Through the weave of her blanket she saw Meredith standing over her, silhouetted in the grey light before dawn.

"It is time to rise," he told her.

Cassia groaned and rolled over. "No it isn't. I've barely got to sleep. Stop doing that."

"No. This is your doing, girl."

She levered herself up onto her elbows, wincing at the aches caused by sleeping on the uneven ground. "What? I don't understand—"

"You wished to learn. This will be the only time we have spare today."

Now the memory returned to her. A couple of days back she had asked Meredith to teach her some skill with the sword. She'd had to settle for a promise to practise with staves, but that had been driven from her mind by the previous day's events. She noticed the Heir to the North held two long, thick staves, freshly hewn and better fashioned than her own, designed for sparring as much as for support. Meredith must have spent the entire night cutting them.

"You did not fashion one for yourself," Meredith noted. "I have done that for you."

"Thank you, sir. I think."

Meredith stepped back and allowed her to stand and stretch her tired, chilled muscles, waiting silently until she was ready. Cassia found herself tidying her bed roll away more slowly than usual, wondering if she was truly ready to face this kind of test when all she had done before was clash with Hetch and his younger cronies in the dirt outside Keskor's walls.

There was no room for her to back out. She found a sliver of relief in the fact that Baum had not yet risen. At least her embarrassment would only be shared with Meredith.

The staff was longer than she was used to, but it felt well balanced and she thought she might actually manage to surprise her new tutor if he let his guard down or under-estimated her skill. She followed Meredith out from the copse onto the damp field beyond and took up position a few yards from him, her left foot forward and her torso twisted to present a smaller target. She held the staff pointing low, to make him think twice about rushing her.

Meredith nodded. "A beginner's stance. But you have seen these contests before. You should not guard so low."

She was stung by the criticism. He had not even seen her fight yet, so what right did he have to make such fun of her? "Why not?"

A single step, his arms blurring across her vision, and the staff rattled from her grasp, her left arm numbed by the impact. The force of the blow staggered her and she dropped to her knees. She wanted to cry out in pain but stubborn pride – and years of experience – kept her silent.

"That is why," Meredith said. He moved back again. "Pick up your weapon."

She flexed her arm to loosen the muscles, wincing at the pain. The flesh above her elbow would darken quickly to a bruise, but it was nothing she hadn't suffered before. At least this time there was a reason for the hurt. She took up her position again, more wary now of Meredith's speed and reach. One end of her staff pointed up at his bare chest.

He regarded her for a moment with that dispassionate stare that so unnerved her. "Now you are awake. Good. Beware also of guarding too high."

She was on the ground again, this time flat on her back, before she could even think to lower the staff or duck away. The breath had been driven from her lungs, and the sky was tinged with strange bright lights. Meredith loomed over her – perhaps it had all been a dream, she thought hazily.

"Is it morning?" she managed to croak.

Meredith lifted her back up onto her feet, supporting her weight for a moment while she rediscovered her balance. "You are slow," he noted, as if surprised by that fact.

"I – I'm a storyteller," she replied, taking two dizzied steps toward her staff. "Not a bloodthirsty warrior. Or a prince."

"Yet you wish to learn."

Cassia pulled free of his hand, aware – too aware – of her skin prickling disturbingly under his cool, smooth touch. She hid her sudden flush by recovering her staff. "I might learn even faster if you tell me how I should stand, instead of hitting me all the time," she snapped.

"If there is no penalty for failure, how will you learn from your mistakes?"

The question was phrased so reasonably Cassia could find no rational argument against it. Her mood already frayed by Meredith's stings, she turned and ran at him without warning, her staff held to impale his stomach. Meredith twisted aside, dodging her attack with ease, and Cassia swung about again, unbalanced and forced into defending herself once more.

"You committed yourself to that move far too early, and you left your flank wide open." This time Meredith had not sprung forward to drive home his advantage. Instead he rested his weight on his back foot, and the ends of his staff moved in loose, hypnotic circles. So far both hits had come from her left, so she began to edge in that direction, hoping to tighten the angle against him.

"Good. You are thinking."

It didn't do her much good. Meredith came forward without apparently moving at all, and his staff cracked across her right thigh, catching her left arm again on the backswing as she spun in reaction. Cassia jabbed with the staff, sore and frustrated, but he was already beyond her reach. Her contests with Hetch belonged to a different world now, she realised. Like the rest of her old life in Keskor, they suddenly seemed very far away.

She feinted right, as though protecting her thigh, showing him the flank he had attacked most often. It was a trick that had always worked at least once in every fight. Meredith's staff dipped and flashed out, taking the bait, and she spun on the spot and brought her own staff down hard across his bare back. Or she would have done, had he still been in the same place. Meredith must have anticipated her move, and now he stood ready exactly where she had left herself open. Over-extended, Cassia could not stop in time and she fell into his blow with a bitten-off curse, landing in a heap on the dewy ground.

Meredith extended a hand to help her back to her feet, but she ignored it and hauled herself up unsteadily, determined to keep some small remnant of her pride. "Don't tell me. My flank was wide open again," she said, wincing. She wondered whether travelling on foot for the rest of the morning might help work off the stiffness that was certain to gather in her muscles. There would be little or no comfort for her on horseback.

Meredith shrugged. "As I said, girl. You must learn from your mistakes."

As much as she wanted to continue and prove to him – a damned prince, after all – that she had some skill in staves, there was still a lot to do before they could set off this morning. Cassia limped back to her bedroll and propped the staff against it before kneeling gingerly by the remains of the campfire. The ashes were cold, but the kettle wedged in their midst still held a little warmth. By the time she had shared the leftovers of the potage between three bowls Baum had risen, yawning, from his blankets and Meredith was absorbed in the rituals of his practice, silent as a wraith.

Baum nodded his thanks as Cassia passed him one of the bowls. "For a girl, you curse like an old soldier," he noted.

She realised he must have heard the sparring. "The curses are my father's."

"So I imagine," Baum said, with a chuckle. "Do you regret your request now?"

"A bit." Cassia rubbed at her arm. "But I won't give up, sir."

"Good. Now then, do you remember what I told you last night?"

Cassia nodded and the warmth that exercise had brought to her dissipated quickly. "Yes, sir. But Malessar – .how will you find him, sir? Does he even still live?"

"Oh, he lives. Be sure of that. Men such as he do not die easily." Baum paused and then shook his head. "Anyway, we are now well on the road to finding the damned warlock. Since the Fall of Stromondor he has avoided that city completely. I know this – I spent thirty years after the sack helping to rebuild the walls there, and I have returned several times since then. There has never been anything to signal his return. But he found new interests in Hellea, and in Kalakhadze, and I have pieced together much of his movements for the last two hundred years."

Despite knowing that Baum was aided by the God of the North, Cassia could not yet accustom herself to the fact that the old soldier had lived through several centuries without visibly aging.

Baum smiled at her. "You may find that difficult to believe," he said. "Sometimes I lose track of time myself. Malessar has moved regularly between Hellea and the southern lands, keeping to the shadows and the background, rarely revealing himself. If nothing else, I have at least managed to sully his reputation through hearsay and folk-tales. In the last half-century I have put most of my pieces in place. Now I plan to move down to Hellea itself and wait for him there. The Betrayer is a man of habit – he will come."

"And then, sir?"

Baum's expression turned predatory. "And then, dear girl, you will have the opportunity to record a confrontation fated by the gods themselves."

But, in contrast to Baum's aims, they did not rejoin the Emperor's March. Instead he led the party out of the dell and further into the hills, with the sun at their backs. Sore and uncomfortable in the saddle, Cassia twisted frequently to survey the ground behind them, fearful of pursuit. The hillsides remained empty, however, with only a few stray sheep, grazing amongst the outcrops, witness to their passing.

Meredith, the Heir to the North, rode out on the right flank, where he had a good view back into the valley. His staff was stowed across his packs, and his sword strapped across his back. He looked every inch a warrior, surveying the land as though it all belonged to him. Which, Cassia reminded herself, it might well do once Malessar was defeated.

Baum seemed in a good mood, singing under his breath as he traced an old herders' path through the narrowing vale. From time to time Cassia caught snatches of the words, hearing enough to understand it was addressed to a lover, as many old soldiers' songs were. Norrow would sing them in barracks towns if he judged there was profit to be made by them, but he did not enjoy performing them – they were often maudlin affairs, testament to hearts heavy through absence and loss. Cassia understood the reason for his aversion, although it was never mentioned aloud. Her mother was a subject guaranteed to bring Norrow's temper flaring into violence.

At last curiosity got the better of her, and she urged her horse forward to ride alongside him. "Sir, what is the song you keep singing? I recognise part of the tune, but not the words."

He took a moment to reply. "An old song," he said at last. "From my youth. It was popular in the taverns after Jedrell came to the throne. I thought I'd forgotten the melody, but it seems to have come back to me. The lyric, however . . . no, the correct words escape me. I wouldn't wish to embarrass myself by singing the wrong words to a storyteller."

"Would you tell me what the song is about?" She was unwilling to let the matter rest. This was her first chance to find out a little more about the man hidden under Baum's ancient quest, as well as being an opportunity to learn a song that might not have been heard in these lands for centuries. "I might know it by a different name."

"Unlikely," Baum told her with a faint smile. "If I recall any of the verses I'll be certain to recite them to you, though."

They rode in silence for a while, and Baum did not sing again. Cassia began to regret asking him about it. *Perhaps I should have just listened more keenly and learnt the song in secret, as my father does.* Norrow was a magpie of sorts, stealing and adapting songs and stories whenever he heard them, never crediting anyone but himself with their success. He would always insist, even to the point of violence, that he had come by the stories on his own.

He would have hunted down Baum's song more eagerly. If I wish to be a better storyteller than him, I must find my own sources and my own material. But the thought of angering Baum by pushing him to say more about a song he did not wish to share made her pause and her resolve crumbled again.

By the end of the third day they had left even the most remote sheepfolds behind and were deep in the Antiachas. Hills rose around them on all sides, dark stone escarpments jutting from the steep slopes to cast shadows over a path that had faded to little more than shallow grooves in the dirt. Thin, cold streams ran down gullies in the hillsides to join the headwaters of the river from which the Antiachas took its name. Baum called a halt here to refill their waterskins before quickening the pace, even though the horses were beginning to stumble in the gloom. A fierce bank of low cloud dominated the northern horizon. It would be an unpleasant night if they did not make camp soon.

She called forward, pointing out the approaching storm to Baum. He slowed to allow her to catch up.

"Shouldn't we stop for the night before it gets much darker?" she asked again.

"No, girl. This is not a good place to rest. Surely you know the history of this land?"

She hesitated. She knew very little about the Antiachas, mostly because Norrow had never shown any interest in the area, preferring to focus on the tales of high glory and tragedy, the great heroes of ages past like Jathar Leon Learth, and the dragons that dominated the Age of Talons. But to admit her ignorance would undermine her claim to be a better storyteller than her father. Baum might even renege on the deal they had made, and where would she be then?

"Not so well as you do, sir," she said, at length.

"Hah, flattery! Or, if not, then a subtle reminder of my advancing years."

He waved her protest away with a laugh, casting a glance at the storm clouds. "Forgive my humour. I've become too accustomed to my own company. We will shelter from this storm, but not here. This path will flood before midnight, and the hillsides become treacherous and unstable in heavy rain. You could break your neck up there in this weather. Many have done so before now."

She glanced nervously at an overhanging crag, half-expecting it to crack and fall upon them. "Then where will we go?

There can't be anybody living up here."

"Not now," Baum agreed. He heeled his horse about. "Apart from bandits and outlaws, of course. We must hurry though."

"Bandits?" To her relief the horse responded to her urgency. She had no desire to be left behind.

Norrow had been lucky, to be gifted with a smooth tongue. In all the long miles they had travelled, the most they had ever lost to outlaws was a half-full purse and a mangy goat he had won in a bet and unaccountably decided to keep. They had been held up several times by scrawny, unkempt men desperate for food and coin, neither of which Norrow ever managed to possess in any quantity. Cassia was sure that on at least two occasions they had only been saved by their own poverty. Storytellers were poor marks, and Norrow was often poorer than most. He would attempt to buy his way free with a fireside tale, and often that would work. Cassia supposed even criminals, exiled from their homes, wanted pleasant company of an evening.

These situations, especially over the last few years, had become increasingly perilous for Cassia. She found it more and more difficult to disguise herself as Norrow's boy apprentice, rather than his daughter, and at the back of her mind there was always the fear that her father would one day offer her up to outlaws in exchange for safe passage. His willingness to abandon her to Almoul's possession back at Keskor stood as proof of his intent. Escaping that fate, only to fall victim to outlaws here in the Antiachas, was not something she wanted to think about.

Meredith was not too far ahead. She managed to make the horse keep pace with him, trying not to let her anxiety show. The Heir to the North seemed calm, though he too cast frequent glances at the looming crags. The weather was closing in fast and Cassia felt rain in the air, blowing against her back. When the storm broke they would all be soaked.

"Nobody should be abroad in this weather," she muttered.

Meredith shrugged. "Perhaps not. But if nobody else is, maybe this is the right time to travel."

She frowned at him. "That sounds . . . unlikely," she said, unwilling to go as far as calling him insane out loud. "I'd rather not get soaked through and catch my death of cold out here."

"Your skin is waterproof," Meredith said. "You will not soak through."

The clouds had darkened further, and the winds whipped around her skirts. She shivered, blinking away the first large drops of rain. "I hope you're certain of that, my Lord Prince," she said bitterly.

Baum called back. "Just a little farther. Rest easy girl. There will be no bandits creeping over our camp tonight."

Oh, and I hope you're just as certain of that, *too,* she thought miserably.

They passed over one last ridge, and Cassia found herself looking across the scattered remnants of an ancient fort, the foundations standing proud from a squared-off mound while stone blocks lay about the base, half-buried in the long grass. Her skin crawled as she realised Baum meant to camp here.

"One of the ancient forts from the age of Caenthell," Baum called, his words almost torn away by the wind. "Once this was the northernmost border of Lyriss, back when it was still a kingdom of note." He nudged his tired mount, its head bowed against the rising wind. "As good a place as any."

Cassia followed reluctantly. She knew of Lyriss, at least. Some of her father's tales were set in that vanished land. The Lyrissans had been peaceful scholars, caught between Caenthell and the stubborn city states of the south. They had fallen quickly, unused to the High King's savagery on the battlefield, and their city had been dismantled and carried away as plunder, the ground salted and all trace of the Lyrissan people driven from history. The Lyrissans now lived only in myths and tales, as did the dragons that, legend had it, provided them with much of their wealth and wisdom.

Her imagination lent her a vision of a grand dragon perched on the wrecked wall, gazing balefully down at them, wings spread to launch into the air. Maybe if the Lyrissans had asked the dragons for help against the marauding armies of the North, their city might yet stand and thrive.

She wondered if Baum would take them past the site of the old city. She seemed to be collecting ancient ruins on this journey: first Gethista, now Lyriss. Soon she might call herself an expert on lost cities, she told herself with hollow humour.

Only one wall of the small fort still had enough integrity and height to serve as a windbreak. The rest were crumbled beyond repair. Meredith and Cassia rigged a lean-to against that wall with the few sheets Baum could give them from his packs, and they huddled inside while the storm broke, unable even to gather kindling for a fire, as everything that lay nearby was already soaked through. For all her fears, Cassia succumbed to sleep quickly, the storm blowing a familiar lullaby, one she knew from her long childhood of weary travel.

She awoke in discomfort to find that rain had gathered in an overflowing pool further along the wall, and was spilling downhill into their rough lean-to. Everything was cold and sodden, made worse by the sharp breeze that pushed the storm westwards.

"Not the best place to raise a shelter," Baum grumbled. His cloak hung from him like grim chains. "But even I cannot influence the weather."

With daylight came the first chance to look at the ruins without the spectres of history and myth casting shadows upon Cassia's imagination. It appeared to have shrunk in the light, becoming a mere collection of tumble-down stone blocks. At the height of Lyriss's fame, the building must have had at least one storey atop the ground floor. The Lyrissans stationed here would have collected tolls and taxes from travellers, and passed on urgent news via a rooftop beacon. They would have shared this lower floor with hens and sheep, as well as the fast horses for courier duties.

She stood at the edge of the walls and looked out into the valleys beyond, dull green and cloud-laden. Not a soul stirred anywhere she cared to turn.

"The hidden valleys," Baum said, behind her. "That's what they used to call this place."

Cassia frowned. "But they aren't hidden."

"No, I suppose not. No grand sorcery to hide their pathways or to turn inquisitive travellers about and confuse them so they follow other roads. Yet hidden nonetheless. After the roads were torn up, it did not take long for people to forget Lyriss had ever existed. And while the lands to the south bowed and paid tribute to Caenthell for a while, and Lyriss was a muttered byword for what would happen to any man fool enough to oppose the High King, that changed too, after Malessar wreaked his evil upon the North."

This was part of the story she already knew. Norrow's audiences revelled in the fall of the southern cities, and some of the most bloodthirsty stories were set against the long, convoluted wars that followed the destruction of Caenthell. Cities and tyrants jostled for primacy on the fertile plains around the Castaria, alliances shifting back and forth in a constant dance of mistrust and betrayal, some discussed, formalised and then violently disbanded in the period between two full moons. It was little wonder some of the more vulnerable cities had collapsed into history and never re-emerged, unable to survive such cut-throat politics. It was a surprise though, that Lyriss had not been able to call upon their ancient allies and protectors to help them.

"What about the dragons?" she asked.

Baum scratched his beard and said nothing for a long moment. Cassia thought he must not have heard her and was about to ask again, when he looked up at the hillsides that surrounded the ruined fort and breathed a tired sigh.

"Dragons," he said quietly. "I'll wager you know hundreds of tales from the Age of Talons."

"Not so many. Dozens, perhaps. I would like to know more," she added, in the hope Baum might relate some grand adventure that no storyteller alive would ever have heard.

"As do all men," Baum said. "That is why they seek out dragons. In my experience, it is never wise to incur debt to a dragon." He flashed a flat, thin smile, devoid of humour. "Often, the results can be far worse than merely incurring their wrath."

He turned away sharply, and it was clear to Cassia that he would not take the subject any further. She wondered if it was wise to ask him about Lyriss's connection to the great beasts while he was in such a closed-in mood.

She felt a presence close behind her and steeled herself not to jump: Meredith still had an irritating tendency to sneak up on her unexpectedly, and she would not give him the satisfaction of knowing he had unnerved her.

"I have heard one story of Lyriss," he said, and she flinched a little. His voice sounded too loud in the stillness of the valley. "It is said the town's elders begged two dragons to stand guard and protect them against attacks from the North. In exchange the dragons asked nothing more than the peace and freedom to do as they would in the hills here."

Cassia was impressed. This was a children's fable that she had heard just once, down on the coast to the east, but the storyteller there had set it in the hills overlooking the Berdellan plains. Try as she might, she could not remember the names of the two dragons who made that compact with the Berdellans. She turned and saw Meredith watching her expectantly, the staves he had carved held together in one hand. "So what happened after that?" she asked, as much to distract him from the forthcoming bout as to hear the end of the tale.

"The High King's armies passed on and came upon Lyriss from the road to the east, of course," Meredith replied. "The two dragons did nothing, because this was not a part of their contract with the city."

"Which goes to show you should never make rash bargains with dragons," Baum finished. "For men may act as cruelly as dragons, but dragons will never act as men do."

She muttered that aphorism under her breath a few times as she poured water into their flasks from the pans she had shoved out into the rain the previous night. The rhythm of the words was not quite right. Perhaps if she worked on them as they passed through the hills she could polish this old story and draw in an audience. People remembered a well-spoken moral as much as they remembered a good dancing tune, and it would be a fine hook on which to hang her reputation.

The Heir to the North still stared out across the landscape, as though lost in his thoughts. A frown creased his face and he cocked his head to one side as if he had heard something Cassia tested her own hearing, but there was only the rustling of trees and bushes as they swayed in the breeze.

"Do you hear them?" Meredith asked, his voice hushed, almost reverent.

She shook her head, wondering what he had heard. Whatever it was, it must be at the very edge of the senses. "What is it?"

"They still sleep," Meredith said.

She stood there for a long moment, trying to work out if he was making a fool of her, but his expression did not change. *Who still sleep? The dragons? No, that would be ridiculous. It was only a story.*

But when they mounted to leave the ruined fort, a kernel of doubt nagged at her mind. It was only a story. But so was Stromondor. And Caenthell. And the warlock Malessar. And now she knew they were all true.

Meredith had laid more bruises on top of her existing collection, and Cassia ached all over as they rode down into the lands that had once been Lyriss. She stared up at the hillsides with fresh eyes. It was her imagination, and nothing more, she told herself firmly, that caused the undulating peaks to resemble the sinuous backbones and tails of monstrous dragons.

Chapter Seven

HERE *WERE* PEOPLE in Lyriss. Moreover, to Baum's evident amusement, a small town occupied the ground where the city had stood in ancient times. They had come upon a road, not much more than dirty ruts in the ground, running from the east and curving slowly to the south, and the old soldier decided to take the southward route, reasoning that travelling east would only take them back to the Emperor's March again.

"They may be cowed right now," he said, when Cassia reminded him of the threats he had made to Vescar Almoul, "but we Northerners are a stubborn breed. There is little sense in tempting fate in such a fashion, and I have no wish to be disturbed in the middle of the night by a disgruntled half-captain who might have just enough courage to put a knife through my heart."

When Cassia thought on that, she pictured Hetch or Rann Almoul himself looming over her in the dark, and she shivered. Rejoining the Emperor's March would not be a good idea.

The following day brought them to the town. There were cattle in the fields around the low walls, and shacks, workshops and small farmsteads dotted the land. Chimney smoke rose and drifted south with the wind, carrying the smells of civilisation away from them. Cassia ran a critical eye over the fields, comparing them unfavourably to those farther north and east. These were smaller, less well-tended, and the livestock looked thin, scouring the patchy grasses with hungry fervour.

"These people are not prosperous," Meredith noted, in a voice that carried across the fields and seemed designed to attract hostile attention.

"I doubt they have much passing trade," Baum agreed. "The March will take all travellers due north, leaving this place to wilt in the shade. Nevertheless, my good prince, I think reminding them too much of this will not make them gracious hosts."

Meredith bowed his head. "I shall remain quiet then," he said.

The town was in better condition than the fields, but not by much. As Cassia rode through the gates, attempting to conceal herself between the two men, the first thing she saw was the gibbet that stuck out from the top of the gate frame. The corpse that hung from it had been there some time, at least a couple of weeks. She had seen it before, in other towns. Many places followed the custom of displaying captured outlaws and murderers over their gates, to discourage others from taking the same path, but it always unnerved her. She imagined the corpse turning gently in the breeze to watch her with hollow, unblinking sockets. Her father often joked that should he murder a good tale, he would swing at the gates by morning. Cassia hadn't found that joke funny. Especially not after Varro.

The corpse set the tone for the rest of the town. A quiet, miserable place, the houses and workshops that lined the main street had their doors and gates firmly shuttered, their windows hidden away. Some looked half-built, while in a few places the ground was scorched where buildings had burned to their foundations, stone slabs overgrown with weeds the only sign there had once been life. There was little traffic on the road – a pair of men hauled a cart, wheels squeaking and complaining, in the opposite direction, never once glancing at the mounted travellers. A few labourers huddled at the side of the road, their hoes and picks abandoned in the mud and dirt as they talked in a close-knit group. There was no noise, Cassia realised abruptly: not the screams of children, nor the cries of traders. The town was as quiet as the grave.

"I don't want to stop here," she said quietly.

"A frequent complaint, I should think," Baum said. "But we need some stores, since your father took much of ours with him. And I believe I have an acquaintance here too."

Cassia hunched down in the saddle, reminded once more of Norrow's failings. *As long as you don't think I take after him*, she thought bitterly. It took her a moment to register what Baum had said, and she wondered who he could possibly know in a dead-end town like this.

The road widened into the town's sorry excuse for a main square. On one side was a small temple, the stone edifice standing almost apologetically amid a motley collection of decrepit taverns and shuttered wooden houses, none of which would have passed muster further north. On the other side of the road was the market, which comprised of a few desultory stalls and half-empty cattle pens. Slender pickings for any pickpocket unfortunate enough to try his luck here. A good thing after all, Cassia decided, that her father had abandoned them.

Baum hauled in before the temple and squinted up at the fascia over the portico. "Dedicated to Feyenn and Alcibaber," he muttered disdainfully. "Vanity."

Cassia glanced over at him, shocked. "You mean they are not real, sir?"

"Oh, they exist." He laughed. "They are real. But they are not gods. Never that."

He dismounted and looped the reins about the post at the foot of the portico. "I have not passed this way in years.

I wonder if the priest still lives. Meredith, remain with the horses. They are worth more than the rest of this town put together."

Excluded from Meredith's instructions, Cassia took that as an invitation. She dropped from the saddle, wincing at the twinges in her legs, and scrambled up the steps of the portico behind Baum before he could change his mind, or Meredith could haul her back. It took her a moment to get accustomed to walking again.

The portico led into an open space, bound on both sides by colonnades. Carved figures stood in alcoves along the walls, and at irregular intervals across the ground. Cassia kept to the stone path that led through the colonnades, increasing her pace to keep up with Baum, who strode across the open space as though he owned it.

The stone figures were a mismatched collection of old representations and new carvings. Men with heavily muscled torsos stared at the sky, the colour painted upon their eyes faded and worn away. Women draped in long gowns, usually with a single breast bared, stood with their heads tilted downward, servile and graceful.

She paused for a moment and turned back. That last figure . . . a man, his stance straight and proud, shoulders pushed back in defiance of something before him. But the features of his face had been chiselled away, jagged craters showing the marks of someone's anger. It was the shape of his back that drew Cassia's eye. It looked far too large, as though the sculptor's talent had failed him at that point. But as she looked closer she realised the figure had been vandalised here too. It had been created with something protruding from behind the man's shoulders, on both sides of his back. She examined the pedestal, but she could not see any inscription.

Why would anybody deface such a thing inside a temple? Why would it be kept after it had been so damaged? She shook her head. It must have some value for the priests to retain it and keep it on display. It was another puzzle.

The sound of voices broke her concentration. She left her examination of the mutilated statue and headed back up the colonnade. Baum had stopped outside the door and was speaking with someone inside. Or, rather, he was being spoken to: the man beyond the doorway had a lot to say and sounded unwilling to let Baum get more than half a word in.

". . . Feyenn was never a Hellean god, you know. Of course you do. You're a learned man, I see that in your eyes. The key to a man's soul is in his eyes – did I mention that before? I must write it down before I forget. They say memory is the first faculty to flee in the face of old age, you know, but – heh – I can never remember who said it to me. Not that anybody ever wants to talk to me any more. Can't think why. Damned ignorant fools, sitting miserably under the hills and wondering if the rain will come through the roof. That's all they want to do. I should never have come here – never would have if *they* hadn't wanted me to keep them company."

He coughed. "Awful weather. Sits on the chest. Nettle expectorant, that's what you need. Did you ask a question?"

"Yes," Baum said. "Several."

"Ah. Oh. Well, never mind. Who's that skulking over there?"

The old soldier turned and beckoned Cassia forward. "An apprentice," he said.

As she approached she saw that the temple's priest was a wizened old man, bent and gnarled like a weather-blasted tree. His hair and beard were patchy and unevenly sheared, and his eyes were rheumy and unfocused. He held himself up against the door frame with fingers thin and dark as a moorhen's foot, and his robe was caked with damp and filth. It was easy to see why the town's inhabitants would not come anywhere near him. Cassia would never have named him as any kind of priest.

"A fair boy," the priest declared. "Very fair. You like the statues, eh? The rippling muscles? The godly thighs?"

Cassia blushed and ducked her head, unsure of her reply. The priest must have seen movement on the colonnade, but his sight was so far gone that, with her hair pulled back and hidden under her storyteller's cap, he had taken her for a boy.

"Ah, if my legs were still as shapely as those . . ."

"We wish to purchase supplies," Baum interrupted him loudly.

The words had a magical effect on the old man. He pulled himself straighter and his eyes grew sharp, the years falling away at the mention of coin.

"Passing through Lyriss, eh? Passing through? Where would you be going that you have to pass through this miserable hole in the ground?" The priest shuffled forward and squinted at the sky. "Be another downpour today, more than likely. Lyriss's tears, that's what they call it. Bawling like a widowed mother. Well then, come on in, don't stand on ceremony. Heaven knows *they* wouldn't."

He re-entered the darkened interior of the temple, gesturing vaguely with one hand and clutching at the doorframe and stone walls with the other. Cassia hesitated, glancing at Baum for guidance. He appeared quietly amused.

"Sir? Is he . . . ?"

"Harmless?" Baum said, in a low tone. "Almost certainly. I would stay beyond his reach, if I were you, but while he believes there is money to be made from us he'll be as honest as you or I."

Still she hovered at the lintel. "Will we buy our supplies from him, then? Why not from one of the market traders?"

"Who would undoubtedly fleece us by charging double or triple the value of the goods, and then give us short measure?" Baum replied. "While our friendly priest may charge a premium, he will deal with us fairly. After all, the townsfolk have donated their food to him to begin with." His smile widened. "Did your father never teach you that trick?"

She shook her head. Norrow had always been strangely

reticent around priests. Now she thought on it she was certain he had never asked at the temples for help, no matter how destitute they were. "The townsfolk will not be pleased with us, sir."

Baum was not troubled by that. "I am not here to make *their* lives any easier," he said.

Like most temple interiors, this one was cold and unwelcoming. Plaster flaked from the walls, old paintings and scenes of worship drifting into dust and destruction. There were brackets on each wall for lamps and torches, but these were empty and the only illumination came from slender windows high up in the walls. Dust, stirred up by the priest's passing, danced through thin shafts of light. Two altars sat against the back wall, offerings of food and slaughtered fowl at the base of each one. Even in this gloom Cassia could see the offerings were days old. The stench caught in her throat.

There was a thick, closed door in the wall on her right, but the priest led them off to the left, towards what were presumably his living quarters. Cassia heard him muttering from beyond the doorway, his voice echoing as he held a conversation with himself. A flickering glow bloomed against the doorframe.

"Come in, come in, don't stand on ceremony," the priest called again, his raised voice cracking. "Feyenn and Alcibaber won't mind."

Well, of course not, especially if they aren't really gods. But I only have Baum's word for that.

Baum pushed her forward and she entered the priest's chamber, her shoulders tense. The candlelight revealed a small, sparse room, with a pallet on one side and a small hearth opposite. There was barely enough space for the pair of low stools and the battered chest that doubled as a table. The fire in the hearth glowed, but gave off no warmth, and the priest jabbed at it before settling on one of the stools.

"Do sit down, do sit down," he said. "Which direction did you come from, do you mind me asking? From the March, or the hills to the west? My money, had I any, would be on the March, as it is rare we have visitors from the west. Sometimes a few caravans venture into the valleys, but they tend to leave sharply once they realise there's not much welcome for them here. Not much wealth either, if truth be told, so honest labour is hard earned. Do you think it warm enough in here? I can stir up the fire, but your boy must fetch the firewood as Gelmik has not been today. Tiresome boy; he takes too much after his father and will come to a bad end if he does not watch his step. I once caught him trying the lock out there, would you believe?" He gestured vaguely towards the heavy door. "He swore blind it was not what it appeared, that he had seen vermin scurry under the door, but I switched him anyway."

Cassia, frozen in the act of crouching against the wall, glanced at Baum. The old man had taken the other stool, so she had to squat in the filthy rushes that covered the floor. He seemed oblivious to this rambling monologue, content to sit with his back straight and his arms folded until, at last, the priest ran out of words and an uncomfortable silence filled the room.

"Is there much news from the road?" Baum asked.

The priest shook his head. "Nothing to mention. Nothing to mention. There was a tax, just before high summer, but they left with their coffers more empty than full. Always the way. They took a few boys for the legions instead. But not Gelmik, of course. Useless boy."

There was an odd expression on Baum's face, one Cassia could not decipher. She thought he might be lost in his memories. "Have you been here long, sir?" she asked, eager to break the quiet. Even the priest's meandering replies were better than awkward silence.

"Hah! An observant boy!" the priest cackled. "Does it look like I came here yesterday? Man and boy now, man and boy. I heard the calling and I came. *They* talked to others too, to begin with, but Fiscum died, and then Hoplar got the wasting sickness, and now *they* just talk to me. When they talk at all. Mostly they just listen. Which is more than that lot do." He jerked his head at the outside wall, indicating the townsfolk, and spat into the hearth. "None of them listen. I told them, I did, I told them it was a bad place for a town, but they wouldn't hear me. Flat land, they said. Flat land and a stream. And the walls of the temple to protect them when the soldiers came, after they'd crept down and stolen the herds off the plains. Then they thought they could be honest men, plough the fields and grow things, but I told them on that too: I said, it's not in your blood and the land knows it. Did they listen? Did they?"

Startled, Cassia could only shake her head. "Um . . . no?"

"No, they did not," the priest continued, as though she hadn't spoken. "A wretched hive of mediocrity, this town. A stain on the history of Lyriss."

Baum shifted. "You remember a little of the tales of Lyriss, then?"

The priest met his gaze, rheumy eyes narrowing. "Did I say that?"

"I believe you did, Dorias."

"Ah." Dorias shivered. "I know you. I know your face. Your voice."

The room grew even more claustrophobic. Cassia glanced from one man to the other, muscles tensed for a swift exit. Baum still smiled, but the priest's expression was haunted.

"I admit I am surprised to see you still alive," Baum said at last. "I always thought your wild schemes were doomed to failure."

"Phah. You are not infallible," Dorias told him. "*They* sustain me. *They* will not be happy to know you've come here. I smell Pyraete upon you."

Baum shrugged. "So . . . don't tell them. They don't pay attention to everything that happens. You call them gods? They aren't immortals, you know."

"What is man to a mayfly?" the priest snapped.

Cassia could not follow the conversation, but she did not dare interrupt. "I should throw you out," the old priest muttered.

"We are not here to cause trouble," Baum insisted. "We are simply passing through this land."

"The March would have been much quicker. Trouble must be on your heels."

"All I seek is news," Baum said. "I have spent the last few years in the far North, and I would like to know the lie of the land before I walk upon it."

"You've come to the wrong place," Dorias said, but the tone of his voice suggested otherwise. "I hear little and less from the townsfolk these days. Only Gelmik ever says more than ten words to me. The legions patrol the March and the eastern woods, and they force the Lyrissans to keep to the valleys. They could crush the town once and for all if they wished – half a legion would do the job well enough – but their commander is a superstitious old fool who still believes in dragons and will not commit his men to the valleys. And there is nothing the Empire could gain by razing Lyriss to the ground for a second time."

"Nevertheless."

The priest sighed. "There are always rumours. Men look North and shiver. I would advise against the March. Even the richest merchants find themselves delayed and questioned on the roads toward Hellea."

"Old fears run deep," Baum muttered. "The Empire has always feared the North. And what do you hear of the name Malessar?"

The priest scratched his head. "Malessar . . . an ill-omened name. Like the warlock from the old tales . . . a certain way to damn a child."

Cassia was surprised. She had not believed anyone would still use that name. Surely the weight of history would choke any boy given that burden.

"*They* know him." Dorias said eventually. "*They* see him. *They* dream of him."

Baum leaned forward. "Where?"

The priest's thin lips twisted in a wry smile. "A fair question. And one I cannot answer."

Baum's expression was fierce and intent. Cassia held her breath, remembering the bolts of pure magic that burned through Vescar's soldiers. Baum had worn the same expression then. She wondered if she might be able to slip away before he lost his patience with the prevaricating priest.

"Cannot, or will not?"

Dorias spat into the hearth once more. "I'm an old man. I've forgotten far more than I'll ever know. But you should know that. He was in Hellea. And Galliarca. But whether that was last year, five years ago, or ten, or even more than that, I do not know. Perhaps he is dead."

"Perhaps not," Baum countered.

"Ah well, if he's like you, if he's a warlock . . ." the priest's words drifted into silence. He shook his head. "Maybe it's for the best that I am old."

Cassia could not endure much more of this. It all frightened her; the priest, the town, the mutilated statues . . . even spending another night in the ruins of one of those abandoned forts would be preferable to staying in Lyriss any longer. She looked towards Baum. "Sir?"

Baum frowned, and returned his attention to the priest. "We will not take up much more of your time," he said.

"If supplying you leaves me in peace, then you can take what you want," Dorias grunted. It seemed he was no longer in any mood to ramble, hunched forward defensively, scowling into the fireplace. He dug into his robe and fetched out a dull and pitted iron key, tossing it to Cassia. "Leave the door unlocked."

She scrambled out of the room gratefully, not caring that her hand landed on something soft beneath the rushes as she pushed herself up.

The conversation continued behind her, words now terse and spare.

"I had hoped you were long dead."

Baum snorted. "Charitable thoughts for a priest."

"My gods are not known for their charity. And neither is yours. What do you really want?"

"The warlock," Baum replied. "His life, and nothing more."

Cassia heard Dorias hawk phlegm. "And the boy? He isn't yours. I can see that much. Leave him here. I'll look after him while you go south. I could use the help. Gelmik—"

"The boy stays with me," Baum said firmly.

"Then it will all end in tears," Dorias said. "*They* have spoken."

Baum laughed. "Your gods? Now, the truth, Dorias. *They* know where he is. I must know too." His voice boomed through the hall, making Cassia jump and almost drop the heavy key. "Boy! Hurry with those stores!"

She hastened to do his bidding, chagrined at having been caught eavesdropping. *It isn't my fault the sound carries so easily in here . . .* She wrestled with the lock, her fingers slipping on cold metal, and tried to block out the sounds from the priest's room.

They left Lyriss before the sun was halfway to the horizon. Meredith's presence had kept the townsfolk at bay, and Cassia felt waves of hostility flow across the square towards her as she stowed the supplies and hoisted herself into the saddle. Potatoes, leeks, and a greying ham were all the priest could spare from his meagre stores.

Two women sat on a step at the far end of the street. Gaunt and hard-faced, the sharp lines of their bodies clear under their shifts, they watched the party pass by, not even bothering to call their wares to Meredith or Baum. Their silence unnerved

Cassia yet further, and she pushed her mount into a bone-shaking canter to escape their unfriendly, calculating stares.

Now they travelled west, into the sunset and directly away from the March. The poor fields petered out into the broken ground that dominated much of the Lyrissan valley, the road once again little more than a rough track. They might almost still be in Gethista, Cassia thought. There was no appreciable difference between the two areas. She kept the brisk pace until, as the path began to climb out of the lowest parts of the valley, Meredith and Baum caught up with her at last.

"I would guess from your demeanour that you did not enjoy your brief visit to Lyriss," Meredith said. There was the hint of a smile around the corners of his mouth.

"The priest . . . his temple was not right." Cassia struggled to find the correct words. "I felt like something was watching me."

"Perhaps it was his god," Meredith suggested. Cassia looked up sharply at him, but that faint smile had not widened.

"Are you mocking me, sir?"

Meredith raised one hand in a calming gesture. "I meant no offence, girl."

Baum spat into the grass and looked back over his shoulder, something Cassia herself had decided she would not do until they had left Lyriss far behind them. "There were no *gods* in that temple," he said firmly. "There never were."

"But why else would the priest be there?" Cassia wondered aloud. "He said they talked to him."

"Dorias has been there for half a century," Baum said. "I hardly think his sanity can be counted upon now."

Another thought struck her and she watched Baum's face carefully as she spoke. "He said he knew you, sir. Was he wrong in that?"

Baum hesitated, looking away for a moment, but when he turned back to her his expression had not changed. "No, he was not."

"Was he a soldier? Like Attis?"

Now Baum smiled, as though remembering the priest as a younger man. "A soldier, yes, but *not* like Half-Captain Attis. Dorias was . . . a delicate soul. He found soldiering too hard for his sensibilities at first. The armour was too heavy, the pikearms too long, his scabbard ever tangled itself with his legs; and he would always march out of time." He wagged a finger at Cassia to forestall her next question. "But nevertheless, he *was* there, in that Berdellan fort when we bested Gyre Carnus. It shaped him. He earned his share of the gold."

Cassia found that hard to believe, recalling the hunched, bony figure living in the midst of his own filth. "But why would he come here after that?"

"Dorias used to say he heard the gods calling him. I never believed him. I know what they sound like, I know the look of a man's face when the gods say his name. And I was here when Lyriss first fell. I know that no god looks down upon this damned valley. But what Dorias heard was enough to cause him to lay down his arms and come to Lyriss to rebuild that temple. A fool's project."

She fought the urge to look back at the dilapidated town. *Perhaps there really are dragons under the hills. Perhaps they found themselves lonely after so many centuries, with only the cracked bones of the past for company . . .* Truth or not, it was a haunting image. One that would give new life to the old stories of Lyriss. *And so I have a tale I can call my own. A tale that will distinguish me from every other storyteller in Hellea.* It was more, far more, than her father had ever given her.

Her mind surged southward, to the Empire's capital. A vast city of grand squares and heaving marketplaces, where women wove gold lace through their hair and noble men declaimed from platforms on every street corner. Where even the rudest servant might have money and a room of her own. Where storytellers might become truly famous and be known by name to the Emperor himself.

Or so Hetch had told her, once. She glanced back at Lyriss as they crested a rise that would at last hide the town from view. *I hope Hellea does not look like that.*

Baum seemed in a fair mood so she ventured another question, angling for more fuel for her tales. "Will we find Malessar in Hellea, sir?"

"Yes, I believe so." Baum sounded pleased. "The Betrayer has always tethered himself to Hellea. No matter how far he travels, his leash always pulls him back to these lands."

His scorn for the warlock's motives was clear. He must have trailed Malessar back and forth across the continent for centuries, biding his time and perfecting his plan.

"Why did you not confront him earlier?"

He scratched his beard and stared at her, his brow raised quizzically. "You are full of questions today, girl. Would you know my whole scheme?"

She almost said *yes*, but bit down on her reply, apologising instead for her forwardness. "My father always told me I should keep my nose out of the business of others, sir."

Baum shrugged. "No matter. It was a fair question. I may be the sword of Pyraete's vengeance, but even a sword must first be forged and hammered, folded dozens of times, tempered, and then sharpened so it may be used. I was a man, you see, nothing more than that, until I was chosen. I had no sorcerous skills, no knowledge of alchemy; I would never have been able to stand against Malessar as I was."

He lifted one hand from his reins and held his thumb and forefinger apart. A blue nimbus sat against his palm, and energy crackled between his outstretched fingers. His horse ducked its head and whinnied, unnerved by what was occurring just behind its ears. Cassia shrank away from the display, remembering the charred bodies of Vescar's soldiers, and the roots of her hair prickled horribly. It was hard not to push her heels into her own horse's flanks and flee. Meredith, impassive as ever and undoubtedly used to these displays, looked on in silence.

"There, you see?" Baum let the unnatural glow expand into a globe that enveloped his entire hand. "I am more than I was before. Now, I am the warlock's peer. I have been taught magic from men who learned their own skills from Malessar himself; I have studied volumes in all the hidden libraries and made practical use of every kind of sorcery and battle magic. No mortal man – no short-lived soldier, reliant on his wits and a blade – could have gained as much as I have, but this is what Pyraete willed me to do. And this is what will bring about Malessar's downfall."

The globe vanished as abruptly as it had formed, though Cassia's skin still crawled. She tried to move the conversation on. Perhaps there was such a thing as too much knowledge, after all.

"But if we are bound for Hellea, sir, surely this is the wrong road?"

Meredith's barked laugh was unexpected, cutting the air like a woodsman's blunt axe might split a trunk. Already rattled, Cassia jerked reflexively on her reins and her horse skipped to one side. She glared at the tall prince, choking back a desire to curse him to the winds.

"The girl has you," Meredith said, over her head. "Even if we seek to avoid the Emperor's March, Hellea is to the south and we are headed westwards. This road will only take us back into the mountains."

Baum turned his frown upon the prince and regarded him silently for a moment before replying. "There are other ways into the welcoming arms of the Empire, Meredith. One may approach from the west as well as from the north. This may be a longer route, but I think Malessar will wait a little longer for us yet." The frown became a smile again and he beckoned Cassia to rejoin them. "We should cook that ham tonight. It will turn bad otherwise, and I do not fancy crossing these hills with an empty stomach. Perhaps you might find more roots to stew with it?"

Cassia nodded in eager agreement. Roots or sprouting leaves – in her experience there was always something nearby that could be adapted. And the search would give her a little precious time alone. Room to breathe, and room to think: *I have a story to polish and rehearse, after all.* Until she could summon the courage to practice aloud before Baum and Meredith, the vegetation of the western Antiachas would be a silent, uncritical audience.

Chapter Eight

AFTER SEVERAL DAYS Baum led them away from the hills of the Antiachas, turning south toward the edge of the Hellean plains. The skies were heavy with storm clouds, gathering over the mountains behind them like sodden masses of cloth in a washerwoman's yard. But the threatened rain held off, and the eastern sky held the promise of better weather to come.

Wrapped tight in one of Meredith's travelling cloaks, Cassia stared out at these new lands with an initial excitement that quickly faded. This part of the world looked little different to Keskor and the North. She had expected something else, something better and fresher, in the same way that all the stories she knew told of heroes who came to new lands and found them filled with magic and wonder.

The real world wasn't much like the stories. She was sure the likes of Renn the Fair never looked down on a fresh, dew-scented valley to find it no better or no worse – or no more noteworthy – than the one before. Perhaps it was just that she had not yet travelled far enough to truly see any difference.

She wondered how the world must seem to Baum, after

so many centuries. Surely, if he had been everywhere and seen everything, nothing would be new or wondrous to him. To wander for endless years, knowing there was nothing new upon the face of the earth . . . she told herself that it was the sudden change in the direction of the sharp wind that made her shudder.

"This is Karistea," Baum told her, sweeping one arm in an extravagant gesture to indicate the dull, barren fields that surrounded them. The ground was uneven, sharp rocks protruding from the thin covering of earth. No crops thrived here, only wiry, thorny brush seemed able to take root. Even the trees were twisted and thin, bent by the prevailing winds and by their own hunger, their roots spread wide through the paltry topsoil.

"It's horrible," she said. "Do people really live here?"

"Not for many years," Baum said.

Meredith's head swung around. "If nobody lives here, then how does it still have a name?"

Baum laughed, a sharp barking sound. "To be more precise, people exist here, from time to time. Not usually for very long. But there is a road that crosses from Hellea to the far west, used by trading caravans – and by adventurous heroes, no doubt." He smiled at Cassia, and she bit her lip, aware he was gently mocking her. "There's always some enterprising soul who believes he can make a living of a sort along this road, whether they be caravan raiders or other exiles, but Karistea is a frugal, selfish land."

"Gelis met the witches in Karistea," Cassia remembered. "They told her if she left the light of their fire she would never find her way home again." It was only one of the tales her father had recited, but Karistea was so inhospitable-looking for it to feel real.

Meredith stared across the scrub, as though he expected to see signs of a fire on the horizon. "Did she?"

"Did she what?"

"Find her way home."

She hesitated, wondering if he too was making fun of her. It was impossible to tell by looking at him. She had to remind herself that he had been brought from far over the mountains. He couldn't know any of the tales that were so common to her lands. "Of course she did – eventually," she said. "How would we know the story otherwise?"

Her father had never ventured far beyond the safety of the old North. There were no distant relatives or old friends to impose upon, and no easy roads to travel, so these lands had no value in his eyes. He envied the wealth that could be earned in Hellea, but he wasn't brave enough to take his own chances there. He told of the legends that passed along the old trade road, but he had never once seen it.

That's one thing I have over you already, father. And I will take my chances and make them work too. Although, with Karistea so unwelcoming and cold, she wasn't sure who had the better deal.

She recited some of Gelis's long history to Meredith as they made their way carefully down the hillside toward the valley floor. Telling these tales gave her some practice now she had claimed the role of storyteller, even if Meredith was the least responsive audience she had ever come across, and it helped pass the time far better than the monotonous silence Baum seemed to prefer. But her own tale, the one she had crafted of the Lyrissan dragons, she still kept to herself, uncertain it would stand up to scrutiny.

Baum rode further ahead, his hood pulled over his head and his shoulders hunched, making it clear he did not want to be disturbed while deep in thought.

True to his words, there was little sign of human life before they reached the road, such as it was. Where the March had been paved along some of its long course, this trade route was little more than a wide series of ruts carved into the ground by the passage of thousands of wheels over many years. They guided their mounts along the side of the track, where the ground was firmer and less rutted, passing occasional signs of burned-out campfires.

"These fires are recent," Meredith observed, as they passed the third of the afternoon. "Less than three days old. We may catch their wagons tomorrow."

Cassia frowned. "How do you know they went in this direction? Surely you can't tell that from their leavings. They could have been heading the other way."

"You doubt my skills?"

"Alright then," Cassia said. "A wager on it. If we don't catch them by tomorrow evening, then you cook the evening's meal."

Baum coughed and turned in his saddle. "Are you trying to kill us all, girl?"

Meredith ignored him, and a smile spread slowly across his face. "And your forfeit?"

Perhaps she should have thought this through before opening her mouth. "I'll stand the night's watch," she said at last. It was the only thing she could think of.

"You really *are* trying to kill us," Baum grunted, shaking his head.

Meredith extended his hand and Cassia took it, half expecting to be pulled from her saddle by his strength. Though his grip was firm it was not overpowering or hurtful, and he released her hand after only a few heartbeats. Still, the contact with his smooth, cold skin was enough to disconcert her.

"Done," Meredith said plainly.

"You had best get some rest tonight," Baum told her. "You will need your strength tomorrow night."

She tried to project a confidence that she did not feel. "Perhaps I should cook a double helping when we stop, in case we find Meredith has the talent to burn water to a crisp."

The old man's shoulders shook as he tried to contain his laughter, and she felt a smile tug her own lips. It was strange, she realised, to be able to laugh at a conversation on the road.

To have fun. It was something she had never been able to do with her father: Norrow's humour was spiteful and selfish, never to be shared with other people, only ever used, like his stories, as a tool to wound and degrade whoever he directed it at.

This was different. This felt more natural, and paradoxically she felt less comfortable with it. *That will change*, she told herself. *It will change with time. This is what people should be like all of the time.*

Meredith frowned down at her as he considered her riposte. "It is possible to burn water?"

Now laughter bubbled up into her throat and she could not hold it in. The puzzled expression on his face was just too much.

Karistea echoed to the sound of laughter for perhaps the first time in decades.

"Your stance is wrong. Again. Move your weight onto your back foot."

"I am." Cassia's arms and her ribs throbbed with dull pain, and she feared, irrationally, she knew, that she had broken bones in the last round of frantic defending.

Meredith stepped back, his staff held one-handed, loose at his side. Hard experience had taught her this meant nothing. He could lash out with that staff at will, without warning, and so swiftly the blow would land before she had even begun to move away. The skin of her thighs felt raw, and she knew she was losing her concentration.

"What's the point of this?" she moaned, half to herself.

He shrugged with one shoulder. "It was your request."

"But I wanted to learn how to use a sword!"

"Would that have gone any better than this?"

For a moment she thought he had made a barbed comment

against her clear lack of skill, and she was about to throw her own staff to the ground and stalk away with the tattered remnants of her dignity intact, when she made herself think about it properly. Putting a sword in her hands would have been a disaster.

She exhaled slowly and tightened her grip on the staff. She *had* asked for this, after all. And Meredith had agreed to teach her. To complain now would be churlish at the very least. She drew herself upright and made sure her weight did actually rest on her back foot.

"Remember the arc of the sun," Meredith said. "And its reflection in the water."

Cassia nodded, but she had already learned to listen less to what Meredith told her and pay more attention to how – and where – he moved. She lowered her staff into a different position, covering her stomach, thinking that might draw him into an attack. This trick had usually worked against Hetch and his friends when they play-acted old battles as children.

Meredith's arm whipped out, and she barely brought her staff back up in time to deflect it, her hands trembling with the impact. *Where next – my legs?* She stepped aside, pulled the staff down and across her flank, and felt it jar violently as Meredith's next swing bounced off it.

A step back to the left, and then forwards, the staff poised to strike against his shoulders – and Meredith's third attack knocked it from her hands completely. She flung herself away, hoping to roll back towards the staff once she had wrong-footed him, but the Heir to the North stood between her and her weapon now, and the knowing smile on his face told her he considered the bout finished.

"I must be getting better – you didn't hit me." A moral victory of a kind, she thought.

Meredith shook his head. "You lost your staff," he pointed out. "You must never let go of your weapon if you hope to win a fight."

"I didn't have a choice. You knocked it—"

"Your grip was too tight. Loosen it." He shrugged and stepped aside to allow her to retrieve the staff. "But you are improving. A little."

She sighed as she rubbed mud from the length of the staff. It was fair, all told. She had already learned a few things from him, even in the short time they had spent practising. If she returned to Keskor now and faced Hetch down, she was sure she could beat him eight or nine times out of ten. With more practice, she might remove that element of uncertainty. That would be something to revel in. The image of Hetch, bruised and broken-nosed, crying in the dirt of the market square, was satisfyingly easy to conjure up.

He would not dare treat her as chattel then.

Meredith's silent return shook her from her reverie. He loomed at her side as though he expected something from her, and finding him in such close proximity, without the staves measuring the space between them, was unsettling.

Did he ask something of me? She was guiltily aware she had been lost in her own dreams of vengeance. A whole legion could have marched by and she would not have noticed.

"The snares," Meredith said.

She blinked. "But I haven't set them yet . . . I mean, I'll set them now . . ."

"No. I said that I will set them, if you wish."

Cassia stared at him for a moment, trying to work out if he was mocking her, but there was no spark of humour in his eyes. "Alright," she said slowly. "But I'd better come with you. There's a skill to finding the right places."

She felt even more off-balance than before as she went to fetch the snares from her pack.

Karistea was not as deserted as Baum had led her to believe. They encountered several caravans that were travelling in the opposite direction, away from Hellea, laden with goods for trade in the far Western countries. The wagons were high-sided and covered against the poor weather, and Cassia envied the traders their shelter. She'd had to stand the night watch as forfeit for her wager, and Baum was concerned the following morning that she might be feverish. That soon passed, although the tea he forced her to drink was foul and made her retch, and she still shivered every time the wind gusted from the north. The only time she felt truly warm was when she lit the fire every evening.

There were smallholdings too, set back from the road, fending off the weather and the outside world from behind raised earthworks and shabby wooden palisades. Families of herders clustered together for the meagre protection that such companionship provided. There were flocks of sheep and goats on the hillsides, although Cassia rarely saw any of the herdsmen. They were a reclusive breed, who disappeared from view as soon as they were spotted, and they were suspicious of strangers. She'd thumped on the gates of one smallholding for what must have been a full hour before a narrowed eye finally appeared at a knot in the wood, the old woman answering her questions in reluctant, monosyllabic grunts. Could they offer space for the night? No. Any food to be bought? No. Was there another farm nearby? No.

"Not a welcoming people," Baum remarked later, watching another herdsman steer his flock away across a broad valley to avoid their small party. "I wonder if they are as suspicious of each other."

"It would be hard to find out," Cassia said.

He nodded. "I suppose it would. Mind you, I suppose they *must* get close to one another from time to time."

He pointed towards the eastern end of the valley, where the road swung away southwards to round a long, sprawling hill.

"A good place to make camp, up on the hill. We will stop there tonight and say farewell to Karistea. Tomorrow we come to the edges of Hellea itself."

"I will be glad to leave this country," Meredith said. "There is nothing here to admire."

Cassia nodded her agreement. If anything, Karistea only served to remind her of her father and home, neither of which she wanted to think about any more.

On their way up the slope, Baum waved a hand at the copse that fringed the hilltop and extended back into a dark and twisted wood. "There should be plenty of firewood for us tonight," he said. "Cassia—"

She sighed, already knowing what would come next. "Firewood. And traps."

The same routine, every night. Just as it had been under her father's rule. No matter that she was free of Norrow's unpredictable temper, or that she had fallen in with a quest to right an ancient wrong – to avenge a whole country, no less – somebody still had to brew tea, skin rabbits and groom the horses. The chores didn't vanish simply because she was out to change the world.

Making history had lost its veneer of glittering excitement as quickly as did reciting it to the same audiences night after night. If the heroes of ages past had ever realised how tiring, how boring, how wet and tedious their journeys would be, they would never have set out.

Baum called her over before she left the campsite to gather the wood. "Stay away from the road tonight, Cassia," he said. "Keep to this hillside. There are some places I remember from many years ago . . ." He trailed off with a frown, looking around as though he did not recognise his surroundings. "Not far from here, I'm sure of it . . . Meredith, go with the girl."

Cassia was about to protest that she was old enough to not need an escort, but Baum had already turned away, unhitching the packs from his saddle.

She smiled across at Meredith. "Do you want to try setting the snares again? You didn't do too badly last night. Then maybe you can try it on your own tomorrow."

"Only if you wish to go hungry," the Heir to the North said, with a straight face.

"What's that?"

Meredith shaded his eyes against the setting sun, staring down at the building. "It could be a shrine. Or a temple."

She frowned, all thoughts of foraging forgotten. "Why would anyone build a temple all the way out here? There's nobody for miles around. And it looks too big to be just a shrine."

Meredith shrugged and turned away, but Cassia's curiosity had bested her again. "Let's go and have a look," she suggested. "It's not far."

"It is best left alone. The day is ending."

Cassia ignored him and started down the hillside, the half-full sling of firewood rattling against her shoulder. "Come on, we'll only be a few minutes. We could even shelter there tonight if it rains."

The building sat a short distance from the road. As she came closer she saw tracks leading from the old road to the building's portico, the ground worn bare by the passage of other travellers over many years, proving the place had not been entirely abandoned. The roof was intact, another good omen, though some of the slates had slipped. This place had not been stripped or plundered, like many ancient shrines she had seen in the North.

She crossed through the long shadows cast by the building and made for the portico, revising her opinions as she trudged across the weed-carpeted grasses. It *was* a shrine, she decided. A temple would require a priest, and a priest would need at the very least a goat, or a small pen of chickens, or a patch of land planted with vegetables. Dorias in Lyriss had nothing and relied on the donations of the townsfolk, but there was no town here, and nothing to support an incumbent priest.

So . . . a shrine. But of such size! She rounded the corner of the building and paused for breath. There were seven steps up to the portico, massive blocks of stone that showed little weathering. She unshipped her load and left it on the first step.

She reached the portico and looked about. Five pillars stretched up to the overhanging roof – a peculiar number, she thought; surely every shrine had either four or six pillars at the front. The school in Keskor had touched on this once, while she listened from atop the wall. Her interest had waned when the tutor turned his lecture into a demonstration of mathematical principles. Now, she wondered briefly if she might have missed something, but she was distracted by the small heaps of charred rubbish in the corners of the portico, where the stone floor was blackened. The remains of cookfires, indicating that travellers had stayed here recently.

Someone may still be here. Perhaps this wasn't such a good idea. She eyed the nearest doorway into the shrine nervously. The sun was fast disappearing below the horizon, and it lit very little beyond the darkened opening.

She padded to the doorway and paused again, drawing up the courage to peer inside, her imagination furnishing the interior with fearsome skeletal warriors and great beasts that hungered for human flesh. There were letters scratched into the wall by the door; someone had left a message here. She traced the letters with one finger and sounded the words under her breath.

This is not a restful place.

Her flesh prickled and she shivered in the dying rays of the sun. *Definitely not a good idea.*

But if this was a shrine, surely it was sacred to a god. Given the size of the place, and the way it was maintained, it must belong to one of the more mighty gods. Cassia could come to no harm by merely looking.

She took a deep breath and slipped into the dark before her instincts could fight back.

She stood with her back against the wall for a minute, allowing her eyes to adjust to the gloom. There were no windows at all, and the only illumination came from the two open doorways and a few shafts of daylight lancing down from between the missing roof tiles.

Two lines of pillars stretched to the far end of the building, creating vaults on either side of the shrine. Statues, life-sized or a little larger, stood in ranks upon low stone plinths, as though awaiting inspection. More figures, visible only as shapes against the darkness, lined the back wall. The air was still and heavy. The breeze didn't seem to touch the inside of the shrine, despite the lack of doors in the frames.

Cassia took a few steps away from the wall, advancing slowly down the left colonnade. Dried leaves, swept in by the wind to lie dead in the unearthly atmosphere, crunched to dust underfoot. She brushed through wisps of spiderwebs, their delicate threads tingling against her bare arms. She watched the stone figures carefully as she moved. They might well be statues, but she had the unnerving feeling they were aware of her presence.

Don't be so daft, girl, they're made of stone.

There were more of them, she realised. Each alcove, behind the pillars, contained a pair of the sharply-carved figures. She squinted into the gloom at the nearest pair, straining to make out their details. They were not gods, she was certain now. Whoever had created them had sculpted them with the full amour of a Hellean legionary, complete with the helmet and shield that she recognised from the Factor's troops.

Stone soldiers . . . do I know this tale? What are they guarding? And why are there so many of them?

Perhaps there were inscriptions on the bases of the plinths.

Cassia was about to crouch next to the nearest plinth, one hand extended to touch the stone, when she heard the quiet scuffing on leather on stone from behind her, in the depths of the shrine.

She froze, breath caught in her throat, not daring to look behind her. The sound did not come again, but that was no reassurance. Her outstretched hand dropped to her belt, and she tugged her knife free before rolling to one side away from the pillar, scrambling back into the darkness of the colonnade.

It struck her that entering the shrine alone, with no light, and with no idea who else might be inside, was one of the stupidest things she had ever done. She had no idea if Meredith had even followed her down the hillside. There could be anybody at all hiding in the gloom. Her heart thumped, and she clutched her free hand to her chest, afraid it might give her away.

She tried to moisten her lips but her mouth was unnaturally dry. She crept forward, away from the colonnade. There were too many places around her for somebody to hide themselves.

Cassia hastened into the middle of the chamber, aiming for the circle of stone soldiers. From there it would only be a short, desperate run back to the doorways. Glancing up, she realised the light, already poor, was fading fast.

This is not a restful place.

Something must haunt this place . . . Another terrifying idea followed hard on the heels of that one, and she wished immediately she had not thought it. What if they came alive after dark? She glanced at the nearest of the stone soldiers. Its features were shrouded in darkness, and it didn't take much to imagine it reaching out to pull her limb from limb, her blood soaking into the hungry cracks between the flagstones . . .

A hand fell on her shoulder and she screamed, tore away and stumbled past the squared plinths, her arms flailing as she lost her balance and crashed to the floor between two of the statues. She twisted, skin scraping against rough stone edges, the knife jarred from her hand and skittering away into the shadows.

It was as if thinking it had made it come true. One of the nightmarish shapes stepped down from its pedestal, one hand outstretched to squeeze the life from the trespasser who'd had the temerity to awaken it. Cassia shrank back as far as she could, another scream bubbling in her throat, but her back was pressed against another plinth, and there was nowhere to go. The creature reached down, and a shaft of fading daylight streaked across its face –

"Meredith!" The scream exploded from her in a shout of pure relief. "Why didn't you say something?"

The Heir to the North pulled her easily to her feet and then seemed to lose interest in her, staring up into the darkened rafters. "Hush, girl. This place . . . listens."

Cassia was suddenly glad of the lack of light, feeling her face flush red with embarrassment and anger. She backed away from the circle of statues, frozen in rigid guard postures, and busied herself brushing the dirt from her dress. "You could have said something. Whispered, even. I was scared." She picked up her knife and tucked it back into her belt. "What do you mean, it listens?"

This is not a restful place.

"We should not stay here," Meredith said. "It is best left empty."

Cassia wasn't about to argue, not while her heart still thudded like a blacksmith's hammer. There was definitely something wrong with this shrine, or temple, or whatever it was, and with the sun now fully gone the fear of something creeping through the darkness towards her caused her to shiver worse than any winter chill. She fled the shrine on trembling legs, almost falling down the steps, and had picked up her sling of firewood even before Meredith had emerged from the dark.

Even Meredith looked perturbed by the interior of the shrine, Cassia realised, as they walked back up the hillside. No matter what she tried, she could not engage him in conversation. He was locked inside his thoughts, even more distracted than usual. Her own thoughts veered back to the eerie chamber, despite her efforts to drive it from her mind. Who would build such a place, and for what reason? The stone legionaries, from what little she had seen of them, did not suit the lowlands and the broad plains of Hellea. They'd had the feel of the ancient North, of mosaics and paintings that glorified the bloody wars of the High Kings and the Age of Talons. But if that was the case, why would modern Hellea allow such a place to stand?

Baum will know. Baum knows all of these places.

As if he had been conjured by the mere thought of his name, the old soldier awaited them at the crest of the hill. He was not, Cassia discovered quickly, best pleased.

"I told you not to stray by the road." He glared down at her as though it was her fault alone. "If you cannot obey even the simplest instructions, what use will you be when we reach Hellea itself? I could leave you right here, you stupid girl."

She blanched, the excuse she had created for her diversion turning into dust in her mouth. *Stupid girl.* Just like her father always told her. No use to anyone. Baum did not really need her. He was only humouring her. Meredith and Baum continued across the hilltop, back towards the camp, but she stood alone for a few moments, her father's voice taunting her with her inadequacies. *You're nothing but a girl. A useless girl. Who will take you on?*

Meredith looked back over his shoulder, and paused. "What is the matter?"

The sling was suddenly too heavy for her to carry. She felt bowed beneath its weight, unable to trust herself to take another step without spilling the firewood onto the ground, along with the tears that threatened to burst forth.

Meredith called to Baum. "Sir, this was not entirely the girl's fault. She did not know precisely why we should avoid the road. Perhaps you should have explained that beforehand."

Baum stared at the princeling with an expression that verged on astonishment. "What?" He shook his head, and glared back at Cassia, but this time with less of the harsh anger he had turned on her before. "If I had to explain every step I took before I made it, I would have talked myself to death centuries ago. Come on – this is no place to linger. When we have set a fire, I will tell you why."

"What did you see?"

Cassia hesitated, still burned by his earlier words. Her position was less certain, she felt less trusting of him than before, seeds of doubt planted by his threat to abandon her.

"It was like a temple," she said, "but it . . . well, it just wasn't. It felt all wrong, and there was nobody there except a collection of statues carved as the likenesses of soldiers. I didn't see much else, it was too dark inside."

Meredith nodded. "I counted at least twenty figures. All were armed and armoured, as though for battle."

"What did you say?" Baum asked. "Did you speak any names at all? *My* name?"

Cassia struggled to piece together the frantic moments she had spent inside that place. She remembered scraping her knees, skinning herself on the edge of a plinth, but very little aside from that.

"The girl called my name," Meredith said. "But neither of us said much more. We did not speak any other names."

The old man relaxed a little at that. "Then the danger is past."

Cassia bit her lip. "It was truly a dangerous place, sir?"

"Oh yes. Make no mistake," Baum turned his hooded gaze upon her. "The wrong words, in the wrong place, and our whole enterprise could have crumbled into dust. It is no shrine, nor is it a temple. The ground is not sacred to any god, unless it is the god of tyrants and demonic magic."

Intuition gave Cassia the beginning of the tale. "This is the warlock's doing?"

Baum favoured her with a thin smile. "The Man of Stone. Exactly so. After he had cursed and destroyed the High King and his lands, Malessar showed his true colours and joined forces with the city states on the Hellean plains. That much is known, how he shaped the Empire and stood as a shadow behind the throne for decades." The disgust in his voice made evident what he thought of the warlock's actions. "To secure his position, to prevent any desperate remnants of the Northern armies forming up to oppose him, he created those things you saw down there."

"The statues?"

"They are not merely statues. They are abominations. Foul mimicries of mortal men, ancient spirits of the earth captured and re-cast in human form, cursed by a geas even the gods would hesitate to use."

Cassia shuddered, and glanced across at Meredith. The princeling wore a troubled frown, matching the mood around the fire. It was little wonder the shrine had felt so wrong, if it was home to such powerful magic. They were lucky indeed to escape unharmed, if what Baum said was true.

"This is not a restful place," Cassia muttered, half to herself. It seemed anybody who tried to rest at that shrine, whether or not they dared enter, would spend an uneasy night, haunted by the strength of Malessar's spellcraft.

"But they did not threaten us," she said. "How are they cursed?"

"While he guided the rise of the first Hellean emperor, Malessar made good use of the knowledge he found hidden in the cities of the plains," Baum said. "He was careful to keep what he found to himself, or so he thought – even he could not create and arrange the experiments that followed without help from others." The smile extended joylessly. "And, of course, he did not realise he was being watched. I found most of those who Malessar employed, and they told me much of his plans before he ended their service . . . and they were silenced.

"When the first emperor ascended to the throne, Malessar came to his apartments and greeted him with the first of his new creations. Two soldiers of stone, marching in unison, armed with greatswords that no man could lift, let alone wield. The soldiers stood guard that night, and defeated the very first attempts on the Emperor's life. The would-be assassins were torn limb from limb, and the last man alive threw himself from the roof rather than surrender to those monstrosities. I watched in anger and horror as Malessar used this demonstration of his unnatural powers to turn the Emperor into a puppet who would accede willingly to everything the damned warlock demanded."

He shook his head. "I tried. Damn him to all the known hells, I tried to stop what was happening. I could see where it would end. But there was only so much I could do without revealing myself, and Malessar would have destroyed me where I stood, without a moment's thought, had I been so rash. You cannot imagine how often I have thought about the choices I made back then; how often I have wondered whether, if I had done things differently, the Hellean Empire might never have existed at all. How different this part of the world would have been now – perhaps Stromondor would never have been sacked, or the great herdsmen of the Berdellan plains might have risen to power instead . . . but we shall never know."

He fell silent, his mind clearly lost to those thoughts once more. Cassia shot a glance at Meredith and found him leaning forward, hooked on the old man's every word. Perhaps Baum had never told him this much before.

We shall never know . . . strange how the whole world might turn on the actions – or the inaction, she conceded – of one man. And yet, nobody in the stories she knew ever stopped to consider this. If they had, then their heroic deeds might never have happened, dashing young swordsmen and feisty heroines alike frozen by indecision and the weight of futures that would never be.

I would need more than one lifetime to think on all this – and Baum has had several such lifetimes! Perhaps it is just as well the gods only give us a short span . . .

"Tell me more," Meredith said. Cassia startled – it was the first time she had heard him take an active interest in any of the tales she or Baum had shared.

Baum blinked, rousing from his thoughts. "Hmm? Ah, of course. I forgot myself." The anger in his voice had diminished, replaced by a more regretful tone. "The remainder is quick to tell. The Emperor wanted to secure his borders and his position, Malessar wanted to bury forever any trace of the Northern kingdoms. They worked together: the Emperor funding Malessar's projects and, within the year, the first cohort of stone soldiers was completed. A great caravan of heavy wagons, each laden with one of the inert creatures, made its way north along the March toward the borders of this new empire. A new building had been erected there to house these monstrosities, the first of a score of such buildings. Call them shrines or temples if you will, but they are not consecrated. They only celebrate the mindless violence that Malessar brought to life. Thus his name, the Man of Stone."

Cassia wished for daylight again. Her imagination was all too good at conjuring up ranks of implacable, silent soldiers, their cold hands reaching out to seize her and crush her neck. She fought the instinct that told her to check over her shoulder. *There is nothing behind me. Nothing. Nothing but an empty hillside.*

"They did not attack us," Meredith said, sounding almost disappointed. Could he really have defended himself against a score of those monsters? Surely even his skills would fail against so many.

"Of course not," Baum said. "You posed no threat to the

Empire. Unless you spoke ill of the Emperor, or of Malessar himself. Or you spoke the names of any of his old enemies. Myself included."

"Which we did not," Meredith said.

"Which you did not. Otherwise you would never have left that place alive."

In the quiet that followed, the crackling of the fire sounded like deadfallen twigs snapping underfoot. Cassia knew she would not sleep easy this night.

"Have they ever awoken?" she asked.

"Not to my knowledge," Baum said. "If they did wake, then the devastation they wrought would certainly be recorded somewhere. Word would spread. I believe that was part of Malessar's reasoning. He intended to cause fear amongst the surrounding cities, to force them into the fold without having to wage war against them."

Cassia knew no tales that mentioned giant, unstoppable stone warriors. Not that her father had known every story ever told, although he frequently proclaimed himself to be the best storyteller in the North. She though Baum was probably right. Perhaps the warriors had slept for so long they had forgotten how to wake. That in itself would make part of a fine story, she decided. Not something to stand alone, it would have to be melded with something else to give it the right degree of menace and tragedy.

"They are under the Emperor's orders?" Meredith asked. "That would make sense. These cohorts would be led against invading armies as well as recalcitrant neighbours."

"Correct," Baum said. "And what does history tell us of successful campaigns against Hellea?" He fixed his gaze upon Cassia and waited.

She squeezed her eyes closed as she recited the histories in her head. The Eastern Hordes were the greatest threat she had ever heard tell of, but the Hordes had never reached far enough to directly attack Hellea itself. Galliarca and Stromondor had borne the brunt of their campaigns against the Empire. And aside from the Hordes . . .

"There are none," she said.

"Precisely."

"A good defence then," Meredith said.

That didn't sound quite right to Cassia's ears, but Baum had seen so much more of the world than she had. The inner workings of an Emperor's court must be second nature to him.

"What did he call these stone soldiers?" she asked, as much to break the sudden silence as to know the answer. An idea had planted itself at the back of her mind. With a tale such as this, told in the right fashion and to the right audience, she could surely make her name as a storyteller. This was something nobody else would have; when she told it, it would be something *new*.

Baum shrugged. "He did not name them. Or at least, I don't think he did. I never heard them called by any name other than the one the Emperor gave to them. Shieldmen, that first Emperor named them." Disgust flitted across his features. "A dull name that doesn't even hint at their demonic nature. That man was a fool, make no mistake. If he'd had any sense at all he would have fled the city and left Malessar to play his games with somebody else."

A disturbing thought occurred to Cassia. "When you defeat him, will these shieldmen rise up against you? Or will they break free of their spell and kill anybody they come across?"

"In all truth, I do not know. I hope the magic will die along with him, but if it does not then perhaps the shieldmen will sleep undisturbed forever, unsummoned and unbloodied."

Baum looked away, and a pensive cast to his face told her this tale was ended. With her own mind filled with thoughts of marauding stone soldiers on the Emperor's March, slaughtering every living creature in retaliation as the North rose up against the Empire's yoke, Cassia barely tasted that evening's meal, and sleep was a long time coming.

I wonder if the Factor knows of these shieldmen? Can he awaken them? If the North is to ever regain its freedom, then Malessar must be defeated, otherwise everybody will die. It seemed a stark choice. She thought she wouldn't have much of a problem with some of those deaths, at least – she had no love for Rann Almoul or his family, nor for her father now, as heartless as that might sound – but her mind rebelled when she tried to imagine Keskor despoiled and unpopulated.

Her dreams that night flitted between glorious visions of Meredith skewering the warlock with his greatsword, and black nightmares in which the shieldmen chased her through a lightless forest, the bare branches of twisted trees scratching at her face and arms. The ground was slippery, and when she fell over she saw her hands covered in a thick, dark liquid. No matter how much she scrubbed with the hem of her dress, the foul stuff would not come off. And the shieldmen closed in on her, their advance rhythmic and unstoppable.

There is blood on my hands. There is blood on my hands –

When that pulled her awake, her heart racing and her hands trembling, she sat by the dying embers of the fire, unable to even close her eyes, until dawn came around once more.

Chapter Nine

ANOTHER WEEK OF travelling brought them past the small town of Lobrith, which to Cassia's eyes looked exactly the same as every other town they had passed. A persistent rain was falling, and she hunched shivering in the saddle, still shivery from the fever that had forced them to shelter for two nights in the hut of a generous shepherd, while she sweated it out and Baum grumbled and chafed at the delay. A small caravan of merchants caught up with them not far from the walls of Lobrith, and the trading master asked them to join him on his way to Elbithrar, going out of his way to praise Meredith's obvious martial prowess. To Cassia's surprise, Baum agreed to the deal.

It made their journey much easier, and Cassia took full advantage of that. To begin with it was enough to find her strength again after her illness, to come afresh to the practice sessions with Meredith. They drew an audience of curious merchants, whose comments and laughter were enough to drive her to red-cheeked distraction until Meredith took their bouts out of sight of the wagons. But it was good to be able to talk to other people as well, and after a couple of nights on the periphery of the cookfires she summoned up the courage to try out a few of the stories she knew. Just to test out her voice, she told herself; to practice the rhythms and phrases her father had wielded so easily.

That the merchants listened at all was enough to raise her spirits, but when they applauded, she thought her heart might burst. She dared to begin thinking ahead to Elbithrar.

Elbithrar, the merchants told her, was joyous and vibrant. A welcoming city of fountains and temples, where the market sold trinkets and rugs from faraway Galliarca, mats of dried and woven grasses from Berdella, and even precious stones from the foreign lands of the far West. She had seen some of these things before, in other markets and other towns, but she marvelled to think of them all in one place.

"And storytellers?" she asked one of the seasoned travellers as he warmed a kettle of wine over the fire late one evening. "Are there storytellers in Elbithrar?"

The merchant's coat had once been splendid, with scarlet ribbons hanging from the sleeves. It was faded and patched now, like the man himself, but Cassia noticed that when he removed it he seemed to cast off a great proportion of his authority and personality. *Like my father*, she thought, surprising herself with the connection.

"Storytellers," the merchant rumbled. He rubbed his expanding paunch, then fiddled with the lid of the kettle, as though he might make it heat faster by doing so. "Real storytellers? In Elbithrar? Oh a few, I dare say a few. Maybe more than a few, eh? You want to go and listen to them, my girl?"

He'd misunderstood, Cassia thought. But it was a simple enough mistake. "No sir, I'd like to join them."

The merchant blinked and stared at her from the other side of the fire. "Join them, eh? A noble ambition, my girl. A noble ambition indeed."

She had the impression he thought there was something wrong with what she had said, so she explained further. "You said last night, sir, that my telling of the lay of Anomae and Dardin plucked your heart to tears. I would like to move an entire crowd of people in the same way."

The merchant nodded solemnly. "May both Movalli and Ceresel smile upon you then, my girl," he said. "For the story was indeed beautifully told."

Elbithrar sat at the bottom of a wide vale. The town's walls were whitewashed and clear, and the patchwork of fields surrounding them were well-tended and busy. The last of the autumn's harvest was being gathered in even as she watched. Gaps in the busy patterns of rooftops showed where the town's squares lay, with the largest of them just off-centre, next to an imposingly pillared temple.

But here, to her dismay, was where Baum decided to leave the caravan behind. "We have delayed long enough," he told her. "The season is turning. We must reach Hellea inside the next week, or else the trail we follow may go cold again."

"I don't understand why the rush," she said, "when you've trailed him for so many centuries." She knew she sounded petulant. *But this is my chance! Such a perfect opportunity to show how much better I am than my father! Why shouldn't we stop here?*

Baum loomed over her, and despite herself she shrank back a little. "And if I allow my course to be dictated to me by the daughter of a storyteller, how many more centuries will I have to spend following the damned warlock?" His anger was more controlled than it had been in the wilds of Karistea, but that only made it worse. Back there he had only threatened to leave her behind; this time there was a much keener edge to his fury.

It subsided and passed as quickly as it had risen. Baum regarded her for a moment as though he could read the broad spread of her emotions. "I have studied him, you know. His habits, his customs. He is as bound to the seasons as a sparrow. If he is still in Hellea, he will not winter there. He will fly to the southern lands before the first snows."

Cassia nodded her understanding mutely.

"And besides," Baum continued, in a more kindly tone, "you will be set up to fail in Elbithrar."

"What do you mean?"

He nodded to the road, where the wagons rolled down into the valley. The story-loving merchant was visible at the head of the convoy. "That man is no friend of yours. If you were to pitch up in the markets and call for an audience, he would be at the head of it, certainly, but only to laugh at you and rubbish your talents. As soon as he reaches town he will be spreading his own tales of a storytelling girl – *A girl! A girl! She thinks she is a man!* – and you will be laughed from the square." He shrugged. "I have seen it happen before."

"But I would have been disguised as a boy," Cassia pointed out. "That was never a problem when I collected for my father."

"That was in the North," Baum said. "In some ways we are more civilised, more tolerant, than the rest of Hellea. Elbithrar would not welcome you."

I'll fight them! Any man who says I'm not fit to tell my stories, I'll take my staff to them and leave them on their backs in the dust, waving their limbs in the air like stranded beetles . . .

No. That would solve nothing. Cassia thought back to her conversations with the merchants, examining their words, the pauses, the sly glances. Everything Baum had said made sense. She stared at the wagons again, then across the fields to the town itself. Suddenly her new life had been pulled away from her, dragged out of reach, and she was an outsider once more.

"Where, then?" she asked.

"Hellea has its faults," Baum said. "Too many to list, sometimes, but the city has always looked overseas to steal its traditions. When I was last there the Galliarcan passion for storytelling was popular again. The idiots may be too blind to realise what lies on their own doorstep, but if they have not been fickle enough to change their opinions every time the wind changes, then you should have a better time there. At least you will be able to take a pitch without that buffoon over there waiting with a handful of rotten fruit."

Cassia turned to her packs with a sigh, checking the straps to make sure nothing was loose.

"To the river," Baum said. "If we are all to meet our destinies in Hellea, we shall at least arrive there in some style."

"You might wish to see this," Baum said, from the hatch above Cassia's head. The sun was high in the sky and sat behind him, giving the effect of a haloed god in a sacred manuscript. Cassia shielded her eyes and squinted up at him. It wasn't such an unlikely simile, she decided. After all, Baum was in the service of one of the oldest gods. Perhaps this was how he had looked when Pyraete chose him to do his bidding.

"What is it, sir?" She dropped her practice sword and climbed up to the barge's deck.

They had passed countless shrines and temples as they pressed deeper into the heartlands of the Empire, and Baum had pointed them all out to her, naming each one and talking about the deities they were sacred to, in tones that were gossipy at best and plain blasphemous at worst. Cassia did not know whether to laugh or be offended when he spoke of Althea, the goddess of the eastern winds, as a wizened strumpet. Or of Periandir, the great giver of grain, as a vainglorious, dithering clot. One large shrine looked familiar to her, but when she asked about it all Baum would say was that it was another of Malessar's monstrosities. That was the only time the old man had been less than good company.

Sometimes the winding course of the great river met with that of the Western Road, and there would be a ford, or bridges held aloft by tall spans of meticulously worked stone. There would always be a town, either nearby or on the very banks of the river. The barges drew up at each one, whether or not the town looked prosperous, and the merchants and sail-rats haggled loudly over bolts of cloth, jewels and ores – and, once, even a weathered stone that an old soldier claimed had come from the long-fallen walls of Stromondor. Baum had laughed at that, but he said nothing more, and Cassia was none the wiser as to whether the relic was genuine.

As the river widened, there were fewer bridges and no fords at all. The towns became larger, their walls extending down to the banks of the river, the jetties busy with traders. Cassia was reluctant to go ashore in these larger towns, and if Meredith was not aboard then she kept her own company. For most of the journey she had been content just to watch the Hellean heartlands pass by. Vast estates sat on the low hills above the fields; the ancestral homes of great families, shaded by groves of lemon trees and set back in lush gardens. The first time Cassia saw one of these estates she had been astounded by the extravagance and the waste of space. In Keskor that land would have been used for more crops, or for grazing animals during winter. But it seemed each bend in the river had brought another, larger estate, and they soon lost their novelty.

Baum moved away from the hatch and the sun blinded her as she climbed up. She had to rub her eyes to clear away the bright spots, careful not to move until she was sure of her footing. There were too many obstacles ready to trip and spill her into the river.

"Here we are," Baum said. He gestured to the open horizon before them.

Beyond the weathered figurehead that decorated the barge's prow, the river opened out into a lake, the far shores visible only as a darkened line on the horizon. The water was becoming choppier, waves licking at the hull and rocking the flat-bottomed barge from side to side.

"Is this the sea?" Cassia asked, knowing even as she spoke that it could not be. This looked nothing like the endless expanses she remembered from the cliffs overlooking the coastal towns of the North.

Baum laughed. "Of course not. This is the Castaria, girl. This is the heart of the Empire."

The barge rocked its way out onto the great lake and Cassia gained a better perspective. The Castaria was the inspiration for scores, even hundreds, of songs and stories. Nearly all of them involved fishermen battling sly demons against great odds, or young women skipping along the lake's fair shores to meet with gods who promised them the world. The estates that overlooked these waters belonged to the richest, most powerful men in the Empire. When Cassia looked north or east, she saw lands that must have sprung fully-formed from the Emperor's commands. The southern shores could only be guessed at, so great was the distance to them, and to the famed waters of the River Meteon.

But to her right, on the western shores, was the ancient city that had spawned an Empire.

Stone piers reached proudly into the Castaria, surrounded by a forest of masts, rocking as the ships berthed there were caught by the light breeze and the rolling tides. The clatter of masts and hawsers reminded Cassia of the coastal towns of the North. Beyond the piers stood row upon row of tenements and workshops, the air above hazed with smoke and dust. The three hills on which Hellea stood sloped away from the shore, and Cassia could see temples and other colonnaded buildings, allowed room to breathe by the wider streets and the squares that Baum told her commemorated the heroes of old battles as well as the gods who once walked this land.

Even from here she could discern the low hubbub of the streets. It reverberated through her stomach, adding to the queasiness she felt from the barge's motion. She wrapped her arms across her body to still her rebellious guts, and wished she had the skill to put all of this into words.

"Hellea," Baum mused, beside her. "A village overgrown with pride and arrogance, wheezing with every bloated breath." It was as though he had read her thoughts.

The barge turned slowly toward the shore. Cassia wedged herself tight against the rail; she had learned to stay out of the way when the crew were battling against the barge's stubborn refusal to answer the helm.

"It looks so big," she said, casting a quick glance over one shoulder to make sure nobody else could hear her. "How will we find the warlock?"

"Through patience and cunning," Baum replied. His gaze was so intent upon the shore that Cassia thought he must be memorising every building on the waterfront. "He does not know we seek him, remember? He will not hide his presence well. And I know his ways, and his likeness. We will let him reveal himself to us."

He made it sound so simple, but Cassia looked at the scale of the city and wondered how long this search would take. To find one man amongst the thousands who lived here . . . it was a search worthy of a storyteller's drama. And that was why she was here, she reminded herself. She *could* do this.

The jetties of Hellea grew closer, and the waters of the Castaria were thronged with smaller fishing boats that picked through the detritus cast aside by the thousands of men and women who lived at the centre of the Empire. Fishermen waved, or shouted for attention, holding their catches aloft. The sail-rats used their long river poles to fend away any who got too close or who tried to board the wallowing barges. Baum went below to see to the horses, but Cassia remained on deck staring at the city, even though she took none of it in. Now she was here she realised her heart beat more in trepidation than excitement.

This is where I wanted to be.

It was not going to be as easy as she had dreamed.

People streamed chaotically through the streets, elbowing their way past each other. Anyone who lost their footing would surely be crushed underfoot. Safe in the saddle and clinging to the reins for dear life, at least Cassia could see where they were going, and the fear and panic bubbling at the back of her mind did not completely take over.

People tried to get out of their path, although there were several occasions when one of the horses must have trampled on somebody's foot. Her shoulders were tight, braced against the possibility of having things thrown at her, but nothing came. Instead she heard wolf whistles, and leering calls, words that made her blush. Were they intended for her? She ducked her head and urged the horse onward, following her companions.

They left the docks and their attendant markets, and Baum guided them up a long avenue of tenements that leaned into each other for support, the buildings merged together under the pressure of years. Everywhere she looked she saw men and women filtering away down alleyways and narrow side-streets. Children gathered in small mobs outside the tenements, gangs parading and protecting their territory. Not so different from other towns then. Perhaps it was all just a matter of scale.

The first shrine they came upon reinforced that thought. It was set back from the street at the top of five great stone steps, and the building's roof stretched out to encompass a pillared colonnade on all four sides, making it look much larger than it really was. Two priests stood at the top of the steps, welcoming – and vetting – worshippers. If she squinted, she could make out the dedication carved into the lintel behind one of the priests. A temple to Periandir, a god who was worshipped if harvests were full. If minor deities could command such respect and devotion here, what would Ceresel's temple look like? Or Movalli's?

"Keep up, girl!" Meredith shouted to her, and she realised she had fallen behind. She heeled the horse ahead, but within a few yards her attention was drawn again by half a dozen men, their tunics covered by hardened leather jerkins, who stood at a corner, watching the thronging crowds intently. Even if they had not worn those jerkins, the short swords at their sides would have given them away as legionaries. Cassia ducked her head quickly, fearing Vescar Almoul had sent messages on to the Imperial capital, appending her description and those of Baum and Meredith so they would be arrested.

They're looking at me. I know they are. They know who we are. We'll be followed through the city until we reach some darkened corner, and then they'll surround us and –

She shook her head to rid herself of the thought. *Look at all these people,* she told herself. *Nobody knows who we are. Nobody.* She glanced over her shoulder at the soldiers once she had passed them, but they had not moved at all, and none of them looked in her direction.

It's only me.

Baum turned off the main avenue as it began to rise into the hills that sheltered the Castaria from the south-westerly winds. Now the thoroughfares were less crowded, but more cramped, and even Meredith could not bully his way through. Their pace slowed to a crawl. Cassia felt conspicuous in the saddle, knowing that people were openly watching her, their faces a mixture of suspicion and curiosity. Who was this slip of a girl who rode a soldier's horse behind a young lord and a hardened old man?

She knew little about the families who owned the lands surrounding the Castaria, but she imagined the ordinary people of Hellea might think she belonged to such a family. That brought a smile to her face – *me, a lady?* – but she suppressed it and tried to maintain an air of dignified hauteur, such as a young noblewoman might possess.

"Do you have a house here, sir?" she asked Baum when the first opportunity arose. They were waiting for a heavily laden cart, one wheel broken by a deep hole in the road, to be pulled aside by a mixed team of tradesmen and urchins. Baum leaned over the pommel of his saddle with his usual sardonic smile, watching the disorganised comedy of errors descend into frustrated shouts and curses. He had not offered to help, even though their well-fed horses would make light work of the job, and although one or two of the tradesmen cast glances in their direction, it seemed Meredith's intimidating presence had warned them away from asking.

Baum shook his head. "No. I never saw the use in that."

"You would not need to pay for rooms all the time," Cassia said. It was something she had always envied in her father's distant relatives. They were rooted in comfort in one place, with a roof over their heads and a door to close against the cold of winter. She dreamed sometimes of having such a house, being able to light a fire with dry wood even in the stormiest weather.

"But I would never have seen any such place as home," Baum said. "My home is lost behind the warlock's curse wards. There is also the problem of the geas Pyraete laid upon me."

"How would that be a problem, sir?"

Baum leaned in and lowered his voice until his words were almost lost amid the uproar of the tradesmen. The cart was almost clear now, a new wheel wedged hastily into place. "It is one thing to spend a mortal life in one place," he said. "It would be another – and not a good thing – to spend an *immortal* life tied to one place. Think how it would appear to townsfolk to have the same neighbour for scores of years: never ageing, never changing. Think how suspicion and mistrust would build. I would not have been welcome for long, even in the largest, most cosmopolitan cities."

Cassia thought about that. Even Malessar himself had moved around; Stromondor, Galliarca, Hellea, the far Western cities; he had to have lived in every great city at some point in the last several hundred years. And Baum had trailed after him, keeping to the shadows, building his knowledge and taking Malessar's apprentices as his tutors.

Such patience, such forbearance. I think I would go insane.
But the tales were filled with heroes who undertook impossible
quests, wandering the earth until they at last reached their
journey's end. If some of them were fantastical, it did not in-
validate their meaning. Baum truly was a legend come to life,
and his journey was truly heroic.

Malessar, on the other hand . . . He had spent long enough
in Hellea to transform it into one of the greatest empires ever
seen. He might not have been so egotistical as to stand openly
behind the throne, or take power for himself, but he had
twisted and tweaked history to suit his own purposes. Baum
had pointed out the warlock's subtle influence to Cassia in
some of the tales she had rehearsed, adding his own commen-
tary to the narrative in such a fashion that she found it difficult
to think of those stories in any other way after that. A ruthless,
twisted man, accountable to none. Even the gods hesitated to
stand against him.

*But he's here now, in Hellea. And this time someone will stand
against him. And I will witness it.*

After another ten minutes or so, in a district of rickety houses
and darkened workshops, Baum finally dismounted, knuckling
his back and waited for Meredith and Cassia to follow suit.
Cassia could see nothing of interest nearby. The lane split into
two even narrower ways further ahead, and the higher, more
affluent areas of the city were far behind them. Dogs barked
in yards hidden behind the tightly-packed houses, the sound
echoing through the street.

"This will do," Baum said. "At least it is still here."

She realised one of the buildings was a tavern, though the
small sign that hung over the door was easy to miss. Crudely
carved, it depicted a stream of liquid pouring from a jug into a
man's open mouth. "We are staying here?"

"If he has any room," Baum said. "Meredith, take the horses
around the back."

From the dilapidated look of the building Cassia guessed

the innkeeper was never so busy he could afford to turn away paying guests. She climbed down from her saddle with relief and passed her reins to Meredith, before following Baum inside.

Her first impression of the inn suggested that it was much smaller than those her father had frequented back in the North, and that surprised her. She had thought everything would be larger, or grander, in the Empire's capital. But as her eyes adjusted to the dim light filtering through the narrow shutters, she realised the room was at least three times as deep as it was wide, and probably much more than that – a thick curtain hid the back of the room from view. The wide hearth held a collection of blackened cooking utensils, and a fire was banked low under the pot that hung from a chain, slow cooking the evening's meal.

The inn even had a few customers. Two of the tables were occupied, each with a small group of men who glanced up at the new arrivals before returning their attention to their drinks. They looked like labourers, but the fact that they were drinking at this hour indicated they had no work. This was the type of crowd her father enjoyed, and he would gladly have taken a seat at either of those tables and shared his misery and preju-dices with them. Like as not, one drink would have turned into a whole afternoon and evening of drinking, and along the way Norrow would have conspired to start a fight.

This time, she thought, he would not be able to spoil things and get them kicked out into the night with no shelter.

Baum looked around the tavern, apparently satisfied by what he saw. He motioned Cassia to a bench and rapped one hand hard against the side of the skeletal stairs that ran up the opposite wall to the fireplace, knocking for attention.

The inn's customers seemed unbothered by the noise, but to Cassia's left a small pile of what she had taken to be rags leapt up with a yelp. On closer examination the shocked mass turned out to be a young boy, dressed in clothes that were clearly too large for him, his frame barely more than skin and bones.

"Weren't sleepin'!" he cried out. "Weren't!" Then he blinked and took in Baum's imposing figure, and his mouth clamped shut. He glanced nervously at Cassia, and bolted for the curtain.

A moment later the curtain moved again. A larger, much older man appeared from the rear of the inn. His arms and torso reminded Cassia of the Almouls – men who had gone to war and done well – yet the innkeeper had gone to seed, the firmness of his muscles retreating along with his hair. He still cut an intimidating figure, however, and the knife prominently sheathed at the front of his apron only added to that impression.

He eyed Baum with short-sighted suspicion for a moment, then spread his hands wide. "Welcome, strangers. I don't stand on ceremony, so take a bench. What will you be having?"

Baum did not sit. "Food and lodging, if you have it. Two rooms. There's three of us, and horses too."

The innkeeper's stare slid across to Cassia. She shrank against the wall, uncomfortable with the attention. "Two rooms. Aye, there's two rooms spare. Boy!" he shouted over his shoulder. "Go fetch the horses in!"

There was a muffled squeak from behind the curtain, followed by the light slap of flesh upon stone as the boy hurried to the tavern's back door. The innkeeper returned his attention to Baum. "How long will you be staying?"

The shadow of a smile played across Baum's lips. "A few days, maybe more."

The innkeeper clearly had no intention of being any more civil than this. Perhaps he would show better manners when he felt the weight of Baum's money. "I only cook breakfast once," he said, wiping the nearest table with the edge of his sleeve. "If you miss it you'll have to wait for dinner."

"That seems fair enough," Baum said affably. He dug a coin from the pouch at his belt. "Perhaps you'll join me for a drink now, Ultess?"

The innkeeper took the coin, his brows creased in thought. "I don't know you, sir, yet you know my name. I don't think I have been recommended – in fact, I know this inn will never be recommended – so how do you know me?"

Baum nodded to the fist the innkeeper had wrapped around the coin. "Look more closely."

Cassia saw his eyes widen momentarily, before they narrowed again. "How do you have this?"

"Because I served with Guhl," Baum said, as if that explained everything. "As did you."

Guhl? That was a name the old man had never mentioned before. Cassia tried to think whether her father had ever mentioned it in one of his stories.

The innkeeper still frowned. "That was long ago," he said, more quietly. "Guhl's dead now. Been dead for years."

"I would be surprised if he were not," Baum said.

Ultess hesitated, seemingly on the verge of movement, before slipping behind the curtain. He returned a moment later with a sealed wine jug and a pair of cups that were obviously part of his best service, not chipped or scratched. He set the wine on the table nearest the curtain, where their conversation was less likely to be overheard.

Baum smiled over at Cassia. "Meredith may need more help with our horses," he said. "That boy looks too feeble to hold his own breath, let alone a bridle."

She recognised a dismissal when she heard it. If Baum still had secrets that he wanted to keep then so be it. She slipped out onto the road to find the path that led around the back of the inn. Through the half-closed shutters she glimpsed Ultess and the former soldier, already deep in conversation. *Everybody he knows seems to be an old soldier*, she thought. The priest Dorias, Attis the moneylender, and now this innkeeper. Baum must have drawn up his plans so many years ago, yet he had everything in place. How much skill and forethought must that have taken? He could have been one of the greatest generals the world had ever seen, with a mind like that.

And Malessar had taken it all from him. She looked around the street at the closely-packed tenements and, feeling sobered, went to find Meredith.

The boy did not have a name of his own, or at least, no name he was willing to share with her. He was so thin and gangly Cassia was unsure of his age, though his voice was shrill enough to suggest he had yet to reach puberty. Cassia wondered if he was the innkeeper's son. There was no obvious resemblance, but then again it was difficult to tell under the boy's shock of straw-textured hair.

He showed Meredith and Cassia where to stow their tack, although there was not much room left in the small shed that served as a stable once all three horses were inside. He was as skittish as a fly around the great beasts, ducking away from their hooves every time they moved, but the horses ignored him. And he surprised Cassia by offering to act as a guide for the duration of their stay.

"I do not need a guide," Meredith said. "But I will need the use of this yard every morning at sunrise."

The boy's head jerked. "Yes, my lord!"

Cassia couldn't hide her smile as the boy's voice rose and fell like a kite. "I would like a guide," she said. "At least for the first couple of days. I'd like to know where all the markets are, and the best places to hear storytellers."

Meredith paused on his way back into the tavern. "You still wish to recite your stories here?"

She bridled. "You know I've been practicing them. And besides, Hellea will be different. Baum said so. They're cultured here – they have a library."

Meredith shrugged. "Men are the same the world over. Do you wish me to accompany you?"

"No," Cassia said, trying to project confidence. "I won't be in any danger."

"As you wish," Meredith said. He looked as unconcerned as ever and Cassia felt irritated by his attitude. Again. That had been happening more frequently since they left the bleak hills to descend to Elbithrar and the river. Nearly everything the lordling did or said got underneath her skin, a nettle rash she could not scratch.

She turned away to hide her frustration and gathered her meagre possessions, hooking the small pack onto the end of her staff. When she looked around again Meredith had disappeared and only the innkeeper's boy remained, staring up at her from under his fringe.

"What?"

"Nothing," the boy squeaked. He fled the stable and ran up the alley to the street. Cassia watched him until he flung himself around the corner, a tangle of limbs, always falling forwards. Cassia shook her head and reached for her staff.

At the centre of the city was a grand square, paved with slabs and cobbles, set in patterns that could only be seen in full by the gods themselves as they passed over the city. The populace flocked there to see the musicians and traders who pitched up in different places every day. The Emperor's palace looked onto the square, which was bounded at each corner by one of the four temples of Hellea's patron deities. Meteon, Casta, Ceresel and Saihri. The river, the great lake, fortune and the goddess who, legend had it, had given birth to the first Emperor, Manethrar. These four elements combined had made Hellea the most powerful empire in the world.

Cassia sat near the top of the steps to Ceresel's temple, her knees pulled up against her chest, and gazed down into the square. Opposite her, behind the gaudy, florid colonnades of the temple dedicated to Saihri, more buildings loomed. A wide lane led to another open space that was used as the city's hiring market, ruled over by an army of clerks from what used to be Pyraete's temple. At this time of the day the market was lined with drunkards and listless, unemployed labourers, hoping against the evidence that they would be offered a job before the sun set. Cassia had stared up at the ancient temple of the God of the North with a sense of sadness, ashamed that such an imposing building could fall to such terrible misuse.

Ultess's boy had abandoned her after showing her this far, disappearing into the crowd as though someone had jerked hard on a string attached to his wrist. He left her to explore the Emperor's Square on her own. It was a more daunting prospect than she had first imagined. Everything happened at breakneck pace, and everyone shouted over everyone else. Cassia was buffeted through lines of stalls, pushed on before she had a chance to see what was on display. She tripped over feet and the edges of stalls, and over children that were dragged, crying, after their mothers. She had to dodge out of the path of horses, mules and handcarts, and once somebody even threw something at her, and she felt an object whiz past her ear.

After half an hour she'd had enough. All the temples were raised high over the square, with wide stone steps before them, but since Ceresel's temple looked the quietest she took sanctuary there. The steps were dotted with beggars, all hoping the goddess would favour them with a gold coin – or a silver bell, or at the very least two copper tokens, not too badly clipped – and visitors to the temple hurried up and down, each harried silently by their own poor fortune, for why else would they bend a knee or make sacrifice to such a fickle mistress?

Nobody came to bother her or sweep her from the steps for making the place look untidy, unlike many of the temples she had waited at in other towns. In some places the priests would descend with their arms spread wide if a man looked reasonably wealthy, but when Cassia or her father approached, they came out with sticks.

If there were storytellers here, she had not found them yet. There were merchants galore in the square and its surrounding streets, but she had not seen a single storyteller. They could be near Pyraete's temple, or maybe there was another square she had not yet found. If the stupid boy had not run off she would certainly have found them by now.

Her feet ached more than they ever had before, even when she had walked all day over the rough terrain of the North. The flags and cobbles of Hellea were bruising and unforgiving, and Cassia did not have the will or the strength to continue her search today. What little she could muster would be needed for the journey back to Ultess's tavern. *If I can find the damned place again without help. Stupid boy.*

"Spare a penny?"

She shoved herself to her feet, pushing away from the voice at the same time. It was one of the vagrants from further up the steps, a gaunt, scarred man, his left hand bound in frayed, dirty bandages. His hair hung in lank strands around his shoulders, and it was hard to tell whether it was dark or greying under the dirt. His tunic might have been splendid, once, but time and the gutter had taken care of that too and the fine cloth was torn so Cassia could see his torso through the fabric. So many bruises and scars – she had never seen the like, not even on the most pitiful of veterans. Some of those scars were recent, as far as she could judge from their appearance.

The man swayed on his feet. He winced and his gaze flicked to one side, as though he listened to someone stood at his shoulder. Then he shook his head. "Only a child. Only a child," he muttered. "Not right."

And he heeled away, shambling along the steps in the direction of another seated pilgrim.

Cassia frowned after him. "I'm no child!"

He looked back. "Hah. Perhaps not. But I have no coin for those pleasures."

Her mouth fell open, the retort unspoken as she realised what he implied, and she knew her face had turned red. She hoped nobody else had heard their exchange.

She hurried along the steps and grabbed the man's arm. "I'm not a whore!"

She had expected her hand to close around little more than bone and flaccid skin, but the vagrant was surprisingly strong. He pulled his arm away with ease and Cassia stumbled. She would have fallen down the steps if he had not reached out to steady her.

The beggar's eyes were clouded by drink, but the stare he turned upon her was hard and penetrating. "No," he said, after a moment. "No, you're no whore. But mark my words, girl, stay on these steps past dusk and you soon will be. Hellea's no friend to country girls."

She managed to free herself from his grip and backed away from him. The meaning of his words was not lost on her, and the sun ducking behind the rooftops brought a fresh shiver of panic. The temple steps were emptying, she realised. There were only a few pilgrims left, sat in a short line further down, near the square. And they were all women: barefoot, wrapped in threadbare cloaks. One of the women scowled over her shoulder at Cassia. *She thinks I'm fresh competition!*

"I didn't realise," she said, appalled. "I only wanted to rest a while. My feet are sore and . . ." she trailed off, helplessly.

The beggar sighed, his eyes softening a little. "This is not a good place to rest. Especially not after dark." He looked her up and down in the calculating manner her father had often used. "You can't afford a guide, I wager. You've come to make your fortune in Hellea, but you don't know where to start."

Cassia lowered her head. "I am so obvious, sir?"

"Nothing I haven't seen before." The beggar shrugged. "If you have lodgings at all, I would return to them now. Ceresel's priestesses will fight for their position on these steps, and they hold grudges like scorned wives."

"They don't look like priestesses," Cassia said. They looked anything but holy and blessed.

"Only what men call them in jest."

Cassia hesitated, then sketched a jerky bow to the man. "Thank you for your advice, sir. If there is any service I may perform for you . . . ?"

He gestured at an empty jug that lay on its side further up the steps. "Unless you can spare a few pennies for another of those, girl. And I do not think you can."

"No, sir."

The beggar waved to the far side of the square. "Get gone then, girl."

Cassia did not wait to be told twice. She headed for the eastern side of the steps, intending to avoid the prostitutes.

"Girl!" The beggar's voice pulled her up short. "Do you *know* where you are going?"

She looked at the roads that led from the square, thought for a moment and shook her head.

The beggar muttered something under his breath. "Fine. Fine. I'm tired of these steps, and people aren't as free with their coins as they used to be. Where are your lodgings?"

Cassia stifled her relieved sigh, still uncertain how far she should trust this man. Nobody else had offered any help, true, but why should a beggar take pity on her? What motive could he have? She had no doubt there were countless unmapped and quiet alleyways in Hellea, and she had no desire to be found in one come the morning, with her throat slit from ear to ear. She should have accepted Meredith's offer. But she was so used to being able to drift freely through the streets of Keskor and the northern coastal towns that she had not considered how different Hellea would really be.

"I don't know the street," she said, "but the sign shows a man pouring wine into his mouth. The owner is called—"

"Ultess?" the beggar interrupted. When Cassia nodded, he surprised her with a bark of laughter that deteriorated into a rasping cough.

"Is something wrong, sir?" she asked, worried by his reaction, and worried too that the coughing fit might incapacitate him. "Is it a fair place to stay?"

The beggar waved her away before she could help him. "Only a cough. I'll be fine." But his breath was shallow and came in a ragged wheeze. He lowered himself carefully onto the steps. "Gods . . . bitches and bastards . . . the damned lot of them . . . I'll be fine."

Cassia hovered nervously for a moment, with a few sidelong glances at the whores at the bottom of the steps, before joining him. She had decided to trust the man. If he did mean her any harm he would be hard-pressed to even catch her if she ran.

"Do you know Ultess, sir?" she asked when the man's fit had subsided.

"I know him. He has *paying* guests now, does he?" The beggar lifted his head to study her more closely. "Might be the day isn't so wasted after all. Come on girl, here's a bargain for you. I'll show you to the Old Soak, and you pay for a drink there."

She did not think Ultess would allow the beggar inside his tavern, but she was reluctant to offend the old man. *Baum will surely buy him one drink if I ask. I can repay him when I start telling my tales.*

The beggar extended his unbandaged hand and Cassia took it.

When they reached the corner of the next road Cassia was dismayed to see the gradient of the hill before them. She knew the beggar would not manage the climb unaided. He had relied on her support ever more over the last half mile, unsteady on his feet and needing regular rests. These pauses were becoming longer, and at this rate they would barely reach the Old Soak before daybreak. But Cassia would not have abandoned her companion even if she had been able to pull away from his clawlike grip. She had given him her word, after all. If she left him here he would in all likelihood go no further and lie helpless in the gutter until dawn.

It was not that he was drunk. Or rather, it was not *only* that he was drunk. The man rambled, the direction of his thoughts changing with every explosion of coughs and wheezes, and Cassia quickly gathered that he had been seriously wounded in recent times. The scarring on his face and body were testament to that, and his wounds had robbed him of his health. Listening to the scattered fragments of narrative, between the bouts of coughing, Cassia was amazed the man was still alive.

"One was as young as you," the beggar said. "Just as young. An' they butchered him. Laughed as they did it. No courage, no principles. That's what it comes to."

Phlegm streaked the corners of his mouth, and he wiped ineffectually at his face with one sleeve. He had mentioned this boy before, a note of bitterness in his voice. "I let him down. I let them all down. Why are *you* helping me?"

"Because you asked me to," Cassia said. She glanced over her shoulder. The street was quiet and only a few revellers and labourers could be seen. For the most part they had been left alone as they made their tortuous path through the city. People veered aside when they saw the old beggar; or were pulled out of the way by their companions and friends. But if any showed a flicker of recognition, none hailed him or offered to help.

"Never asked."

"You did, sir."

He spat against the wall. "More fool you. And don't *sir* me."
"Then what am I to call you, sir?"

"Fool. Idiot. Gutless. Drunkard. *Coward.* Fake." He lifted his head for a moment and saw the hill before them. "Sweet

Matias. Leave me be."

Cassia gritted her teeth and hauled him upright once more. "No. We have a bargain, sir."

"Stupid girl."

"You're worse than my father," Cassia retorted. She would have to drag him up this hill, but if that was the only way she could move him, that was how it would be.

This far from the grand squares and precincts that were at the heart of Hellea, there was little light to see by. Flickering shafts escaped through the missing slats or gaps at the sides of the shutters in the tenements that crowded the narrow lanes. But Hellea was dark and becoming darker, and now Cassia began to fear for her safety. If any man chose to attack her now, she would be hampered by the beggar's weight, and he would be unable to defend her. Right now he couldn't even defend himself.

"How much further, sir?"

The beggar spluttered. "Why didn't they run?"

That made no sense at all. She cursed under her breath and started up the hill, half-dragging him along with her. After a few steps she realised propping him up from behind and pushing him up the hill might prove more successful.

The man's weight vanished suddenly, pulled up and away from her as though Althea herself had descended from the skies to pluck him from the streets. Cassia overbalanced with a squeal and tumbled forward into the dirt at the side of the road. When she looked up, the dark shape before her had far too many limbs, until her shocked senses finally caught up with her.

"Meredith?"

He held the old man's unconscious form in the air as if he was nothing more than a rag doll. "You have worried us."

Her strength leaked out from her body as she lay on the cobbles. It was a struggle to lever herself back onto her knees. "That stupid boy ran off and left me."

Meredith reached down with his free hand and hauled Cassia onto her feet. She eyed the lordling nervously. In the dim light he looked as frightening as he had back at the shrine that housed Malessar's shieldmen. He wore his sword openly, the bejewelled pommel flashing as it caught a shaft of light from a nearby window. Cassia imagined the tales that would circulate around the city as Meredith made his presence felt. *A Northern lordling, seeking the great Warlock – there will be trouble . . .*

The beggar wheezed, and Cassia realised his breathing was more shallow than ever. "Meredith, take care with him. He's ill."

The lordling lowered him gently to the ground and the beggar's breathing eased. "He was not attempting to overpower you?"

"No. We were helping each other. He was going to show me how to reach the Old Soak. He knows Ultess."

"I can smell alcohol." Meredith bent over the man. "Cassia, this man is dying. Ultess will not welcome him."

It was hardly a surprise to her, but she could not leave him here like this. "Can you carry him? Please, Meredith?"

There was a puzzled frown on his face. "Why?"

"Because he helped me. It's the right thing to do."

"I will help you," Meredith said. He lifted the old man with barely any effort. "Come with me. The inn is not far."

Ultess was sat at one of the tables in the front room, a half-drained tankard at his elbow. His only reaction to the sight of the beggar in Meredith's arms was a weary sigh, and a resigned shake of his head.

"Look what the dogs dragged in. My errant doorkeeper."

This beggar – the only man in the whole city who had talked to Cassia this afternoon – was Ultess's man? Surely that was such a coincidence that only storytellers would use? She watched as Meredith laid the man on a bench behind the door, handling him more gently than he had in the street, and her thoughts tumbled over each other. *But this* is *a story. Or it will be. Who is to say what will happen?* Only the gods knew for certain. This must have happened for a reason. *I was on Ceresel's steps – the goddess herself heard me! She* meant *for this man to find me!*

The man groaned, but did not wake. Already he looked more comfortable, his breathing becoming more regular. Ultess snapped at his hearth-boy. The treacherous child was hunched by the fire, and Cassia glared at him as he hurried to cover the old man with a blanket.

"Sir, who is he?" she asked, once the room had returned to normal. There were still several men occupying a table in the far corner of the tavern. They had offered a few muttered comments at Meredith's entrance, but their attention had soon wandered.

"Didn't he tell you?" Ultess said. "No, I don't suppose he did. Not one to shout his own name. He never was, and these days even less so. I believe he thinks himself cursed. And there's always the bloody Gentarrs to watch out for."

"I don't understand," Cassia said. "The Gentarrs?"

Ultess winced and motioned her to lower her voice. "Softly, girl. Even here there are eyes and ears. This is political."

She looked around guiltily, but none of the other customers appeared to be listening. She was reminded of Rann Almoul and his quiet campaigns amongst Keskor's richer families, and the thought left a sour taste in her mouth.

"He may tell you if he sees fit," Ultess said. "If he actually remembers who you are from one day to the next."

Meredith loomed at Cassia's side. She was oddly grateful for his presence now, and a small part of her wanted to edge closer to him for warmth and comfort. She wasn't sure where those thoughts had come from, and she shied away from them.

"He was a soldier," Meredith said. He nodded to the wall over the bench, where a sheathed sword was mounted. Metal brackets secured the weapon in place; it would not be easy to remove it. "Was that his sword?"

Ultess stared at the lordling as though weighing his answer. "The last he ever wielded. I don't think he even sees it now."

"But what is his name?" Cassia asked again.

Ultess glanced at the man. For a second Cassia thought she saw a shade of sympathy in the tavern keeper's eyes. "Arca. Arca the Brave."

The old man muttered and shifted, as though the mention of his name had penetrated his exhausted mind. Then he rolled onto his side, curled away from them and away from the dim light of the tavern's lanterns.

"Baum says you are a storyteller's daughter," Ultess said. "Well, here's a tragedy for you. Arca the Brave, one of the last heroes of Cape Magister, the man who held the line at the Usurper's Fields, who saw even the mighty Guhl fall and die."

"What happened to him?" Cassia asked.

"He grew old. His body failed him. He went to drink. Then he sold out a contract and his honour. His guilt got the better of him – if it had not, then Lianna of the Castaria would most likely be dead. Arca himself barely survived. Now he sleeps on my floor and begs for scraps like a dog." The tavern keeper sighed. "Perhaps there are some wars that are not worth fighting."

Chapter Ten

By the time Cassia rose in the morning, Baum was gone. When she asked Ultess where he was the tavern keeper shook his head.

"I never asked him, and he never told me," he said, in a tone that brooked no further questioning.

She was disappointed, but she supposed she only had herself to blame. It was little wonder, after the exertions of the previous day, that she had slept far into the morning.

She peered through the shutter, down into the street. Stains and unsavoury lumps marked the ground beneath the window. Thankfully, she did not need to avail herself of the pot. Yet.

Meredith, after scaring the hearth-boy half to death with his intense practice of forms and stances in the yard, had also left for the day, and Cassia was alone. She glared at the hearth-boy until he retreated behind the curtain. He still had not apologised for abandoning her the night before. Arca slept, and every so often a snore like dry twigs breaking underfoot came from his bench. Ultess was busy with chores, moving endlessly from the fire to the stairs, casting an occasional frown in her direction. Cassia had the impression that he was uncomfortable with her presence. And that served to inflame her own discomfort.

Finally she fled back to her room and gathered her robes, tying her hair so she could hide it under the cap. The patched clothing hid the curves of her figure, so the people of Hellea would see her as a boy, just as her father's audiences in the North had done.

Ultess looked up as she descended again. "Going out? Don't get lost again, girl. Arca won't wake today."

She decided not to answer him.

The hearth-boy might not have been one for words, or directions – or cleanliness, come to that – but his route into the city was easy to follow. This time she took care to watch the way behind her as well as the road ahead, memorising landmarks, buildings and small shrines. She was confident she would not lose her way today.

She navigated her way past the Emperor's Square and paused before the temple of Pyraete, marvelling at the building's overbearing columns. It had been built in the Northern style, blunt and aggressive, threatening to take over the entire square. In the evening the temple would cast grand shadows over the square, asserting its dominance over the city. For a moment she felt a twinge of homesickness. There were still buildings with such a profile in some towns in the North, and she had sheltered in their deep porticos during many savage winter storms. She forced herself to veer away from the steps of the temple. She had more important things to do than remember those days, she told herself. She had a future to make.

Still there was no sign of even one storyteller on the streets. Cassia felt conspicuous in her robes, but nobody seemed to be paying her much attention. As the sun reached its zenith she found a large market area that sprawled through streets and open spaces alike, clogging up all passage like pondweed. Where the stalls in the Emperor's Square were piled with yards of rich cloth and fruit from overseas, the traders here clearly catered to a less affluent market, selling grain, roughly milled flour, old and sweating cheese and, on a few stalls, even cuts of greying meat.

She shuffled through, struggling against the press around her. The sun and the dust made her queasy, and the streets stank. At last she could stand no more and, checking her cap still covered her hair, she found a tavern just off one of the broader alleyways and ducked cautiously down the steps.

This tavern was a dingier affair than the Old Soak. The rushes covering the floor were rank and strewn with rubbish, and even the light from the candles seemed dirty and greasy. The men on the benches that lined the damp walls only emphasised the run-down and squalid nature of the tavern, and Cassia almost turned on her heel immediately, intending to find a better place. Even her father would not be seen dead in this horrible dive.

But she had been noticed. The barkeep glared at her, his eyes too close together and the shape of his face rodent-like. "Whatever you want, you'd better be able to pay for it, boy."

Cassia coughed, praying her voice would not give her away. "I think you'll find my tales are more than worth a tankard of ale." It was one of her father's lines. When he used it he sounded full of bluster, but it always seemed to work. From her mouth, the words sounded ridiculous.

The barkeep shook his head and turned away. "We don't need another bloody storyteller," he said. "We already got one. No coin, no ale."

They already *had* a storyteller? Cassia's eyes were still adjusting to the gloom, and she became aware of one of the tavern's patrons pushing himself to his feet.

"But surely if you hear me—" she started.

"Country boy," the customer snapped. "You heard him. I'm the storyteller here. You find your own place. If you can."

Now she could see him more clearly. He was a large man with a storyteller's cloak draped around his shoulders, the hems frayed and the patches faded. His jowls sagged and his hands were fat, and he moved as though his joints had seized up and turned to stone. *This is how my father will look in ten years*, she realised, taking an involuntary step back toward the door.

"Country boy, is it?" the barkeep echoed. "He won't know our ways then, will he?"

"What ways are those, sir?" Cassia asked carefully. She reached behind her with one hand to find the reassuring solidity of the door.

The storyteller smiled. It was an unpleasant sight, reminding Cassia of some of the thugs she and Norrow had encountered over the years. Men who demanded money to allow them passage, or to sleep unmolested outside the walls of a town. It made sense they would flock to a city such as Hellea.

"There's a guild in this city," the storyteller said.

"And I have to belong to it?"

Both men nodded. "And you'll need sponsors," the barkeep added, his smile as predatory as the other man's. "It's not a cheap process, you know."

Cassia had guessed as much. This had happened to her father once or twice. Usually Norrow had settled the argument by packing up and leaving, refusing to play their game. Only once had he agreed to pay, and on that occasion he had to borrow against the promise of his future earnings. That had ended badly; Norrow would not be visiting Iltridor again.

"If it's all the same to you," she said, as lightly as she could, "I think I will find my sponsors elsewhere."

"You don't want to offend Marko," the barkeep said, shaking his head. "Perhaps you should buy him a drink."

The man named Marko was too close for comfort now and Cassia realised with mounting panic that she had trapped herself behind the door. She would need to push the man aside to be able to open the door far enough to escape. Marko had clearly seen that too.

And when I need Meredith . . .

Marko reached out to grab her shoulder. Cassia ducked inside his grasp, driving her elbow forward into his chest. It was a desperate move, she knew, but it had always worked against Hetch.

Marko staggered back with a shout of pain. Before he could recover Cassia kicked out at his knee and he toppled sideways into the nearest rickety table. She dashed back to the door and heaved it open, the hinges squealing in protest. Light struggled down the stairwell, motes of dust swirling in the air around her.

"Try telling that one to an audience!" she shouted back at them.

As she scrambled up the treacherous steps, Marko's fury erupting behind her lent fresh impetus to her flight. She flung herself into the alley beyond the narrow lane that sheltered the tavern and soon lost herself in the crowded market.

At last, when her heart stopped pounding and her breathing slowed to a normal level, she paused inside an off-kilter doorway and gathered her thoughts.

That was stupid. He won't forget me. And he'll tell other people about me. They won't let me into their damned guild now. If there really was a guild. She still wasn't certain about that. It was equally possible Marko and his tame barkeep had been trying to con her.

In any case, the experience had put her off trying any other taverns. She circled back around to the square in front of Pyraete's temple, threading her way between the clusters of labourers and flapping her robes ostentatiously to make sure people saw her and paid attention to the symbols that lined the hems and sleeves. Back in the North her father would have drawn an audience almost instantly, but to her dismay nobody seemed bothered by the storyteller passing through their midst. After two passes through the crowd, feeling more ridiculous and frustrated by the minute, she gave in and slumped onto the temple's steps.

I'll never be a storyteller.

Hellea carried on regardless all around her and, for a while, she chose to ignore it in turn. She could not understand how the city could relegate the telling of its history into the care of horrible men in damp, seedy cellars. How could they express the noble traits of honesty and bravery in such surroundings? Hellea, she decided, had lost its way. And perhaps she was not the one to lead it back.

She hoped Baum was having better luck in his search to uncover the warlock's traces. How did one search for a warlock anyway? Where would you begin? *Excuse me, have you seen a warlock in this city? You may have recognised him by the magic spitting from his fingertips and the cold shadow that engulfs everybody in the immediate vicinity. No? What about a trail of reanimated corpses or murderous statues?*

It could be told as a farce, she thought, shuffling through stock scenes that her father used to pad out some of his shorter stories; a thin narrative that might be twisted to contain some of the hoarier, well-used jokes Norrow relied on with certain audiences. She was sure she could fashion such a tale and make it a success in Hellea's taverns. The trick, of course – and a daunting barrier to be sure – was to gain access to the closed ranks of the city's storytellers.

With the stone of the temple steps numbing her rear, she decided to move on again. Maybe it was time to try another tavern. Marko *must* have been lying about the guild.

This time she picked her target more carefully: a larger tavern, not far from the Emperor's Square. A few minutes spent watching the entrance satisfied her that the customers actually had money to spend and were not just crawling in from the gutters. The place even had a small yard, though the high walls surrounding it were topped with vicious metal spikes to discourage climbers. If there was a yard, there had to be a stable. And that in turn suggested this tavern hoped to attract travellers as well as the more moneyed locals. Even if they did not need a storyteller here, at least they should be more polite than the denizens of that horrible dive a few streets away.

This time she held her head high and flourished the cuffs of her robes so the tavern's customers could not mistake who she was. It made little difference; the large main room was busy and filled with chatter, and her pace was checked by the men clustered in groups all across the floor. She was forced to skip aside at least twice to avoid being barrelled over by other customers.

She paused, in the lee of one of the thick posts that supported the beams of the floor above, to catch her breath and orient herself. The upper part of the post was decorated with small bronze plates representing the Hellean gods and myths, hung to bring good fortune to the tavern and all who came under its roof. She reached up to touch the lowest plate with one finger and hoped that luck would rub off on her.

It took a few minutes to gain the attention of the harried barkeep, and even then he barely looked up from his casks and tankards. "Make it quick, boy. Time is money."

"Sir, if I might introduce myself—"

He shook his head, pulling loose strands from his greying queue. "Cut the flowery horseshit."

She did. "I'm the best storyteller in Hellea. Or I will be, if you let me tell my tales here."

Now the man glanced up. Once, and then again, more appraisingly. "You're not guilded. If I take you on and the guild men find out, I might as well throw every coin I own from the windows. Where are you from?"

Cassia felt her shoulders drop. "Keskor, in the North."

The barkeep grunted. "Thought so. I can hear the accent. And you ain't the first to run up against the guilds either, boy." He stared for a moment longer, and the harsh lines around his eyes softened. Cassia wondered if she truly looked as miserable as she felt. "Go and sit down. That corner – out of the way." He pointed. "But don't try telling any stories, or I'll throw you out so hard you'll bounce off the palace temple itself."

She hesitated, then nodded. She wished she could loosen the band around her chest. Perhaps if the corner he indicated was secluded enough she could make some delicate adjustments . . .

A rickety bench was wedged between two posts at the far end of the room, furthest away from the fireplace. From the letters scratched into the old seat, it looked as though this was where visiting merchants or other rich travellers might deposit their servants. At the moment it held two small errand boys, their bare feet swinging above the ground as they placed wagers with each other, using nutshells for coins. The boys clammed up, staring at her with a mixture of curiosity and suspicion as she took a seat at the other end of the bench. Cassia glared back at them until they scooped up their nutshells and disappeared into the tavern's crowds.

She sighed, leaning against the post. How could the world be so cruel? All she wanted to do was be a better storyteller than her father, but it seemed at every turn there was a new obstacle in her path. In her experience guilds only meant trouble – though mostly for her father – but the very idea of a guild of storytellers sounded wrong to her. Would the guild decide which stories could be told and which were seditious? Would they lay claim to her earnings? And would they be enlightened enough to believe a girl could be just as good a storyteller as any man? Cassia knew she still had much to learn, but she thought she already knew the answer to that last question. And there was no way she could fool a whole guild into believing she was a boy. Not for very long.

The barkeep loomed over her, a dripping tankard held out in one hand. Cassia looked up, blinking. "Sir, I have no money," she started.

The barkeep thrust the tankard at her. "At least you're honest. I can't take what you haven't got. Call this hospitality."

She took the tankard with both hands, and ale slopped over the rim to splash down her wrists. "Thank you, sir."

The barkeep paused. "If I'm right, you're the boy who caused an almighty clamour over at the Gallows Cellar earlier. Well?"

Cassia wasn't sure if she should own up to that, in case this man turned out to be Marko's friend, but the barkeep stared down intently at her and seemed reluctant to leave without an answer. "A man said he would sponsor me into the guild," she explained, "but I didn't believe him. And then he didn't want to let me go."

The barkeep's face twisted into a scowl. "I hope you never paid him. You'll not see that coin again."

She shook her head. "But why is there a guild anyway?"

"Too many storytellers. Or so the Emperor said." The barkeep grunted and spat on the floor to show his disdain for that law. "Every one of them had to apply for a licence. It took days for the heads of the new guild to hear the auditions. At the same time the Emperor decreed no tavern could employ more than one storyteller."

The barkeep glanced round and then crouched lower, his voice dropping to a whisper. "This bit's only hearsay, but apparently there was a man who told stories that openly criticised the Emperor and his father. Haroam, I think his name was. I heard people used to come away fired up and angry, and a few times there were fights and stonings. Fires of retribution lit on the streets. The legions used to bloody their pikearms after those stories were told. The guild was instituted not long after that."

Cassia nodded her understanding. "The guild stops those stories from being told again?"

"Those, and others besides." The barkeep's eyes narrowed. "Don't get me wrong, I'm the Emperor's man through and through. It may not be just, but it's the way it is. If you go plying your trade, unlicensed or on the streets out there, you'll soon be parted from your tongue."

"How do I find the guild?"

"You walk around dressed like that a while longer, they'll

find you. And they won't let go of you until you've paid your dues."

Cassia sipped the warm ale. "Thank you, sir," she said quietly. "I don't know how I can repay you for all of this."

"By not getting caught," the barkeep said. He indicated with a jerk of his head in the direction of the main square. "They make a public show of pulling out tongues. It's bad for business, boy."

As the barkeep hurried back to his work, she drew up her feet and huddled into the corner between the bench and the post, making the ale last as long as she could. She did not want to hurry back onto the streets, not if word had got around and Marko was still looking for her.

She could not think what to do next. Her dreams of success had been founded upon Hellea. The warlock Malessar was here, Baum had come to throw him down, and Cassia was here to record the tale. But if she was not a member of the city's guild, nobody would hear the story. At least, not here. Perhaps Baum would know how she should proceed. He *had* to know.

It's that or I go back home. And that was unthinkable.

There were more charms and tokens fastened to the posts at this end of the tavern, she noticed when she looked up again. The ones nearest the top, out of reach, were sculpted bronze, but most were crudely fashioned from iron or even stone. She squinted to make out the scenes on some of the older charms, worn down by the passage of time and the touch of countless customers hoping that good fortune would rub off on them.

One of the charms, close to her eye level, looked familiar to her. An oval stone plate, fastened by a fraying leather cord nailed to the post, appeared to be one of the oldest charms in the tavern. The figure of a man stood in relief, his arms outstretched and braced against the mountainsides that formed the sides of the plate. If the figure had ever been carved in detail, his features were long gone, and the script that ran around the plate's rim was barely legible. Cassia traced the letters with one finger, wary of the charm's fragility.

. . . steel to their enemies . . .

"All true Northerners should bare steel to their enemies," she muttered under her breath. "*The Call To The North*."

Then it was Pyraete, and he was raising the mountains, not holding them up or forcing them apart. How strange to find this here, and how old was this piece? How did it get here, of all places?

The leather cord chose that moment to give way and Cassia caught the plate only because she had kept her hand close underneath it. She looked around quickly, but her nerves were unfounded. It appeared that nobody had seen it fall. She closed her hands tight around the plate, feeling the rough edges cut into her fingers, and her thoughts whirred. In the tales this was a sign from the gods, but what were they trying to tell her? *Can it mean I have Pyraete's favour? Should I take this with me for Baum to see?*

For a long moment she sat frozen on the bench, caught in a dilemma. The barkeep would not appreciate it if she repaid his kindness by stealing his ornaments, but the more she thought about it the more she believed this had to be a message from Pyraete.

All true Northerners should bare steel to their enemies . . . and stand true to the course they have chosen, for when the heart is divided by fear then the battle is already lost. Cassia snaked the stone into her robes as unobtrusively as she could. *Stand true to the course*, she told herself.

She gulped down the remaining ale and slipped through the crowd while the barkeep attended a party of ship's officers who had just entered the tavern. The stone plate weighed heavy inside her robe, and she feared it might fall and crack on the floor as much as she feared the sudden weight of the barkeep's fist, but she made it through the doors unscathed. She realised she had been holding her breath, and she drew the city's air gratefully into her lungs.

She decided against spending the remainder of the afternoon scouting through the city. There seemed little point since she would not be able to try out her storytelling skills, and Marko was probably still looking for her, so instead she retraced her steps wearily back towards the Old Soak.

Baum and Meredith had already returned. Their travelling cloaks hung behind the door, and Baum sat at one of the tables with his eyes closed. Cassia heard the familiar sound of steel being whetted to a sharp edge and guessed Meredith was in the back yard. The potboy was in his usual place by the fire, sullenly tending the evening's meal.

"Your day went well?" Baum asked, without opening his eyes. Cassia started at the sound of his voice. She had intended to go up to her room and examine the stone plate, but now she made her way over to the soldier's table instead.

"Not especially well, sir," she said, drawing up a stool. "The Helleans don't like storytellers much. Perhaps that's why my father never bothered to travel this far south."

Baum's shoulders rolled in a dismissive shrug. "Perhaps. I was told the last Emperor was not keen on the effects of what he called slanderous gossip and fairy-folk fancies. It would seem his successor shares those opinions. I hear there is a guild now?"

Ultess clumped past behind her, on his way to the stairs. "There's a bloody guild for everything," Cassia heard him mutter.

Baum leaned forward, lowering his voice. "And the man we seek? Have you any news?"

She had thought Baum and Meredith were working on that themselves, and she shook her head. The slight narrowing of Baum's eyes reminded her that although he had saved her from a life of slavery at the hands of Hetch and Tarves Almoul, he still owned her. She had to pay her way and prove her worth. *And I've been pulled off-course by Hellea itself,* she thought. *The city has blinded me.*

"I didn't know what to ask," she said. "Or how. Surely people would think me mad if I asked after a nine-hundred year old man?"

Baum's gaze did not move from her for a long moment, and then he shrugged again. "Perhaps. Perhaps not. Think about it for yourself. How much do you know of our man?"

Cassia was familiar enough with Baum's manner now to know that he would only ask that question if he thought she already knew the answer. She tried to dredge up from the depths of her memory any instances where Malessar had been described as a major character in any of the stories she had learned. The warlock passed only lightly through history and folklore, and where he did enter into a scene – like the Fall of Stromondor, for instance – his presence was peripheral, usually overshadowed by the nominal hero or heroine of the tale. So while there were physical descriptions of the noble Jathar Leon Learth and cunning Verros the Younger, Malessar was an intangible, looming threat. Every storyteller she had ever heard used that lack of description to their advantage, giving Malessar features and qualities that matched the needs of the story they had chosen to tell. In one he might be tall, skeletal and ravaged by the effects of his own cursed sorcery; in another he might appear as a cutting reflection of the local nobility, dignified and aloof, but reeking of corruption. One ribald tavern song painted him as a capering, twisted fool, dancing to a tune nobody else could hear. If any of these tales gave him one common feature, aside from the fact that he was a terrifying and evil warlock, she had yet to uncover it.

But Baum clearly believed otherwise. And she could not see where he was trying to lead her. "In all the tales I know, he is always a different man," she said. "That is all I think I know – but how can I begin to look for a man who always changes?"

Baum appeared disappointed by this, but to Cassia's frustration he did not hurry to correct her. Instead he turned his stare upon the beams above them as though there might be some absolute truth hidden in the pattern of the boards. "Think on this a while longer," he told her. "Perhaps what you should look for is not so close to the surface of your tales?"

That confused her even further and she excused herself and made her way out to the yard where Meredith sat on a stool, sharpening the blade of his greatsword. His shirt lay discarded on the ground next to him and she could make out the traces in the dirt where he had stepped and twisted through the patterns of his daily practice.

His head was lowered as he concentrated on the blade, and he did not appear to have noticed her. Cassia paused to watch him. The movement of the sculpted contours of his arms was fascinating, almost hypnotic, and of late it had even imprinted itself into her dreams. Even the thought caused the heat to rise in her cheeks.

I should not be thinking these things. He is a prince. The Heir to the North. But the images – and the faintly nauseous sensation that accompanied them – refused to be banished easily. She had a vague memory of a dream in which those arms had been wrapped around her . . .

"Are you well?"

She jumped, shocked from her reverie by Meredith's voice. He was looking up at her, a frown of concern on his face. He laid his sword aside with care and rose from the stool, towering over her even though she stood on the doorstep.

"Oh, I . . . that is . . . yes," she stammered, her blush deepening as she tried to get the words out. "I . . . I was just watching you."

Well, even a blind man would have seen that. Bloody daft girl.

Meredith did not seem to have noticed her discomfort. If he had, then he clearly was unconcerned by it. "I have been waiting for you."

The rest of her thoughts fled. "You have?"

"We did not practice this morning. Your staff is over there."

Cassia wasn't sure if she should feel relieved or not. She slipped the stone plate from her sleeve and laid it safely beside the step, wrapping it in her storyteller's cap before collecting her staff. She tried to slow her breathing and concentrate on the forms Meredith had taught her as a warming-up exercise, but she felt so self-conscious she kept mistiming her steps. Once she came close to dropping the staff, and that only made her worse.

"You are not concentrating," Meredith noted, stepping into place opposite her. He had not bothered to reclaim his shirt, and the sight, which she should be used to by now, was more than just intimidating, it was distracting. Cassia bit down on her lip and launched into her first attack.

Meredith side-stepped easily, and Cassia had to alter her swing to avoid leaving herself open. Just a few weeks ago she would have been hard pressed to make it, but this time Meredith's counter-move rebounded off her staff. It quivered in her hands and she almost dropped it again, but she felt a surge of pride at having successfully defended herself. *Now do it again.*

When she turned he had already moved. She ducked into a crouch and Meredith's staff whistled over her head. She jabbed out at his knees, forcing him to step back.

And with that she managed to forget, however temporarily, that the Heir to the North had made such an impression on her dreams. Bare-chested he might be, but she was focused on the staff that spun in his hands and the way he balanced his weight on the balls of his feet. That meant he would push to her right flank. She was beginning to recognise more of his moves now, having watched him practice almost every morning.

Can it be? Is he really so predictable?

She feinted to her right and as Meredith's staff swept toward her legs she nipped left and brought the end of her own staff hard against his calf. He stumbled onto one knee, forced to put a hand to the ground to steady himself. Cassia skipped back, her heart fit to burst in triumph and disbelief.

Meredith drew himself up and looked at the dirt on the palm of his hand. It seemed to bother him more than the bruise that must inevitably appear on his leg. "That was well done, girl," he said.

Was that a smile? Cassia blinked. Surely not, it had to be her imagination.

But Meredith's lips twitched as he settled back into a guard position. "Once more."

She reined in her thoughts, making certain she was still beyond his reach. He would have to come to her and if she could see how he intended to move, she could try to counter his attack again. She could prove her last blow was no fluke.

"Best of three, then." She challenged him without thinking.

The staff spun in his hands for a moment, and he leaned to the left. Cassia shifted her feet in readiness, but she was completely unprepared for the sheer speed with which he launched at her. She had barely enough time to duck aside, her own staff held across her body to ward off the blow, and by then he had turned to continue the attack, snapping both ends of his staff at her in multiple feints until she had no idea where she should defend next.

In desperation she fell back. It was a trip more than a deliberate move, but she was pressed too close to correct herself. One end of her staff caught on the ground and it tore from her grasp. She landed hard on the ground, skinning her elbows and the back of her head, the breath forced from her body. Meredith – gloriously invincible, his hair flowing loose around his shoulders – descended upon her like a god, crouching over her with his staff poised over her throat.

All coherent thought fled from her mind. She could only stare up into his hard brown eyes, not daring to let them move further downward to take in the broad curves of his chest. He remained there for what felt like an eternity, and she was frozen in place by that impassive stare. She was all too aware that her chest rose and fell with every shuddering breath she took.

"That evens the score," he said. He had not even broken a sweat.

He stood, abruptly, and the sight of him rising was dizzying. His proportions were firmly imprinted upon her mind now, and Cassia knew she would see them every time she closed her eyes. She rolled onto her side and reached for her staff, stabbing it into the dirt to haul herself up. Unlike Meredith, her body was damp with perspiration – not all of it the result of her exertions – and the dirt of the yard clung to her arms as much as her robe stuck to her skin. She took a moment to brush away the worst, forcing her breathing back into a deep, slow rhythm, and only then did she turn to face him again.

Her heart sank and despite herself she felt her shoulders drop when she saw him standing on the opposite side of the yard, his staff held ready once more. It had taken all of her strength to make that single hit count, and she had no reserves left to draw upon. At least this would be over quickly.

She brought her staff up, rolled her shoulders, and loosened her knees. "I'm ready," she said, wincing at the tremor in her voice.

Meredith's staff spun, just as it had before, and he began to lean to the left.

Just as he had before.

Cassia had a single heartbeat to recognise the pattern of his movement – and it was barely enough. Acting upon instinct more than rational thought, she spun in place, her hands shifting along the length of the staff until she held it at one end. Meredith rushed past her, already twisting and reacting to her, but she thrust her staff down at his legs and he tripped over it. The only thing she had forgotten to do, she realised far too late, was let go of the staff. Rather than it being pulled from her hands, she was jerked off-balance and pulled down on top of him.

His chest moved evenly beneath her for a moment, just long enough for her to marvel at the firm smoothness of his skin, and then she realised where she was and she scrambled to her feet, the heat rising faster on her face than a mountain storm.

Meredith remained on the ground, propping himself up on his elbows to stare at her. There was clear and frank admiration on his face, and that only caused her flush to deepen. "I am not accustomed to being beaten," he said.

"I'm sorry." Cassia wrapped her arms around herself to hide from his gaze. "It was – I mean, I was lucky."

"No, girl. You were persistent." He reached down to rub at his shins. "Persistence and desire, when refined and channelled through your training, will overcome more enemies than ability alone. Hold on to your desires."

From him, that was akin to a hero's monologue in one of the epic tales, but if there was one thing Cassia did not need it was a reminder that *her* own desires were bubbling perilously close to the surface. She retreated to her room as quickly as she could, remembering almost too late to pick up the stone plate and stumbling over the threshold as a result. Her clumsiness was appalling and embarrassing. The potboy stared at her as she hurried to the stairs, his lips twisted into a smirk, but she ignored him.

It took all of her will to slow her heartbeat. She could still feel his touch, his breath upon her skin. The air inside the room was too thick and, unaccountably, held reminders of his smell. To divert her thoughts, Cassia unwrapped the stone plate and examined it more closely. Now it seemed the figure in the centre of the plate was rising from the mountains. Even that reminded her of Meredith.

Perhaps I should give it to him, she thought. It was an attractive idea, but in the back of her mind she knew she was being swayed by her emotions. She traced the shape of the figure with her fingers, resting her palm gently upon its chest, and imagined she could feel the chill winds of the North.

Chapter Eleven

SELLEA WAS A city without a soul, Cassia thought.

The days had followed the same pattern since they arrived. Each morning Baum and Meredith disappeared like morning mist into the mazed streets and left her to fend for herself. And each morning she wondered anew how she might be able to conduct her own search for Malessar, every plan collapsing half-built as she considered how little she knew about the warlock and the city. Most of the time she would drift down to the temple markets, careful to avoid the dingy taverns where the guilded storytellers would undoubtedly be looking out for her. Sometimes she would end up along the bustling docks, marvelling at the bright-coloured foreign ships and their outlandish crews.

Either way, she always wound up hungry and miserable, returning to the Old Soak for a bowl of the unlikeable stew that always simmered over the cookfire because she could not afford to buy her own food. Once or twice she considered stealing from one of the market stalls, but she had quickly discovered the city-dwellers were just as vigilant as those in the North, if not more so. She had not been caught yet, but the stallholders had clearly marked her out as trouble. The last one had glared menacingly at her, weighing a stone in his hand, and when she turned to keep out of his reach she heard him call out: "What, you think it grows on trees, boy?"

Cassia had left her robe at the Old Soak, but elected to maintain the rest of her disguise. She had bound her chest to flatten it, and her hair was tucked up under the storyteller's cap, but without the robe she looked like any of Hellea's scavenging urchins. She thought she might at least gain sympathy from that quarter, but a lack of trust must have been passed down from one generation to the next, and when she hung around the fringes of the gangs they cold-shouldered her, sneering with suspicion. It was worse than anywhere in the North had ever been.

The only people who had any time for her were Meredith and the drunkard, Arca. Her feelings for the Heir to the North unsettled her to the point of distraction, and she was sure Meredith could see that for himself – all hells, even a lump of rock would be able to see the effect he had upon her! Outside of their training bouts, she tried to avoid him as much as possible. That left only Arca who, she was certain, had latched onto her simply because she helped him stagger back to the Old Soak that one night.

But the old man was harmless enough, and over the course of a few days she grew used to his company, and then actually began to seek him out. Usually he would be on the temple steps where she first met him, content to watch the city's routines play out before him. What manner of company he provided depended on how successful he had been during the early morning. If he had begged a few copper coins then he would already have spent those on wine, and by the time Cassia found him he would be half into his cups. If he was still sober, he might have managed to beg a helping of soup, stew or even the off-cuts of dried old fowl that a butcher had abandoned as unsaleable. And, best of all, he was willing to share.

Arca squinted at her and wiped one sleeve against his nose, drawing a trail of snot onto the fouled cloth. "He's hunting that warlock, I heard."

She hesitated, then nodded. If the old man already knew then it couldn't hurt to do that, at least.

"Myths and legends," Arca muttered. "Like catching the wind."

"You don't believe he exists?"

"I didn't say that." Arca poked at the contents of his bowl. The surface of the cold stew was covered in a layer of congealed fat.

The way he refused to meet her gaze inspired her to a leap of intuition. "You've seen him, haven't you? You know what he looks like. Arca – sir – you have to tell me! Please!"

Arca shook his head and warded off her pleas, twisting his bony frame away and shielding the wooden bowl close to his chest. "I saw him," he admitted at last. "I saw him once. And that was all, just once. But that was long ago, and so far away from here . . ."

Cassia realised how closely she was crowding him and forced herself to sit back. Arca uncurled and sat a little straighter. He scooped a handful of the stew into his mouth, although much of it ended up smeared through his beard. He chewed quietly, his face dropping into a frown that was lost in the past. Cassia had no choice but to wait for him to continue. Even if she could force the whole tale from him, she was afraid she might hurt him, for Arca looked as frail as a new-born lamb.

"I was a soldier, once," Arca mused at last. "I took the Emperor's bit. It was a life, you see."

"Were you in Berdella?" she asked.

Arca sniffed. "They gave me to the Glorious Fourth, and they sent me South. I went over the sea, to Kebria."

Kebria was an old country. It was said, in some of the tales

Norrow knew, that dragons still dwelled in her inhospitable wilds, dreaming beneath the shifting sands of the promised return of the Age of Talons. The Kebrians were an insular people, suited to such legends. In the stories they were as mystical and obtuse as dragons themselves. They rarely ventured into the Northern seas, but Cassia had seen a Kebrian ship once, on the Bay of Varro. Angular and needle-sharp, with bright sails, it cut through the sea effortlessly, making the boats around it look drab and heavy by comparison. For such a close-guarded people they certainly went to great lengths to stand out.

She might not be allowed to tell her stories in the city, but there was no reason she could not continue learning them. "What was Kebria like?"

"Strange," Arca said eventually. He stuck one finger through the congealing stew. "A man could lose himself there, sink into the sands and vanish without trace, as easily as that. You could look around at the temples, or step into a bar . . . or a brothel . . . and when you turned around again you would be lost."

A few names rose to the surface of Cassia's mind. "Oscorier Bay?"

He shook his head. "Never went there. We landed outside Jetuhen and joined up with the Stromondorians, and we laid siege to the city. They opened their gates within the space of three days, and we believed the whole land would fall to us so easily. More fool us." He fell silent again and Cassia shifted position on the stone step.

"Vaile's standards flew over the Glorious Fourth back then. We were renowned for pushing forward and never giving ground. Half-captain Guhl led our company. He looked for land and gold, as he always did. He pushed us even harder than Vaile drove the rest of the legion, and we came to the gates of Kebria four days before everybody else." Arca paused for breath. Cassia reminded herself that he was not the same man he must once have been. He was frail and battered, his breath rattling with the exertion of so much talking. When was the last time he said this much?

"Such life in that city. Such colour. We disguised ourselves as natives – darkened our faces and blackened our hair. Buried our armour, wrapped in cloth, in the shade of a stand of palms off the road." He barked a quiet laugh. "They let us in! Even as they dug their trenches and built their palisades!"

He was overtaken by a fit of coughing and Cassia scrambled for her flask. Arca drank gratefully, water spilling from the corners of his mouth. Then he returned to the dubious pleasures of the bowl of stew. "Kill myself laughing one day," he said, through his next mouthful. "If I'm lucky. Kebria. Guhl ran us through the streets like a hound on a trail of blood. Swear he could smell it. Damned if I could. He was touched by the gods, that one. Touched and cursed. Drove us through the markets so quick we never saw anything of them. And there it was."

"What?"

"The palace. There was no gold in Jetuhen, see. We weren't in the vanguard for that action and the city was plundered long before we got through the gates. Guhl was enraged. That was why he pushed us to Kebria so far ahead of Vaile's army. It was said the Queen of Kebria had sheets woven of gold. Great statues with eyes of diamond. Sandals made of dragonscales that would let a man fly. They'd make us rich, and bugger the Emperor's coins. Guhl handpicked a dozen of us to climb the walls, in the dead of night, and sack the palace for ourselves."

As he spoke Cassia looked around to see if anybody else was listening, but the pilgrims and passers-by paid no attention to an old beggar and an urchin sat close together on the steps. *Does this count as storytelling? I am his audience, after all. I wonder what the guild would make of this.* She could picture Marko's sneering face, apoplectic with indignation.

Arca might have been reading her thoughts, as his eyes narrowed in suspicion. "You're thinking to make a tale of this? I doubt anyone would listen."

"Not to me, not here," Cassia agreed sourly.

He grunted. "I wish I could have seen more of Kebria. More of the palace. All I can remember about the gardens is how dark they were. How smooth the stone paving was against our bare feet. The sweet smell of the night. We only looked for the Queen's treasures. Guhl led, and every so often I heard the slink of metal and muffled grunts up ahead. Once, I stood on a man's arm, a shape in the dark. Guhl didn't care how many corpses he left in his wake."

Cassia imagined the small company of men skulking through the palace gardens, the weak light of distant lanterns glinting from their unsheathed blades. She thought of them as similar to Verros the Younger and his cousins, when they set out to capture the crown of the Old King of Galliarca. Such a scene would be easy to set up and tell. The rhythm of the dialogue and the rest of the narrative would only need a few small alterations. Maybe Guhl had even been inspired by that story; it was a common tale, after all.

"I remember climbing up to a balcony overlooking the gardens. I was the lightest, and the youngest. The walls were crumbling, and it was easy to dig out the footholds. With the light that came through the window I saw a grand bed against the far wall. For a moment I thought it was occupied, but that was just my nerves. I took the sheets – they weren't gold – and twisted them together. Tied them to the balcony, let the others up. They went through the room like locusts. I got sent to the door, to listen for the guards."

Arca paused again. It would be a miracle, Cassia thought, if this tale was done before nightfall. It was engrossing, despite his halting monologue, and it was uncannily similar to that of Verros and the Old King. She wondered if he might have heard it years before and, befuddled by the years and by drink, conflated it with his own experiences. But his story was populated with characters that surely could have come from nowhere but his soldiering past. Guhl was a mercilessly focused man of no fixed principles, driven by the lure of treasure. Arca described him as dark, of both mind and body, with the cunning and hunger of a mountain wolf, and Cassia was able to picture him instantly.

The other soldiers in the company were less well-defined, as though they had faded from Arca's memories, but he spoke of them fondly, and tantalising glimpses of their personalities shone through his words. Breal, a tall Northman, stooping at every doorway to avoid the frame; Gunt, who had stepped on a nail while barefoot and limped around the palace wincing in pain; Tovemor, a hulking giant who climbed the walls without the aid of the knotted sheets, his belt studded with curved knives he took from the murdered guards.

Arca seemed to grow a little as he recalled them, fresh life drawing his emaciated frame from its hunched position. His voice was still raspy, but he spoke louder, punctuating his phrases with a few wavering gestures. The wheezing cough that afflicted him became less pronounced. The soldier he had once been was visible once more, a ghostly apparition beneath his skin.

The tale progressed, with the company accumulating trinkets and silver jugs in the rough sacks they had brought with them, until at last they reached the palace's grand hall. Here servants slept on woven mats between the pillars, and lanterns hung from high pins, creating flickering shadows in the dark colonnades. Guhl split the company in two and they crept down either side of the hall, picking their way between the mats and the huddled shapes. When one or two servants stirred in their sleep, Arca paused in mid-step, his breath frozen in his throat, one hand hovering nervously above the hilt of his knife. But the servants did not wake, and the company gained the steps that led to the next tier of the hall with no difficulty.

Now their adventure became more dangerous, for these were the Queen's own apartments and her personal guard stood watch through the night. The company had to wait in uncomfortable silence while Guhl sent the sneak thief Yonn to scout ahead. The echoes from the great hall were a potent reminder that a servant might awake and discover them at any moment, and Arca found himself at the rear of the cluster of men, peering back into the gloom, imagining he could see movement in the furthest recesses of the hall.

There were two guards outside the Queen's bedchamber, armed with short spears and wicked longswords, Yonn reported when he returned. And there were another two pairs of guards patrolling the enclosed garden between these apartments and the annexe Guhl believed housed the treasure chambers. There seemed no other way through. The company slumped, deflated: they would never be able to fight their way out of the palace if the alarm was raised, but the odds against sneaking past half a dozen elite guards were slim.

Arca spied a small corridor that seemed to lead around the side of the gardens, and they took that route instead. The corridor turned sharply, several times, until it ended abruptly at a sternly decorated door, stained deep crimson. Guhl pressed up against it, and after what felt an age, he nodded, his hand dropping to the bronze latch. The door swung inward and he disappeared into the gloom. Weighed down by the fact that the night was passing, Arca hurried after him.

The room was pitch black, no glow of moonlight reflected from the gardens. Arca came to a halt and Breal collided with him, hissing a curse. A scratch of flint, ahead in the darkness, marked Guhl's position, and a few seconds later the faint nimbus of light expanded as he found a candle. The silhouettes of tables and tall shelves loomed around the room.

"He was like a ghost, stood there in the middle," Arca said. "But we paid him no heed – this was the treasure chamber, or so we thought. All kinds of strange devices laid on the tables and on the shelves all around us. Silver, brass, gold and iron. Great glass lenses. Other things . . . I never knew what they were. And books. And scrolls, rolled up in gold-rimmed cases. Just one of those would have bought me a house on the Castaria's eastern shores." Cassia could picture the room. She looked up, aware the day was flying away from her. The crowd on the temple steps was changing, and the prostitutes were taking their places further up; again they stared down at her with narrowed eyes. "Sir, did you find the treasure Guhl wanted?"

He shook his head. "Let me get to it, girl. Let me get to it." He abandoned the bowl at last, and spat onto the steps between his feet. "We lit more candles. The room never seemed to get any lighter, as though the darkness sucked all the light away. Guhl went through the shelves, and Yonn and Attis picked over the tables. I wanted to join them, but something felt wrong. My head was tight. I stayed by the door and kept watch on the corridor."

Every sound the company made seemed to echo through the room. Arca winced with each scrape, cough and clatter. He imagined the guards approaching through the darkened gardens, how they would fall on the intruders without mercy. This was no way for a soldier to fight, and he had no desire to die like a common thief.

He opened his mouth to tell Guhl his misgivings, but the words refused to come. He counted the shadowed members of the company with mounting alarm. They should have numbered eleven, excluding himself, but twelve men moved about the room. Again he tried to speak, but it was as though his jaw was frozen. Guhl, focused on his search for the Queen's treasure, was oblivious to the danger.

You will not find what you want here. A voice cut through the darkness. The soldiers spun, dropping into crouches, blades glinting in the candlelight, scrolls and trinkets abandoned on the tables and shelves.

Show yourself! Guhl snarled.

Light bloomed at the far end of the room. The man held up a shuttered lantern, and the candles the company had lit guttered and died, snuffed out by invisible spirits. Arca saw the shape of the man's robes and his mantle, and the staff he held in his other hand. Although the lantern obscured the details of the man's face, his eyes burned clear, sharp and hard, resting on each of the intruders in turn. When that gaze turned on Arca, he shivered, feeling his fingers loosen their grip on the hilt of his knife. It took an almost physical effort of will to keep from dropping the weapon.

Helleans, the man said. He had seen right through their disguises. *Is one empire not enough?*

I don't want an empire, Guhl said.

The lantern moved to illuminate him more fully. Arca was relieved the man's attention had turned elsewhere. *No, you do not. But, again, you will not find what you are looking for in these rooms.*

Guhl backed against one of the shelves. He held his knife close to his chest, as though the other man might reach out to seize it. *How do you know what we seek? Who are you?*

He appeared from nowhere! Yonn said. *He must be a god – or a dragon!*

Neither, the man replied, in a sardonic tone. *These are my chambers, and you are not welcome. Leave now, or I shall regret the consequences.*

Arca paused and looked across at Cassia. "A strange thing to say," he noted, "and that is why I still remember it."

She hung eagerly upon every word now. Even with a lack of clear description it was plain the man was Malessar himself. How many men could say they had faced down the man who murdered the North? She had no idea how Arca's story might help her locate him – after all, he surely would not still be in Kebria after all these years – but right now that did not matter.

"We did not realise," Arca said. "Not until later. If we had known – even if we *had* known – I think Guhl would still have challenged him. I saw him duck down, and spring forward. Yonn and the others followed him." His sigh caused his shoulders to slump once more. "And so did I. Only a step.

That's all I had time to do. He shouted a word, and swung the lantern high, and we were all blinded. It was like staring at the sun. We cried out in pain and terror. I reached for the wall, so I could turn around and flee, but it was not there and I stumbled to my knees. I felt sand between my fingers. Sand!"

He curled his fingers in the air before his face. "It was quiet. I felt the wind touch the back of my neck and I knew I was not in the palace. I was too scared to move. Scared I might be surrounded by silent enemies, or magical traps. Or by a sheer drop. I could not even bring myself to call out for my companions. I did what I could: I crawled over the ground, blind and helpless, until I found the shelter of a thorny bush. I lay there and prayed to every god I could name."

The deep silence that followed was heavy with shame and embarrassment. Cassia thought no soldier would ever want to admit to such helplessness for fear of being branded a coward. Arca was much braver than he probably felt himself to be.

"I might have slept. I don't know. But at last my eyes recovered and I saw it was not long past dawn. I lay at the edge of a field, not far from the city walls. There was a great haze on the horizon, in the north and the east. Vaile's armies."

For a while he had just sat there, so shaken by the brush with the warlock – who else could it have been but Malessar? – that he could not decide how to proceed. He dared not return to Kebria, in case Malessar had alerted the palace guards, but he was painfully aware that he and the rest of Guhl's company had deserted the legions to carry out this raid. Vaile would be less than sympathetic to their plight.

In the end it was Guhl who decided the matter. He staggered across the fields, his clothes torn and ragged, his face set in grim anger. He too had been cast out of the city by magic, buffeted by winds that ripped the air from his lungs, but rather than lie whimpering in the dark as Arca had done, Guhl had crawled through the night, plain luck and the taste of the air guiding his way. Ceresel had favoured him, this time.

Of the other men of the company, there was no sign at all. Arca never knew what had happened to them.

I will not let this stand. Guhl ground out the words.

There are only two of us now. How can we fight against such magic?

Guhl brooked no argument. *Two can go unseen, where twelve cannot. Even a warlock will be helpless against a knife in the back.*

They took a mule from a farmer who was too slow to realise his danger. Taking it in turns to ride the beast, they reached the gates just before noon. Now their appearance worked in their favour, for they looked so pale, panicked and worn that the guards simply waved them through.

Kebria was in chaos, and Guhl swept through it unerringly, swift as a javelin and with the hunger of a starved hunting-dog. At the palace gates he claimed to be a native guide who had escaped Vaile's ranks to bring news of his formations to the Queen herself. A loyal Kebrian, he told the guards. Honest and true. That they believed him at all was testament to his exhausted condition, for where could these two beggars have come from but the vanguard of the invading legions?

Once inside the palace Guhl and Arca turned on their escorts and rolled them into the shadow of a kindling shed, stealing their tabards and the bright scarves the Kebrians wound about their necks and waists.

They marched through the palace unmolested. The servants and courtiers were far too busy to worry over a pair of guards. Guhl led the way down the long colonnade of the great hall, and Arca kept his gaze lowered rather than acknowledge the activity there. Generals competed to advise the Queen, while her own advisors fought to make their voices heard. It seemed Kebria might surrender without the need for a siege, which only added urgency to Guhl's mission.

When they reached the warlock's rooms, they discovered the reason for the clamour. The shelves were empty, the tables bare. Malessar had left Kebria without warning or reason, just as he had done at Stromondor centuries previously. Again Arca guarded the door, the leather-bound hilt of his knife damp and sticky with sweat, while Guhl prowled the room. He kicked the few remaining items across the floor: a battered tin jug skittered between the shelves, the sound ominously loud in the empty chamber.

The bastard. Damned coward. We might have been rich!

Arca was privately glad Malessar had gone. He held no illusions about his ability to defeat such a man. But he said nothing while Guhl raged. There were other riches to steal before Vaile's legions plundered the city.

A glint of something, in a corner beneath one of the tables. Unwilling to leave the door, Arca pointed it out to Guhl instead. It turned out to be one of the gold-rimmed scroll cases that had once filled the shelves. Perhaps Attis or Breal had dropped it before the warlock banished them, and it had rolled away, out of sight. Guhl tucked the case into his belt.

There was not much left to tell. Arca's tale trailed off, along with her interest, with Guhl's realisation that the majority of the Queen's vast treasure had already been removed from the city – safe from the grasping hands of the Hellean Empire. Guhl and Arca bent their efforts to rejoining the legion without arousing Vaile's suspicions, and their hunt for plunder was suspended. Only after Vaile and the other noble generals had taken their shares were the ordinary soldiers allowed to scavenge what remained. The pickings were slender indeed. There were no sheets of gold, no dragonscale sandals.

"All he gained was that one case," Arca said. He shook his head. "He was bitter ever after. All hells, was he bitter!"

Cassia felt a little disappointed by the tale. She had expected to hear more of the warlock himself, yet he had made only a fleeting appearance, just as he did in so many tales. It seemed there was nothing new to learn of him. He lived behind the scenes of the world, like an insect beneath a rock, scurrying away when exposed to the lights of humanity.

But at least Arca had seen him, however briefly. It proved he existed, that he still lived, as recently as those Kebrian campaigns. And he was dangerous too, Baum was right.

And Baum believes he is in the city now. I can't give up on this. What a tale it would be to see Malessar defeated at last – for Meredith to take revenge for the North! A story that would be told over and over, even by the guilded men of Hellea . . .

Arca looked across at her. "And here, I'll tell you. That case is still in Hellea."

She blinked, her interest reawakened. An artefact! Surely Malessar would want it back? "Does Guhl still have it?"

"No. He's dead." Arca bowed his head in the direction of the old temple to Pyraete, now home to the army of clerks who manned the hiring halls. "Ganx took him in the end. Years back. His creditors took his chattels. They wanted mine too, but I had nothing left by then. May their cocks rot off. I thought he would have stripped it, sold the gold, but the damned fool kept it in one piece. He owed some useless bastard scribe for penning two petitions, and the scribe used it to pay off his own debts to the library."

"The library?"

Arca waved across the square, toward the Emperor's palace. "Over there."

"Would you show me, please, sir?"

He coughed, a rasping noise that was almost a laugh. "Not a chance. I hate the place. Filled with braying donkeys and useless arseholes who love the sound of their own voices. Talking about talking about things. Drives me to drink." He raised his arm to Cassia. "Help me up, girl. The cold's settling in my bones. Ultess will be wondering about us."

The building was anchored at one end of a wide avenue that was almost a market square, looking back toward the walls of the Emperor's palace at the other end. A wide set of steps had been built into the man-made hill the library sat upon. It was lower than the palace buildings, for nothing could be raised in the Temple District that was higher than the Emperor, but for all that the library looked more like a fortress than a seat of knowledge. The estates built by Factors in the North were built in such a fashion, to ward them from outside attacks. Cassia wondered if the effect here was intentional. *Do they seek to keep people out, or to keep the knowledge within?*

The steps were busy and Cassia paused, suddenly uncertain. Even this early in the day men gathered to discuss weighty matters. They ascended in twos and threes, dressed in plain, heavy robes, heads bowed to listen or to speak, looking like a great convocation of priests or pilgrims to the Seat of the World. Cassia had never seen the like. Not a single man amongst them could be described as young.

I would not stand out more if I ran naked up those steps, screaming at the top of my voice.

She sighed and almost turned away, but the stubborn, prideful part of her soul that still wanted to search out a new story, pin down the warlock, and watch Meredith take the North's revenge on him urged her forward. *And I will take my revenge on Hellea's bloody guild as well*, she told herself. Cassia shifted her grip on her staff. She had brought it with her hoping it would make her appear more mature. She pushed her shoulders back before starting towards the steps once more.

She felt as though everybody was watching her, and it was difficult to not look around. She waited for somebody to call out, or put a hand upon her shoulder to prevent her going further. Her muscles tensed to pull away and run, but nothing happened. The stone under her feet was worn in places, bowed where it had seen the passage of so many men. Cassia had not asked how old the library was, but she remembered a tale which mentioned that the ancient kings of Hellea had once lived upon this site, many centuries ago in the Age of Talons. The present Imperial Palace must be a relatively new construction.

Halfway up the steps, her confidence returning once more, she paused to look back. She could see over the palace walls from here, into the formal gardens beyond. Stone figures lined one of the paths – more of Malessar's shieldmen, she decided. On an artificial hill in the centre of the compound, towering over every other building in the Temple District, was the palace. Pristine whitewashed walls, steep roofs supported by slender fluted columns, flags and pennons rippling across the skies – the palace radiated a godlike aura.

For one moment she thought she saw a figure that looked much like Baum further down the great avenue. She frowned and squinted, but the figure was obscured within the crowds thronging the road. *If that was really Baum, why would he follow me?* she wondered. Aware the men passing her on either side were beginning to frown at her, for she had halted in the middle of the steps and was causing an obstruction, she lowered her gaze, muttered an apology, and hurried on.

The gates at the top were sheltered behind four columns that supported an overhanging roof. They were thick, iron-bound wood, coated and stained so dark it was hard to tell the difference between the two materials. Cassia brushed a hand against one of the massive beams for luck as she passed through, on the heels of a knot of earnest, bearded scholars. They veered off to the left into a colonnade as soon as they passed through the long gatehouse, and Cassia was left alone to take in the grandeur of Hellea's famous library.

It was a tremendous sight. The schools and estates of the North were nothing but cattle sheds next to this. The walls of the library enclosed a rectangular yard, paved level with slabs of stone that interlocked in a pattern too complex to comprehend from here on the ground. On Cassia's left, life-sized statues stood atop pillars of differing heights, set into a squared-off horseshoe. Men wandered between the pillars, some small groups in animated discussions. At this distance she thought the stone statues were gods, but she recognised none of them. Further away, more scholars had gathered on plain wooden benches that faced each other. They debated in loud arguments that, overlaid and confused, made no sense at all.

On her right hand, on foundations of white-painted stone that lifted it above the business of the main yard, stood a small temple of the kind she had seen in towns along the river. It was hidden behind thick columns and, unlike the rest of the yard, it was curiously silent and empty.

The covered colonnade surrounded the yard on all four sides. Men rushed along, half-seen between the pillars, with scroll cases or writing boxes held tight underarm. There were doors visible on the far side, leading to what Cassia thought might be the chambers of the library itself.

That's where she would find Malessar's scroll case. It could hardly be anywhere else.

She took a deep breath and began the long walk toward the opposite side of the yard. There was no obvious place to start looking, so she might as well pick a room at random.

Nobody else appeared to have noticed her presence. The men were all engrossed in their own little worlds and esoteric subjects. Her earlier thought bubbled back up to haunt her. *They really* wouldn't *notice me if I ran naked through their precinct!* She raised a hand to muffle the laugh before it escaped and betrayed her.

Cassia walked the entire length of the colonnade twice to discover how the library was set out. Most of the rooms that led from the colonnade were small cells with whitewashed walls and ceilings. There were no windows, but closed lanterns sat above each pair of desks, mirrored glass amplifying and directing the light. Some of the scholars glared up at her presence, while others were engrossed in their work. She stood behind one for several minutes, watching him carve intricate designs into the margins of a single sheet of manuscript. Unrecognisable creatures curled through the borders of twisted colours, licking at the words as though on the verge of devouring them. She was reminded of Rann Almoul's copy of *The Call to the North*, yet these designs flowed with such ease that Almoul's scroll seemed raw and untrained by comparison.

Opposite the main gates were two larger halls. One was a kitchen where a large cookfire burned in a deep alcove along the back wall. The library's boys came in from time to time with small braziers, loaded them with coals from the fire, and then scurried out with them to the reading rooms. Some of the scholars Cassia had seen were little more than skin and bone. She saw the need to keep them warm as they clearly could not look after themselves.

The other hall contained a flight of stone steps, sweeping down into the hill beneath the library. Three scholars sat on stools over to one side, conversing in low tones about this year's grape harvest. On the other side of the room stood a younger man, muscular and attentive, his eyes tracking her tentative steps. He looked as though he could have been a soldier, and when she approached the steps, he moved forward to loom over her.

"You're not allowed down there," he said.

"My master needs the third book." She kept her tone as deep as she could. If anybody saw through her disguise it would be him.

"Tell him to send one of our boys."

Cassia nodded and ducked away before he asked a question she could not answer. If the bulk of Hellea's library was kept below ground, it was effectively out of her reach. She allowed herself a sigh and wandered back into the yard, looking down at the pattern of the slabs under her feet and letting that guide her steps.

When she looked up again she realised she was close to the base of the small temple. One boy knelt nearby, scrubbing industriously at the steps with a brush, but otherwise she was alone. There was no indication which god the temple was sacred to; no inscriptions, no figures, no decorations at all. It was as if somebody had built it as an empty shell. She took the steps cautiously and peered within, and her suspicions were confirmed. The altar block at the far end was plain stone, unmarked and devoid of offerings. This was a temple without a god. For a moment she imagined rows of Malessar's shieldmen standing their silent vigil here, as they had at the shrine on the Western borders of the Empire. The warlock had set himself up as a god, after all. Might this be a monument to his works?

"You look confused, boy," a voice said behind her. She jumped, alarmed by the sudden sound, and turned quickly, gripping her staff tight with both hands.

The speaker was one of the scholars. He was a hard-faced man. Weather and age had drawn lines upon his face, and his mouth wore a thin, emotionless smile. She was put in mind of a hawk, staring down unblinkingly at its prey. His robes emphasised his stern countenance, sleek, grey cloth lined and hemmed with deep emerald, which made him stand out from the other scholars in the yard. Unlike them, he was clean-shaven, his silvered hair cut short and flecked with purer white.

Cassia opened her mouth, but then realised she did not know what to say.

He came up the steps toward her. "This is your first time here."

She had to steel herself not to back away from him. "How do you know that?"

"It would be easy to see, for any *man* who cares to look." The emphasis in his words, combined with that mocking smile, made her flush.

"I'll leave," she said quickly. "Please don't have me thrown out, sir."

The scholar shook his head. "Your secret is safe with me, *boy*. If we punished curiosity then mankind would never learn anything." He lowered himself onto the top step and motioned for her to join him. She did so reluctantly, holding onto her staff and making certain she was beyond his reach. The scholar's smile twitched, but he did not comment on her caution. "You are not from the city."

Cassia did not like this sensation of being examined like a dragon's new toy. "No, sir."

"The North, I think," the scholar said. He waited for the boy scrubbing the steps to move out of earshot. "The accent is plain. And a girl with a storyteller's cap – your father's?"

Could he unravel her entire life just by looking at her? Cassia shifted uncomfortably, avoiding his gaze.

"You would be lucky to merely be thrown out," he told her. "There was a case once of a woman who entered the library, disguised as you are. She went about the scholars and contributed to their debates, and made several important philosophical points. She became a valued member of this community. But when one of her rivals became jealous, he followed her and discovered her secret. The next day he assaulted her in the precinct, over there." He pointed to the benches on the other side of the yard. "He ripped her robes to her waist and uncovered her."

"What happened to her?" Cassia did not want to ask the question.

"They wanted to weigh her down with carved tablets from the depths of the library and drown her in the Castaria," the scholar said. The slight smile had vanished completely. "Drown her with knowledge. She appealed to Casta and Saihri. During the night, there was a storm, and the temple cell where she was being held flooded and the stone walls burst out. Casta claimed her for her own." He looked across at her again. "I would not rely on the gods to save you."

"Then what do you want from me?" Cassia felt the muscles of her thighs tense in preparation for a burst of speed. If she was lucky, she could be at the bottom of these steps and away across the yard before anybody responded to a shout from the scholar. She hadn't felt this threatened since that last night in Keskor.

He laughed softly. "What do I want? Nothing, for myself, other than to satisfy my curiosity. The question is, why would you risk your life like this?"

She thought for a long moment, wondering what she should tell him. She doubted anyone would believe she was on a quest to find a centuries-old warlock to overturn his curse. This did not seem to be the place for such a revelation. "Stories," she said at last.

The scholar nodded. "Not as strange an idea as it might first appear," he said. "What would you do with these stories?"

"Tell them," she said bluntly. The scholar seemed to appreciate her honesty so far. "Not here, though. Not in Hellea."

He laughed again, but this time with genuine humour. "I can see why. Where, then?"

"I would go back to the North," she said, warming to her new theme. "I could build my reputation there."

"Then you have already made a gain on the day."

Cassia took a breath to embolden herself. "I did not realise, sir, how much of the library is underground. I don't want to debate with the others. I just want to read and learn."

The scholar stared at her, his fleeting smile gone again. That penetrating gaze remained, however, and she felt pinned to the steps of the empty temple. "If you are serious, then we *may* make a deal. I find myself in need of a boy – bright, trustworthy and obedient, mind you – to assist me in the archives for the next few days. The help the library hires out varies quite appallingly in quality. Irritating, fickle children. Will you do exactly as you are told, without question or delay?"

"Yes, sir," Cassia said without hesitation.

The weight of the scholar's stare was disconcerting. "Then I will meet you here tomorrow, boy, when the Saihran acolytes ring their prayer-bells."

He stood abruptly and began to descend to the yard. Cassia

picked up her staff and followed. "Sir, may I ask a question?"

"Already?" He did not pause.

"What is that place? Is it really a temple?"

"It is sacred to the god of knowledge," the scholar said, over his shoulder.

"So why is it empty?"

At last he looked back and the skin around his eyes creased in a knowing smile. "It should be clear, *boy*. There is no god of knowledge but man."

Chapter Twelve

The rain was a penetrating drizzle borne on a sharp wind from the north-west. Cassia shivered beneath the white-washed portico and drew her cloak as close as she could around herself. The weather had forced all but one or two of the philosophers from the library's yard and she felt self-conscious again. Any moment now, somebody would come to ask what she wanted or who she waited for, and her disguise would not stand up to the scrutiny.

She told Baum she had found work at the library in order to see if Malessar was there. To her surprise he approved of her idea and, when she described her new employer, Baum clapped his hands. "A man of authority and seniority," he said. "Stay with him. If Malessar is inside the library, then he will lead you to him."

"How long have you waited there?" the scholar called from the bottom of the steps. She had not noticed his approach, and she hastened down the temple steps in case he decided she was hopelessly lazy.

"Only a few moments, sir," she said. It was almost the truth: the bells at Saihra's temple had rung several minutes ago, just as she reached the top of the flight of steps that led to the library. Since then she had struggled to quell her fears that the scholar had already grown impatient and gone on without her.

The scholar looked her up and down as though he had not seen her before. "You will pass, I think. But speak only when directly addressed, and keep your eyes down. Once we are in the lower archives, you will need to cover your mouth, and that will make your disguise even more effective."

He strode toward the rear of the yard and Cassia fell in a few steps behind him. "Sir, what should I call you?"

"Karak will suffice for now," he said. "And you?"

"Cassia, sir. What are you looking for in the library?"

"Two questions already, and the day has only just begun," Karak observed. "You seem intent on making the best of our bargain."

His voice was dry, but Cassia ducked her head so he could not see the fresh bloom of red on her cheeks. It would not do to aggravate the scholar, she told herself furiously.

This time they were waved over to the stairs without any comment. If anything Karak was given more deference than the library's other scholars, and Cassia's presence was not commented on at all. Karak had to bend low to squeeze through the entrance to the underground archives, and even Cassia had to twist her body to fit through the gap. The space below, at the bottom of the short, steep flight of steps, was a small squared antechamber built between a set of rough-hewn pillars. Wooden doors were set into two of the four walls; after a moment Cassia found her bearings and realised the archives must run beneath the buildings above ground, forming a great loop.

Karak had collected a small lamp from the table at the bottom of the steps, along with a handful of spare wicks. He passed them to her without comment and waited as she fumbled to settle the load so she could hold the lamp aloft without dropping everything else. Then he pushed one of the doors open and disappeared into the dark beyond. Cassia hurried to follow, less certain of her step. The lamp illuminated a few feet, enough to show Karak's back and the edges of the shelves to either side, but nothing more than that.

This space was a catacomb, like the burial chambers of the nameless family that she and her father had once sheltered in, stranded on the high moors in a sudden storm a few years ago. At the time she had been grateful to stumble across the broken-in barrow entrance, never thought to question why it was there. Now she knew a little better. The place could have been one of the outlying reaches of the old Northern kingdoms. Perhaps that family, whoever they had been, were leaders of Gethista, or another town like it. Gone now, lost to history, their goods stolen long ago by robbers, or rusted and decayed to nothing.

Like the barrow, this passage was tight and claustrophobic, with deep alcoves and shelves on both sides. Instead of caskets, these held dozens of cylindrical scroll cases, of different widths and thicknesses, their ends strengthened with leather or rings of iron, dulled silver and other metals. On the lower shelves were flat wooden boxes with handles on each side, similar to the box in which Rann Almoul kept his copy of *The Call to the North*. For a moment Cassia's imagination burned with the thought of what wondrous stories she might find in those boxes, but then she looked up at the rows of scroll cases, and remembered what it was she wanted to find.

A single case, which once belonged to Malessar the Warlock. One single case amongst thousands. Perhaps even more than that. It would take weeks, if not months . . . if the warlock had not taken it already.

Side passages appeared from the dark, tilted down into the depths of the hill and lined with yet more shelves. Her heart sank even further, and she struggled not to sigh at the sheer scale of the task she had set herself.

Cassia hurried to keep up with Karak, though the scholar

appeared to be so certain of his footing that he did not need the light. She wondered how well he knew this labyrinth of tunnels; whether he might even know where Guhl's purloined case was stored. But how to broach that sort of question without arousing his suspicions?

Karak finally halted, peering up at the top shelves. "Here we are." He motioned her to raise the lamp higher. "Yes. This was the place, I think."

"What are you looking for, sir?"

"Old stories," Karak said with a wry smile. Cassia bit her lip, glad the lamp cast her face in shadows. "I apologise. But in all seriousness, you could say that *is* what I am looking for. The things written by past generations of scholars. A few small paragraphs in particular that will resolve one area of difficulty in my research." He reached up to the dark shapes on the top shelf. "If I can ever find them."

He lapsed into silence. All Cassia could hear was the scraping of the cases on the shelf as he rummaged through them. She kept the lantern high, moving it as he directed so he could examine inscriptions and carved rims. Only once did he unseal a case to unroll the flimsy piece of parchment inside, twisting forward to catch the light. The decorations on the borders were faded with time, the script almost illegible. Karak's lips moved as he read, his brow creased into dark lines. Then he resealed the case, dismissing it with a shrug.

They moved along the archive to another set of shelves. Karak repeated the exercise, rifling through the lower shelves, sending up dust that hung in the air and caught in Cassia's throat. Other than the sound of their own breathing, the scrape of leather against the shelves, and the occasional muttered echo from far down the passage, there was little else to hear. The space closed up around her, shrinking the world to what could be illuminated by the lantern. Cassia began to feel that the world outside the library might as well not exist.

Her throat tickled, and the corners of her eyes itched, but

she dared not rub them for fear of disrupting Karak's concentration. The lantern was heavy too, the muscles in her arms ached, and the effort of keeping it aloft started a quiver that affected how the shadows fell. She shifted her grip as carefully as she could, adjusting her stance and flexing her free hand to bring her fingers back to life, but nothing worked well for very long.

"Hold the light still, please," Karak said at last. He looked up from beneath lowered brows, his eyes alarmingly pin-bright. "This script is difficult enough to read as it is."

"Yes, sir," Cassia replied. She changed position again, using one arm to support the other. This was not what she had expected to be doing. Perhaps this whole adventure was a waste of time and energy. If she hadn't listened to Arca's far-fetched yarn, she might even have stumbled across the warlock's townhouse by now!

Her mind drifted, rising from the depths of the city's archive to float over the temple district. She imagined that the clouds had passed over, and the sun now warmed the stones of the streets and markets. Meredith would be stalking through the crowds, men and women parting before him like waves against a steadfast rock. Cassia still did not know how he and Baum spent their days, or how they had organised their own search for Malessar, so her fantasy fell short quickly, reverting to the same image over and over again. After a while Meredith's face gained a smile and he reached out a hand to her, just as he had done in the tavern's yard . . .

"Wake up, boy."

It was not Meredith's hand that shook her arm. She jerked upright and managed to catch the lantern just before it fell from her fingers to smash upon the floor.

Karak took the lantern from her firmly, and set it down on the edge of the nearest shelf, as far from the dust-covered scroll cases as possible. "That would have been interesting," he said. "In any case, it disproves one hypothesis."

She was still too dozy to understand what he meant, and her confusion must have shown in her eyes, as the corner of Karak's mouth quirked upward. "Every single boy I have employed so far falls asleep on the floor halfway through the day. A small number of men here have speculated on whether the same would happen to a girl."

Cassia checked over her shoulder in alarm, but she saw nothing at the edge of the lantern's dim light. Out there in the dark, however . . . she shuddered and prayed nobody was near enough to have heard.

The scholar had already turned back to attend to the lantern. The light flickered and then brightened, revealing more of the tight corridor; Cassia could have believed that it went onwards into the dark forever, if she had not known that this was built into the base of the hill. But what if there were archives even further down, beneath these ones? She chased the thought away quickly.

"The air does not move well down here," Karak said. "That affects some more than others. What I need is not here. We must move on."

He passed the lantern back to her. Cassia had enough time to notice that it was indeed burning brighter and hotter before she had to hurry after him. She didn't want to be left alone here.

"Sir – sir, what is written on these?"

Karak paused so abruptly she almost thumped him with the lamp. "These ones here? Who knows? Most of these have not seen daylight for hundreds of years. There was a filing system, once, but it was eaten by mice." There was a note of disgust in his voice. "That was a time when even the librarians of the Castaria did not value the knowledge they held."

He shook his head, lost in his own thoughts. "Since you are somewhat closer to the ground than I am, boy, perhaps I can put your enquiring mind to good use." With a fingertip he drew a glyph in the grime that lined the nearest shelf. To

Cassia's eye it looked like a pair of inverted V shapes, one stepped in front of the other. Those shapes were intersected by a sharp horizontal arrow. "If you see this mark upon any of the cases, shout out immediately. It will mean we are close to what we seek."

It was dull, fruitless work, but it kept her busy for long enough that she did not recognise until deep into that evening why he had set her that task. It meant that Karak could work undisturbed by questions. That realisation, in the middle of her practice against Meredith, caused her to lose both her concentration and her footing as the Heir to the North effortlessly cut beneath her guard. The pain of the landing served to emphasise her own bitter thoughts. *I'm a fool. A fool, useless, and out of my depth.*

"Your thoughts are elsewhere," Meredith said as he reached down to help her to her feet.

"Of course they are," she snapped, "or else I'd have put you on the ground already."

One of the subtle smiles Meredith was increasingly fond of began to form upon his lips. It still looked unnatural, as though an outcrop of rock had learned to express itself, but it was enough to take Cassia's thoughts from her chores at the library. She had found herself wanting to see that smile more and more, and it had even made its way into her dreams. Something else that discomfited her as much as she desired it.

"Then put me there," Meredith said. "If you can."

He was making fun of her! *I'll teach him . . .*

One rolling lunge brought her staff back to hand and she came up swinging.

On the third day she finally plucked up the courage to ask the one of the questions at the forefront of her mind. "What did you mean, sir, that there is no god of knowledge?"

Karak did not answer for a moment. Instead he paced further down the passage and held the lantern out around the corner, staring intently down the dimly-lit archives. As the light retreated and darkness closed in around her, Cassia held onto the nearest shelf. It was reassuringly solid, even if the wood was cold.

The scholar seemed satisfied with whatever it was he looked for. He came back and hooked the lantern onto a peg that jutted out from the uppermost shelf. "The gods are not rational beings," he said, lowering his voice to confidential tones. "In fact, they are exactly the opposite. They are primal and emotional. There are gods of anger, of joy, of love, and desire. Gods of war, of luck, and of fate. They are all of the heart, not of the head."

That did not sound quite right to Cassia. "But Periandir is a patron of great harvests, and Meteon weighs the waters of the river."

"In those aspects, yes," Karak agreed. "But Periandir is, at his deepest roots, little more than a totem of fertility. These gods are earthed, grown in the fields of mankind."

She struggled with that concept while he opened another case and passed it to her so he could examine the contents. "So you say they are not real?"

The scholar's brows peaked in clear surprise. "Ha! Be careful where you ask that question, boy. Even here, men are superstitious and live in the grip of the gods. No, I do not *deny* them. I am a rational man, not a stupid one. The gods play with us all, and more fool us if we try to get involved. My own theory is that they have been afflicted with base human emotions even as they have affected us. Not a theory that makes me popular with priests of any temple or discipline, by the way. You came from the North – you should know as well as anybody how close to our own world the gods dwell."

She spent some time mulling over his words. "But, sir, that still does not explain why there is no god of knowledge."

There was a flicker of annoyance in Karak's eyes, but it disappeared as quickly as it took for him to blink. He sighed and hefted a case in one hand. "No, it does not. What do you think the answer is, boy?"

How am I supposed to be able to even guess at such an answer? She shook her head in apology and Karak returned his attention to the scroll.

"Well, if you *could* answer that question," he said, "you would accomplish more than all the learned scholars in this institution together have done in their entire lives. The real answer, I'm sure, is that nobody knows."

"The *gods* should know." By now Cassia had become irked by Karak's lofty attitude and the words slipped out before she could stop them. "Why hasn't anybody asked them?"

Karak did not take offence; in fact he appeared amused by the thought. "I dare say somebody has. What answer they received, however – if they even got an answer at all . . ." He lowered his voice still further, even though it was evident nobody else was near enough to hear them. Cassia had to move in close to hear him clearly. "The truth of the matter, I suspect, is that knowledge requires questions. Tests. Proof and disproof. There is no god I can think of who would be happy to see his worshippers questioning the tenets of their faith, questioning that god's very existence. That, I think, is why there is no god of knowledge but man himself."

"But *you* know a lot about the gods," Cassia said.

"Enough to know that they are vengeful and unforgiving, Cassia. Leave them be while they cannot hear you."

It was impossible to measure the passage of time other than by the frequency with which she had to refill and relight the lantern, and she quickly discovered that time warped cruelly here in the cellars of the library. Several times she convinced herself that the day was ending and she should hurry back to the Old Soak before the library's gates were closed, only to find that the sun still sat high above the horizon, autumnal light slanting down across the city. But she had always prided herself on being a quick learner, and by the fifth morning she was certain she knew how much oil, and how many wicks, she would need for the day.

Even the library's custodians were becoming used to her presence and she breathed much more easily when she queued with Karak to descend into the archives each day. It seemed strange there were not more scholars rooting through the darkened shelves. Even though errand boys disappeared down the steps before her, she never encountered them in the tunnels. There, apart from faint voices in the stale air, she was alone inside a flickering globe of light with Karak.

He was abrupt and obtuse, and fond of his own private jokes, but perhaps because they shared the biggest joke of all – that Cassia was no errand *boy* – she found herself more comfortable around him than she was with Baum. And Karak seemed to enjoy her presence, on more than one occasion he had slipped and used her real name, although thankfully never in the presence of the library's elders or the boys who skittered through the colonnades like startled rats.

There was a weight tugging at her thoughts, however. The days were passing, each faster than the last, and Baum was ever more certain the warlock would emerge from his hiding-place to escape to the warmer lands of Galliarca and Stromondor. But Cassia had still come no closer to finding either Guhl's scroll case or the warlock himself. Not an hour went by that she did not wonder whether Arca had told the truth. Perhaps he misremembered. Perhaps it had happened to someone else. That was quite likely, some men adopted common tales as their own, changing details to suit their own circumstances, though they were never told as anything other than pale copies in her view.

Perhaps he just lied.

There were thousands of documents in this archive, all sealed against the elements inside cases that had blackened with age. She couldn't even tell how far beneath this hill the tunnels reached, but she was certain she hadn't seen half of them yet.

"Have you run out of questions?" Karak asked, shocking her out of her thoughts. "I will be disappointed if that is the case."

She toyed with the idea of asking him outright about Malessar's scroll case. He knew so much about the library, after all, that why wouldn't he know where to find it? But discretion won the day. "Would you like me to ask more questions?"

That drew a smile from him. "No, for my part. I feel I must have struck the most uneven bargain known to man. Never have I given so many answers for so little payment!" His smile took the sting from his words. "But the company is pleasant. Perhaps you might grace these mean passages with a tale or two?"

Cassia blinked in surprise. It was the last thing she had expected him to ask. Her mind froze – what story would a scholar want to hear?

Karak looked down at her. "You've come from the North," he reminded her. Not a day went by that he did not comment on her origins, a trait that was starting to bother her a little. It made her think of Pyraete, and of Meredith, and the way that time was running out in their search for the warlock. "What about the *Call to the North*? Do you know that?"

It seemed odd that a scholar from the south would want to hear the Call, but she could feel the first lines shuffling into place, ready to be said, at the mention of the title. "Some storyteller I would be if I didn't know it," she said, more boldly than she truly felt. Even if her father had counted it amongst his most popular tales, Cassia would have been hard pressed to keep it word-perfect all the way through. The Emperor's Factors had tried for years to suppress the telling of the *Call*, and Cassia had only ever seen the whole text once, in Rann Almoul's study. Norrow always improvised the parts his wine-soaked memory could no longer recall, and there were far too many of those. If this performance was not to be a disaster she would have to think damned hard and fast.

Karak raised his brow in expectation, his head cocked to one side – like a hawk waiting for its prey to bolt. "Amaze me, then," he said.

They were drawing an audience now, Cassia had noted in the fleeting seconds between her bouts. The Old Soak's pot-boy, wide-eyed and limp as autumn's dying flowers, stood at the corner of the stables, afraid to come any closer. The buildings that surrounded the inn had windows overlooking the yard, and these were packed tight, heads and shoulders leaning out precariously to watch the sparring. There were mutters and catcalls, and even wagers shouted between the tenements. They needled their way in, distracting Cassia's attention from what she *ought* to be thinking about, and her cheeks burned with a heat that wasn't entirely due to her exertions.

She spun her staff up, jabbed out as she side-stepped past Meredith's attack. He was so close his hair whipped across her face, and she breathed in his scent.

Now all ye Northmen, will ye never be free?
Shake off your shackles and shout in the air!

Now she went to ground, having learned a fight could be won from the floor as well as on two feet. She used her staff to propel herself back to her feet, beyond Meredith's reach, ducking away immediately. The man was so hellishly fast that he had to have been deliberately slowing himself when he first started teaching her.

Like bright rivers that break from the banks that they run!
Let –

Meredith's staff tapped her shin, enough to unbalance her and send her back down to the dirt. She skinned the knuckles of her left hand, but she didn't have time to hiss a curse. It was her own fault for not giving this bout her full attention. The verses of the *Call* kept running through her head and, no matter what she did, she could not drive them out.

A few cheers greeted her as she drew herself up again. Meredith had stepped back, his own staff held nonchalantly across his shoulders. The position forced the muscles of his upper body into shapes that distracted her yet further. Cassia directed her gaze down to his feet instead. *Watch them, not him. See how he balances, see him poised to spring . . .*

He flowed into motion, one end of his staff cutting through the air with a sharp whistle, and she was already moving. She spun into his attack, arms tight against her body, and struck out at the last moment. To her shock her movement was stopped dead by something that should not have been there. Meredith, clamping her firmly into the crook of his arm to stop her falling over.

She could not find the breath to protest. All she could do was to stare up at him, losing herself in those piercing brown eyes. She felt herself leaning back into his arm, yearning forwards at the same time . . .

"What did you do there?" Meredith said. It took her a moment to realise that, by the tone of his voice, he'd had to repeat the question at least once already.

"I . . . I wanted to get closer," she managed. It was no lie.

"You should not have beaten that form." Meredith stared down at her with his brow creased, his eyes wide with surprise. "Nobody should ever beat that form. How did you do that?"

He seemed in no hurry to let her go, but that was alright. Every line of his face, every strand of hair that hung down and brushed her cheeks, were imprinted indelibly upon her mind like the scars of a war. "I don't know."

She willed Meredith to lower his head further, to bring his

lips closer to her own. *A prince will kiss me!* Surely such a kiss would set her nerves afire.

But Meredith paused, seemingly frozen in position for a long moment before straightening up again and gently – but quite firmly – pulling Cassia upright. When he released her arm she felt unsteady, as though she had been in the sun too long.

The innkeeper stood in the doorway, regarding them with a faint frown. "I never saw a girl fight like that before," he said. "In fact I don't think anybody ever saw that before. What next – give her a sword?"

With her emotions so unsettled, Cassia could not hold her tongue. "Why not?"

Ultess shook his head. "That's just not right. Not here."

He disappeared back into the tavern, wiping his hands against his hips to clean them. Cassia shifted from foot to foot, her body boiling with unexpended energy. She looked across expectantly at Meredith, but the Heir to the North had reached for his shirt, his unspoken signal that the day's training had finished.

"But we still have time for more," she pointed out. "The light is still good, and I'm not that tired . . ."

Meredith smoothed down his sleeves, giving more attention to the dirt than to her. "No, but that is all for today. I have business in the city tonight."

That caught her interest. "Business? Have you found . . . *him*? Let me come with you, Meredith!"

"No. I have not seen him, but Baum believes he is still here, and this work may be dangerous. Baum will not give you leave to join us tonight."

"How am I supposed to be able to make this history, if you don't allow me to witness it?" The energy she felt was fast turning into frustration, caught like a hunting dog in a kennel, with nowhere to go. She had been in Hellea long enough to be able to judge the passing of days through the bells and prayers of the temples and the sudden surges of traffic through the squares and precincts, yet she had still seen only a small part of the city. Between the Old Soak and the library. And back again. *It's not fair. I'm a part of this venture as much as either of them!*

"There are no living storytellers now who have borne witness to the tales they tell," Meredith said, in a tone so matter-of-fact Cassia could not find a reply. After he had gone she dug the end of her staff repeatedly into the ground, sending small stones skittering across the yard until Ultess came to the doorway again to glare at her. She sighed and retired to the bench she had appropriated as her own.

It was not fair, but she told herself she had work of her own to do. Her first full recital of the *Call to the North* had not been the success she hoped for. Karak had not laughed, but he might as well have done. He held up one hand to halt her even before she reached the fourth stanza, with a list of corrections so comprehensive she was glad that the light helped to hide her shame. Just as her defensive stances before Meredith had taken her in hand, her technique was apparently quite awful. *Old mistakes, magnified ten-fold*, was what Karak had actually said. *Not your fault.* But she felt as though it was.

Old Arca was sprawled across a bench beneath the window, comatose, so still that he might be dead. At least if he had been awake she could have practised her new phrases upon him, but for now she would have to sit alone and mutter under her breath. Just like her father, penniless in a corner of some tavern. The irony was too painful to consider.

"That was better. Your diction was more fluid, and the rhymes you used were not so clumsy. You thought about those before-hand, yes?"

Cassia nodded, pleased even though the comments were faint praise at best. Although what did a scholar from overseas know of the old stories of the North and how best to tell them? That question had haunted the edges of her thoughts all night, but she had forced herself to concentrate on the more practical matters of choosing the right words and creating a tale Karak would not instantly dismiss as woefully childish.

As the sky lightened and the background murmur of the city rose again, she had come to another conclusion. Perhaps her father was not as skilled a storyteller as he believed himself to be. Some of the lines Karak had called risible came straight from her father's version, rather than from the generally accepted recital of the ancient manuscript that circulated across the North.

Clumsy. Unnecessary. She wondered what the merchants on the road outside Elbithrar must have really thought of the tales she told at their fireside night after night. Little wonder Baum had not let her try her skill in the town's square. That would have proved embarrassing. And Hellea itself? She worked to hold back a sigh, hoping Karak would not notice.

Even if I am better than my father, that's nothing to boast about.

Karak was saying something about the need for a martial beat. Cassia dragged herself away from her thoughts to listen again. One thing she had learned quickly was that the scholar did not like to repeat himself.

As he talked he was still methodically searching the shelves, one by one, opening each and every case and leaving her to follow him with the lantern. "The emotion is there. The passion, the will, the drive to entertain. That much, at least, has not been lost. But I thought the North was the fount of form and technique. It seems I was in error. Even the Stromondorian river songs have more to recommend them. The Southern lands have developed a passion of their own for rhythms and rhymes."

"It's the Emperor's fault," Cassia decided sourly.

"Hardly," Karak said before appearing to reconsider. "There

may be something to that, now I think upon it. There is a fashion for music in Hellea, and for dancing, but I have not seen many storytellers on any of my last visits to the city. Your trade has become heavily regulated within the city walls, has it not? Euandros made those decrees – I remember he detested the effects of scandalous gossip. I'll wager his son inherited that along with the throne."

"Euandros created the guild," Cassia said, remembering what she had been told after dodging Marko on that first, failed attempt to make her own way in the city.

Karak acknowledged the point with a sharp flick of the case he held. "And a guild brings rules, closed minds, and stagnation. Something you will have felt even as far away as your little northern towns, in time."

She wasn't so sure about that. Even under the watchful eyes of the Factors, her father had never felt himself restricted in the stories he could tell. The *Call to the North* was the obvious exception of course, but that had still been passed from mouth to ear: a kind of whispered defiance.

"Sir, where *do* you come from?" she asked. A part of her was surprised she had not asked the question before. Another, set slightly deeper within her mind, noted that she should have been able to identify his home from his accent and the manner of his dress. "Does your land have great storytellers?"

Karak's eyes were hooded by the shadows thrown by the lantern. Cassia, discomfited by his attention, pulled her legs more tightly beneath her. "Where have I come from? A small town on the banks of a wide river, set against the sea, under golden sunset skies. You might know of it."

She recognised the description immediately. So many stories made use of it, and Norrow had never been above decorating his tales with stock phrases. "Galliarca! Really?"

"Why not? Every man must come from somewhere."

If Hellea had seemed grand at first, how much more overwhelming must Galliarca be? A land so far away she had little chance of ever seeing it. Here, she had seen illuminations and border illustrations in some of the scrolls, and they confirmed her visions of grand whitewashed houses and bustling, colourful squares. The world was a place of wonder and surprise, and she knew she had done the right thing in leaving Keskor.

She sighed. "If I had come from there, I would never have left."

"If you had come from there, you might well have envied the North for its vitality, fertility, and the strength of its convictions," Karak said. "The Northern lands have always been so much closer to their gods than the great cities of the south. There is also the small matter of the never-ending war to keep the Hordes at bay, and that's something you will never have to worry about in Hellea. There are other things too. No place is perfect."

"But, sir, how do you know so much about our stories?" It felt odd to be taught the forms of storytelling, especially Hellean forms, by a Galliarcan scholar.

Karak waggled the scroll case in her direction. "Knowledge and learning, *boy*. Mind your work."

Cassia lowered her head and focused on the task of readying a fresh wick. Knowledge and learning. Perhaps Karak could be a god of knowledge, and that thought made her smile.

"Wait please," Karak said as Cassia jogged the last few steps to the square beneath the library. The last supplicants were leaving their temples, the stalls that depended upon them had already closed for the day. It was a cold evening, with a breeze sharp enough to be uncomfortable. Cassia felt the chill working through the layers of her clothes, and she did not want to wait around too long. The hearth at the Old Soak was calling her.

Karak took his time in descending. He looked deep in thought, his gaze sweeping across the square as if seeing it for the first time, yet he also seemed tired and jaded. Cassia waited as patiently as she could.

"I would like to thank you for your help," Karak said. "Your presence has enlivened the tedium of these last days. It is rare I employ assistants; all too frequently they are dull, unimaginative boys, looking only for ways to take advantage of the situation."

She didn't know what to make of that, but his meaning struck her suddenly and she gasped. "You're leaving?"

He reached for her hand and she felt the weight of a small purse pressed into it. A decent weight too, more than Norrow ever managed to carry from town to town. But this was it; she was being paid off. As much as she had wished the length of the days away, she had not thought the end of her employment would come so soon.

"You have made me feel welcome, but this is not my home," Karak said in formal tones. He nodded back to the library. "I cannot recommend you repeat your incursions there without my company, Cassia. You *will* be uncovered and if I cannot be there to dig you out of trouble . . ."

He left the sentence unfinished, but he did not let go of her hand until she nodded her understanding. "I wish you luck in your endeavours. I hope that, if you return to the North, your talents are recognised for what they are."

"Thank you, sir," Cassia said quietly, unable to meet his eyes. "May the gods favour your voyage."

Karak's smile was unexpected and unforced. "I would rather they stayed well away from me, but I appreciate the thought. Now, I have work to oversee before it gets too dark. My ship's master does not want to miss the morning tides."

She watched him cross the square, moving through the thinning crowds with long, purposeful strides. She had become used to the new routine, and for some reason this departure hurt her more than her father's flight had done. Karak might be older than him, but he had helped her like a father should have done. Like Norrow had never done. And she had felt comfortable around him in a way she did not with Baum and Meredith.

Of course that was something altogether different. There was a contract between them; they had common cause against Malessar. Her relationship with Meredith was developing much faster than that of a student and teacher, and the thought of it caused her heart to thump. As she walked back through the streets to the Old Soak, she allowed the daydreams to rise again. Visions of Meredith, triumphant over the warlock's cowering form, his blade slick with blood. He turned and beckoned her, his palm open, and she reached out to accept his hand. He pulled her towards him . . .

The fact that Meredith had invited her to join him in his morning exercises to hone her expertise in the forms only served to feed her fantasies. Meredith still took to the yard bare-chested, the keen edge of his blade glinting in the fresh light of dawn. The sight took her back to Rann Almoul's house and the very first time she had watched him. She struggled to follow most of the time. Her staff was a poorly-weighted substitute, and she was too self-conscious to truly give in to the movements the same way that he did. But her mind's eye gave her images of them flowing through the forms together, and she poured as much effort into this chapter of her training as she had into learning the more basic skills. Soon, she thought, she might be allowed her own blade.

She could see the meaning of Meredith's forms now; the way each movement flowed seamlessly into the next. With the jarring aggressive edge taken off the exercises, she had come to appreciate how her own skills had improved, even in a short period. By moving in one direction, her staff leading in another, she might pull an opponent off-balance. Another set of movements could take her beneath a swordsman's swing, close enough to knock his weapon away. If she went back to Keskor now and challenged the likes of Hetch Almoul, she could beat him every single time.

Cassia paused at the end of a narrow street to allow two boys to push a cart heaped with rags past her. They bickered with each other as they wheeled it around the corner.

But what now? She had not found either the warlock or his fabled scroll case. She doubted it really existed. Arca must have been feeding her a story and, like a fool, she had been all too ready to believe it. Without Karak's authority she had no access to the library, and going back in alone would be too dangerous. So what was left that she could do?

There was nothing, she decided, resuming her journey. She had to rely on Baum to locate Malessar and pray that the old soldier still included her in his plans. She was sure she could find *some* way to be of use, even if it was just keeping watch on one particular house, or a tavern, or waiting at the docks to see who was taking ship that day.

He might allow her to go with Meredith. Her mind rose to the challenge and showed them sharing a quiet corner of a balcony, notionally watching for movement in the streets below. Even crouched by her side he dwarfed her, but the warmth of the autumn sun still reached her face.

That fantasy sustained her all the way back to the Old Soak and into the yard behind the tavern. It took her a moment to realise Meredith was not in his usual place beside the stables, waiting for her to return. She scuffed the ground with one foot and reached back for her staff. Her breathing deepened and steadied, and she settled into an approximation of the stance Meredith always began with. It felt peculiar to be here alone, without the weight of his presence by her side.

She saw the hearth-boy peering out at her from the empty stables, but she ignored him as she started into a slow circular defence, imagining her staff was a sword as brilliant as Meredith's. These forms were very simple. She had learned them simply by reacting correctly to Meredith's own movements. But today was harder, and not for any reason she could think of. Her concentration wavered as her mind tried to focus on something else, something just beyond her comprehension. It was like listening to the rhythms of her father's stories when he was on the cusp of inebriation.

After a few minutes she became aware that somebody else was watching her. Ultess stood in the doorway, staring at her with a vaguely surprised expression. "Is something wrong?" she asked, breaking off in mid-step to face him.

Ultess rubbed his chin. "Could be," he said. "I thought you were all on the boat, away down the eastern Castaria."

"What?" The staff became a leaden weight in her hands. She must have misheard. Or Ultess was mistaken. "On a *boat*?"

"Didn't the young lord find you?" The large man's face, lined with age, wrinkled further as his frown deepened. "Obviously not. You'll need to hurry, girl, or you'll be left behind."

For one moment her feet remained rooted to the ground, and then she raced into the back room of the tavern after him.

"What do you mean? They've *gone*?"

"That's what I said."

She felt the panic rising in her gullet, pressing hard against the back of her head. Even her father's cowardly departure had not felt so terrible. "But . . . why?"

Ultess paused, a rough chunk of bread poised over the bowl before him. "You think Baum ever told me anything? Great gods, child, he goes where he wills, and he does what he wants. Not my place to question him." He sighed. "He said the warlock was done with the city. He was going to the coast. That means one of the grain barges, down on the far quays. You might be lucky . . ."

The far quays . . . She skipped around the edge of a bench that was in her way, and bounded up the stairs. Her pack – the one meagre bundle of clothes and small charms she still possessed – was gone, along with the saddle and riding tack. Her patched-up storyteller's cloak remained, hanging forlornly from a nail. She snatched it up, feeling the weight of the stone charm hidden in the lining.

Her breath caught as she burst through the door into the room Baum and Meredith had shared, a door which had always been closed to her. Baum had kept it locked when he was not in there, and she never dared to intrude on his privacy. Even if she knew for certain Meredith was in there alone, she had never knocked on the door.

The room was bare. All their packs, the weapons and Meredith's armour, the canvas shelters rolled into tight bundles behind the saddles . . . all gone. Her breathing sounded loud in the empty space.

He might still be there.

She took the stairs at a run, momentum carrying her forward before she could fall, and swung through the main room of the tavern. Arca was gone too, and she called a farewell to Ultess over her shoulder, not waiting for the reply.

Luckily the streets were quieter now. She still caught herself on the sides of barrows and the corners of tenements, squeezing through tight spaces and small groups of people. By the time she reached the temple squares her robe was torn in several places. She regretted spending so much time in the cramped confines of the library, as her tendons howled with pain and her throat burned with the effort of running. The daily sessions in the yard had never prepared her for this.

She forced herself to pause for a moment to take her bearings, remembering the shrines she had passed on the day she arrived in Hellea. The spires were visible over the temple roofs. She only needed to work out which was which. The far quays lay on the eastern side of the city, which meant she needed to be on the *other* side of those spires . . .

A hand fell upon her shoulder, almost knocking her to the ground. She twisted around, wincing as the grip tightened, and realised she had to crane her neck to see the man who had seized her. A large man, his face blotched and livered, his cloak tattered and patched. A storyteller's cloak, she realised, her memory tolling an urgent alarm.

"I think we have unfinished business, my young storytelling friend," Marko said. His voice was thick with drink. She tried to pull away, but he was far too strong.

"You owe the guild their dues," Marko said. "Shall we see what you have?"

She kicked at his shins. Marko simply pushed her back until she could not reach him.

"Let me go!" she shouted.

The man's eyes narrowed, focussing on her more intently. For a moment Cassia could not think what she had done. Then cold reason pushed past the anger and panic. Back in the taverns she had deliberately lowered her voice, in keeping with the rest of her disguise, but Marko had heard something different now. A higher-pitched cry.

He grabbed at her breast with his free hand, causing her to cry out again, and now his smile turned thin and hungry. "Oh, *here's* a tale! Cress! Cress – come see this!"

She spat into his face, thick spittle sprayed his cheek and the corner of his eye. Marko pulled one hand back, and with a bright clap of pain he sent her reeling to the ground. Her shoulder jarred on the flagstones, and she heard her staff clatter a few feet away. The side of her face was numbed, her vision blurred. But despite the pain and the suddenness of the blow, her instincts kept her moving to avoid the follow-up; she'd lived with her father's temper for years, after all.

A tiny corner of her mind was rational enough to tell her she had suffered worse at Norrow's hands. This was nothing. There was no real strength behind the strike. Marko hadn't had to move around all his life, hauling his possessions along steep trails from town to town.

A boy could hit me harder than that.

I *could hit* him *harder than that.*

She was rolling back onto her feet, blinking the bright lights from her vision and looking for her staff. Marko had half-turned away, waving another pair of men towards him. He was eager to humiliate her, to gain revenge for that encounter in the tavern. And it wouldn't end there. She knew that her body – maybe her life – now hung in the balance.

Cassia grasped the end of her staff and pulled it towards her, staggering upright as though she was dazed, scraping the wood against the stones. At the same time she looked around and tried to judge whether she might be able to call for help. But the crowds of the day had disappeared, vanishing like mist, and only the whores and the drunkards still populated the square. There were no city guards within sight. Even if they were called to the scene, they would arrive far too late.

So I'm on my own. Again.

Fear, panic, distress, coalesced inside her, hardened into a core of iron anger. And now she had a target.

Marko turned back to her, his fist drawn back to strike her again, to beat her into submission. "This time you won't run, bitch."

"No," she agreed. Her grip shifted down the staff. As she set one foot forward against him, she felt her body relax. *Fluidity. Speed. Use your opponent's size against him.*

Marko came at her. She batted his forearm away, pushed around to the opposite flank, and smacked the end of her staff against the back of his knee. His leg gave way, and Cassia swung back around to attack his unprotected right side. She jabbed his midriff and landed two solid blows before he keeled over with a cry.

That cry was echoed by the other two men, approaching at a run. Cassia had not forgotten them. She sidestepped away from Marko and reset her stance.

Both were shorter and less bulky than Marko, though they showed the same symptoms of a dissolute lifestyle. The nearest looked ready for a fight; the other was hanging back.

She stepped into the first man's path, forcing him to rebalance in mid-step. Meredith had done this to her so many times she knew how to see it coming. Marko's friend did not.

The staff caught him square beneath his chin, and the force of his momentum almost jerked the weapon from Cassia's hands. The man crumpled into a heap on the flagstones.

His companion paused. His hands were raised, but more defensively than anything else. When she took a half-step towards him, he bolted.

Marko had come to his knees, wheezing and clutching at his side. His expression blazed, cruelty replaced by murderous anger. "Bitch."

Without thought, she altered her grip and brought the staff around like a two-handed sword. Marko's head snapped back and he hit the ground with a horrible crack.

All she could hear was her own breathing, sharp and raw against the faint echoes of chants inside one of the temples. She turned in a full circle, poised to charge at another opponent, but there was nobody left to stand against her. The nearest figures were the whores, scattered across the temple steps, curious enough to watch, but not enough to come any closer. There were other people at the edges of the square, some shouting and pointing in her direction.

She looked down at the two sprawled forms. Neither one moved, and she could not tell if they still lived. A vision of the hillside below the Antiachas rose unbidden into her mind – men lay bloodied and charred, their limbs twisted in the air like lightning-struck stumps. *Oh mercy, I did this. Oh, mercy.*

Warm spots of blood shone dark on her back of her hand. She wiped it against her cloak and the blood smeared, staining skin and cloth alike. The shouts were getting louder. If she stayed here, she would have to answer for this assault. *My word against his. If he lives. And even if he does, who would believe me?*

There was strength yet in her body. She ran on, outpacing the cries from behind her, not allowing herself to think of what might still lie ahead.

The docks were still busy. Even in the small towns of the north-east coast people stopped after sundown and retreated to the warmth of their homes. Business could always wait for the dawn. But that did not seem to be true in Hellea.

This tide, at least, was set against her. Her progress slowed to a crawl as she forced her way through the streets. The last time she had passed through this district, she'd had the advantage of height and a horse, and people had moved out of her way. Now they only noticed her if she trod on their feet. She clutched her staff close and skipped into a fleeting gap in the crowd, then flinched as a man shouted in her ear, loud and angry. For a moment she feared the pursuit from the temples had caught up with her at last, but the shout was a curse, rather than a hue and cry.

She was losing time. With every heartbeat she imagined Meredith and Baum stood at the prow of a ship, drawing away from the quays and disappearing into the gloom of the Castaria, hard on the trail of the Betrayer. But they might still be there – the crew might not have cast off – she could get there in time. If only everybody would get out of her way.

At last she made the broad street that fronted the docks. The grain barges left from the eastern end of the docks. Baum had already told her that from there other ships left for the ports of far-away lands. Stromondor, Galliarca, Kalakhadze . . . she had seen the ships of those countries before, moored along the Northern coasts. They had mesmerised her. Now she spared them less than a glance as she hurried along the quays, only enough to be sure that Meredith did not stand tall on the deck.

And there, at the end of the docks, where the bay of the city curved around and became too shallow for such great vessels to be moored – there sat the grain barges.

Or they should have done.

The quays were empty. A few labourers rested there, slumped against mooring posts, sharing wine from chipped jugs. One or two glanced up at her breathless arrival. But the barges had gone. She could not even see their silhouettes out on the water. They were long gone, and her headlong dash through Hellea had been for nothing. She stumbled to a halt and collapsed onto her hands and knees. Her world felt as dark and hopeless as the eastern horizon.

All of her strength, all of her anger and desperation, evaporated into nothing, draining from her like the blood of a slaughtered animal.

First her father, then the scholar Karak. And now Baum and Meredith too. They had all abandoned her.

She thought that the tears, when they came, would never stop.

Chapter Thirteen

HE HAND THAT fell upon her shoulder was as unexpected as it was gentle. At first Cassia did not even realise it was there. When at last she registered the warmth and the weight, she lifted her head a fraction to see a man stood at her side. The Emperor's guards, she thought miserably. They had come to see justice done for her attack on Marko and his friend.

She did not rise, but tightened her grip on her staff. If there was no future for her in Hellea, at least she might direct some of her anger against the men who had been sent to seize her.

"What are you doing here, girl?"

The voice was familiar enough to make her hesitate. There was precious little light here. The last vestiges of daylight had ghosted from the sky and the dockmasters had taken their lanterns with them, so the remaining labourers drank and conversed in the dark, but she recognised the shape of the man's face and the way his shoulders hunched forwards.

"Arca?"

"You must be lost," he said. He sounded weary but, for once, she could not hear the slurred tones that poor wine lent his voice.

Cassia nodded, to herself as much as in agreement. "Yes. I think I am."

"They waited for you for as long as they could," Arca said after a long pause. "But the tides beat them."

"You saw them, sir?"

"Aye. Best get up from there, girl. There's better places to be miserable."

She levered herself to her feet and allowed Arca to use her arm for support as they made their way back along the dock. As they passed a couple of open tavern doorway Cassia thought she could see an odd cast to Arca's face. Like before, when he had told her of Malessar's scroll case, he seemed lost in the past.

"Were they angry, sir?"

"Hmm?" Arca blinked and shook his head. "No. Perhaps. I never could tell. He was impatient. And the young one . . . hard as stone. I would not get on his wrong side. If I'd had a company with him – and three, maybe four, just like him – I might still be a soldier . . . Hah, that's what you think. Shut up. Shut up."

Startled, she almost pulled away from him, but the invective was not aimed at her and Arca fell quiet abruptly.

"Where are we going?" she asked, to break the awkward silence.

"Near here. A small place." He twisted around to regard her. "You'll do, but pull your hair in. And don't talk to anyone."

Her fight with Marko and her flight through the city had loosened her cap. She tucked her hair back under it and tugged at her tunic and cloak so the cloth fell more loosely over her body. They had come to a low door set in the wall of a waterfront tenement on the waterfront. Beyond was a long hallway, masquerading as a narrow room. There were benches down one side, and a bar at the far end. Some of the benches were occupied, but the men were little more than shadows slumped against the wall in the dimly-lit room.

Arca moved past them and drew Cassia to one of the empty benches. "We'll not be disturbed. I spent three whole days here once. Nobody said anything to me."

It was not hard to believe. Cassia let herself drop onto the bench. It felt as though she was surrendering herself to fate at last.

Arca lowered himself slowly, with a hiss of pain. They sat in silence for an age, the harsh rasp of Arca's breathing gradually easing. Cassia strained to make out the murmur of conversation from the closest benches, but the voices were muffled and slurred. She gave up the effort, closed her eyes, and let the evening pass her by. That was what Arca had brought her here for, she thought, to give her space of her own. He was trying to help her in the only way he knew.

"You won't be able to stay here," Arca said eventually. She turned her head. She could barely make out the shape of his face against the light from the door.

"But . . ." she hesitated, coughed, and lowered her voice. "But you said . . ."

"No, girl, not that. I don't mean that. I mean here. The city. Hellea. I know you got into the library. But you won't be able to do that much longer, will you?"

How did he know about that? Did everybody know? He had to have guessed though, as he had told her the story of Malessar's missing scroll case to begin with. But he was right. She knew that disguising herself as a boy would not work for much longer.

"I don't know," she said. "I don't know what to do. I thought they needed me to record their tales. I thought I was part of their company. I thought Meredith . . ." She let the words tail off, rather than voice her most private fantasies. That was all they were, in the end. The fantasies of a stupid girl. Baum had bought her, and now he had discarded her. Her eyes flooded with tears again, and she wiped them away with one sleeve.

"Maybe you should go home," Arca said. There was

kindness in his voice, but he sounded as though he was talking to a wayward child. "Back to the North."

Cassia shook her head. "No. No. Never back there."

She couldn't go back there. Not on her own. For one thing, she did not know the route back up the Emperor's March. Summer was well over now, and winter would not be long in coming. With no shelter, blankets or thick clothing, it was rank stupidity to head north in the autumn months. And her father was up there, somewhere. She could easily imagine encountering him outside the first tavern she came to. It would not be pleasant. The humiliation she felt already burned hard at the base of her spine.

Arca was silent for a time. Cassia forced herself to stillness. There must be something she should be doing, something that might correct her course and lift her from this pit she had stumbled into. But no matter how she tried, she could not bring anything to mind.

Arca started to speak again, but Cassia had to strain to hear the words. It took her a moment to realise he was talking to himself. "There's a way, you say. There's a way. But it ain't a good one. I can't do that. You say that, but it ain't right. Not right. No, you can't call me that. I'm not that. Never was. I proved that, didn't I? Proved it. Damned near killed me too." He broke into a fit of coughing. "He'll never know. Ha."

She waited, but Arca seemed to have forgotten she was there. Drained and exhausted by her earlier flight, she was on the verge of falling asleep when Arca gripped her elbow and tugged her back into wakefulness.

"Listen to me," he said. His tone was taut, his bony fingers dug painfully into the flesh below her elbow. "I think you might catch them up, if that's really what you want to do?"

She didn't stop to consider the question. "How?"

"Those barges stay close to the shoreline, and they make frequent stops between here and Corba, where they take on more cargo for the coastal towns. You could catch them, if you can find a place on one of the ships leaving tomorrow morning. One of the sea-farers."

Cassia sat back with a sigh. "Sir, no captain would take me as a passenger. Not a girl on her own."

"Perhaps not," Arca agreed, "but there's always ships that need crew. I could find one for you. You could sign on with one and jump ship at Corba, before the barges arrive." He hesitated. "But you don't have to. It would not be easy."

Ocean-going ships. Other lands. The thoughts struck a chord in her mind and she searched back, piecing together something that evaded her. "A ship," she murmured. "There *is* a ship. Tomorrow morning – a ship for Galliarca."

It was a slender thread of hope, and she struggled to keep it from overwhelming her. She felt Arca's gaze upon her, though she could not see his face in the dark. Somebody had lit a lantern at the far end of the tavern, but the light, smoky and guttering, did not reach this far up the room. She wondered how she might approach the ship's captain, the phrases she could use, and how she might recommend herself. It wasn't easy; she had no experience to draw upon.

What can I do aboard a ship? Coil ropes? Climb the mast? Take the oars? That last thought was so absurd it brought a smile to her lips, but it vanished quickly as she ruled herself out of task after task. The crew would laugh at her efforts.

She wondered if she could plead directly to Karak. Would he listen? He had listened to her stories, and he had helped her get into the library, but this was something different. It was her best chance though. Even the ship's captain would listen to such an eminent passenger.

So . . . how to snare Karak's attention? What could she offer to a scholar?

"Stories," she breathed. That had to be the answer. It was all she could think of. Karak knew the *Call to the North*; he was interested in tales as much as histories. Their friendship had bloomed quickly once they began to share the different versions of tales they both knew. That was her way aboard his ship. And from there to Corba . . .

But one step at a time. Stories . . .

She thought she knew the very one.

"Arca, are the city's gates still open at this time of the night?"

He grunted. She had to shake his shoulder and repeat the question before he would answer. "Open? Hah, they never close, girl. But why? You'll never catch them by road."

"I need to find some open fields," Cassia said, the words rushing from her as the idea rose into her mind straight from the old verses. "Or an orchard. Yes, an orchard. That'd be best. And I need some small offcuts of wood – almost like kindling."

"What good will that do?"

"Wait and see." Cassia felt her spirits lifting. At last, there was something she *could* do. Something worthy of her father's creaky tales of heroics, perhaps even of Gelis and Renn the Fair.

The night was a rushed affair, and Cassia got no rest. Her thoughts spun far too quickly for her to think of closing her eyes, no matter that every movement was a truly monumental effort by the time that the sky showed the first signs of dawn.

If there was a cry raised against her, she did not hear of it. Perhaps she had managed to flee the temple square before anybody got a decent look at her. Perhaps Marko and his friend had not yet regained consciousness, or maybe they had preferred to walk away from the whole affair, ashamed they had been bested by a mere girl. In any event, Cassia was not stopped when she passed through the Summer Gates, even though the guards frowned at her and wondered aloud where a young boy might be headed at such a late hour.

Hellea had spread far beyond the walls that once contained it. The streets were wider here, the houses had fewer storeys, and some were surrounded by walls and fences. Cassia had started to worry about finding her way back into the city when she finally reached the fields and orchards Arca had described. Beyond the silhouettes of the last buildings, the world vanished into utter blackness. She realised she had become used to the press of tenements and temples around her, and the empty night sucked at her soul, causing her to shiver.

There was no time to waste. She left the road, prowling along the length of the last wall until she reached a point where she could wedge her toes into the cracks between the stones, and hauled herself up onto the top. Pear trees stood below her in regimented lines, like the mustering of a legion. She nodded in satisfaction – the orchard might be a little too tidy for her liking, but it was also so large that, at this end, she would never be seen from the windows of the house.

She spent a moment listening, trying to pick out sounds from the rustling of the leaves and the barking of distant dogs. That could be a problem, and she prayed that if the house-holder owned any dogs they were muzzled and tied up for the night. Then she dropped down into the garden.

The cold grass came up to her ankles. Bending low, she brushed one hand along the ground, searching until she found the telltale pellets.

Yes. Thank you, Ceresel.

Arca had managed to provide her with a few pieces of kindling suitable for building a snare, and she snagged some short lengths of twine from beneath a trader's stall before leaving the city. It was a simple task to construct the traps, even in the darkness. She had done it dozens of times before. Once they were set, she retreated to the top of the wall and forced herself to wait in silence and in stillness. That wasn't quite so easy.

It seemed to take an eternity for anything to happen, and Cassia's mind had time to distract her with hundreds of unpleasant and miserable scenarios. The litany of misfortune ranged from simple failure to total humiliation and several times tears flooded over her cheeks as she cradled her head in her hands and cried into the sleeves of her robe.

But Ceresel must have taken pity on her. A quiet *snick*, followed by a flurry of panicked movement drew her back to the job at hand. Jumping down, she discovered that both snares had been triggered. One had fallen apart in the process and was empty; the other held a small rabbit, the animal's free paws digging furiously at the surrounding earth in its desperate attempt to break free. Part of her was surprised she had managed to catch even a single rabbit. It was far easier to kill game than to take it alive, and she felt a thrill of optimism as she bound the animal's paws together and tied a hood over its head. At least something was going right. Perhaps this was a sign.

The thought lent her determination and vigour, and she ran back to the city with a smile upon her face. The rabbit bounced against her back, twitching and turning frantically inside the bundle she had made of her robe. The first fingers of dawn were touching the sky, illuminating the heavy clouds gathering behind her. Summer was definitely over, those clouds said. It was time to migrate towards fairer weather and more southerly lands.

True to his word, Arca waited on the quays outside the dive they had sat in earlier. When he saw her he shook his head, wonder plain to see on the ruin of his face.

"Girl, you must be touched by the gods," he said. "How else could you believe this hare-brained scheme will work?"

"*Rabbit*-brained," she corrected him with a grin. "It all depends how well he knows the tale." If he knew it at all, she did not add. She could not admit that possibility to herself. Not now. "Is the ship still here?"

Arca nodded, levering himself away from the wall that supported his gaunt frame. "Away down the main pier," he said. "With a bright green pennant. You should not miss it. But hurry, the tide's almost at its highest now."

She took a step away, then hesitated. "Will you come with me?"

Arca shifted his gaze from her, looking away down the quays. "No, girl. I would only spoil your chances. But take my prayers with you. Now – get gone. Bugger off."

Cassia leaned in to brush her lips against his cheek. "Thank you. I'll think of you."

"That'll give you nightmares, then," he said sourly, pushing her away. The corners of his eyes creased as if he was in pain. "And don't thank me yet. Now, I told you – bugger off."

She hurried along the road, the bundled robe slung over one shoulder. The rabbit kicked at her, but it seemed to have tired itself out. The city's dockside workers were already filing out from the alleyways, forcing her to slow and dodge around them, ducking away from carts laden with last minute purchases, supplies, coiled rope and canvas. She wondered if anybody else in the city ever slept. All the while, she scanned the forest of masts to find the green pennant. At first it was too difficult, the sky wasn't light enough and she was too distracted in her struggle to keep her feet. But then she forced herself to pause, ignoring the curses from behind her, and focused her attention on the banners that flew high above every single ship.

There. That was green, wasn't it?

And then she saw another cart, a pair of large, brass-bound chests secured upon it, pushed out from a street that led back towards one of the city's more upmarket districts. Karak strode behind it, the scholar keeping a close eye on his porters. Cassia pushed forward, her pulse pounding. This would be a performance of sorts. And there was much more at stake than a few grubby coins.

"Sir!" she called out. To her embarrassment, her voice came out as a cross between a wheeze and a squeak, immediately lost amidst the clamour. She had to reach him before he boarded the ship. She imagined Karak would not wait on the ship's deck, such an important passenger would have a private cabin.

If he took to his cabin, the captain would not dare to call him out just to speak to a lone, desperate girl.

The porters manoeuvred their cart to the bottom of the gangplank, wheeled it around and began dragging it up. A few of the ship's crew joined in, Karak directing their efforts from the quayside. Cassia called out again, but he didn't seem to have heard her. To mirror her frustrations, the rabbit began to buck again, throwing her off-balance for a few steps.

Finally, as the two chests were hauled aboard, Karak looked across at her. His face was blank for a moment, and then he straightened in surprise.

"Sir! Please, let me speak with you!"

Karak held up a hand to forestall her. "I have no time. The wind is with us, boy. The captain has called his lines."

She dodged around a barefooted sailor who leaped past her onto the gangplank. "Sir, please, just one moment. My friends—"

A large man, even taller than Meredith, leaned over the ship's rail and shouted down. "My lord, the pilot is ready to tow us out. You must come aboard now."

Karak looked at her and shook his head firmly. "No more, I'm afraid. I need no apprentice, Cassia. My work is not of that nature."

"But, sir," she started forward in desperation as he ascended the gangplank, "I don't need to be your apprentice. I only want to go to Corba! My friends have gone ahead without me!"

He turned at the top of the ramp, and for a moment she thought she saw disappointment in his eyes. By his side, the captain muttered into Karak's ear, and Karak made a gesture with one hand. The captain wheeled and barked a series of half-incomprehensible orders to his crew.

"But I can be useful!"

"My captain has a full complement," Karak told her. "There is no room for passengers. Girl, this is no trader's scow."

She took a deep breath. This was where her plot stood or

fell. It depended on how well Karak knew his folklore, and how well his captain took her next trick. "Sir, do you have aboard anyone who can catch rabbits?"

The captain looked irritated, his attention spread between this and his crew's attempts to reel in the lines that held the ship fast against the dockside. Karak tilted his head and regarded her with a thin, piercing gaze. She might have been wrong – it was so hard to interpret his expression – but she thought the corner of his mouth turned upward. A twitch, perhaps.

"What?" The captain shouted. "Of course not!"

"Then let me aboard, sir! I can catch rabbits!"

Karak's smile was obvious now. He knew what was coming. But the captain, and those of his crew close enough to catch the exchange, only burst into laughter.

"You ridiculous child!" The captain shouted. The ship creaked, and a pair of sailors knelt to take hold of the gangplank, ready to haul it back aboard. When that was gone, it would take her chance with it. "There's no bloody rabbits on this ship!"

Oh Ceresel, I love you!

She had already slipped the tied bundle onto one end of her staff. Now she raised her arms and whirled the staff in a looping circle as though it was an oversized sling. She only had one chance. If she judged the arc poorly, the bundle might fly over the entire deck and splash into the Castaria.

One last heave, and the bundle, rabbit and all, sailed through the air. She watched it turn end over end. In mid-air, the loose knot that held it together finally came free. The rabbit, hooded and tied, skidded over the deck. Sailors shouted and leapt aside to avoid being hit by the twitching missile. Stunned, the poor beast must have managed to work free of the bindings, because there was uproar, a cacophony of shouts as the crew fell over each other in their attempts to seize it.

"There is now!" Cassia shouted up in triumph to Karak and his captain. The two men appeared torn between apoplexy and crippling laughter. The ship's deck was in absolute disarray, the crew abandoning their posts to chase the confused rabbit. A small part of Cassia was appalled at the chaos she had caused, and she hoped it wouldn't make matters worse. The captain might refuse outright to give her passage now, and she would not blame him. She shifted her feet, her calves tense as she prepared to flee the scene.

Karak shook his head, but at least he was smiling. "Even Gelis herself was not so brazen," he called down to her. "Her rabbit was dead!"

She had not known that. A familiar flush settled at the base of her neck. "Sir, will you at least return my cloak?"

Karak glanced over his shoulder. It seemed that her furry invader was still on the loose. "Can you catch this blessed thing?"

Cassia nodded eagerly. Her heart was fit to burst.

"Well, then, don't just stand there, girl. Lift those feet. Hurry, now, before the pilots tow us clear."

She was already halfway up the gangplank.

The last she saw of Hellea was the view from the rails of the ship's hind deck. Obscured by a floating wall of masts and hulls, canvas drawn in irregular curtains across the scene, Hellea already seemed more than a world away. The ceaseless clamour of the streets was gone, swept from her ears by the morning breeze, and the sour taste of the air came only in brief waves. The towers of the temples stood bright in the dawn, highlighted against the horizon, and the palace itself peered from between flapping sets of sails. Just a place now, a name and a history, rather than a collection of individuals and a set of hurts and bruises. Memories.

She said a swift prayer for Arca, to thank him for his help. He deserved better. *One day perhaps I can come back and thank you properly. But for now this will have to do. Ceresel, please intercede on Arca's behalf – bring him better luck and the path he deserves.*

Catcalls and laughter rang across the deck. Not aimed at her, she guessed – the rabbit, finally caught, was caged in a wire-fronted basket that hung from the central mast, and the crew appeared to have adopted it as a mascot. Two of the men hung from the rigging next to it, baiting the poor beast with handfuls of grain. It looked to be a contest to see which of the two would be bitten the least. They had even called it Cass. She wasn't sure how she should take that.

Karak had not stayed to watch the games, disappearing into the cabin beneath the hind deck as soon as the pilot tug had disengaged. That left Cassia alone again, but it was a feeling she was becoming used to now. And, besides, it was probably a very good thing the crew wasn't paying her too much attention. She'd failed to realise how confined the space aboard a ship might be, or that she would be the only girl aboard. She had assumed there would be other passengers, also bound for Galliarca.

She wrapped one arm around the rail and watched the sailors as they grew bored and agreed to call the contest a draw. They compared the bites they had received as they descended, as proud of them as of battle scars. What a strange story this would be, when she finally came to assemble it.

The captain thumped towards her, his face fixed in the half-scowl he had worn earlier. "Don't know what your game is," he said without preamble. "Or his, for that. But you better keep out the way."

"I will. I'm sorry about the rabbit, sir."

He glared down at her for a moment. "Anybody tries that again, I'll lash 'em to the anchor. How good are you, then?"

The abrupt change of tack confused her, until he pointed at her cloak. Frayed, and stained with the rabbit's droppings and urine, it was still the mark of a storyteller. It lay bundled at her feet, all she had left of her old life.

"Fair enough," she said. "My father was Norrow of Keskor, the best storyteller of the North. Have you met him?" There was nothing to lose now, so she might as well try to impress the man.

"Never heard of him," the captain said.

Cassia shrugged. The words felt wrong upon her tongue. "But now you can say you met his daughter."

The captain continued to stare at her, as though waiting for her to wilt and look away. She willed herself to stand firm, and at last his mouth cracked into a dry smile that did not touch his eyes. "Keep those guts, girl. You'll need 'em for this crew."

He waved one hand at the deck, where a few sailors had gathered to sit and pull cups of water from a barrel. Cassia watched them for a moment before she realised what he meant. He wanted her to recite for them? For her passage?

The ship lurched through the water, leaving her stomach a few feet in the opposite direction. Cassia gripped the rail again, as though it was the only thing keeping her safely aboard. The only thing she could think of was Gelis's escape across the sea. It might be a good idea to find some quiet corner and sleep for a little. The day, after all, had only just begun.

She woke with dried lips and a peculiar warm ache beneath her ribs. She shifted to one side and dug into her robe, pulling out the stone charm. She turned it over in her hand uncomprehendingly. Why was it so warm? Was that supposed to mean something? She had prayed upon it several times over the last few weeks. Could Pyraete really hear her prayers? *Oh, mercy, what if he has? What should I do?*

She scrambled up to her knees and was about to push the charm over the raised edge of the ship's bow when she hesitated, coming fully awake. Gods? Sending messages to her? When she thought of it like that it sounded ridiculous. This was no godly artefact, just a charm from the wall of a tavern. Gods sent messages through dreams, or by golden animals or fish that could speak. Or they sent great weapons of power . . .

"So this is where you got to."

She almost dropped the charm again. Karak had appeared without warning, although in truth she had been engrossed in her thoughts. She pulled herself upright and looked about. It was difficult to judge, but if the ship was still headed east, she had slept through most of the day. There was a haze over the horizon ahead, the accumulated smoke and dust indicating a town in the distance. In the west, the sky was dark with storm clouds. Summer had ended for Hellea, and the winds blew the ship freely before them. There was no need for the sweeps when the weather was this favourable, so the crew also seemed relaxed. Cassia was sure that wouldn't be the case once the river ejected them into the sea.

"My captain is none too happy with you," Karak said. Cassia flinched, but there was no real anger in the words. If anything, the scholar sounded amused. "Oh, have no fear. He'll not throw you overboard. Unless your tales are truly horrendous, of course. But the crew have taken a liking to your pet."

"He's not a pet," she said.

"That's just as well, as you're unlikely to get him back. Unfortunately, they now want to rename the ship, for luck."

She had believed that nothing could be more embarrassing than having the *rabbit* named after her. Little wonder the ship's captain was upset. She hunched her shoulders and looked down at the deck so Karak could not see her face. "I don't know if they'll listen to me, if I ask them not to."

"Oh, I should not worry," Karak said. "The captain will come around to the idea eventually. Perhaps he will even paint the letters onto the hull himself."

The humiliation was absolute. Cassia wondered if she should just throw herself over the side now, to save everybody else the trouble later. Then Karak laughed.

"*Rabbit*, girl, *Rabbit*. You must admit, it sounds a thousand times better than *Warlock*."

She thought she preferred the latter, but there was most likely no chance of convincing the crew to change their minds.

"We will be at Corba early tomorrow morning," Karak said, his tone brisk and remote again. "If you confine yourself to this part of the deck, you will not be in the way. As far as payment for your passage, Sah Ulma asks you entertain his crew this evening."

She had expected it, but she felt as though the ship had leapt high from the water and taken her stomach with it. All she could trust herself to do was nod, and that none too firmly.

Karak turned away, but paused before he left her. "I would not try the *Call to the North*," he advised dryly.

The deck was lit with braziers, the canvas of the sails lifted high to prevent them catching alight. The captain, Sah Ulma, had brought the ship back across the Castaria and closer to the shore, and now the newly renamed *Rabbit* was anchored not far from the low sandstone cliffs. Cassia had thought they would sail on through the night, just as the great ships did in all the stories she knew, but one of the sailors had set her right. That might be fine on the open seas, but the Castaria was only a lake, after all. Nobody wanted to risk running aground or smashing into the cliffs. For a few minutes Cassia stared nervously into the dusk, watching to make sure the cliffs were not coming any closer.

The crew gathered around the braziers, sat on tasselled cushions and bales of cloth hauled up from below deck. The ship's stores of fresh food were still full, so they ate from plates of cooked meats and fruit from wicker baskets. There was wine too – watered down heavily, Cassia realised. With neither

Baum nor her father to watch disapprovingly, she poured a large mug and sat back against the curved rail to enjoy herself.

She wasn't sure what Sah Ulma had said about her to his crew, but her fears remained unfounded. She caught a few grins, and she was certain at least a few muttered comments were about her, but the sailors left her in peace and did not bother her until the end of their meal.

She grew aware of a slow, rhythmic drumming from the raised hind deck where Sah Ulma and his officers sat apart. It was a quiet but insistent one-two, one-two-three beat, that made her tap her fingers on the deck in time. When she looked up she saw Sah Ulma stood watching his crew, beating out the rhythm with one foot.

One-two, one-two-three, one-two, one-two-three.

Gradually the crew took up the rhythm, slapping the deck with their palms, or drumming against their plates. One or two drew out small flutes and piped competing melodies over the top until all fell into the same tune, almost by accident. The deck was alive with music, and the rhythm had sped up into a bright jig rather than a heavy march.

Cassia realised belatedly that this was her cue. Norrow had always built the rhythm for himself, wandering through markets to draw people along with him. But this was an audience that *commanded* her performance. They were here, they were ready, they wanted to be entertained. Unlike the people of Hellea, they seemed not to care that she was not a man. This was the greatest opportunity she'd ever had.

She didn't have the faintest idea what to do.

Her father had told stories to sailors, but that had always been inside taverns, and Cassia had always been outside, minding the bloody mule in the cold and rain. There was nothing in her own stock of tales that suited this audience.

One-two, one-two-three, one-two, one-two-three.

She came slowly to her feet and gathered her robe around her. She could delay the moment by walking amongst them, encouraging them and driving the rhythm, but she could only delay for so long. And then . . . there was a yawning gap in her thoughts that she could not fill.

She thought about the rhythms her father used. The kinds of stories that belonged with each one. One-two, one-two-three, one-two, one-two-three. That was something she wasn't familiar with. She couldn't feed a story into it. But if she could lengthen the phrases . . .

Cassia stepped across the deck to join the loudest of the drumming crewmen. His grin was wide and infectious, and he called up to her in a thick accent she could not penetrate. She raised her hands in reply and clapped out a different beat. A longer, less disjointed phrase, more suited to the way she had learned from her father. For a moment the two rhythms collided in a cacophonous battle before the drummer swung effortlessly over to her side. The men around him followed suit and the rest of the crew picked up the new rhythm within seconds. Now they were playing her tune. But still she did not know the words . . .

Just like Pelicos, she thought.

It was as easy as that. She almost shouted in relief. Pelicos the Illuminated! The hero of Kalakhadze, of Stromondor, of the plains-built fortresses and more besides; the man who left a trail of broken hearts and enraged husbands in his wake. Only a few winters ago, watching sails disappear over the horizon from the clifftops south of Oemonia, she had likened herself to Pelicos – as free as the wind, breezing from town to town, unshackled by the Factor and the Emperor's laws. It had been a child's romantic notion, and it lasted only as long as it took for her father to be hounded from the town for the money he owed, but it had haunted the far edges of her thoughts ever since.

Why didn't I think of this before? What else could so perfectly suit the crew of a ship bound once more for distant shores? The beauty of Pelicos, she realised, as she looked out at the variety of men in her audience, was that he was truly a man of the world. Stromondorians, Helleans, Galliarcans, Northerners and Kebrians alike – they all became the butt of his jests and tricks; he was one with them all, but he belonged to none.

She spread her arms wide and leaned forwards. The musicians played more softly, the flutes descending the scales into low monotones while the drummers seemed to brush the deck with the palms of their hands.

How would her father have begun? A prayer to the gods. But which ones? There was only one prayer she could truthfully make tonight.

"In praise of Ceresel, who favours the brave," she sang out, "who gives us the heroes whose stories we tell, who walks hand in hand with the fickle winds of fortune, and who slips out of reach of those who depend on her – Ceresel, Ceresel, lend me the gift of a honey-coated tongue and the wits of a hare—"

Shouts of laughter came from the crew, and several pointed up at the basket that swung from the rigging, where the rabbit had been left in relative peace. Cassia skipped a beat to let the noise die away and hoped her embarrassment would not show.

"The wits of a *hare*," she repeated, "to best tell the tales of your favourite son!"

"Pelicos!" one man shouted. His neighbour echoed the call.

Cassia pushed her palms flat through the air, and the music subsided, so that she did not have to raise her voice too much. All eyes were upon her and, to her surprise and satisfaction, she could not see a single hostile expression. It was so different from Hellea, from Elbithrar, from all the towns in the North where folk still regarded her and her father with some degree of suspicion.

But tonight had changed all of that for her. For the first time she knew she was doing the right thing, that she was destined to be a storyteller. Like her father.

But better.

"Pelicos the Illuminated," she said with a broad smile. She twitched her palms upwards, and the rhythm leapt back in.

It was a long night. One story was not enough. After she completed her first tale, collapsing exhausted onto one of the mats spread across the deck and gulping long draughts of wine that the sailors pressed upon her – bitter, stronger, and unwatered, she realised – they crowded around her and begged for another. Fuzzed by wine, flushed with adrenaline, she had trouble picking out Hellean phrases and proper names from the jumble of dialects the crew used, but at last she struggled to her feet and managed a slower, more sombre rendition of one of the histories of Gelis, set against the soft, entrancing drones of the flutes. She stumbled over several parts and managed to repeat one speech twice, but nobody seemed to notice. The slow pace of the story helped settle the crew, and by the time she trailed off with the heroine now within sight of safety, many had laid out on their mats, covered by thin blankets.

Cassia's head felt horribly tight, and she was certain the boat was rocking far more than it should. She found her way back into the prow and wrapped herself in her robe. Her thoughts splintered and scattered, and all she could bring to mind before she fell asleep was that given time she might be able to get used to this life.

The storm caught up with them in the early hours of the morning. The first Cassia knew about it was from the man who accidentally kicked her in the ribs as he reached over her to pull one of the lines. She moaned, curling into a tighter ball, only to realise that both the deck and her clothes were soaked through, and the ship was rocking like a baby's crib.

Her stomach lurched in the opposite direction. She crawled out from beneath the prow and narrowly avoided having her fingers stamped on.

"Out the way!" somebody shouted. A spray of water lashed against her side, washing her flat across the deck. Her limbs felt as though they belonged to somebody else, and they would not hold her up.

"Aft anchor's loose!" The cry came from further down the ship as she swung again and Cassia swallowed a mouthful of bile. This was as bad as any winter night in the mountains, sheltering in vain against the cruel winds and the whiplashing rain. At least up there the ground didn't move beneath her . . .

One of the sailors shouted in another tongue, and Cassia heard the fear in his voice. Sah Ulma's booming tones cut through the end of his sentence. "No – no sail! The wind will rip us to shreds! Ship the oars! We have to get out into the current, or we'll be dashed against that shore!"

More sailors ran past Cassia, several leaping over her body as she huddled on deck. She yelped and squeezed her eyes tightly closed. Somebody picked her up, one arm wrapped effortlessly around her waist, and threw her over his shoulder. She was too startled and nauseous to even think of screaming, instead covering her mouth with her hands in a desperate attempt to keep from vomiting.

The man carrying her did not care how sick she felt. After a few strides he swung her down again and held her as a farmer might a newborn calf. Cassia found herself rolled from his grip onto softness. She blinked, but saw only his back, bare and patterned with tattoos, water streaming down the curves of his shoulders as he hurried out into the storm.

Out. There was a roof over her head. Low, wooden planking. She guessed she was beneath the hind deck, as she could hear the thump of Sah Ulma and his officers.

The booming sound of a man chanting reached her through the boards. It sounded as though Karak was up on the hind deck as well. The chant circled through her mind, soaring like an eagle riding the winds that blew down from the mountains. It made her feel that if she slipped off the pallet she would just keep falling, never hitting the deck. Her skin prickled, a horrible surge that crept along her arms and legs and made her bile rise in her throat. *Oh no. No, not now.*

The ship swung again, and her stomach cramped. This time she could not hold it in. She rolled to the edge of the pallet, saw the bowl half-tucked beneath it, and grabbed it just in time.

Afterwards, she was too exhausted to do more than fall back onto the pallet. The shouts of the crew chased those strange surges, cramps that were not cramps, through visions of soldiers tossed like chaff before sorcerous flames and back down into unquiet sleep.

This time it was the thumping headache that woke her. Her mouth felt like she had eaten manure for a whole month. *Is this how my father wakes up every morning?* That thought revolted her into a groan and she stuck her head over the edge of the pallet to spit into the bowl. Somebody had covered her with a thick, woollen blanket that was not hers. She let her fingers brush against the scarlet weave for a moment, puzzled, but unable to form the right question in her mind.

"I was beginning to think you would sleep through this day and into tomorrow," Karak said.

Sleep fell away like an avalanche. She lowered the blanket slowly and lifted her head to see the rest of the cabin.

The scholar sat on a stool at a low, slanted table, a scroll of parchment pinned across it. Daylight filtered through an opened slat in the hull behind him, bathing the table in flat shades that spoke of a lull in a storm. The rest of the cabin was dim, shadowed and haunted by the silhouettes of travel chests and rails of hung robes.

"Perhaps you should not have drunk so much," Karak continued. "Stromondorian wines are famed for their strength, even when watered."

Cassia winced. No wonder she felt this way. Her father had once bought a cask of what a vendor claimed was a genuine Stromondorian vintage. He swore he would not drink it until he had made his name in the towns of the Empire. But Norrow never left the North – through fear, Cassia understood now. The fear of having to make his reputation again, in lands that might not be so tolerant of his manners.

The cask remained unbroached for close to six days, and Norrow's temper worsened by the hour, until at last he drove a metal spike through the top and consumed the contents over the course of a single day and night. At long last, just before dawn, he passed out and did not stir for two whole days, pissing and soiling himself, leaving Cassia to fend for herself outside the walls of whichever town they had just left. Those had been the most fearful nights of Cassia's life up to that point. She thought her father's deterioration could be marked firmly to that cask. He had been a bully before then, but after that he became worse. His moods veered more violently. He distrusted even his closest friends. He began to plan and mutter to himself, and cast looks at his daughter that made her shudder even now.

"I won't do it again," she said, her voice halfway between a croak and a dry rasp.

Karak twitched one shoulder. "Perhaps. The folly of exuberant youth."

"I'm sorry, sir," she said, remembering her manners. It dawned on her that there was only one pallet in this cabin. "I did not mean to take your bed."

Again, the twitch, a shrug which suggested he was not giving his full attention to the conversation. Cassia glanced under the covers to make sure that she was still clothed. Her robe had gone, but she still wore the thin tunic and holed breeches she had used in her disguise at the library. They felt clammy and damp.

"At my age, I find I don't need as much sleep as I once did," Karak said. "Little wonder most of the philosophical thought in this world is done by old men, when none of us can sleep through the night. Your sandals are to the left, there. Perhaps *I* should apologise."

That threw her. "For what, sir?"

"For disturbing your sleep last night. It was my suggestion to bring you from the deck. Sah Ulma was concerned you would be underfoot while his crew fought the storm."

It could have been meant in one of two ways, but Karak's tone gave her no hint as to which. The scholar tapped his stylus against the side of a small glass bottle, then dipped it into the ink and scratched a few lines onto his paper. As he leaned forwards the incoming light illuminated his pale skin. He had not looked so pale in the library. In fact, he looked ill.

"Such storms are uncommon on the Castaria. Winds blowing from the North. Very unseasonal. Almost unnatural."

Winds from the North. The way he said it sent a shiver up her spine. That was what she had thought herself to be, in one mad moment when everything had been right, back in the hills, on the edges of the Empire. She and Baum and Meredith – a fresh wind to sweep away the ancient tyranny of a terrible warlock.

"Sah Ulma was also concerned the storm would run us aground before we could reach the freedom of the open sea," Karak continued. "It required all his skill, as well as my assistance, to keep the ship from being overpowered by the ferocity of the elements."

Cassia had a faint suspicion that she should be apologising. But why? It wasn't as if the storm had anything to do with her. Did it? She struggled to recall the stories she had told. Could either of them have offended one of the gods? Meteon, or Casta? Or perhaps – and her skin grew cold as she thought of the one god who might have most cause to be displeased with her – perhaps Pyraete sought to punish her for her failures.

"As such, we have had to alter our sailing plans. I had no desire to be stranded on the Castaria while the weather attempted to capsize us at every turn. The clouds building beyond Hellea promise to dwarf last night's storm."

It took her a moment to understand. "You are putting me off the ship, sir? But, please, I can make myself useful – I promise!"

"Putting you off? Oh no, girl, exactly the opposite." Karak sighed and shook his head. "I am not used to this," he said, as though to himself. "Perhaps it *was* a poor idea. Sah Ulma should make the apology."

Cassia was now thoroughly unsettled. Following the scholar's musings was difficult enough when her head did not ring like a bell. "What apology?"

Karak tipped his head to the open slats. "Corba lies a full day behind us. The Meteon carries us into the ocean as we speak. I could not put you ashore even if you wished it. If your friends do still wait for you at Corba, then I am afraid they will have to wait a while longer."

Cassia sank back down onto the pallet, unable to trust her legs to keep her upright. The drive and determination that had kept her going for so long, against so many obstacles, failed her at last – the solid core of her soul turned to sand and blown away.

"How long?" she forced herself to ask in a voice that sounded frail and hollow.

"A year. Perhaps two. Unless you can purchase your own passage back to Hellea." Karak's tone made it clear how unlikely he thought that possibility.

"Where from?" she asked at last. Karak still regarded her from his seat at the low table, his brow creased by something that could have been concern.

"Galliarca, of course," the scholar said.

She shook her head, wondering why that no longer excited her as it would once have done.

Lost. Like pollen on the winds. Like Pelicos on the Seas of the Damned. It struck Cassia how far from home she was. How far from her old life.

Chapter Fourteen

THE SHIP WAS smaller than Cassia had first thought. Beyond Karak's cabin there was no space for a passenger. Despite her best efforts she got underfoot of the crew or the officers, and she lived in fear of Sah Ulma's scowl. When the captain made his rounds of the ship she retreated to the steps that led to the hind deck, but even that was only a temporary shelter. The cabin itself, Karak told her, was out of bounds unless she was invited. He had been polite but firm on the subject, and Cassia judged that she was in no position to argue.

The nearest thing she had to her own space was the mat laid out behind the prow. There, at least, she had enough room to practise with her staff and try to work herself into the state of mind that Meredith had taught her. The sailors thought her antics hilarious, but their ridicule washed over her like the ocean spray, and affected her just as little. She could fix her sight on the featureless horizon, and block out the catcalls; they were good-natured for the most part, and they soon subsided when the sailors saw how graceful and fluid her movements were.

She spent the remainder of her time making desperate

repairs to her clothing, so she looked less like a beggar, and staring out over the rails at the sea. The sheer scale of the ocean awed her more than Hellea had ever done, and she began to understand how the crew of the *Rabbit* were bound together against it. *And if history is an ocean too, then where am I?*

The crew had split into shifts, working day and night to keep the ship on course. There was no longer any time for stories, and every hour brought another adjustment, another reading of the sun or the stars, sails to be trimmed or let out. The constant activity was a welcome reminder that she was not on her own.

On the third day, one of the senior officers came to her and pointed down at the deck. Another sailor stood behind him with a brush and a wooden pail. Cassia looked up at them and sighed; the man's accent was difficult to understand, but his meaning was not. Her stories had paid her way as far as Corba, but only hard work would take her any further. At least it would pass the time.

The crew called her "Rabbit", despite her protests, and after a while she decided it was more trouble than it was worth to try to stop them. As names went, she'd heard much worse, and they meant no harm by it. Even though she was the only woman aboard there seemed to be an unspoken agreement between the sailors that they would give her the same respect they gave each other. One of the sailors even donated a thick cotton shirt to replace her ragged tunic.

Karak did not emerge from his cabin until at least the sixth day, although by that time Cassia had begun to lose count, settling into the rhythm of life on the ship. He climbed slowly up onto the hind deck and sat on a stool there for an hour, exchanging low words with Sah Ulma. Cassia assumed he must have been ill, as she remembered how pale he had looked after the storm, how slow and deliberate his movements had been. She felt there were some unresolved questions from that conversation, but she could not pin them down in her mind. And, besides, Sah Ulma's officers kept her far too busy for talking.

In the end, the scholar came to her. She grew aware of his presence behind her as she worked through one of the exercises Meredith had taught her. She had added her own twist to a couple of the movements, a flourish here, a half-step there, to distract the invisible foe before her. The memory of her fight against Marko and his cronies was never far away, and she remembered how close he had come to overpowering her. She would never let that happen again.

"You have a distinctive style," Karak noted. His voice sounded stronger.

She let the staff come upright at the end of her swing, using the momentum to turn in place so that she faced him. Karak's dry smile was something of a relief to see now. In some ways he reminded her of Meredith.

"I was taught by a prince, sir," she said.

Karak laughed. "Of course you were. By Pelicos himself, I'll wager." His smile broadened at her discomfort. "On that evidence you should thrive in Galliarca. Even Sah Ulma tapped his foot."

She had known the captain was listening to her story, but she had not thought Karak himself was also there. Galliarca was something she had not yet let herself think about, lest she cause her luck to run foul again. But now she could not help it, and visions of spires overlooking great paved squares crowded at the edges of her mind. She lowered the staff with a sigh, knowing she was too distracted to continue.

"Do you really believe so, sir? I left the North for what I hoped would be a better life, but I didn't find it. And now I'm leaving the Empire as well . . ."

Karak shrugged. "All of life is a series of departures, girl. But why write off a place before you have arrived there?"

"Because men are the same everywhere."

"You are far too young to have such a philosophy," Karak said. But Cassia noticed he had not contradicted her. She felt the ship rise as it rode through a wave crest, and she shifted her stance to compensate for the pitching of the deck.

"Stories are only stories," she said. She had already begun to think that more than a few of her father's tales might have been woven from whole cloth. Perhaps even Malessar did not exist. If that was the case, Baum was nothing more than a sorcerous madman, chasing a shadow from shore to shore just as other men wasted their lives in pursuit of dragons.

"Not always," Karak replied. "Every story finds roots in the truth. Even Pelicos the Illuminated."

That piqued her interest, despite her low mood. The scholar knew her well enough to drag her attention back around. "Was he real, then?"

The scholar's lips twitched. "Do you doubt your own wares? Oh, Pelicos existed. He did not achieve everything attributed to him, but he did live. I have encountered him in my enquiries."

The idea that occurred to her was a startling one and it must have shown in her expression, because Karak watched her expectantly. Cassia stepped down from the prow and thought how best to phrase her questions.

"Sir, you must know a lot of stories," she said hesitantly, waiting for him to nod before continuing. "I think you could tell the *Call to the North* even better than my father could. And I'll wager you've seen every library in the world, too. If there are such stories in them, I would like to see them too. Do you think I could learn from you?"

Karak laughed. "I have been waiting for that question since our second day in the library," he told her. "If you had asked then, you might have saved yourself whole days of trouble!"

She stared at him in surprise. "Really? You mean that?"

"Of course. I am a man of my word." Karak sounded huffy that she doubted him. "I will give you a room and a roof, and I will teach you some – only *some*, mark you – of the stories I know. In return, you will be on the staff of my household, carrying out any tasks and work I deem necessary."

Cassia felt herself recoil. Her memory of the last night she had spent in Rann Almoul's yard echoed unpleasantly against Karak's words. Somehow she could not believe he would force his will against her, but neither could she bring herself to trust him completely. Hetch's duplicity would not let her do that.

The scholar watched for a moment, frowning as though able to read her thoughts. "The door to the street will always be open," he said. "You have my word on that as well."

"Does that mean you would be . . . my patron, sir?"

Karak nodded. "A fair description. They must still have patronage in the Empire, though possibly not in the Northern lands. The tradition died out centuries ago there."

"My father sometimes spoke of it," Cassia told him. Usually that had been in disparaging tones, mixed with unhealthy doses of bitterness and envy, and anger that no merchant or high-ranking noble would ever admit him to their household. Karak did not need to know that. Her own voice was bitter enough for the truth to show through.

"Pelicos was an apprentice in Galliarca," Karak noted.

"Truly?" Cassia was beginning to suspect he was misleading her. How could he know so much?

The scholar nodded. "That was where he learned his swordsmanship. You already have some skill with the staff. Perhaps a visit to Galliarca will make your name as well."

She wanted to believe it, but she felt too unsettled to let his encouragement affect her. All the heroes in the great Galliarcan tales were acrobatic, athletic and possessed of quick wits and godlike features. Next to them, what was a Northern girl dressed in a patched robe?

Again her thoughts must have been clear upon her face, because Karak sighed. "I could tell you that you have more skill than one of Sah Ulma's officers, but I do not think you would believe me. Perhaps I should show you. No, perhaps you should show *yourself.*"

This perplexed her, but Karak did not offer an explanation.

The crew had cleared an area of space below the steps to the hind deck. The sleeping mats were rolled up and wedged beneath the rail, bales and chests piled around the mast. Karak gestured to the space and Cassia moved hesitantly into it, feeling the weight of her audience's attention. She tightened her grip on her staff and drew it closer to her chest. What was this?

Karak reached over her shoulder and pulled the staff up and out of her hands. "You will not need this."

She twisted to seize it back, but he had already stepped beyond her reach. Sah Ulma's voice brought her around again, poised to run at the first gap she could spot in the crowd.

The captain stood with his arms folded, his expression cool and unreadable, but two of his officers had joined Cassia in the ring. The youngest was most likely Sah Ulma's son, the resemblance could hardly be coincidental. Even though he was younger than Cassia he still possessed the airs of a man twenty years older. The other was more of an age with Vescar Almoul. He spent the majority of his time up on the hind deck with the captain. Ulma's son held out a slender blade to her, hilt first, and she took it reluctantly.

The blade was wrapped with cloth to blunt the edges, the rags bound tight with fine cord. Cassia hefted the weapon, impressed to find it perfectly weighted. The few times she had been allowed to lift Meredith's greatsword, she had struggled to keep the blade level. But this was a one-handed weapon. She wondered what she was supposed to do with her other hand.

"That blade should suit the forms I have seen you practise," Karak said. "Galliarcan duelling styles often rely upon swift movement, rather than reach and weight."

"Oh good," Cassia said. Her opponent easily outmassed and outreached her, but that didn't matter. She supposed that was meant to make her feel better.

As she tried to remember how Meredith might have stood,

the younger of the two officers skipped back into the crowd, leaving her with his larger counterpart. The man held his own cloth-wrapped blade, looking more at ease with it than she could ever hope to feel. Shirtless, his forearms decorated with tattoos that snaked around his biceps, he contrived to appear both more and less intimidating than the Heir to the North. *My prince.* Meredith would not be scared of him, Cassia thought.

"Sir, this is hardly a fair contest," she protested. "I don't know how to fight like this!"

"Ah, but consider – Yaihl does not know that," Karak told her. "And he does not know the full extent of your skill."

"But he's seen me practising in the bow!"

"Nevertheless. Trust me, Cassia, you will surprise yourself."

Sah Ulma held up a hand and the crowd hushed.

"Three touches!" the captain shouted. "Three, and no more. No blood!"

That made sense. No captain would want his crew injured or crippled in a fight, even if it was a practice bout and the swords were wrapped and blunted. Cassia watched Yaihl bow courteously to her, and as he came back up she saw his gaze was wary and hooded, his weight shifted back in a defensive posture. He clearly did not want to make the first move, uncomfortable engaging in a fight against a woman. Against a *girl*. Karak might be right. Cassia dipped her own head to him and lifted her blade, just as Meredith would have done.

"Begin!" Sah Ulma barked.

Cassia felt the muscles of her legs snap taut. She pushed right, to lead with the blade. It would leave her open, invite Yaihl in to attack her. She missed the reassuring weight of the staff, and her whole left side felt wrong and unbalanced.

Yaihl responded, but not in the way she had hoped. He circled in the same direction so they remained on opposite sides of the circle, holding his blade out before him, slanted down across his torso. Packed tight around the edge of the space, his fellow sailors called out encouragement. There were one or two jeers as well, and Cassia's cheeks burned. She saw Karak in the corner of her vision, watching the first moves of the fight with little more than his usual distracted disinterest.

Tiring of their circling, Yaihl suddenly broke forwards and aimed at Cassia's unguarded upper arms. She ducked under the swing and brought her blade around in an instinctive block. Her arm quivered, her fingers numbed by the impact, and she dropped to roll out of the way. But Yaihl was a close shadow above her. Cassia's blade rang out under the next few blows, and she was lucky to have stopped them at all. She caught a glimpse of Yaihl's face, saw the dark frown of concentration there, and then he was gone.

Not far though, she thought. And he was still on his feet. Meredith had taught her to use feints to make space for herself. Cassia made to roll to one side, and pushed herself in the other direction instead. She came to rest at the very edge of the circle, with sailors stumbling over each other to get out of her way. A sudden peak of murmuring told her she must have confused them, as well as Yaihl himself.

She came back to her feet, just in time to block again. Yaihl looked put out, and a little embarrassed. Cassia was not meant to last this long. She feinted again, whirling as Meredith would have, like a child's spinning top. Yaihl's reactions were too slow, and she tapped him across the back of his shoulders before he could turn.

The deck was still, the sailors hushed. Yaihl's eyes were wide with surprise. Cassia backed away, keeping her blade raised, hardly daring to blink.

Somebody called out, a Galliarcan jibe, from Yaihl's reaction. The young officer rolled his shoulders, called out a reply that brought scattered laughter, and stepped back in towards her. This time his strokes were stronger, more direct, testing her ability to shift from stance to stance. She was forced around the edge of the ring, the space expanding as the watching sailors ducked away from the fight. When she tried to change her direction or get in behind him, he anticipated her every movement.

It was more exhausting than any bout she had fought with Meredith. Had he been more gentle with her, reined in his power to allow her to compete? Was this what every fight should have felt like? If so, what did that mean? He didn't want to hurt her – he *loved* her . . .

She faltered and mistimed a block. Yaihl's cloth-wrapped blade stabbed at her collarbone and sent her reeling. The crew cheered, but Cassia, sprawled upon the deck, could not tell who they favoured. As many urged her back to her feet as called out encouragement to Yaihl.

"Rabbit!" one man shouted in harshly-accented Hellean. "Rabbit!" The cry was taken up across the deck. Even a couple of officers joined in. Cassia levered back up with a wince, feeling the stiffness in her shoulder.

Three touches. She wasn't sure she could survive a third round. *But it's nearly over. Already.*

Her arm felt numb. She would have a terrible bruise in the morning. Yaihl's strike had been deliberate; he had hit her on her leading side, and he must have seen her discomfort. Cassia glanced across at Karak. The scholar was regarding her intently. He nodded, as though answering a question she had not asked.

I don't understand. What does he want from me? What am I supposed to do?

Yaihl waited for her to stand straight, half-turned, to present a smaller target. Cassia did the same, but her arm wobbled as she held the blade out before her and she cursed silently. One last glance at Karak before Yaihl came for her . . .

But the staff is a two-handed weapon – I can't use this!
Trust me, Cassia, you will surprise yourself.

Yaihl shifted his balance, the precursor to his attack. Just like Meredith in that way. So dangerous, but also so unvarying. Predictable, even. That was how she had first come to beat him.

You will surprise yourself.

Yaihl stepped in with a cut aimed at her numbed right side. Cassia had already turned to avoid the strike. She knew that would leave her left side undefended and, without thought, she switched the blade to her other hand. Yaihl's inevitable follow-up snapped one of the cords that held the bindings tight and she twisted her wrist to force him away, onto the defensive.

The sailors called out appreciatively – at least she hoped it was appreciation – and Yaihl looked startled. Cassia skipped backwards, using the respite to regain her breath and settle her grip on the sword hilt. The ridges of the leather had been moulded under the fingers of a right-handed man, and the damned thing felt unwieldy, even less familiar than before.

Is this what you meant? She could lead with either hand when using a staff, she realised. Meredith had insisted she practice in such a fashion. It wasn't so difficult to transfer that skill. Now Yaihl would have to change the way he fought her.

He hesitated, his caution plain upon his face. He was unsure of his approach now. Cassia pressed her advantage, trying to draw him into the centre of the circle. Her strokes were weaker than she would like, and Yaihl easily batted them away, but he could not find a way past her defence.

"Rabbit!" the sailors called behind her. Their cries battled against those who were backing Yaihl, and were beginning to drown them out. The tide had turned in this bout. Yaihl's smile had disappeared, and his face was creased in concentration.

As she forced him out from the edge of the circle she glimpsed Sah Ulma, stood amongst his officers. The captain looked concerned, and he held another of the younger officers back with one arm. The boy wanted to come to Yaihl's aid, she understood immediately. This was how close she was to winning the bout. *I can win this. I really can win this.*

She came close to flicking her blade across Yaihl's thigh. Yaihl stepped back and lowered his guard further, his torso twisted awkwardly to keep behind his sword.

But what will happen if I do win? Perhaps Sah Ulma would

not be able to hold his officers back. Perhaps they would see her victory as a mortal insult. This was a practise bout, but she was a girl; surely they had never thought she might win. *And even Sah Ulma will not want me aboard if I humiliate one of his officers.* Anger flared as she realised Karak had placed her in a position where she could only lose. She glanced over at him, to see that infuriating knowing expression still on his face.

You will surprise yourself.

Bastard, she thought. Two sharp strokes brought her to the point of victory. She had only to feint back to the left, forcing Yaihl to leave himself open. She hesitated for half a heartbeat, and the answer to her dilemma flashed into her mind. Instead of moving left, she swung to the right, presenting her unguarded flank to her opponent. Another half a heartbeat for him to recognise the opportunity, and he thumped the base of his blade against her wrist and knocked the sword from her hand.

It was an anti-climax. They stared at each other for a long moment before Yaihl raised his sword in salute. Cassia inclined her head to acknowledge his win, and to avoid his gaze. *He must know. He must be able to tell.* But when she looked up Yaihl had already turned away to be congratulated by his fellow officers.

Cassia sighed, leaning back against the ladder that led to the hind deck. She prayed the rest of the crew would quickly lose interest in her and leave her alone. Surely the novelty of a girl waving a sword about would soon wear off. Particularly as she had contrived to lose the bout.

"I told you that you would surprise yourself," Karak said, from one side.

"But I don't *understand* . . ." Cassia trailed to a frustrated halt. If she had learned anything about scholars it was that they did nothing in a direct manner. Karak's explanation, if he even offered one, would be high-minded and oblique, forcing her to discover the meaning herself. At this moment, aching and embarrassed, the last thing she wanted was to be taught the meaning of a bloody fight.

Karak waited, a shadow above her, and she sighed again. "What would have happened if I had beaten Yaihl, sir?"

"He would have made your waking hours a misery," Karak said. "Until I ordered him to stop."

That gave her cause to shield her eyes against the sun and look up at him. There was no trace of humour in his features. Jests did not come easily to this man, and those he did make seldom appealed to anyone other than himself. He was too much like Baum in that way. Cassia wanted to ask him to explain further, to square her own suspicions about who really owned this ship – Karak was no mere passenger, to judge by the way Sah Ulma talked to him – but she bit down that question in favour of another that crossed her mind.

"But you couldn't have known that I would . . ." she lowered her voice, but the crew had scattered across the deck and into the rigging. Yaihl had disappeared below. "That I would deliberately lose. You never said anything like that, sir."

"No," Karak agreed. "I did not. So you lost. Yet, at the same time, you won."

"Won what?" she asked cautiously.

"Should all rewards be so immediate?" Karak said. Cassia could not tell whether she should answer, so she waited. "Very well. Your style has distinctive Galliarcan elements, and so that sword is an apposite weapon."

"Apposite?"

"Fitting," Karak said. "It once belonged to a man who was famed in his lifetime for his prowess with the blade. For the time being, it is yours."

She still held the sword, she realised. She passed it back into her right hand, so the hilt fitted snug against her palm. It was just the right length and weight for her. She could never have managed a weapon like Meredith's greatsword for long.

How many times did my father tell the tale of Gelis and the Queen of Blades? How many times did I wish I had fought alongside her?

"Mine?"

Karak held out a slender scabbard, the ends cased in scarred silvered metal. The stitching on it was frayed with age. "A loan. Just as it has never belonged to me, so it does not belong to you. Look after it, Cassia."

Startled, she could only nod, but he had already turned away. Cassia moved from her perch before someone spotted her and decided to give her a job, returning to her usual place at the prow. There she had the privacy to examine the sword more closely, to remove the thick cloth that bound the blade and hold it up so the edge, slightly pitted, and otherwise well honed, caught the afternoon light. She trailed her fingers along the blade's length, as if she might feel some hidden truth in the cold steel.

Why give this to me? What have I done to deserve this? The sword, unlike the one Gelis had wielded, remained mute. *Patronage. Is that what this is?*

She tried to imagine herself striding the streets and squares of Galliarca with the sword strapped at her side. It seemed a ridiculous image – all the more so in that it would soon be true. Cassia shook her head and breathed out in soft disbelief. What would Baum say if he could see this? Surely the old warrior would scoff at her temerity. He had always regarded her bouts against Meredith with wry amusement, as if barely tolerating a girl's game. And Meredith himself – what would he think?

I know what he would tell me. He would tell me to respect it, to know it. He'd already know how to include the blade in everything he did. She felt a smile creep onto her lips as she thought of the Heir to the North. Even though he had abandoned her, he still held some power over her heart. Perhaps it was not his fault. Baum must have led him away. Perhaps he still thought of her.

With one hand securing the sword against her lap, she fished through her old robe to find the stone carving. The figure of Pyraete resembled Meredith every time she looked at it. Strangely, the surface of the carving still felt warm. She must have left her robe out in the sunlight.

The breeze whipped spray through the air, reminding her of her new duty of care. She sheathed the blade, making sure it was secure within the scabbard before wrapping it inside her robe along with the carving.

"Good," Sah Ulma said, behind her. Cassia jumped in fright, narrowly avoiding dropping the whole bundle. She tucked it safely aside before standing and bowing her head to the captain.

"You know enough to take care of it," Sah Ulma said. His coarse accent made his words even blunter. "Yaihl should have watched you."

"He was better, sir," Cassia said, keeping her eyes lowered in deference.

Sah Ulma spat over the rail. "No. You beat him."

That was awkward. Cassia did not know what to say.

Sah Ulma was close enough to touch her bundled robe with one foot. "Do you know why he gave you this?"

"No, sir."

"Nor do I." The captain's gaze pierced her. "My father's greatfather knew that blade. And Karak had it then. It is not his to give away."

"He told me that," Cassia said. "He said it was a loan. Sir, who does it belong to?"

Sah Ulma grunted. "Waifs and strays," he said after a moment, seeming not to have heard her. "Always waifs and strays. They all leave him seeking magic and glory. Or they flee. You're the first he has trusted this much, and I wonder why. It cannot be the story alone."

Now Cassia was growing nervous. Her mind snatched at the captain's words, trying to make sense of them, but she was certain she had missed something important. "Flee? Surely Karak doesn't mean me ill?"

"You miss the point," Sah Ulma told her. "This sword was entrusted to his care. Now he entrusts it to you. Can you live up to that, little rabbit?"

She felt her cheeks redden. "Of course I can."

The captain shrugged. "Then perhaps Pelicos will be proud."

Cassia stared down at the wrapped shape of the sword. "Pelicos? What? Do you mean . . . ? But . . . but that can't be true. It was a story. And he . . ."

Her throat dried up. Sah Ulma's silence, and his refusal to contradict her, was more potent than anything he could have said.

Pelicos went into the Tombs of Treba barehanded. He left his sword and his pack with his companion – a sorcerer, aloof and taciturn, always the foil for Pelicos's wit. Norrow always played him as a fool, a lucky survivor. Could it really be?

A sorcerer. Oh sweet gods.

"Your father's *greatfather* . . ." she said weakly.

Sah Ulma nodded. He seemed unaffected by her shock, as though this sort of revelation came naturally to him. *And I have a sorcerer as a patron.* Half a year ago she would have scoffed at such a tale, but that was before she met Baum, before she had seen fierce sorcery burn the flesh from Vescar's legionaries. She covered her mouth with both hands to muffle the panicked squeak that wanted to break free.

Sah Ulma offered her a wineskin. "This usually helps," he said.

It was unwatered, she spluttered on the first mouthful. *I have encountered him in my enquiries.* That was an understatement, if it was true. And the surging rush she had felt on the night the storm pushed the ship from its moorings on the Castaria – that had been sorcery, of course. No wonder Karak had been so pale afterwards. It all made sense now.

"What should I do, sir?"

Sah Ulma shrugged. "Be as Pelicos. The rest is up to you."

"Enter."

Cassia lifted the latch and moved cautiously through the doorway into the cabin. As before, it was lit dimly by sunlight through the slats at the rear of the cabin, but two reflecting lanterns hung from the low beams, swaying with the ship's rolling movement. Karak was a shaded figure at the desk, bent once again over a densely scribed manuscript. He did not look up. Cassia edged over the boards until she stood before the desk. She turned the scabbard over in her hands. The leather felt comforting under her fingertips, but she was not at all comfortable.

"Sir, I must return this."

Karak peered up at her. "I see. May I ask the reason?"

She'd had time to think this over. There were as many reasons as there were sheep in the mountains, but only one really mattered. "Because it is not mine."

"I see," Karak said again. "Well, I can hardly argue with that. Sit."

Cassia found a small stool in one corner of the cabin. She sat on the other side of the desk, the blade held awkwardly across her lap. Karak had returned his attention to the scroll, making occasional notations in the margins until Cassia finally mustered the courage to break the silence.

"Sah Ulma says you knew his father's greatfather, sir. And you knew Pelicos too."

"And you believe him. I am always interested in how so few would believe me if *I* told them the truth. Somehow facts have greater veracity when recounted by others. Have you never found that the case?"

Cassia forced herself to think through that question. She had a nagging suspicion the scholar was making fun of her. "Um, yes?"

"Yes," Karak repeated. He scratched another note onto the

scroll.

The sword seemed to have gained weight. Cassia shifted on the stool.

"Tell me what you know of Pelicos," Karak said. "In brief."

"He was a hero. He was brave and daring. He loved wine, women and stories. He told jokes and played tricks, and he was the greatest swordsman of his day. He never stood down from a challenge."

Another nod. "Good. And all true. Especially the last. How many of those qualities do you recognise in yourself, Cassia?"

He *was* making fun of her. "Not all of them, sir."

"Pelicos told me I would know who should inherit his sword," Karak said. "Until now, I had despaired of ever possessing that knowledge."

"But I don't *want* it!" Cassia managed to keep her voice from rising to a shout.

Karak laid his pen aside and stared at her. "Are you certain of that?"

"Absolutely, sir. I am a storyteller. That's all I want to be."

"Then the sword is yours. Just as Pelicos intended."

Cassia shook her head despairingly. "But I'm a girl – just a girl!"

Karak no longer smiled. "*Just* a girl? Hardly. In Hellea, you were a boy, a storyteller, a rogue who infiltrated the deepest cellars of the greatest library in the world." He counted off each description on his fingers. "A born trickster as well. Before that, what were you? A warrior trained by a prince, a storyteller's daughter. And more, I should think. But never *just* a girl, Cassia."

She was on the verge of tears, and she angrily pulled her fingers through her hair to obscure her face. Her ribs felt they might burst outwards at any moment. "But what if I don't take the sword? What would happen then, sir? What would you do?"

"Nothing," Karak said at last. His own tone was calm. "It

would wait for someone else. As would I. And as for the matter of my patronage; that would not be affected."

So far he had never lied to her. Not directly. She thought she could trust what he said this time as well. Although . . . "You're a sorcerer."

"Naturally. Many men of *my* age are sorcerers." At least his sense of humour had returned. Matters couldn't be that bad. A teary snuffle became a stifled giggle. "That doesn't frighten you?"

Of course it frightened her. Not a night passed that she did not think of Vescar's soldiers, aflame in the grass. *That* was sorcery. And what Malessar had done to Caenthell, laying waste to a whole kingdom in his wrath, sealing it behind a curse of eternal torment – that was sorcery at its most evil. The unnatural surging Cassia had felt when Karak stood on the hind deck to battle the elements was what even the smallest of sorceries must feel like. Only the most witless dullard would not be scared by that power. But her obstinacy flared up and refused to allow her to admit that.

"You never spent a night watching my father taunt the crowds in Lathynak," she said. "That would frighten you."

Karak chuckled. The cabin's atmosphere lightened, and even the beams of sunlight seemed to grow in strength, as though following a storm. The scholar scratched another few lines onto the scroll. "And there is the spirit of the North," he said. "To laugh in the face of danger, to believe that you master your own destiny. Good."

Should I be scared? Am I in any danger? Aside from being in the middle of the ocean on a ship bound for Galliarca, with a sorcerous master and a crew that seems to think I'm some kind of lucky charm? If she was master of her own destiny then she wasn't doing a very good job of it. There were more important questions.

"Sir, may I ask something?"

He shrugged. "It is difficult to stop you."

She ignored the jibe and thought how to phrase her question. "Are there many sorcerers left in the world? I mean – I know all the stories of the North, and the Age of Talons, and my father said there were evil warlocks in the far south of Kebria, but they all lived hundreds of years ago."

"And they may yet be there," Karak said. "We live long, Cassia. We are sustained by the energies we channel, though that sustenance is as much a burden as a blessing. The town where I was born no longer exists. My line has scattered and dissipated like drops of blood in the ocean. What would you say if I was to tell you I am older – much older – than the Hellean Empire itself? That I helped rebuild the broken walls of Stromondor?"

"I would say you look no older than my father." All the while Cassia thought she had heard some of this before, from Baum – she thought she already knew much of what Karak would tell her. *But perhaps he knows something of Malessar. Perhaps I can learn his location and wait for Meredith there.*

Karak looked down at his hands. "I feel my years. I feel the weight of ages upon my shoulders. We all do, Cassia. It is no easy thing to live this long. There are few of us, and we seldom meet. Time magnifies all faults, you see, and we find it all too easy to fall into enmity. A fight between sorcerers is not pretty. So we live in seclusion and we keep apart from ourselves. We are never ourselves, we are always someone else. I may keep a name for twenty-five years, perhaps more, and then have to uproot and become a different man. We hang from the tails of immortality, with few of the benefits and all of the disadvantages. But that does not answer your question. If my sources are correct, and I have read news from other ports correctly, then there may be a score or so of my brethren still living in the world."

His lips quirked. "Does that alarm you now?"

A whole score of sorcerers and warlocks. It did surprise her in some ways, not least that they would choose to hide themselves away. But there was something in what Baum had told her, that he could not stay too long in one place, otherwise he would risk his longevity being noticed by the townsfolk.

"You are an unusual girl," Karak remarked, still watching her intently. "Your reactions are quite atypical. Most ordinary people, on discovering the presence of a sorcerer in their midst, cannot hide their suspicion, fear and hatred. Armed parties sent to drive the ungodly from their towns. Poison, flames and stones. Men such as Sah Ulma and his fathers before him are rare indeed in their tolerance of my magic."

He seemed to have read her mind. Even if nothing else had truly alarmed her, that was enough to send a shiver along her spine. *Meredith – no! Stop thinking of him! Think of yourself, girl!*

"But why would you look to be a patron, then?" she asked. "Doesn't that only create more trouble for yourself?"

"Capricious whim. We are onlookers at the world, though we can never be a full part of it. You, Cassia, men and women like you, are a breath of fresh air in the darkened chambers of our memories. You help us recall what humanity is. Thus we live, renewed, for a short while at least." He sounded apologetic. "It is parasitic and ill-minded. The gods are no different – in fact they are worse."

They sat in silence, Cassia reeling beneath the weight of his words and the black depths of the emotions contained within them. She had thought Baum's attitude towards the world was dismissive and harsh, but Karak made his own life sound even worse. *If all sorcerers are like this then no wonder the tales they leave behind are so full of anger and tragedy.*

"I have said enough. The day is still fair."

She recognised his words as a dismissal and came to her feet. The shaft of light that framed him looked as much a prison cell as illumination. Karak did not appear to notice her as she edged past the desk, back to the door. She felt she ought to say *something* – to try to lift his spirits a little – but what could she say to ease the passage of so many centuries?

Karak spoke again as she lifted the latch. "You still have the sword, Cassia."

She looked down and realised that, with no conscious thought, she had slipped the scabbard through the fraying length of cord that served her as a belt. She felt his gaze on her back and she hesitated. "Yes, sir," she said at last. "I do."

"Good," Karak said. And, in a lower tone that she suspected she was not supposed to hear, he added, "Thank you."

It was easy to tell they were approaching the Galliarcan coast. The horizon was speckled with the bright sails of fishing fleets, emerald greens, rich earthen browns and wonderful cloud-clean whites bobbed up and down at the far edges of sight. The sky was filled with gulls once more, not just the brave few who had accompanied the *Rabbit* all the way across the sea. A fresh vein of humour bubbled amongst the officers and crew; not quite erupting forth, ever wary of tempting fate, but un-mistakably present.

Even Karak seemed affected by the new mood, spending more time on the hind deck, talking with Sah Ulma or staring out across the waves. There was an uncomfortable distance between Cassia and the sorcerer, a barrier she was not sure how to overcome. In any event, she found herself too busy with the tasks the officers set her to spend any time with him. In some ways that was a blessing. She settled back into the ship's routine, using what spare time she had practicing her forms, alternating between her staff and Pelicos's ancient blade. She had added a loop of cord at the sword's hilt, tying the other end to her wrist, in case she was clumsy enough to drop it over the side. It may not have been his to give, but she was certain Karak would not want it to end up buried in the depths of the sea.

At last, a dull smudge of land painted itself along the

horizon. Yaihl shooed Cassia away from her tasks and the crew began to ready the ship for port. She had to confine herself to the small space at the bow until the shore was close enough to see the great stone wall that jutted out into the sea to enclose Galliarca's famed port. Then Yaihl came again, this time to deliver a summons to the cabin.

She turned away from the looming city reluctantly, ducking around the work parties to knock on the cabin door.

"You asked to see me, sir?"

Karak stood in the middle of the cabin, staring distractedly at the bulkhead. She would have thought him wrapped inside his own thoughts, but for the spider-crawl sensation that made the hairs on her arms stand on end. The air tasted of dust and copper. Cassia took an instinctive step backwards, pulling at the door as though it was a shield, but the sorcerer raised one hand to halt her movement. Clutching at the latch so tightly the metal dug into her palm, Cassia stayed where she was. Her heart, however, was racing for the comparative safety of the ship's bow.

"Hush. It is almost done." Karak lifted his other hand and traced a web in the air before him. The web had an unnatural glow that reminded Cassia of Baum's destructive powers, but it was completely unlike the savage fire that had killed Vescar's men. Even as she watched, the web became translucent, stretching itself through the air like gossamer threads blown on the wind. One of the pieces came close to her skin and she shrank back. Then, abruptly, the magic was gone. A sharp gust dispersed the fine web with no sign it had ever existed. Cassia allowed herself to breathe again.

"Sir, what was that?"

"A small thing," Karak said. "The winds that brought us across the ocean are free to leave us. The breeze is changing already."

A novice sailor she might have been, but Cassia had lived in the hills long enough to recognise a change in the weather.

The wind was swinging around, bringing the taste of dry land with it. The *Rabbit* creaked and reared up against the waves as the sails caught the fresh winds. Sah Ulma shouted new orders, and the crew hurried across the deck and up through the rigging once more.

While Karak rolled his shoulders and rubbed his palms together like a craftsman at the end of his job, Cassia struggled to understand what the sorcerer meant. "You caught the winds, sir?"

"No, not caught," Karak said. "Employed might be the better word. Perhaps. But the effect is the same. Artrevia's winds have carried us safely across the ocean, and far sooner than Sah Ulma would have made this journey otherwise."

A magical breeze had carried them all the way to Galliarca. Cassia marvelled at the thought and the wonder must have been clear upon her face. Karak smiled, and dismissed his work with a single gesture.

"How else do you think we escaped the storm that swept onto the Castaria? Artrevia is my major patron now, girl. If I must often go where the winds take me, then sometimes I may ask that those winds take me where I wish to go. Such are my privileges. And Sah Ulma's sons must see their home again. They have been away since early spring."

Another dismissive gesture. "Enough talk. A task for you, girl. I would like you to accompany my goods while I pass on to my house. Your first charge."

"Are they magically sealed?"

Karak laughed. "If you wish. But ensure they all arrive at the house. Intact, please." He drew a thin coat over his robes. "Meanwhile, I must supply Sah Ulma's payment and deal with the city's officials."

He stalked past her, ducking through the door, and left her alone in the cabin. Cassia realised her mouth was hanging open, and she clamped it shut. She surveyed the half-emptied rails, and the chests that sat open beneath them. *So is this what patronage comes down to? I'm to be his servant?* A spark of indignation, an echo of her father's temper, threatened to flare up and she smothered it quickly. *I'll have a roof over my head, and meals, and I even have a sword. And not just any sword. Can I complain? Really?*

To judge by the rising level of noise outside the ship was drawing closer to the docks. She set to work, folding the sorcerer's robes down into the chests. There was a muslin bag of dried rose petals between two of the chests, and she sprinkled small handfuls over the top layers of clothing before closing the chests and slotting the bolts home.

The rest of Karak's goods were already stowed away. He did not travel light. Some of the chests looked too heavy for even two of the sailors to manage between them. *Did he pack his entire house? Or has he stolen the contents of Hellea's library?* That idea made her smile.

Waiting for the sailors to arrive and help, she sat cross-legged before one of the chests, scrutinising the scarred fittings of the locks and the corner braces. The designs carved into them were old, and looked naggingly familiar. They made her think of the North. Of course, it was likely Karak had been into the North at some point in his long life. He might have acquired these chests in any of the coastal towns.

They might even be as old as this sword, Pelicos himself might have lifted this chest. She felt herself teetering on the crumbling cliff edges of history. If she looked down she might lose her balance and fall. *Try not to think about it too much.*

She had a little time to gather her ideas now. To think of how to *begin* asking questions of Karak, and tracking down Malessar.

Two sorcerers in one city – surely one would know how to find the other. She considered that for a moment. Something didn't feel quite right.

We live in seclusion and we keep apart from ourselves. We find it all too easy to fall into enmity.

She shook her head. The thoughts would not fit together. Why would Karak come to Galliarca if Malessar already lived here? In fact, why would Karak and Malessar both visit Hellea at the same time? It sounded as though if they came upon each other they would have set fire to half of the city. And if Baum had known Karak was also in the city surely he would have mentioned it? He was a sorcerer as well, after all. If it was rare to find two sorcerers in the same city, then three must be nothing short of apocalyptic. Such coincidences never happened. Not even in stories.

Cassia lifted one hand to her mouth.

Stories . . .

How do you know so much about our stories?

We are never ourselves; we are always someone else.

I helped rebuild the broken walls of Stromondor.

Malessar had been at Stromondor when the city was sacked by the Hordes. Everybody knew that story. And people still lived there even now, though the sea power was a pale shade of its former self. *He left the battle. He left the whole city to die.* But what if he went back afterwards? What if he went back to make amends?

Surely not. That did not fit with what Baum had told her of the man. Malessar had thrown fire into the crowds of Jedrell's courtiers. He had seized the High King's heart and torn it from the man's chest and, while Jedrell breathed his last, he had seared Aliciana from existence. Such a man could never let guilt or remorse sway his thoughts.

But still there was something that did not fit.

If you should see this mark upon any of the cases . . .

She traced two V-shapes into the dust between the chests. Then she sat for a long moment and considered that shape. Karak would have drawn it from the other side, she realised. They were not twinned V-shapes at all. They were mountains.

Or the letter M.

Her fingers were numb. She forced herself into motion,

scrambling up from the deck and wiping away the scribbled letters with one foot, as though erasing them could also erase the avalanche of awful ideas flooding into her head, pushing at the sides of her skull. Fractions of thoughts, gathering together into one terrible and unwelcome revelation.

Oh, I must be wrong. Please, I must be wrong.

There had to be a way to be sure. She cast an anxious glance at the door, perhaps she had enough time. She bit her lip and her hand hesitated over the clasp of the first chest. *I have no right. I have no right.*

She held her breath and flicked the clasp aside. Nothing happened. Foul demons failed to rise to drag her away to fiery hells. Sorcerous magic was conspicuous by its absence. She leaned across and flicked the other catch, lifting the lid before she could have second thoughts.

Karak's writing materials were inside: the table folded down into the base of the chest, and the space around it tightly packed with boxes of pens, cushioned bottles of ink, and long, slender scroll cases. Hardly breathing, and with no deliberate choice in mind, Cassia let her hand fall onto one of the scroll cases. The golden-rimmed ends were cool to the touch. It seemed to weigh so much more than it should.

She turned it over in her hands and realised that she had no real idea of what proof she needed. Something caught her eye, a design scratched into the leather. Like an old tattoo, it had faded with time, but it was simple enough that she could make it out with little trouble.

A stylised M.

Cassia dropped it back into the trunk and picked up another. Again there was an M stencilled into the leather. And on the one after that too. She lowered the lid slowly and refastened the catches with trembling fingers. The chest sat accusingly before her.

Oh dear Ceresel, what have you done to me?

Baum's instincts had not been wrong. Malessar had been in

Hellea all along. He had indeed left the city with the turn of the season. And somehow the gods had conspired to send her, alone, with him.

And – even worse – she had become his ward. She had allied herself with the warlock who devastated the North and destroyed Caenthell.

Now she sat alone in the quiet of the cabin, surrounded by Karak's effects – Malessar's effects – and she knew that she was running out of time. The sailors would come to take these chests away, and Malessar would expect her to accompany them. To his house. Her first instinct was to run. Run as fast as her feet could carry her, until Galliarca was a distant memory. Forget about Baum and Meredith and everything she had done over the last few months. Start again.

But this was not her home. Beyond this cabin, beyond the deck of the *Rabbit*, was a strange land, even more alien to her than Hellea had been. She didn't have the first idea how to survive, how to get through her first night in this new world.

If I go with him, I will have a roof over my head. Food and clothing. He has given me a sword. I made a bargain with him.

There was a stubborn streak inside her that demanded she keep her side of that bargain. *Bloody stupid girl. You leapt at the chance to get away from Keskor, and you sided with Baum and Meredith first. Baum is sure to follow you across the ocean eventually, and when he does you can lead him straight to Jedrell's murderer. You got yourself into this mess – now deal with it.*

"I only wanted to tell the story," she whispered. The solid travel chests gave no reply.

She stood again, her legs unsteady beneath her, and wiped her eyes, taking a few moments to steady her breathing. It would do no good if Yaihl came to find her crying her eyes out. Or if Karak – Malessar – was to return unexpectedly. Questions would be asked.

Now the *story* was telling *her*. That wasn't right; it wasn't fair. This wasn't how it was supposed to happen. But the gate was open and the herd had wandered, as the old saying went. If there was nothing she could do about where she found herself and how she had gotten there – blind, stupid, fickle chance, Ceresel's poison kiss – she might still turn the situation to her own benefit. It would not be easy, and it would most likely be dangerous. But she could be like Malessar's shieldmen, hard and steadfast, weathering all storms. If she was a lamb jumping for the knife, well, she had her own blade now.

She crossed to the door and leaned on the frame, staring out beyond the rail to the harbour. The *Rabbit* was being pulled by one of the port master's pilot boats, tugged to within a few lengths of the outermost piles. Dock workers waited to catch the ropes the crew had coiled ready. They were dark, wiry men, shirtless for the most part, their skins baked by the sun into shining armoured carapaces. They wrapped rags and lengths of cloth about their heads, and their leggings were loose and flowing, tailored in fashions Cassia had never seen before coming aboard the *Rabbit*.

The heat and the dry wind picking up from inland made it feel like midsummer. The winds Malessar had harnessed to bring the ship here had sheltered her from the heat. Her storyteller's robe, thin and patched as it was, would soon become uncomfortable in this climate. She would have to find some more appropriate dress.

Yaihl approached from the bow, shouting and gesturing at somebody above her on the hind deck. There was a fresh swagger in his stride, a bit of homecoming pride, and a fair amount of showing off. She'd seen Hetch do the same. *Men* are *the same the world over*, she thought.

"Where's Karak?" she asked, stepping back to allow him into the cabin.

"Gone ashore now, little rabbit," Yaihl said. "Gone by oar. Over the side, understand?"

She nodded, she had seen the rowboats that cluttered the harbour. Clearly the warlock had much to attend to, and she could not help but feel disappointed and relieved in equal measures. Disappointed because she had been left behind again. And relieved for much the same reason.

"You go with these, yes?"

She shook her thoughts free and nodded. "Yes. I go with these. Do you want me to help lifting them?"

Yaihl pointed to where young Genjis hovered nervously at the door. "I have help! You, help? I put box under that arm and you under this one!" The officer laughed, not unkindly.

Cassia braced her fists against her hips in mock indignation. "I'll fight you!"

This time both Yaihl and Genjis laughed, but Yaihl took a small step out of her reach. Cassia tried not to smile too much.

Be as Pelicos.

Perhaps she could do that.

Chapter Fifteen

"Cloth! Red cloth for your shirts, young master! Six pennies a bolt! The best colour!"

"All designs sewn! Birds that fly!"

Cassia ignored the calls. She skipped past a small crowd of men gathered outside one of the ovens that were wedged into every small corner in the heart of the city. One hand held her leather scabbard flat against her leg to keep the sword from tangling and tripping her, and she flashed a grin at the stall holder who offered such lifelike embroidery. His birds were indeed wonderful, and if she had the coin she would not hesitate to commission a design, but the man simply could not draw any four-legged beast. His rabbits were awful.

As with most of the narrow, twisting streets in the *mede* of the walled city, the afternoon sun slipped through slats and dried palm fronds latticed over the tops of the buildings. The heights of the walls differed with every pace, so the shade was unevenly distributed, illuminating small windows and odd corners that drew Cassia's attention every time she looked up. She loved to take to the streets in the early afternoon, when much of the city retreated indoors and relaxed or dined. There was so much more space, and she danced into each patch of sunlight as though working through one of the forms. That garnered odd glances from the few passers-by on the streets – but she didn't care at all.

She'd picked up some Galliarcan aboard the *Rabbit*, and even more since then. A part of her was surprised by the speed and facility with which her language had improved. That was how she knew she'd made a ripple of sorts in the city, hearing people call her the *nord lapa*, or *the story girl*. It made her flush with barely suppressed pride.

I haven't even done anything yet! Just wait!

It had taken several days to work out even a small part of the maze of alleys that made up the *mede*. The sheer profusion of stalls and awnings, and tumble-down buildings leaning over each other to prop themselves up, made it difficult for her to differentiate one narrowed, uneven lane from the next. She'd got lost on her first venture and hadn't found her way back to Malessar's *dhar* until late in the evening, exhausted, hungry, and on the verge of tears. Hellea had been intimidating enough; Galliarca was simply terrifying. That night she had cried herself to sleep, wishing she had never come to the city.

But that had been weeks ago – a lifetime. She was as comfortable in the *mede* as she had ever been in any town of the North. Each day brought something new to astound and enthrall her: new spices, strange beasts brought by traders from beyond the mountains to the south, Kebrian dancers, slender golden chains dancing like rain from their outstretched arms . . .

Oh, and the stories. The wonderful proliferation of stories.

So much of them still went over her head – the language was so rich, and every word seemed to have three or more meanings – but there were some she already knew, and that made things easier. She could go to a different corner of Fahrian Square each night, join the edges of another crowd, and hear a tale she'd never heard before. There were storytellers from across the known world; Kebrian, Stromondorian, Hellean and Northern, and even plainsmen from Berdella. Malessar had pointed them out to her one evening on one of the few occasions he had accompanied her, naming all the men he knew, listing each man's tendency for tragedies or heroic humour and explaining the particular tales they counted as their own, until Cassia felt her head would burst with the volume of new information. There was no way she would ever be able to remember it all.

That night stayed fresh in her mind for more than just that reason. It was the first time, she realised afterwards, that she had not felt afraid.

It was a peculiar revelation, one she pursued only reluctantly, as if in doing so she might break this dream. So she threw herself headlong into the city, all it could offer to her, and all she could take from it, and tried her best to ignore the dark thoughts massing at the edge of her mind, walled up with her memories of the North. Of the past. Of a *different* girl.

Every corner and twisted alley led deeper into the heart of the *mede*. Yet there was open space in the most unexpected places. Here for example, at the far end of a lane so narrow two men could not pass side by side, Cassia knew there was an empty square with an old hay cart abandoned against one wall. The cart's presence was a mystery, it was much too wide to have ever entered through any of the lanes. Had somebody built it here, in this square? Or was it an accidental relic of a long-forgotten magic? Her imagination leaped upon it. And in another part of the *mede*, a small, anonymous door set into a long, blank wall had been left open to reveal a vaulted, airy temple, the glazed columns suffused with sunlight. Cassia stared into the space in awe – it far outstripped any of the Hellean temples she had seen – but when she tried to find the place again, she could only trudge in frustrated circles through the *mede* and nobody seemed to understand what she was looking for.

And so it was with Malessar's *dhar*. It confounded her expectations at the same time as it reinforced everything she thought she knew about the warlock from Norrow's tales.

She had thought Malessar would live in an opulent palace, with an army of quiescent servants to cater to his whims. How else would a warlock live, after all? But when the baggage train halted at last before an iron banded door, she thought there must have been some mistake. The alley was a dead-end, and a small group of young men watched her from a doorway further along. The wailing of children echoed faintly through the air, over the muted murmur of the wider streets they had left behind.

"Where are we?" she had asked. "Are we lost?"

Yaihl slid the travel chest from his shoulder and laid it on the ground before her. "No, we are here," he said. He knocked on the door and waited. The porters they had hired to carry Malessar's other goods had already grounded their own loads and were gathering around Genjis to receive payment. Cassia was too exhausted to do anything but slump down on top of the nearest chest.

A rattle of bolts drew her attention back to the door. An old man, his lined face hidden beneath a thick beard still flecked with black, scowled out at them. He and Yaihl exchanged a few short sentences and then the man fixed his glare upon her. "Another one, eh?" he said in Hellean. "Gods above and below, another mouth to feed."

Cassia coloured, and bit down on her reply. The old man sighed and disappeared, leaving Yaihl and Genjis to haul the chests through the door and down one uneven step to the tiled antechamber beyond. Cassia had to wait until the last one had crossed the threshold before she could follow, acutely aware of how the men watched her. Her sword, she thought, wouldn't make much difference. It certainly didn't shield her against their eyes.

The antechamber had given her pause for thought. The walls were plain, but their ochre sheen was richer than she expected given the house's weathered exterior, and the candles the old man lit bathed the room with warmth – but then she was ushered across and into a short passage that led . . . into a *garden*, of all things. She halted, staring around and up at the lush plants and shady trees that grew in enclosed beds, between neat paved paths. At the centre of the garden was a stone fountain where water bubbled pleasantly. Rows of arches created small colonnades on all four sides of the garden, like a miniature version of Hellea's library, but there was a second set of arches on the floor above as well. Doors and windows indicated rooms on both this side and the far side of the garden, creating two separate wings with the garden enclosed between them. The house had turned its back to the city and created its own world of calm here.

How fitting, she had realised later on. Malassar had raised walls against the world, disguised himself as a scholar, and turned inwards. How could his house have reflected him in any other way?

She swung into the alley and took the last turn. The thick sack bumped against her back. She was probably late, but she was certain Narjess wouldn't mind too much. The old gardener was a grump, but he never stayed in a mood for long.

The *dhar* was wide enough to warrant two doors onto the street, with the nearest of the two a narrow, duck-down affair that led straight into Leili's kitchen. Unlike the main door at the other end of the alley, this one was always open during the day. Leili could be found cooking, baking or salting meat, usually singing or chattering at high speed to one of the women from the neighbouring houses. Cassia slung the sack through first, clasping her blade to her side as she ducked through after it. "Hello, Leili!"

The short woman barely paused for breath, cursing some poor boy who'd had the ill fortune to short change her in the market. Her companion nodded agreement each time Leili jabbed her filleting knife into the air. Cassia grinned, snatched up the sack again, and headed for the door at the far end of the kitchen. It never ceased to amuse her that, for a man so insular, Malessar had surrounded himself with servants who never stopped talking.

These doors, at least, were more correctly sized. Curved and ornamented, they opened onto one of the colonnades. Cassia slowed, taking her time through the garden. She had never been ordered *not* to run here, but it didn't seem like the sort of place she should hurry.

Narjess was down by the far wall, nursing a creeping vine towards the upper balcony. He muttered under his breath as if chastising it for not growing faster. He didn't look around as Cassia approached, but he had clearly heard her come through the kitchen. "Great fates, girl, I could have gone twice myself for the time you've taken!"

"There was a wedding," she started, and Narjess sighed.

"If not one thing then another," he said. "Newborn babies have a greater attention span! Don't tell me, don't tell me, there was food, and dancing . . ."

"And a storyteller for the wedding party," Cassia said. "I could not stay too long though."

Narjess grunted. "Just give me the bag, girl."

He examined the table legs – three, hand-turned in the artisans' district and bound together to keep them from damaging each other on the journey – and shook his head, his muttered words never quite audible. He seemed to do a lot of that when she was around. That, and sighing. There was plenty of that too.

"I suppose I can sand out these knocks before I paint them," he said at last. "But great fates, girl, do try to be careful."

"I'll try," she said. "Narjess, is the master in his rooms?"

"No. Still not back."

She glanced up at the balcony, at the shuttered windows sheltered behind it. That whole half of the *dhar* was private and out of bounds, she had been told early on. There were layers of privacy beyond anything she could penetrate. Even when

Malessar was within and the windows were unshuttered, the doors were firmly closed. Leili was the only person to enter there, and even then only at the warlock's bidding. If Cassia saw him at all, it was here in the garden, or on the terraces that enclosed it, or when he decided she needed to learn something.

Secretive as he was, he had already disappeared from the house at least twice without telling anyone of his intentions. The first time, Cassia had panicked, thinking she had been abandoned already. But Leili dismissed her alarm with a brisk clucking. "The master's life revolves around the master, not around you," she said. "I certainly don't want to know what he's doing, and neither should you. Now, if you don't want to help, get out from underfoot. This meat won't spice itself."

It hadn't been much comfort, which was part of why she still felt happier away from the *dhar* than within it. Out in the *mede* she was not surrounded by proof of who her patron truly was. She didn't have to pretend the walls of the Galliarcan house were not decorated with scripts, hangings and other objects that were all unmistakably of the North. Or, more, that some of the scripts didn't actually name the towns that Baum had mentioned to her. Gethista. Aelior. Kennetta. The memory of riding through the cold grasses towards the ancient ruins of Gethista was still clear in her mind, and thoughts of the curse upon Caenthell and Baum's centuries-long search for vengeance inevitably followed close behind.

On some nights she lay awake, listening to the sounds of the *mede* echoing through her small window and wondered what sort of mischief and subterfuge Malessar was about now. There had to be something. After all, hadn't he been in Kebria, working ill magics in the queen's palace there, before the sudden arrival of Guhl and Arca's squad of soldiers caused him to disappear overnight? He'd be plotting something now, Cassia was certain. Everything Baum had told her of the warlock pointed to it.

And neither Leili nor Narjess appeared concerned. Cassia

was convinced they had to know the truth of his identity, yet they referred to him, and addressed him, only as their master. She had been careful not to let slip the extent of her own knowledge for fear she would find herself ejected onto the streets once more. Or worse.

I assume they know. Perhaps they assume that I know. And Malessar – what does he assume? What does he know? There was danger in everything she said, she had quickly realised, a terrible danger that she would betray either herself, or Baum and Meredith.

She crossed back to the shaded table at the other end of the garden and poured a measure of the minted drink that Leili always maintained there. The Galliarcan staple was an acquired taste, but it refreshed her more than water alone, clearing her palate of the fine, dry sand that seemed to hang in the air. There was time enough to doze and regain her energy before the market stalls were broken down in the Fahrian Square and the crowds began to gather for the night's festivities.

And tonight she would wear her storyteller's gear, the gown repaired and repatched, the colours fresher and less Northern, embroidered designs flowing in a fashion that Norrow's never had. Her cap was brand new, hemmed with thread that sparkled in the lamplight. Tonight she would try her own tales in the Square.

She'd spent enough time listening to others, hearing the rhythms they used and the ways they drew their audiences into their stories, and she had tried out some of those techniques on the children who infested the top end of the alleyway. Whether they had listened because of her skill, or because of the sheer novelty was debatable, but the point was that they had listened. When she lowered her voice and brought the tale to a slow build-up of tension, they leaned in closer, ballgames and playfights forgotten; then with bold jests and heroic deeds she whipped fire into them. And, the following day, they wanted more.

In one wild moment, buoyed by their excitement, she even wondered if she might have been inspired by a spirit that still watched over Pelicos's sword, or perhaps even by Pelicos himself. As unlikely as that seemed, she realised she was far more ready to believe in such things now she had seen sorcery for herself.

I'll tell my tales just as he fought, she decided. *Lightfooted, daring, the breeze that licks the darkened corners of a room. Swords and words – the two aren't so far apart, are they?*

Leili and Narjess slept in the long room between the kitchen and the entrance hall, a room they had clearly occupied for a number of years to judge by the possessions they had accumulated, which stood as a bulwark against the Northern-styled furnishings that prevailed in the rest of the house. Malessar had offered Cassia the room above that, but she spent no more than half an hour in it, marvelling at the thought that she should merit so much space, before she began to feel uncomfortable.

The waifs and strays Malessar had taken in before haunted the room. Every step Cassia took echoed through the air and against the walls before seeming to disappear up into the dark ceiling panels. There were hundreds of other sounds up there, she thought, left by its previous occupants. She felt them looking down at her. She could not lie on the bed without feeling exposed and vulnerable.

"It's too large," was all she said to Malessar. For once the warlock actually looked surprised.

She had spent that first night on a mat in one of the garden colonnades. It was much colder than she had expected, but she was too exhausted to care. In the morning, after some negotiation with Narjess and Leili, she appropriated a small room just off the entrance hall. It had been used as a storage room, but once it was cleared and swept and Cassia had dragged in an old, lumpy pallet, it was a lot more comfortable than the empty room on the floor above.

There were other considerations too. Here, she was closer to the *dhar's* front door. If she had to leave, she could do so quickly, and without having to let the warlock's servants know. Malessar might have promised she would be safe in his house, but there was a nagging uncertainty, as that promise came from the man who had destroyed the North.

She dropped onto her pallet and felt beneath it for the stone charm. It was virtually the only thing she still owned from her time in Hellea and the North. Peculiarly, it always seemed to retain some warmth, even when left in here, in the cool. She ran the tips of her fingers over the worn contours of the figure. It was easy to imagine she was touching Meredith's skin, caressing his cheek or his lips. From there her memories of his touch, of his body so close to her own that an inhalation would have pressed them together, would lull her to sleep every night.

There was no time for that right now. She shoved those thoughts to the back of her mind, the warmth she felt not entirely caused by her journey through the streets. *Ceresel, be merciful tonight. And Movalli, patron of storytellers, please look down in favour.* She hesitated then, and looked at the carved figure once more. *And Pyraete, should it please you, I am your servant.*

If any of the gods heard her, they did not answer.

Fahrian Square was a cacophony of noise and motion. Polyrhythmic drumming echoed between the buildings, the beats chasing themselves through the air like playful spirits. Young boys shinned up studded posts to light the braziers, baiting each other with catcalls. Below them the stalls in the square moved like a tide, collapsed and lifted aside by expert teams who had performed the same task every day for their whole adult lives. Behind them came the carts that held the open-air ovens, the rickety benches, the spice traders . . . and the storytellers.

They were there all through the day, but the best storytellers came out in the evening. That was where Cassia wanted to be: among the very best.

She threw out her elbows as she entered the square, her cloak billowing out behind her. The silvered thread flickered around the edges of the patches she had sewn onto the cloak, catching both the light of the braziers and the eyes of the nearest onlookers in equal measure. She felt the corners of her mouth twist upwards into a grin. *This is what my father must feel when he does this.*

All the prime positions were already taken. There was an established pecking order amongst the city's storytellers, it seemed, and Cassia had not found her own place yet. Some of the stares turned in her direction were speculative, others less friendly. A few were cold and openly hostile. She threaded through the gathering crowds, making sure to step in time to the dominant beat. When she looked back over her shoulder after her first circuit of the Square, she was delighted to realise a couple of men had begun to follow her. A handful of young boys, including one or two she thought she recognised from Malessar's street, were gathering just behind them.

An audience. In Fahrian Square. My father would bite his own tongue out.

She cast about for a space to set up, and spied a pitch to her left that a stallholder had just vacated. There was no sign that another vendor would take his place. *So I'll go there. At least until they try to move me on.* She swatted the thought away. *One problem at a time, girl. One at a time.*

The boys flooded in to the space before her, around the ankles of the few men who had come to hear the Square's newest storyteller. The canopy flickered with the reflected light of the nearest braziers, and the air was filled with smoke from the cookfires and the burning tang of spices and stewing lamb.

She reached up to adjust her cap, making sure her hair was tucked safely underneath it, using the moment to examine her audience more closely. The boys would want something thrilling, a tale of heroics and treasure. Dragons were always appreciated, she had discovered. She was less certain of the men. Would they look for old-fashioned epics, or more modern tales? Something that matched the rhythm of the Square, perhaps?

"Who remembers the days of old?" she asked aloud, falling into the cadence of the introduction as though she had recited it every night of her life. "Who remembers the great and the good? Their deeds and their trials? Who remembers the battles of times long passed, when the heroes and generals are blown to the sands? Who will remember our times, when we too are gone from the world, when our lives are done and our last breaths escape to rise past the tallest peaks of the mountains?"

There was something that might suit. Her father had told it as a bawdy story in taverns, while Cassia huddled below the window outside, close against the wall to keep the night winds from chilling her bones. She could shorten it by stripping out some of the less palatable jokes, but there would still be enough humour in the tale to please her audience.

I hope.

"So thought Pelicos, Pelicos the Brave, Pelicos Bedstealer with his sheets to the wind – the wind that had borne him away from the shores, into the seas that took him to wife . . ."

With the final words, she swept off her cap and flung it to the ground, and raised her arms into the air to show the gods she was done. Her mouth was dry, and it felt as though there was no air in her lungs. Her eyes itched from the smoke that drifted across from the next stall. Throughout her tale she had focused on the front rows of her audience, switching her attention from one set of eyes to another as she paced the small space she had claimed. It was a little wider now; she had decided to illustrate one of the tale's fights with her staff, marrying the rhythm to Meredith's training, and the boys had scrambled backwards with excited cries.

Now she looked out and realised her small company had grown. Behind the boys, and the men who had followed her across the Square, there was a wall of bodies. Twenty at least, perhaps more, Cassia thought in surprise. *Surprise? No – this is what I wanted!*

The boys at her feet cheered and begged for more, just as they had in the alleys by Malessar's *dhar.*

"A *girl?*" she heard one man's voice question. "And a *Northern* girl at that?"

Cassia felt her cheeks colour.

"But better than Dromic ever told it," his neighbour said, sounding amused. He tossed a coin down into her hat.

Another clinked in after it. And then a third. Cassia leaned on her staff and exhaled heavily.

It was a start, she thought. Thank Ceresel, it was a start.

Chapter Sixteen

THE WARLOCK REAPPEARED in his *dhar* one morning as though he had never been away. Cassia stumbled over him as she carried the morning's tray of minted tea to the table in the centre of the garden. He was kneeling at the side of the raised flower bed, his attention focused upon one of the plants.

"I had hoped this specimen would thrive in this environment," he said, without looking up at her. He cupped one of the blooms in his hand, tilting it back and forth with a surprising tenderness. "It has taken, but still it struggles. A troublesome transplantation."

Cassia felt awkward all of a sudden. It was clear the warlock was referring to her, as much as to the flower. She could not tell if he meant her to answer.

"You still sleep in the cupboard beneath the stairs."

She nodded, realising that he still had not looked up. "Yes, sir."

"You would fare better upstairs."

She hesitated before replying. "I think that would be a troublesome transplantation, sir."

Malessar's shoulders stiffened, and then he relaxed. "As you will, Cassia. As you will."

Cassia took the tray to the table and set out the small glass cups. She forced herself to concentrate on pouring the tea, aware of the warlock moving through the garden behind her. As ever, he brought a massive weight to the atmosphere of the house. Even the near-constant chatter from the kitchen had diminished.

I don't know who – or what *– he expects me to be. I am not Pelicos, no matter what he thinks.*

Her skill with the sword was improving all the time, and Malessar had been right to suggest the Galliarcan style would suit her, but in her heart she knew she was not a born swordswoman. There was a burden of expectation that she could not shift, and she was reluctant to face up to it.

Is it my fault? Have I misled him? Or myself?

Usually either Leili or Narjess joined her for the meal, but today neither were present. Instead Malessar sat down opposite her, picking at his food with the slow grace of a stork, apparently unaware of how he discomfited Cassia. His robes were worn and stained by travel. It was as though he had walked into the city directly from the scrubland that stretched south towards the mountains.

What could be out there to catch a warlock's interest? She itched to ask, but diverted herself instead with another flatbread, even though she was already full.

"You appear to have made yourself at home everywhere in the city but here," Malessar said, tilting his cup at her to emphasise the point. "Fahrian Square, the rest of the *mede*, they even talk of the Northern Rabbit in the lower circles of the Court."

For one moment Cassia was too shocked to speak. "But I haven't even been to the Court!" she managed at last.

"Indeed," the warlock said. "A fine achievement. It seems my first instincts were correct."

He sounded proud of that. Proud of her, or of himself? It was a strange idea to have to consider. Almost as strange, if not more so, as the idea she might be talked of in the circles of Galliarca's court. But wasn't that what she wanted, after all? The glory her father could never achieve? And if she had help to achieve it – well, there was nothing wrong with that. Again, it was more than her father would ever have. He had spent so much of his life grasping for anything that glittered, greedy yet unambitious, but never once had he been offered any help.

She almost felt sorry for him in that moment.

But what of Malessar? What does he gain from my rise? Why would that please him?

You help us to recall what humanity is, he had told her.

Could it be as simple as that? The fell villain of the Northern sagas, the warlock who destroyed Caenthell with a curse so forceful even the gods cried out, the master of a thousand foul and secret plots – he did this for no other reason than that he *wanted* to? She was not a small, easily manipulated piece in one of his grand and evil schemes? Baum would tell her otherwise, Cassia was certain. His centuries of experience, spent constructing Caenthell's revenge on Pyraete's behalf, were worth so much more than Cassia's meagre handful of years.

But Baum was not here.

She looked around at the walls of the *dhar*. A world turned inward. Private and reflective. Not obvious aspects of a power-crazed warlock.

Malessar had turned his attention back to the meal. Cassia watched him for a moment, hesitating over the question she desperately wanted to ask. She chose the more obvious question instead.

"Instincts for what, sir?"

"For potential, of course. The North has ever been a land of unfulfilled potential. And of *wasted* potential," he added darkly.

"So what would you have me do in the Court?"

Now he looked up at her, apparently surprised. "Do? What

would I have you do? Cassia, why do you think I would have you *do* anything, other than tell your tales?"

There was nothing for it. She took a deep breath. "Because of who you are?"

The warlock was silent. He took a small, ivory-handled knife to carve an apple into slices, each movement quite deliberate. Cassia wanted to flee onto the streets, her heart felt like it was pulling her physically across the length of the garden. But she could not make herself move. Instead she gripped the edge of the table so hard her knuckles were white beneath her tanned skin. It wasn't magic that kept her in her seat, she knew. It was fear.

"My reputation goes before me. Always." Malessar shrugged. It was a small action, but it held far more emotion than any great outburst would have done. "No matter how I might live, or where, or whether I go by a different name. Always there is something – or someone – to remind me of my mistakes. And it hurts twice as much to hear it from a girl of the North. Of the North and . . ."

He shook his head. "It does not matter. I would wish that your tales were wrong. In so many respects they *are* wrong, but not in the most important aspects. But *this* is my house, Cassia, not the apartments of a minister deep inside a palace or high in the main tower of a castle. I am nothing to Galliarca's princes, nothing and nobody. I have no interest in how they rule their state, as long as they do not interfere in my work or my life. If there is any work to be done at the Court, then the Court can do it itself."

"I only thought . . ." Cassia began, but the cold steel of Malessar's stare froze her words in mid-sentence.

"You thought I have some degree of influence in Galliarca's court," Malessar said. "That I am the power behind the throne, just as I was in Stromondor, or Hellea, or Kalakhadze during the Golden Rule."

Or in Kebria, she thought, remembering Arca's story. But

this was not the time to say such things.

"And I was all of those things." His voice was as hard and bitter as Baum's had been when the veteran described the aftermath of Caenthell's demise. "All of those, and more besides. And so I have become an embodiment of evil – of treachery, avarice, dark, inhuman gods and destruction. The fall of Stromondor was my fault; that the Golden Rule was twisted into perversion and depravity was also my fault. Shall I list them all for you, Cassia? All the stories you will have heard, and the ones you may not already know? Wouldn't you like to know what I have done in the cause of peace? What I have sacrificed?"

She could barely manage to shake her head. It was a reflexive action far more than an intellectual response.

"Your audiences would not want to hear such things from my perspective, I think. No, they have their villain. All for the one thing I wish I had never done. The one thing I can *never* take back, no matter how much I do in penance."

"Caenthell," Cassia breathed. "You cursed the North."

The words, even spoken so quietly, seemed to fill the courtyard and echo beneath the columns that surrounded the garden. The air felt cooler, as though the wind blew from the North, ignoring all the walls that stood in its way.

"Exactly so," Malessar said. "And everything I have done since has been an attempt to redress the balance. Without the presence of the High King, watching from the mountains, there has been nothing to check the advance of the barbarians, high beyond what you call the North. Nothing to stop the slow spread of Hellean civilisation across the shores of the Middle Sea. Nothing to keep Hellea from invading these shores and laying siege to Stromondor or Kebria. Stromondor weathered that storm, but it was too weak to hold off the Hordes that came after, and I could not defend the city by myself. By the time I marshalled the necessary help, it was far too late. All I could do was to assist in burying the dead. Even when I have intervened personally in Hellean affairs, I have failed to stem the flow of history. My efforts to limit their progress, to foster a fear of the lands beyond their own and make them into a more insular people, only backfired and caused an even greater streak of imperialism instead. How can I hope to engineer a solution to that problem? By tinkering with Galliarca as well, to cause ever greater wars in every land known to man? By giving such advanced knowledge and magic to the Hordes that they could easily drive the inhabitants of every land into the sea?

"Or should I bring myself into the open once more and rule the world for myself? Fill the bodies of the ruling families with fire, scatter their ashes to the winds, tear down their citadels and appoint pale puppets to dance at the ends of my strings? Well, Cassia? What should I do?"

"I'm sorry," Cassia said.

"Not half so much as I am." Malessar ground out the words.

"But you could lift the curse." The idea was a sudden revelation. Of course – if Malessar was the greatest sorcerer in the world, then surely he could reverse what he had done. If she could persuade him to do that, then Baum need not try to defeat him! "You could bring Caenthell back. Couldn't you, sir?"

He stared at her, and though the rest of his expression remained opaque there was anger in his eyes. Anger . . . and something else . . .

"Bring it back?" he repeated. "Bring it back? Revoke a curse laid in the name of a god? A curse laid with all the power Pyraete had given to me?" He shook his head, and his mouth twisted abruptly into a smile. "Oh, Cassia, if it was as simple as that I would have done it centuries ago and let them all rest in peace."

In all of Baum's stories recounting the history of Malessar's evil works, there had never been anything to suggest the warlock would be so repentant. That he actually wanted to revoke his own curse. Cassia cupped her hands protectively around her tea. All this time – all these years – and Baum never knew. *Oh sweet gods!*

"But they are all dead and gone, and I am nothing more than a demon – a god-touched warlock. Everything I have ever done to try to protect the North from its predators . . . and most likely nobody even remembers my name, let alone what I have done."

It was Cassia's turn to disagree. "No, sir. They still talk about you. About . . . Caenthell." Her mind worked furiously to keep her from disclosing too much. She knew she could not mention Baum or Meredith directly, but she could still try to persuade Malessar to lift his curse. It might not be as difficult as it appeared, if Malessar truly regretted his actions. "Some people – I've heard that some people long for the North to rise again. Surely you'd know a way to help them?"

Malessar looked away. "There is no way to lift that curse, Cassia. And even if there were, it would not be safe to do so."

Cassia knew she was pushing her luck with more questions, but she had come this far, and not to have the answers would be an affront to her natural curiosity. "Why, sir? Surely it would be a better thing?"

"I have had ample time to reflect on my mistakes," Malessar said, "and I have learned far more about this sort of magic than I ever knew when I had the temerity to believe I could challenge the world. Curse wards are terrible things, Cassia, and not to be placed lightly. Over time the magic will warp and infect the thing that is warded. The wards themselves become not so much a prison as a containment. Do you understand the distinction?"

"I . . . I don't know . . ."

A small gesture dismissed her ignorance. "I have applied tests to small creatures, and to the cages that housed them. With even the slightest of curses, the creature inside the cage sickened quickly and visibly. And, in the second week of confinement, it became infected by the wards themselves. After a season, it was no longer safe to continue the experiments. The beasts had to be destroyed and burned before they could test themselves against the restraints of their cages."

He stared at her until it appeared he was satisfied that she understood. "That was after one *season*, Cassia, and with a single small creature. I cursed an entire kingdom – over eight hundred years ago. What do you think might be harboured behind those wards now?"

She struggled to imagine anything on the scale he was suggesting. The closest she could come to it was the short time she had spent in the forgotten and long-faded land of Lyriss, where the land itself seemed to repel her feet. There was nothing in any of the stories she knew, not even from the Age of Talons, that she could use as a comparison. But surely it could not be as terrible as Malessar suggested?

"I don't know," she said quietly.

"Neither do I," Malessar said. "And the world should never have to find out. I hope – I believe – that Caenthell's caged spirits will devour themselves over time, before the wards fail at last, for nothing endures forever. But that is not certain."

Cassia envisioned the figure of Pyraete, carved upon her stone charm, rising up between the mountains. Perhaps the spirits of the North would surge forth in such a way if the curse was lifted. She could not decide if that was a good thing. Baum would doubtless have said that it was – it was what he had fought towards for hundreds of years, after all – and Meredith would have nodded his wordless affirmation, but Cassia was no longer so sure.

Something had happened to the wonderful tale she had wanted to witness; the great heroic tale of an evil warlock brought down by the rightful Heir to the North. Meredith was still her prince, but . . . it wasn't the same. It wasn't wonderful now. It wasn't quite so heroic.

It was real.

The revelation was sour and frightening, and she ducked her

head to drink her tea before it cooled completely. It helped her avoid Malessar's mountain-stone stare. She was convinced he would see right through her if she looked up at him, that all her duplicity would be laid bare before him. The warlock would fly into a rage again. He would tear Baum's plot to pieces, and scatter her own body and soul to the winds so absolutely that the gods themselves would never find her.

This wasn't what I wanted, was it?

It took her another silent moment to realise that her own agenda had been naive and selfish. She'd tried to use Baum's quest to drag herself away from the North, away from the interminable drudgery of Norrow's life on the road, the endless cycle of wheedling, anger and abuse. And who could blame her for that, if the only other option had been allowing herself to be sold into the hands of the Almouls? She had allied herself to Baum because he had given her a way out.

But what if he was wrong?

Malessar had, ironically, performed the same service for her in Hellea, and given her an avenue of escape. A way forward. He had brought her to Galliarca as her patron, and she had never felt more alive. But he was also the man who destroyed the North, the man who had abandoned Stromondor just before the city's walls were finally breached. *And I owe him as much as I owe Baum.*

I cursed an entire kingdom. There was no pride behind those words, only pain. Centuries of self-loathing.

I can't do this. He deserves to know.

When she looked up at last, drawing in the breath to begin her apology and explanation, it was to find Malessar already gone, his meal half-finished. The door to his apartment was closed.

The momentum propelling her thoughts vanished like smoke. In the kitchen, Leili began to sing under her breath, the low tones of an old Galliarcan rhyme serving as an odd counterpoint to the quiet of the garden.

Her hands trembling, Cassia gathered the plates and cups. They rattled on the tray as she carried it back to the kitchen. Then she returned to her small room, the cool air prickling her skin as she collected her staff and the thin sword of Pelicos. The sun illuminated the top of the western wall of the *dhar* if there was no passing cloud the day would soon become very uncomfortable.

It already is uncomfortable. It can hardly get worse.

She started up the winding steps to the rooftop. Meredith had taught her one way to calm herself and clear her mind. Now, if it took her all morning, it was time to see how well it worked.

She blinked in the light of the lantern, pulling the blanket up around her as she sat up on the pallet. "Who . . . ?"

The lantern moved aside, up to the shelf high on the wall, illuminating Malessar's deeply furrowed features. The warlock looked even more distracted than usual, as though he heard voices. He wore a high-collared thick coat, with another bundled under one arm.

"I cannot rest," he announced. "Our earlier conversation has given me cause for concern. You have focused my thoughts on something I have tried to keep from my mind these past few hundred years. And your news that there is growing momentum for the removal of the curse wards . . ."

Rapidly awakening now, Cassia shook her head. "More rumour than news," she started, but Malessar raised his hand to stop her.

"Unheeded rumour topples thrones," he said. "I have been studying for hours, but I can find nothing to satisfy myself that I should not worry. This is something I should have taken care of a long time ago."

He tossed the spare coat down to Cassia. "I would have you witness this."

It took her a moment to understand this was a request, rather than a demand or an order. Still, she hesitated. "Sir, may I ask why?"

Malessar looked away, wiping the tip of one finger along the edge of the shelf and examining it for evidence of dust. It was a distraction, she realised. He wasn't sure how to answer the question.

"Because I will require an independent and honest verification of my findings," he said at length. It didn't sound like the entire truth to Cassia's ears. She waited for more, but Malessar had fallen silent again.

And that wasn't the answer to the question I asked. There was much more to this than Malessar would admit, especially to her.

Malessar appeared to wake himself from his reverie, tutting under his breath as he turned to leave. "Come to the roof when you have dressed," he told her over his shoulder. She listened to his measured tread on the tiled stairwell until he had ascended past the first landing, then fished for her warmest clothes, the blanket still wrapped around her shoulders.

He listened to me, she thought. *But I still don't know if that is a good thing. I don't know if I should tell him everything.*

Despite the warmth of the daylight hours, long habit had driven Cassia to invest in shirts of thick cloth, and convenience kept her in the divided skirts she had seen the dancers wear in Fahrian Square. She threaded Pelicos's blade onto her belt and shrugged into the fur-lined coat Malessar had left behind.

She took the lantern with her up the switchback stairs. By night, lit by the flickering glow, the masks and carved figures in the alcoves took on more sinister aspects, leering at her as she ascended.

The night was cool and clear, the moon gibbous and low in the starry sky. There was no wind to speak of, but she could still taste the acrid tang of the tanneries beyond the old walls. Few people in the city had reason to be up at this hour, and she saw no lights in the maze of the surrounding district. Malessar had picked this time with deliberate intent, Cassia thought as she ducked under the lintel and emerged onto the rooftop garden.

A brazier had been lit in each of the four corners, radiating small circles of warmth with a banked, hungry glow. Cassia set down the lamp and let her eyes become more used to the night before crossing the stones to join Malessar at the other end of the roof. He stood shaded between two of the braziers, apparently deep in thought.

She remained a pace behind him, wrapping her arms around herself to ward off the cold that was seeping into her bones. Slow to anger, she remembered. Fishing in dark, undisturbed waters – you may not like what you catch.

She shivered. *And what have I caught?*

He faced North, she realised. Seeing the ancient mountain fastness in the depths of his mind, perhaps, as though the hundreds of miles between Galliarca and Caenthell did not exist.

"Sir," she said softly. "Perhaps I am wrong. It might be nothing. I must have misheard, or misunderstood . . ."

Malessar raised one hand from the wall to silence her. "Hush. Our course is set," he said grimly. "Stay close, but do not speak or interfere. Follow my instructions exactly. Understood?"

"But—"

The hand waved again, this time more brusquely. Malessar's attention had turned skyward and he appeared to be searching for something. Searching and listening.

Cassia tipped her own head back and turned on the spot, wondering what he sought. She knew it was possible to divine the future by reading the patterns of the heavens, yet the warlock had disdained that practice, dismissing it as unreliable. And what did he mean about their course having been set?

High above, a small constellation blinked as it was briefly

occluded. Something had passed in front of it, Cassia realised, with a shiver that had nothing to do with the cold.

Another few stars disappeared for an instant. This time she thought she saw the dark shape that commanded the skies over Galliarca, and the breath froze inside her lungs.

It banked and curved, describing a slow, ponderous circle above the city's walls, descending all the while. The lack of grace was deceptive, it required the merest twitch of a wing to tighten or alter that curve. Those wings, fully spread, would stretch across the entire width of the Square of the Princes. And the sinuous tail that flicked, lazily, for over thirty feet behind the scaled body . . .

She backed up against the wall at the edge of the roof, her hands gripping the bricks tight as another myth came alive before her eyes to wreak havoc upon her beliefs and fears.

The dragon's gliding spiral kept Malessar's rooftop at its centre. The beast's long neck twisted under its body to keep the city under close scrutiny. Malessar had begun to pace around the roof in the opposite direction to the dragon, muttering a low chant. Each brazier he passed flared up of its own accord, green flames briefly illuminating the walls and silhouetting his figure.

Cassia sweated with terror inside her fur coat. All the tales she had ever recounted of the Age of Talons jumbled inside her head: heroes, villains, august generals and vicious demons alike, all speaking their lines atop each other, random verses piling into a meaningless hubbub of words that stopped her from thinking of anything else.

Uhlwe of the Deeps. One-eyed Krol, scourge of the Hordes. Sabita the Mighty, who created winter by blocking out the sun. The legends were legion, told around fires on cold winter nights to thrill and scare children.

The dragon flexed its massive wings slightly, and a cold down force licked over the coals. The only sound came from Malessar's even chanting. Cassia could only watch, transfixed, as the beast hung in mid-air while its huge hind claws reached out to the balcony at the far end of the roof.

A rasp of bone against fired clay. That was all. The dragon perched lightly on the wall, head arching to look at Malessar, who stood on the opposite side with his arms folded.

"Craw," Malessar named the dragon. "Old friend."

The dragon's head tilted to one side, the left eye coming level with the warlock's head.

Centuries have passed. Yet you have not.

The voice that sounded in Cassia's mind was deep but androgynous, and it carried an edge of humour. Craw had made a joke, she belatedly realised, and that further astonished her.

This city sleeps, Craw pronounced. *This is your work?*

Malessar nodded. "It would not do for this city to know that you still live," he said. "Even less that you consent to come at my request. Panic is an ugly emotion."

Of course, Cassia thought. Galliarca was preternaturally quiet, even given the late hour. The warlock must have cast a spell to make certain the populace slept soundly. Little wonder she had fallen asleep so quickly earlier.

Craw's head moved again, and a huge golden eye stared unblinkingly at her. *This one is awake.*

She shuddered, pinned to the wall by that cold regard. The dragon seemed to see right through her, through her clothes, skin and flesh, to her heart itself.

"I have need of her," Malessar said with a shrug.

The eye was mesmeric. Cassia could not tear herself away from that vast, all-consuming well. Finally, just as she believed herself lost forever in the gates of the dragon's mind, Craw blinked and raised its head. The moment was gone, and she slumped against the wall in relief.

Yes, the dragon said, settling back on its perch once more and returning its attention to the warlock. The braziers cast flickering light on the burnished scales of its underbelly.

Your scent is troubled, Malessar. And you have called upon me.

Is this indeed a dire situation? There is no siege at this city's gates, no sorceries in the air other than your own. I do not perceive a challenge.

Malessar frowned. "The challenge is not at hand, Craw. But I am troubled nonetheless by what may come to pass."

He paused, as if uncertain of asking his next question. "Have you been close to Caenthell recently?"

No. I have neither reason nor desire to cross those lands. There is nothing of worth in that past.

Malessar sighed. "I need to examine the wards I placed upon the land there, to ensure they still hold fast. But I dare not spare the months it would take to travel north, so I have called on you, Craw, to beg your favour."

Craw was silent for a moment. *You fear your wards will fail.*

Malessar moved restlessly along the rooftop, his face falling into shadow as he spoke. "They should not fail, unless the curse itself is lifted. But I researched the long-term effects of curses on the living earth many years ago, and I was reminded of that research earlier this afternoon. This is a journey I should have made centuries ago, but I could not . . . I could not face returning to Caenthell. Such wounds do not heal with time, Craw. I fear I have delayed too long."

There was a raw edge to his voice as he spoke of Caenthell, a combination of sadness and anger, his bitterness directed at himself. How could he still be so angry with the High King after so many centuries? It was as if there was an empty space in the middle of this tale – pages that had been written but then torn out and hidden away, and Cassia could not work out what was missing.

Now you have the courage, Craw said. *And I am intrigued. I would see this for myself. Very well, we fly north.*

"Fly?" Cassia gasped.

Both heads turned to look at her and she clamped a hand over her mouth. She had not realised she had spoken aloud.

Malessar actually sounded amused. "But of course – how

else should we reach Caenthell quickly?" Malessar actually sounded amused. "Remember, I must also attend the Crown Prince's banquet this week."

It is an interminable journey on foot, Craw said dryly.

Cassia blinked, startled by the dragon's words, not sure how to interpret them. Had Craw just referred to the long trek she had made from Keskor with Baum and Meredith? If so, how on earth could it know?

She shivered, all too aware of Craw's gaze. Could the dragon read her as easily as she would read a book? No, she told herself, surely it couldn't be possible. But there was one thing she was suddenly certain of – Craw had spoken only to her. Malessar had not heard the comment at all.

She stared up at the dragon's bulk, wondering how a person might ride on its back. The stories were vague on the subject, or skirted around it altogether, but then, how many storytellers ever actually saw a dragon, let alone rode one?

I am told the ridges of my spine are most comfortable, Craw said, as if it had again heard her thoughts. *You should grip with the muscles of your legs.*

The whole scene struck Cassia as absurd: she was stood in a rooftop garden in the heart of Old Galliarca, listening to a dragon advise her how best to seat herself on its back. *Shouldn't we be speaking of gold, or philosophy, or ancient wars? This is nothing like the tales of the Age of Talons!*

She looked around for Malessar, hoping for some indication of how she should ascend, not confident in her own ability to climb up. The warlock, however, busied himself with putting out the braziers. Once more he was aloof and unreadable, and the cracks in his façade had disappeared.

"I don't think I can do this," she said. "Surely Narjess would be more useful to you?"

Malessar's lips twitched. "Narjess does not believe in dragons," he said, as though that explained everything, extinguishing the last brazier with the wave of one hand. Smoke curled from the darkened coals, along with a faint tang of spices that made Cassia's nerves tingle when she inhaled.

She could not help but glance up at the beast towering over her. If Narjess stood in her place, he might well change his mind.

Then Malessar was at her side, urging her up onto the dragon's back, and there was no more time to think. Fear rose in her mind, taking control of her muscles as she struggled to make herself comfortable between Craw's great shoulders, scared of toppling back onto the roof or even into the narrow alleys below.

Sat behind her, Malessar said something she could barely hear. Craw's body shifted up from the rooftop and she flung her arms around the dragon's massive neck, the scales cold but oddly soft under her hands.

Craw's wings snapped out to their full width and Cassia felt her stomach wrenched by gravity. She caught a glimpse of rooftops retreating into the dark below her, a sight that so shocked and frightened her she could not bear to watch. She squeezed her eyes tight until tears streamed from under her eyelids. She felt the dragon bank to the left, a movement that threatened to empty her stomach, and cold air plucked at her exposed face and fingers as her hair streamed out behind her.

You are safe, Craw told her, but that did not reassure her. She dared not reply, nor did she open her eyes or relax her grip on the dragon's neck. Her heart hammered and she thought she might pass out.

Craw flexed and pulsed underneath her, a solid rhythm that accompanied each sweep of its mighty wings. It was supple and exotic, a flowing movement that only heightened Cassia's distress. She prayed fervently to any god that might hear that she would not throw up, dreading what might happen if she insulted or annoyed the dragon.

After a while, her nausea subsided, and Craw's tireless movements lulled her back into an uneasy half-sleep. Malessar's presence close behind her was a reminder that she was not alone, and it was a greater comfort than she could have imagined. The effort of keeping her arms wrapped around Craw's neck made her muscles ache, but she could not bring herself to relax her grip.

Cassia gradually became aware of a sound tickling the back of her mind, a low murmur; a susurration. It was like listening to a conversation taking place two or three rooms away. She realized it was Malessar and Craw talking privately to each other, and that caused her even more anxiety. What if Craw had indeed read her mind and was, even now, explaining her part in Baum's schemes to the warlock?

She felt herself tensing further, readying herself for sharp questions, or an even sharper push. With no wings of her own, how simple it would be for Malessar to throw her from the dragon's back . . .

You are safe, Craw repeated its earlier words to her, its tone warm and soothing. *You have nothing to fear.*

But Cassia could not shake her anxiety, especially when she wondered whether the dragon had been inside her thoughts. Was it mere coincidence that Craw sought to calm her now? She could not tell one way or the other.

The private conversation resumed, plucking at the edges of her consciousness. With her eyes still closed against the cold air, Cassia concentrated on the faint sounds, fighting to bring them closer and make sense of them. In part she wanted to know how dangerous her situation had now become, but another part of her had eagerly seized upon this distraction from her new-found fear of flying.

Craw's voice came again, this time sounding amused and – Cassia believed – a little surprised.

Hush child. Sleep.

Frustration welled up inside her, adding to the tumult of emotions. She opened her mouth to snap at Craw, and yawned instead.

"What—"

She yawned again, unable to complete the sentence. Her thoughts were unravelling before she could put them together, and now she wanted to open her eyes she couldn't even manage that.

The whispered conversation had become a low, rhythmic chant, she realised, just before she plummeted into a deep, dreamless sleep.

The ground was cold, the dew-scented grass damp against her cheek. She rolled onto her back and groaned as she discovered her coat was soaked through, a most unpleasant sensation that drove her towards wakefulness. Cassia levered herself up onto her elbows and blinked against the heatless glare of the morning.

The air was sharp and bitter, her breath forming wispy clouds before her. She struggled to her feet, unsteady as her limbs felt stiff and leaden. She guessed that was a reaction to the stresses and strains of the previous night's journey.

She turned, trying to work out what had happened to her. The dragon – she remembered clinging in terror to Craw's neck, then hearing the hypnotic chant of a spell being cast in the back of her mind . . . and now here she was, with no sign of either Malessar or the dragon. Had they abandoned her?

The mountainous peaks to the north and west were caught in the full glare of the new morning, their snow-capped crests blinding bright. Cassia stood on a wide ridge halfway up a grassy hillside dotted with clumps of ancient, weathered firs and pines. Further up the hill lay the edge of a more ancient, virgin forest. A cobbled road, perhaps older than the trees around her, followed the length of the ridge, passing around the side of the hill to vanish from sight. The road was wide and level, but buried and corrupted by time.

Back toward the south and the southeast the land fell away into undulating, sparsely vegetated hills. Cassia thought she knew where she was now, although she had never come this far north before. Nobody dared live so close to the cursed borders of Caenthell, and her father had not reckoned the more northerly villages to be worth visiting.

Caenthell – just behind this hill . . . the shiver that ran through her had nothing to do with the cold. She dropped one hand to her belt, checking her knife. She was fortunate not to have rolled over on it while she slept.

She was about to take her hand from the knife when she saw a figure striding easily into view along the old road, coming from the direction of Caenthell. Her fingers curled around the hilt, gripping it tight, and she felt the muscles across the back of her shoulders tense as the distant figure raised one arm to hail her.

It wasn't Malessar.

She took an uncertain step back, only to realise that she had nowhere to run, nothing to hide herself behind.

An odd man, she saw, with a slightly exotic appearance that hinted at a sorcerous pedigree, just as the warlock's did. His cheeks and his nose were too long, too smooth, echoing sculptures of antiquity she had seen in Hellea. His eyes were too wide, his mouth far too thin. The hood of his plain woollen robe was down, and she could see faint mottling across his bare skull, as though he had suffered from a disease many years ago. He seemed on the cusp of middle age, yet somehow beyond that too. As he came closer, and Cassia noted with apprehension that he would have towered over even Meredith, she saw the mottled effect extended to his hands and his bare feet.

He carried himself with such confidence that even though he bore no weapon, she really did not want to provoke him into a fight.

"You are awake," he said in an oddly familiar voice. Cassia could not quite place it, but it sounded wrong coming from his mouth. "The way is clear and safe ahead. You may join us now."

"I would if I knew who you were," she replied, more boldly than she felt. "And where is Malessar?"

The man looked surprised, then dismayed and hurt. "Child, you clung to me last night as you might to a lover, and you say you do not know me? Think upon your lore! Are tales no longer told of noble Pyarre's adventures amongst your kind? Or of Grist the Unfaithful, or even Gera the Unnamed, who ruled with a golden fist in the lands of the West?"

Cassia's jaw dropped wide in disbelief. "Craw?"

The dragon affected to look offended. "It would seem the storytellers of this age do not learn their craft well."

Now that she knew, Cassia could see what appeared so wrong about the woollen robe he wore. It did not move at all in the morning breeze, but it rippled whenever the transformed Craw moved. It was tight against his torso and she suspected that it was in fact a part of his body, changed to resemble human clothing for modesty's sake.

She began to relax a little, forcing herself to take deeper, slower breaths. "I'm not a proper storyteller," she told the dragon. "I wish I was. I've never been apprenticed to one. My father is a storyteller, but he'll never accept me as one. I'm sorry I didn't recognise you, but I've never met a dragon before."

Craw seemed mollified by her apology. He gestured back along the old road. "Malessar awaits further on. There are the remains of a pre-Hellean fort at the entrance of the next valley. In centuries past it marked the border with Caenthell. Malessar did not wish to venture past that point without study and certain preparations, and he did not wish to risk your safety. That is why you were left by the road, out here beyond those cursed lands." A wry smile slipped across the face of the dragon's human form. "But you were perfectly safe, have no fear. There are no wild beasts courageous enough to venture into this region."

"None save dragons," Cassia muttered, struggling to keep

up with Craw's long-legged pace.

Apparently that tickled Craw's sense of humour, because the dragon laughed out loud and repeated the comment to himself, chuckling all the way to the ruined fort.

Chapter Seventeen

THE ROAD TURNED northwards to enter the deep valleys between the mountains, where the ancient and cursed lands of Caenthell lay. Wild bracken and grasses had encroached upon the untended road, although the route was still easy to follow. Cassia could imagine the High King's feared legions marching out to make war on the lands below. It felt strange to be walking along a road nobody else had travelled in hundreds of years.

If the place itself was unnerving, her guide unsettled her even more. Craw strode ahead, perfectly at ease. Cassia hurried to keep up with him, marvelling at his transformation. Fragments of stories and half-remembered lore rose into her mind, jostling for attention, but she could not focus on any of them.

The one thought that stuck, circling around and around, was how solid the dragon was in his human form. She could feel his presence from several paces away, and his every movement spoke of immense power and weight. Dragons passed through many of the legends she knew, walking disguised and unseen in the world, but Craw's obvious and otherworldly appearance made that hard to believe.

Craw paused at the crest of a rise, waiting for her to catch up. He might have been an imperial lord surveying his domain.

"Now we approach the borders of ancient Caenthell," he told her solemnly.

Cassia looked ahead, half expecting to see the massed ranks of an undead army arrayed before her, ragged pennants hanging limp from rusted spears. She was almost disappointed – almost – to find the winding vale deserted and still, with only the treetops stirring in the morning breeze.

A short way down the vale, the road split to pass around a great mound, too regular in shape to be natural. At the summit of this steep-sided hill sat Caenthell's ancient border fortress. Three circular towers formed a triangle, pointing out towards where she now stood. Centuries ago, it must have looked formidable and unbreakable, but while it still dominated the valley time had wrought savage damage on walls and towers alike. There were jagged gaps in both the walls she could see, and giant stone blocks lay half-buried where they had fallen on the hillside. The tower to the far right of the fortress sagged, pulling the wall out with it. It looked on the verge of collapse, held up only by the winding vines that had taken root in the cracks between the blocks.

"Nature seeks to reclaim the land," Craw said. "But the stone is strong, and memory persists."

Cassia shifted nervously. It felt like the fortress was waiting for something, biding its time until . . . she shivered and cursed her imagination, raising her head to look beyond the fortress.

"Can you see the castle of Caenthell itself from here?" she asked.

Craw shook his head. "No. And we will go no further than this fort. You should stay close to me."

She smiled, despite herself. "I won't argue."

Craw led the way down the slope, glancing frequently over his shoulder to make sure Cassia was still with him. Although he said nothing, she thought he was being more cautious now, his attention focused on his surroundings. She felt the back of her neck prickle uncomfortably, and her heart raced no matter how hard she concentrated on keeping calm.

She unsheathed her sword, hoping to draw comfort from its weight in her hand. That brought another of Craw's careful looks, but the knife was absurdly tiny against the looming presence of the fort.

They kept to the road, passing around the base of the hill. Here Craw turned aside at last and they began to climb the far side, following the remains of a wide, winding track that looped back on itself several times. Parts of the curtain wall had fallen here too, ancient stones spilling like crumbs to be devoured by the grass and heather that clung to the hillside. Cassia looked up once and saw the two rearmost towers reaching blindly to the sky, leaning out at angles that pulled at her stomach. She kept her eyes firmly on the ground after that.

At last the track levelled out on a promontory in front of the fort's gateway. Cassia looked up at the slits in the walls of the two towers, visualising a company of archers silently watching their approach, arrows nocked and held steady. Any attacker would pay dearly just to get this close to the fort.

The gates had long since gone, rotted or plundered, she could not tell which. The fort lay open. Craw, who had regained a little of his previous good humour now they had reached the gateway, smiled and gestured onward. Cassia hesitated for a moment, but as the breeze shifted she caught the tantalising smell of a cookfire, and hunger pulled her through the darkened arch into the yard beyond.

The ground beyond the gatehouse was overgrown, strewn with weeds that tugged her ankles. The gutted remains of buildings lined both walls ahead as they narrowed toward the tower that watched over the entrance to the valley. Daylight filtered through their collapsed slate roofs to reveal hollowed-out interiors. The open-fronted building on her left had probably been a stabling block, while the garrison's barracks had been built against the opposite wall.

Malessar sat in the entrance to the stables, tending a fire banked with loose bricks that had fallen from the walls. A covered pot hung from a wire frame rigged over the flames. The warlock poked at the fire distractedly with a stick, but looked up and smiled as Cassia approached.

"As you see, I've not lost all my talents over the years," he said wryly. "I can still make a fire without servants to assist me, although finding dry kindling here presented some difficulties."

Cassia found a larger stone nearby that she could roll into position on the other side of the fire. Craw joined them, gazing up with great interest at the towers and the ramparts that linked them.

Malessar seemed content to stare into the cookfire, losing himself inside his mind while the contents of the clay pot warmed. The silence began to unnerve Cassia once more. Her imagination placed ghostly observers at the arrow slits high in the towers, and malignant spirits waiting inside the old barracks to ensnare her if she dared explore the fort on her own.

Had this place died when the kingdom fell? Had its commander fought to the last, or had the garrison fled out of the mountains, leaving the fort to wither in nature's grasp? Cassia suppressed a cold shudder, thinking of men chained in dank cellars, screaming desperately, but in vain for somebody to help them, their cries smothered by the empty towers.

"What is this place?" she asked, unable to bear the quiet any longer. Her voice sounded too loud in the enclosed bailey.

Malessar sighed. "The border fortress of Karakhel," he said. "One of the great strongholds of the old kingdom. Solonel, son of Forochel, had it built. There was a town once, a little further down the road. Where you have soldiers, you have a need for ale and wine, and the town of Karakhel grew quickly, supporting the garrison and trading with the lowlands."

"There was an inn of some ill-repute," Craw said, his gaze resting on the crenelations above the gatehouse. "A place for young men who thought they were immortal."

The words were softly spoken, but Cassia saw the warlock flinch. "The Dragon's Cup."

She hesitated. "I didn't see a town as we came up. What happened to Karakhel?"

There was a long, awkward pause, and she wished she had not asked the question. When Malessar raised his head she saw the tumult of grief and anger in his eyes.

"It died."

She shrank back, wrapping her arms about her to ward off the sudden chill. It had been hard to believe this was the man who had destroyed an entire kingdom almost overnight. Baum's tales and memories had sometimes seemed exaggerated, or too remote. But now she saw the age-old fury under Malessar's measured exterior, and for the first time she felt truly frightened.

His face softened, as though he realised what he had done, and he lowered his head. "I am sorry. These are memories I thought I had locked securely away."

Craw leaned forward. "We are all here. What will you do next?"

Malessar raised one hand to pinch the bridge of his nose as he gathered himself, and Cassia took a deep breath, grateful for the dragon's intervention. She was so far beyond her depth now that all below was grim darkness.

"This fortress is secure," the warlock said at last. "Or, at least, as secure as even I can make it. I shall use it as a base for the work. I intend to anchor myself here while I make brief explorations towards Caenthell. To that end I will need both you and the girl to remain here to tend this fire."

Craw's face was impassive. "You believe you are strong enough to confront this on your own?"

"These are my wards. I know the feel of them. I will know if they break."

"You should have assistance," Craw said. "I will go with you."

Cassia blinked. They were going to leave her here on her own, poking at the damned cookfire?

Malessar shook his head firmly. "I am still not certain what I am looking for, old friend, and your presence will overwhelm my senses. Apart from that, if the wards are indeed failing, I may . . . have some trouble returning here."

As one, they both turned to regard Cassia, and she felt her indignation bubbling into anger. "Wait! Did you bundle me all this way just to watch a pot boil? Why can't I go with you? Why won't you tell me what you're doing?"

"This is no mere cookfire, girl. These bricks are inscribed with bonds and glyphs of protection. While the fire is lit it will shield me as I walk in the old kingdom. The strength of this fortress will be added to mine. But only while this fire remains lit. This is your task."

She stared at the bricks laid around the fire, stunned into silence. Sorcery? So close at hand and she was commanded to watch over it?

Malessar cleared his throat. Clearly he expected some kind of response. Cassia glanced sidelong at Craw, but the dragon had turned his attention to the skies again, having evidently decided the discussion was done.

"Alright," she said. "I'll do it."

Malessar nodded. "Good."

"I shall remain here," Craw said, as though it was his idea. The warlock shot him a sharp look, and Cassia hid her smile as the dragon ignored him. "I will assist Cassia in her task."

"How long will this take?" Cassia asked. "I mean – how long will we need to keep the fire burning?"

"A good question," Craw said.

Malessar frowned again. Cassia wondered if he had

forgotten to think on this more practical side of the sorcery. "A good question. And I admit I do not know the answer."

"Then we'll need more wood," she told him. "If you don't mind, sir, I'll go looking now, before you make a start."

The warlock's smile was warmer this time. "This is why I requested your help, Cassia. But be careful. This place is not beyond crumbling around our ears. Watch your step."

She was already on her feet, eager to be away from the fire and the increasingly ominous conversation.

She left the stables behind and headed back toward the gatehouse. She had spied a small building, with a thick chimney stack on one side, squeezed in a corner of the yard between the gatehouse and one of the towers. Any building with a chimney would need fuel, and a fort with stables would probably need a smithy. It seemed the most logical place to start; scavenging for firewood was a skill she had learned quickly while traveling with her father.

Her father . . . What was he doing now? She had no doubt he had fled back to Keskor, but what kind of story had he told? Had he replaced her with somebody else? Did he think she was dead?

Did he actually care at all?

He was somewhere in the lands below these mountains, she thought, a hollow pang of something like homesickness tugging at her stomach. It wasn't all that far really, not when she thought of the distance she had travelled in just one night.

She glanced over her shoulder at the stables. Craw and Malessar were talking in low tones. They were so different, so beyond her comprehension – and so frightening. But even if she could wish herself back to safety in Keskor right now, she wasn't sure she would. However this strange tale turned out, she was far too caught up in it to pull herself away now.

"I'm a storyteller," she muttered to herself. "I have to know how it ends."

The hut had indeed been the fort's smithy. The forge took

up the whole of one wall, opposite a collapsed pile of rusted and pitted blades and spear tips. A rotting mass that had once been a workbench sat between them, against the far wall. Cassia grimaced and stuck her hands into the pile, searching for something usable. The wood was almost too rotted to use, and she came out with barely an armful of fuel that was crawling with scurrying insects.

When she returned to the fire she found Craw sitting alone, staring placidly into the flames.

"Craw? Where is Malessar?"

There might have been a hint of tension in the dragon's voice as he replied. "He has begun his exploration of the wards."

Cassia dropped her wood by the fire and wiped her hands clean on her coat. Despite her disappointment at his departure she was getting used to the warlock's sudden and often unexplained movements.

"Will you stay here while I search the towers for more wood?"

"Of course. But remember Malessar's warnings, girl. And do not stray beyond the gatehouse."

She had already decided which of the three towers she wanted to explore first. The two on either side of the gatehouse had small, recessed doorways that made them look less important than the tower watching over the entrance to the valley. That third tower must have been the main watchtower, and there must be something worth finding in there.

Three wide stone slabs led up to the thick door, which sat firmly closed. Cassia quickly discovered it had rotted into place, the timbers expanding with damp and the door's hinges rusted. She did not have the strength to force it open.

But to her left a set of steps had been built against the wall, climbing over the roof of the stables to the ramparts above. Another short set of steps led from the rampart to the top of the watchtower, and she wondered if there was a way down into the tower from there.

There was only one way to find out.

She climbed carefully, mindful of the warnings Craw and Malessar had given her. The steps appeared solid underfoot, but she tested her weight on each one. That aside, it was no worse than any climb she had made before, and her confidence grew as she reached the rampart with no difficulty.

She paused to take in the view. This face of the fort looked out toward the northwest side of the valley, guarded by a long, forbidding ridge. Blotches of bold purple heather, hardy enough to grow even on the rocks near the crest of the ridge, shimmered in the sunlit breeze. It would be good land to graze goats upon, she thought, and tried to picture a few herders' cabins dotted across the hillside, wood smoke drifting from their chimneys.

This land might not be so bleak and unwelcoming if anyone still lived here, Cassia decided. Then a cloud drifted across the face of the sun. The air was suddenly colder, and the shadows upon the land much deeper than before. She felt an odd pressure build in her stomach, as though the hills themselves gazed down balefully at her.

She shivered. Caenthell was cursed – how could she forget *that*?

She made her way along the rampart, eyeing the crumbling edges with renewed trepidation, until she reached the shorter stair up to the top of the watch-tower. Now the way had become easier and she felt a smile break out on her lips as she clambered over the crenulations and slipped down onto the tower itself.

Just as she predicted, there was a trapdoor set into the stone flags on one side. Like every other door she had seen in the fort it was heavily bound and reinforced with iron plates, though the metal had not weathered well. A rusted metal ring was set into one edge, and Cassia pulled at it eagerly, hearing the trapdoor creak, but the hinges had seized up many years ago. After several attempts all she had achieved was to run out of breath.

She stepped back and glared at the door, thinking hard. Had she missed something, or was this hatch just as stuck as the door at the base of the tower?

She stooped to grasp the ring again, twisting it this time. First to the right, then to the left. Now the ring moved a little, accompanied by the dull scrape of metal against stone. She twisted it again and again, doggedly working the catch loose until the ring spun free and the sudden lack of resistance spilled her awkwardly onto the stone flags.

Cassia picked herself up and crawled over to examine her work, just in time to see the trapdoor tumble away into the space below, the old wood finally rotted away from the hinges holding it in place.

She peered cautiously over the lip into the gloom, waiting for her eyes to adjust. A steep stone stair followed the curve of the wall, illuminated patchily by arrow slits. A thin shaft of light played across the stone flags at the bottom of the stairs.

It looked solid enough, she thought, chewing on her lip as she pondered the wisdom of descending into the tower. Craw was nearby. Surely he would come to her rescue if her adventure went awry?

If he heard her at all, a far more cautious voice muttered in her mind.

She slipped her legs over the edge and tested her weight on the first step. It was solidly set into the wall, and she ducked under the lintel and took the next few steps down before she could second-guess herself.

The room below was empty but for a large, heavy table that sat in the middle of the floor. Sheltered from the elements these past centuries, it was in much better condition than anything else she had found so far. She circled it slowly, testing the wood with the point of her knife. It had suffered from damp, and woodworm had infested it over time, but she didn't think it would come apart too easily. Perhaps Craw would be able to dismantle it.

As barren as it was, this chamber had an almost noble air to it. Arrow slits pierced the thick walls in several places, the largest of them facing the head of the valley. The flagstones were smooth, laid out in a geometric pattern that looked oddly familiar to Cassia's eye. The old table – the garrison commander's table, she decided – sat in the middle of this pattern, with the stones radiating out from it. There must have been a chair too, once, she thought, searching the floor for a sign of where it had stood, but it must have been looted once the fort was abandoned.

Partway around the circumference of the room, past an empty hearth, another stone stair wound further into the tower's depths. This time it descended into pitch blackness and Cassia shuddered as she considered it. There were clearly no arrow slits down there to let in light, and without a torch or lantern she had no option but to return the way she had entered.

It was no bad thing, really. If there were cells under the commander's tower she had no wish to discover what they might still hold.

She wandered back to the larger arrow slit and gazed out, trying to imagine how this chamber would have looked in the High King's time. The hearth would have roared with a fire to keep the room warm, and maybe the commander would have slept on a pallet nearby. Great soldiers of noble bearing would have gathered at the table, discussing plans and intelligence brought to them . . .

Her reverie trailed off as she felt warmth prickle against her side. Flickering firelight gave her arm a rosy glow. Caught by sudden tension, she turned slowly back to the room, hardly daring to breathe in.

She realized immediately that this was more than mere imagination. A group of soldiers stood around the table, dark presences silhouetted by the blazing hearth, studying maps and scrolls. These were not the handsome and virtuous men Cassia had pictured in her mind. These men were stern-faced and scarred, responsibility and duty weighing heavy upon their shoulders, their eyes shadowed and haunted. They moved carved markers across the maps, their voices indistinct.

In their midst stood a tall man, resting with his hands splayed across the table top, his head bowed as though already defeated. He did not seem to be part of the discussions around him, brooding instead on something only he could see.

Cassia held her breath, frozen in place. This was Malessar's magic, she realised, the thought bubbling up through her growing fear. The protective spells he had cast around the fort had brought these wraiths to fleeting life – ghostly echoes from the long-dead past, blurred and fuzzed at the edges.

They can't hurt me – they're not really here, she told herself firmly, almost believing it. *They can't hurt me.*

As if he had heard her the man at the centre of the gathering raised his head and stared across the table at her. Firelight flickered over his features, highlighting the distinctive long nose that sat between eyes filled with haunted despair.

Cassia's heart thumped and she threw her hands over her face, unable to bear the harsh sorrow that lashed her senses. She slumped to the floor, heaving voiceless sobs as the wraith's emotions battered her.

When she could piece her thoughts together once more, and her crying had subsided into ragged sniffles, she peeked through her fingers at the table, dreading what she might see.

The apparitions had vanished, leaving no trace behind. The chamber was dark once more, the hearth as dead and cold as it had ever been. Cassia struggled to her feet, blinking away tears, her breath fast and shallow. The watchtower felt oppressive and dangerous now, the air stale and choking. This was no place for the living.

She staggered to the stairs, leaning heavily on the wall to keep herself upright, desperate to regain the safety of daylight and fresh air. All thoughts of dismantling the table were forgotten. She wished she had never left Keskor, that she had never come to this forsaken place, that she had never ventured into the watchtower.

And most of all she wished she had not looked into the garrison commander's eyes.

The warlock's eyes.

"Craw, may I ask you a question?"

For a long moment the dragon did not reply; indeed, Cassia believed he had not heard, so faraway was his gaze as he absently stirred the contents of the pan.

She had sat at the top of the tower for what seemed like hours, her thoughts skidding as wildly as her pulse. By the time she managed to calm down enough that she no longer trembled visibly, the sun was high in the sky and her stomach grumbled. Craw made no comment when she picked her way down the stairs from the ramparts with only a meagre armful of deadfall to feed the fire, and she was grateful for that.

Since then Cassia had ventured only as far as the barracks on the other side of the yard, picking through the rubble of the collapsed roof to find pieces of old timber, and she had been careful not to lose sight of the fire.

After a while she noticed the cookfire did not appear to be consuming as much fuel as it should have. Part of Malessar's spell, she guessed, but it did mean she could stop scavenging for now.

A smile crept over Craw's face and he folded his arms. "Yes, Cassia, you may ask me a question."

Now she wished she had not said anything. Her mind whirled with the questions she had thought of – was Malessar born here? Why did he leave? Had he truly been the garrison's commander? – but there was also a sudden rush of fear, as though she stood on the edge of an awful precipice. Had she forgotten something? Despite the warmth of the fire she shivered and wrapped her arms around herself.

Craw waited silently.

"What—" she began, then changed her mind. "Why—"

She was aware her cheeks were colouring. How could it be so hard to ask a simple question? That thought gave her an escape – an easy question. If there was an easy question.

The words tumbled out before she could think about them. "Why don't you give yourself hair? I mean, if you can change your shape to look human, why not have hair so you really do blend in and . . ."

She trailed off, deeply embarrassed, ducking away from Craw's intent gaze.

The dragon was quiet for a moment, and when he spoke he sounded disappointed. "Child Cassia, I did expect better. Of course, it is long since I answered a mortal's questions. Long indeed since I had need to seek answers myself. Perhaps these things are forgotten. But I will answer. As a dragon I have no use for any kind of hair. Why should my human form be any different? I have no hair because I have no hair."

He leaned forward, his voice sharper. "Now. My question to you."

Alarmed, Cassia shrank back. "Your question?"

"Ah, I was right. These things have been forgotten, even by the storytellers." Craw lifted the corners of his mouth. A hint of a smile, but no more.

Old tales rose to haunt her once more, and she kicked herself for not recalling them in time. Some legendary heroes had sought out dragons to ask questions of them – about the future, or how to beat the evil that threatened them. But such answers never came free, if they came at all. The dragons were said to ask questions of their own. Hard, riddling questions. And if they could not be answered . . .

"Why have you not told him the truth of who you are?"

Craw asked.

Her thoughts stalled. "I – I don't understand. I'm only a storyteller – not even that."

Craw shook his head. "That's not an answer."

Cassia felt herself drawing close to panic, her throat tightening around her words. "But that's all I am, I swear it! I never asked to be a part of this, but Baum—"

She clapped her hands over her mouth, appalled, but the damage was done and Craw did not let it pass.

"Baum. The soldier. The picture becomes clearer. Turn your head to the side, girl."

Mute, she did as he asked, flinching as cold fingertips brushed her cheek and pulled her hair away from her face.

"A resourceful man, firm in his convictions. There are ancient wrongs that must be righted, a curse that must be lifted. He will see it done. It is his life's work."

Tears welled up in her eyes as the implications of her slip came to her. Not only had she failed Baum, but she had betrayed Malessar's trust in her. Surely he would think nothing of killing her, just as he had destroyed the High King so long ago.

"And so he has brought the heir to Caenthell with him," Craw continued, laying the scheme bare. "The surest way to break the curse on these lands."

Cassia drew in a ragged breath. "How can you know about Meredith too? You – you've taken all this from my mind?"

Craw shrugged diffidently. "Enough to see clearly. Perhaps you realise now, child, that seeking answers from dragons was never a fair bargain for mortal men."

She shivered. "You'll tell him."

To her surprise Craw shook his head. "No, child. I will not interfere. I count Malessar as a friend, but this tragedy is of his own making. I have no desire to become entangled in these schemes. I have brought you both here, and I will return you both to Galliarca, just as Malessar has requested, but that is the end of it."

"Then—"

"All of your secrets are safely kept," Craw confirmed, turning his attention back to the fire. "All of them."

Cassia wiped her eyes with one sleeve, discovering with embarrassment that her nose was running too. "What should I do now?"

Craw continued stirring for a moment. "I cannot give you an answer, child. What do you believe is right?"

The trouble was that she no longer knew. She had become convinced by Baum's words and tales, and by the sheer force of his spirit, that revenge against Malessar was proper and justifiable. But as she spent more time in his household that view was being eroded by her own experience of the warlock. And who was she, a slip of a girl from a ratty town at the very edges of the Empire, to pass judgement on men who had lived for so many centuries?

"I don't know," she said miserably. "I just don't know any more."

And it wasn't just Baum and Malessar who were caught up in this tangled tale. Meredith was there too. The young prince had been led to believe he would sit upon the throne of Caenthell, reclaiming everything Malessar had torn so violently from his ancestors. What right did she have to deny him his birthright?

She drew her legs up, resting her chin on her knees. She felt as though a yoke hung from her shoulders, the load on each side becoming heavier with each passing day, every hour. How was she supposed to deal with such terrible issues on her own? She was no hero, in the mould of Jathar Leon Learth or Pelicos the Indomitable. They were both men, after all.

"How can I make this right?" she asked, hating the pleading tone of her voice.

Craw sighed. "I cannot give you an answer, child," he repeated. "Truly, I am sorry—"

The fire guttered, the flames dying back without warning

before roaring up again to lick the edges of the pot. Craw cursed, raising his arms around the banked fire as if to embrace it, and Cassia flung herself backwards out of harm's way, just in time to avoid another fiery bloom.

Flames quested outward as though blown by the wind. But here inside the walls of the fort there was nothing more than a light breeze. Her skin prickled: magic. Something was wrong, out there on the borders.

"What is it?"

Craw looked distracted. "Quiet, girl. The gate – go. Tell me what you see."

She scrambled to her feet and ran for the gatehouse. Behind her she heard the cookfire roar like a caged beast, waves of heat pressing against her back. The urge to look back was almost too much to resist, but she knew if she did she would be caught and devoured by whatever pursued her. Only as she flung herself through the dark arches of the gatehouse did the intense pressure subside, though the low roaring sounds shook her bones.

She gasped as she took in the land beyond the fortress. The valleys at the edge of Caenthell had changed beyond all recognition. Deep mists roiled, washing against the hillsides, masking everything. The sky above was bleached of all colour, pale and insipid, the air itself sucking at her lungs rather than giving her life.

Shadows rose from the depths of the mists, clustered together in the middle distance. Straight, squared outlines, with angled roofs. Figures flitted, half-seen, half-imagined, in the gaps between the buildings. Man-sized, she thought, chilled with fear.

Karakhel, risen from the grave.

Chapter Eighteen

SHE TORE HER gaze from the ghostly town, and shouted back towards the yard. "Caenthell! It's coming alive!"

The firelight flickered angrily, reflected against the arch inside the gatehouse, the burning roar fearsome and animalistic. Craw might not have heard her.

"Craw! I can see the town – there are people moving in it!"

There was still no sign he had heard, or that he could reply. She backed into the gateway, far enough that she could still see down the hillside, hugging the arch for protection.

Where was Malessar? He must have gone down into the valley. Had he conjured these grim visions of Karakhel? Or were they a product of the terrible curse he had wrought? Perhaps, by accident, he had triggered the wards he had set against trespassers into the kingdom. The sorcery might have torn him apart, or he could merely be trapped within its bounds, like one of the tragic heroes who fell foul of such snares in the tales of the Age of Talons.

While the town and its inhabitants were still indistinct, the mists surrounding it were spreading, creeping up the valley toward the fort. It would not take long for the first questing tendrils to brush against the base of the walls. There was no way to block the open entrance, so the fortress would provide no degree of protection. Cassia's heart pounded and her breath came in shallow gasps as she wondered how anyone could fight against something so insubstantial. Even Craw would be engulfed by the curse-laden mists.

She realized her slender blade was in her hand, as though she could cut her way to safety with it. Swordsmen in her father's tales always gained courage from their weapons, and now she knew that for the fiction it was. She swallowed, and retreated into the courtyard.

The cookfire blazed with a heat and intensity that far outstripped the wood that fuelled it. Cassia shielded her eyes with her free hand. "Craw? There's something in the town – it's coming up here!"

For a moment she could not see him but then there was a hint of movement above her, and the sudden weight of a massive presence – a gust of air flicked dirt up into her eyes and Cassia flinched and stumbled back against the wall behind her.

I see it. The voice slid through her mind.

Craw had transformed again. It sat on the edge of the battlements above her, with its wings fully extended as it twisted its sinuous neck around to examine the valley. Craw's tail flicked the ground, scoring fresh lines in the earth.

Your shape constrains me. But I cannot protect our boundaries and *tend the fire.*

She glanced at the swollen fire as it flared, reaching out as though sensing her presence. "How do I tend *that*?"

Craw did not even look at her. *You must. If it dies then you will die too.* The wings snapped straight and the dragon tensed. *You have the authority.*

"Authority? To do what?"

Craw did not reply. Instead the massive muscles that supported its hindquarters pushed it effortlessly into the air, dislodging blocks of stone that tumbled into the yard. Cassia yelped and dodged out of the way, and by the time she raised her head again Craw had disappeared beyond the walls of the fortress.

The skies were bleak now, grey and soul-sapping, as though the mists that enveloped the town drew strength and life from the air itself. The mountains were always cold, even during summer, and despite the presence of the engorged fire Cassia shivered.

Tend it? There is hardly any wood left to fuel it. Surely it was Malessar's craft that was keeping it alive? She clenched her fists, feeling hopeless and useless. It wasn't as if Craw or the warlock had left her with any choice. *Stay here – watch the fire – should I boil a pot of water too? Is that all I am good for?*

Furious, she took a step toward the gateway, then halted as the fire dipped, seemingly in response to her movement. Another step, and although she could now see that the mists had completely enveloped the surrounding hillsides, the fire had weakened yet further. It was key to her survival, she understood that much, but the real question was whether she trusted what Craw had told her. *That I do have a part to play in this.*

Did she trust herself to play that role? *Oh Ceresel, I only ever wanted to tell the stories. I never wanted to* live *them.*

The first wisps of sorcerous mists licked the edges of the outermost arch and she realised she had been wool-gathering far too long. The fire no longer baked her back, and when she turned she saw it had shrunk in strength, a normal cookfire once more. Cassia darted back to her place at the fire, scrabbling on the ground for the last poor offerings of firewood.

She poked the fire back into life, taking care not to stifle it by piling too much fresh wood onto it. Her very presence at the fireside seemed to make the flames leap higher, as they had done when Craw tended the simmering pot earlier. Cassia had not seen the dragon do anything that looked remotely sorcerous, yet the fire was supposed to be the heart of the protective wards Malessar had laid around the fort.

The contents of the pot bubbled under the ill-fitting lid; they should have been burned away by the ferocity of the fire, and Cassia wondered what ingredients Malessar had left to cook. She was tempted to lift the lid to find out, but a more careful part of her mind warned that she might break the spell's efficacy. Instead she reached out for another sliver of the scavenged wood and jabbed it into the base of the fire.

The courtyard had darkened. Fresh shadows lingered in the corners and the doorways looked hungry and unwelcoming. There was no sound from beyond the walls. The valley had been quiet before, but now the encroaching mists had suffocated it completely. Firelight illuminated the ground for a few yards, and she was careful not to step beyond the clear bounds of that light.

If the wards fall, how will I get away? It was a thought that refused to leave her head, even though she kept telling herself that Malessar was too powerful to be defeated by a curse he had laid himself. *And Craw is a dragon. What could ever defeat a dragon?*

But the old tales did speak of heroes who had won great battles against the beasts. If they were anywhere close to the truth, then dragons were not invulnerable. The curse had sat, silent and gathering power for hundreds of years. It might now be more than a match for Malessar's skills.

Cassia could not imagine herself battling Caenthell's vengeful spirits on her own. She knew she would never make it to the base of the hill.

She poked the fire again, raising a small shower of sparks. There was something peculiar here, though the fire burned fiercely now it did not seem to be consuming the splintered wood any faster. Malessar's fire was burning some other fuel. The warlock had said the strength of the fort would be added to his own, and she thought of his words as she looked around at the darkened walls. He had commanded this outpost, centuries ago. The wraith had been proof of that. With a flash of intuition she was suddenly certain that Malessar had somehow created a reservoir of his own power here, stored for just such a desperate situation.

Just how much strength did he leave here?

The cursed mists had broached the top of the battlements, and tendrils curled in through the gateway, questing across the ground as though it knew she was there. Cassia felt the wild rush of terror surging through her body, urging her to panic and run, and she could see no way to prevent it seizing control.

You have the authority.

What had Craw meant? What authority? The fire flickered, distracting her, and Cassia could not keep her thoughts in order. For one moment she believed she saw the warlock's face in the flames, twisted into a scream, and the edges of an idea followed close behind. She grabbed at it, as a drowning man might thrash toward the end of a thrown rope.

I must defend this place. That was what Craw had been telling her, in the frustrating and oblique fashion of all dragons – that she had permission to use the reserves of power embedded inside the very stones of the fortress.

But I'm no witch! Common sense rebelled in a flare of panic. *I am a storyteller – a girl! I wouldn't even know where to start!*

But you do, another part of her said. *Verros the Younger was left to guard Black Govou's horde of riches against the greedy townsfolk, and he made good use of the magic the dragon had left behind.*

She knew the tale, it was one of her favourites. Verros was an enterprising character and all the stories he featured in made full use of his initiative, bravado and penchant for witticisms and punning putdowns. Cassia loved the more light-hearted tones, finding them a welcome relief after Norrow's more strident tragedies. She had never thought that one day she might emulate his deeds, as well as his words.

What did he say? How did Verros begin his case?

"Spirits, hear me!" Her voice came out as a squeak and

she cursed under her breath. It felt wrong to be addressing an empty courtyard. "Oh, revenants and wraiths, come defend your walls against invasion. Your captain, Malessar, commands you to service!"

She fed the last of the wood to the fire and repeated her lines in a stronger voice. If they had any effect it was difficult to tell, though the flames appeared to be tinged with a shade of flickering blue. She wondered if that was due to the mists.

"Revenants and wraiths!" she called once more, and as she drew her next breath the harsh sound of metal scraping on stone froze her words unspoken. Cassia turned and peered through the gathering murk, but she could see no sign of movement.

Yet . . . the sound came again. Somebody was moving inside one of the towers.

"Revenants and wraiths," she called once more, a fresh quaver spoiling the bold tone she had put on. "Rise up and serve as you have been bound!"

This was a risk. Even if this was what Malessar had intended, the spirits that haunted the stones of the fortress might not listen to or recognise the authority he had left with her. Such had happened to Verros, she recalled. Dark and angry ghosts had poured out of the mountains to ravage the countryside and Verros had spent the next two years on a quest to ensnare them and return them to Black Govou's lair. *And with my luck it'll be worse than that . . .*

The cookfire flared and she shied back, throwing an arm up to protect her face. The heat seared her skin and she yelped.

When she lowered her arm again, she was not alone.

A shadowed figure stood before the door of the main watchtower. The silhouette was that of a soldier, cloaked and armoured, a crested helm tucked under one arm. A sword sat at his hip, and he held a pair of slender javelins in his free hand. He might have been one of the men she had seen inside the watchtower, but she could not see his face.

The man raised his hand. In response to his silent orders

other soldiers appeared from inside the barracks, and at the doors of the other towers. Their forms were all tinged with the same flickering shades that coloured the cookfire.

"Hold these walls!" she commanded, with as much authority as she could borrow from the tales of Verros the Younger.

The first shade stared at her and jerked his head. He donned his helm and raised the javelins into the air in silent salute. Cassia looked up and saw the battlements were now manned by these ancient spirits. They all stood facing outwards, javelins held ready as though the fortress was besieged by mortal forces. Others had converged on the gatehouse, their forms merging with the mists that rolled along the ground there.

The cookfire was settling down again and Cassia stabbed the heart of the blaze once more to keep it burning fiercely. Embers flew upward, stinging her face, but she dared not move back any further.

The hissing of steel rang through the courtyard. The soldiers at the gate had drawn their weapons, advancing to meet the mists that reached out for them, tendrils extended like the fingers of a great, grasping hand.

As one, the soldiers launched their javelins or plunged their swords into the mists. Cassia could not see how such an insubstantial enemy could be harmed, but the tendrils recoiled as though stung, the severed ends dissipating into thin air. The soldiers pressed their attack, striking again and again until the ground around them was cleared. Cassia shouted and cheered them on, caught up in their fight. For a moment she even forgot her own danger. But the fog beneath the gates piled up, thick and dark and swirling with hate.

The soldiers on the battlements threw all of their javelins down into the mists. They drew their swords and attacked the tendrils that whipped through the sky against them. If Cassia had not conjured up these defenders then the fort would already have been overrun and she would be dead. She forced the thought away before she had time to dwell on it. She punched the air again and shouted even louder.

A dense length of mist curled around the legs of a soldier nearest the gates and pulled him down to the ground. His arm flailed through the air, the rest of him lost to sight, and then *something* pulled him away through the gates and he was gone forever.

Another man, struck across the face, tumbled from the battlements. His body landed on the broken roof of the barracks, disappearing through the remaining tiles without disturbing them, as though he had never been there at all.

The fire guttered for a moment and Cassia, remembering the importance of her own task, searched about for fuel. With horror she realised that nothing remained. She had already fed the last of the scavenged wood to the fire. Worse yet, the fire was actively consuming these last planks and branches, at such a voracious rate it would surely burn itself to ashes in a matter of minutes.

"Ceresel save us all," she gasped, praying the goddess would hear her. TThere was nothing else to burn. The fire would die, and Malessar's spell of protection along with it. Then nothing could prevent the cursed mists from swamping the fortress.

Her summoned defenders, their own strength surely linked to that of the fire, were flagging as the mists forced them back from the gates. Another man had already fallen, and a second looked winded, favouring one side to protect his ribs. *How do you injure ghosts?* Cassia wondered before damping the thought quickly. It mattered only that they were on her side. She had to do something to help them.

What would Meredith have done? But she knew the answer: the Heir to the North would already be lost to sight, his sword a blur as he worked through the forms that no man could withstand. Would he be able to drive the mist back? She wanted to believe so. If only he was here. *But if I can imitate even the least part of his force . . .*

"Stand!" she shouted. "Stand or we shall all die!"

Not one of the soldiers looked in her direction. They were too busy fighting this physical manifestation of Malessar's centuries-old curse.

In desperation she tore off her coat and threw it on the fire. If she died it would not matter if her body was cold.

That the coat burned was no surprise, but the flames engulfed it so eagerly, rising up with an intense heat that forced her away from the fireside once more, and that did shock her. With no time to think over her decision she flung off as much of her clothing as she dared, stripping down to her shift and her boots, piling it on top of the coat. She felt as vulnerable as a babe in arms, but she ignored the sudden roar of flame as she scooped up Pelicos's sword and abandoned her place to join the defence of the fortress.

Close up, the soldiers appeared drab, grey and insubstantial, and they moved, hacked and died without a sound. The nearest man looked around and gave her a curt nod of acknowledgement before returning his attention to the coils that threatened him. Cassia took a deep breath. Her heart bursting in her chest, she edged in alongside him and jabbed at the swirling cloud that poured through the gates.

"For the North!" she shouted. She could not tell whether the soldiers heard her, but they pressed forward with renewed strength and the mists dispersed before them. Cassia saved her blows for the tendrils snaking out to flank them, beating them back so the soldiers could attack the thicker base of the mist. One coil brushed her leg, leeching and clammy, before she severed the thing and it disappeared into a fine spray.

At one point she glanced at the fire and noticed it still burned with an intense flame, but then the mist redoubled its attack and she had no time to wonder. As redoubtable as her wraiths might be they still fell, dragged to the ground, or throttled, or thrown from the battlements, and Cassia's force was soon pushed backwards once more. The man beside her overstretched, hacking into the depths of the mists, and something beastlike whipped up to grab his arm and pull him off his feet. The last Cassia saw of him was his face, twisted into a silent scream of agony.

She looked up to see that she had become the vanguard. Only half a dozen soldiers remained behind her, their attention drawn by events above them on the battlements. She edged back, lifting her gaze, and saw the mist pouring over the ramparts like water, pooling in the courtyard with such speed already it was hard to see the watchtower.

We're surrounded. So much for my heroic defence.

She flailed out of the way of the grasping tendrils, warding them off with her sword, and fought her way back to the soldiers. They looked resigned to their fate, their eyes darkened to near invisibility underneath their grim helms. At least they still had the protection of Malessar's sorcerous fire. *While it still burns, at any rate. After that . . . nobody will tell this story.*

"Gather around the fire," she told the soldiers. "If we can defend that there's still a chance."

Again only silence met her words. She could not tell if they understood her, let alone believed her. Yet they formed the last line of defence with her; one would step forward to jab and slash at the pearled murk while his colleagues guarded his flanks, and by attacking in turn they kept the mist at bay. Cassia felt the heat of the fire at her back and was glad of it. With each breath the courtyard was becoming colder. Nimbly avoiding a portion of the mist that sought to separate her from her companions, Cassia thought she might die of exposure before the fire went out. If it was no longer as fierce as before, it still channelled Malessar's sorcery and fed upon her own clothes, and it showed no sign of abating before it was engulfed at last by the relentless damp of the clouds pouring over the walls and through the gates.

The seconds stretched and blurred, until she could not tell how long they had been battling the ancient curse wards. The soldiers fought silently beside her, grim and determined, but even so she was glad for their company and she felt an odd stirring of emotion that lent fresh strength to her tired muscles. Pride, she thought in the spare moments between hard-pressed defence. *I can be proud of this.*

A sudden refracted flare of light from high above, as though the sun itself was cleaving through the gloom. The throaty roar echoed through the skies a bare moment later, and Cassia realised the shrill cry that followed was her own. Her legs had lost their strength and she rested on her hands and knees in the clammy dirt, her sword fallen half a pace away.

Craw!

A cold touch brushed her arm, resting then gripping hard. Cassia tried to pull away, reaching out for the sword. She managed to tilt the weapon back into her hand and slashed frantically at the air before her. The mists released her and she fell back. The phantom soldiers struck out, over her head and beyond her, to cover her while she crawled back to her feet.

The flare, like the slow lightning of a nightmare, erupted again in a different quarter of the sky. This time the roar was accompanied by a brutal hiss, like water burning away from the outside of a kettle. She fought against the instinct to panic and cower.

"Craw!" she shouted. "Craw! We're down here!"

The mists drew back and then surged forward, desperate to overcome the last ghostly defenders and smother the fire that channelled Malessar's spellcraft. Cassia had no choice but to step back, closer to the fire, stabbing and swinging for her life, even though her limbs were leaden and she felt the last of her strength had already been driven from her.

Another soldier fell, backwards this time, into the fire, and his image dispersed like the seeds of a dandelion, before he hit the ground. The remaining soldiers were barely enough to encircle the fire.

Be like Meredith, she told herself. *Be strong. Be a hero.*

It was not easy.

Dragonfire ripped through the sky once more, directly above the ancient fortress. Cassia's knees buckled against the dragon's fearsome presence. Yet she remained standing, and she was certain Craw's efforts were forcing the mists back from the hilltop.

We cannot hold. Craw's voice sounded in her head, as clear as if the dragon spoke right beside her. *Flee this courtyard, girl.*

That made her falter. "Where to?" she called out. "Where should I go?"

The sky lit up over the watchtower, the mists burned away to reveal Craw's immense form looming overhead. Craw could not fit into the small courtyard, so if she wanted to escape she would have to make her own way up to the battlements. The climb had not been difficult earlier, but now the steps and the rampart were damp and slippery, and she could picture herself tumbling down, to be engulfed by the mists and the unseen creatures that haunted them . . .

Hurry, girl.

She shook the thought from her mind and glanced around at the spirits she had summoned to her aid. While the mist had retreated from Craw's presence, they stood at guard, weapons raised as they awaited the next assault. The nearest man met her gaze and indicated, with a jerk of his head, that she should head for the steps beside the stables.

"But what about you?" she asked him.

His eyes held no emotion. None of the ghosts had yet uttered as much as a cry, though their mouths moved to shape words, but this time the soldier only held up his sword in a salute. Cassia touched her own blade to his. The hilt of her sword suddenly felt ice cold, leeching warmth from her hand, but the blade gained a brilliant silvery hue.

Touched by magic, she thought, too exhausted to be awed as events and impossibilities piled atop one another. She could scarcely take it in.

Cassia broke the salute and sprinted across the ground

toward the steps. She had already decided not to look back. These soldiers had already died once for their homeland and she did not want to see their bold spirits snuffed out a second time. Not when she was responsible for those deaths.

The stone was as damp as she had feared, but Craw's intimidating presence overhead kept the mists at bay and there was nothing to trip her or seize her limbs as she skidded over the rampart. It was only nervous energy that kept her going, she knew. Exhaustion dragged at her heels and weighed her down, and she was barely able to haul herself up to the top of the watchtower.

The mists swirled below her, covering the hillside. Dark shapes moved within, just as she had seen in the resurrected town of Karakhel. Cassia kept her sword high and ready, circling anxiously, but it seemed the effects of the curse wards were concentrated on the courtyard.

"Craw!" she shouted.

The force of its passage overhead knocked her to her knees once more. She raised her head and watched the dragon sweep into a graceful curve that brought it back toward the watchtower. The mists curled away, repelled by Craw's presence.

Craw reared up, wings fully extended, and its hind claws closed on the crumbling battlements. *Swiftly, girl. We are not out of danger yet.*

The dragon raised one of its smaller front limbs so Cassia could scramble up onto its back. She was far too tired to complain when Craw rolled that limb to tumble her into place at the base of its long neck. Her stomach heaved as Craw thrust back into the air, the watchtower dropping quickly away from view. She caught one brief glimpse of the courtyard before it was lost within the murk, and if the fire still burned at all, she could not see it. There were tears in the corners of her eyes; tears she wanted to ascribe to the cold air that stung her face, but she knew she was mourning the wraiths she had called up.

To die again. With my authority.

Craw banked, the dragon's great wings pushing it beyond the reach of a thick tendril of mist that whipped across the sky. *Hold on, girl. If you fall . . .*

"Where are we going?" The mists covered more than just the hillside and the ruins of Karakhel, she could see from this height. She could not make out any of the valley's landmarks, and with no sun visible in the grey sky, her sense of direction was confounded. Another thought occurred to her and she glanced over her shoulder. "Craw, where is Malessar?"

A fair question. Where are your clothes?

Her hands were already numb, and the rest of her body was not far behind. Even on the worst winter nights, huddled beneath scrubby bushes by the side of a frozen mud track while her father drank himself to insensibility by the fire, she had never felt this cold.

"I burned them," she admitted.

Whatever the dragon thought of that, it kept its own counsel. *Malessar is nearby. The wards must be sealed again.*

Craw dipped, following the curves of the landscape. They had left the valley behind and now flew low between the inhospitable peaks of the mountains. Mists curled over the ground below, hugging the contours of the land and disguising the few stands of trees that grew there. She could not work out their heading, but Craw seemed to be making for a high ridge that ran the length of the range to her right.

The ridge was clear of mists, and Craw slowed to circle a wide promontory that looked out over Caenthell's valleys. A figure stood there; the warlock leaned on his staff, head bowed. She was so glad to see him alive that the scale of his exhaustion did not register until Craw reared to a halt and she scrambled from the dragon's back to run to him.

"Sir, I thought—" she began, but Malessar raised a hand to stop her.

"No apology is necessary," he said. "The fault is mine. I should not have brought you to this place. The wards are

disintegrating. Caenthell is far too dangerous, even for me."
He frowned. "What has happened? Where are your clothes?"

He tore off his cloak and wrapped it around her. "Gods
above, girl, you will catch a death of cold up here!"

"I used up all the fuel," she explained. "I had to keep the fire
burning, or you would be unprotected, and the soldiers could
not hold back the mists, and I thought I was going to die . . ."

Malessar tied the cloak tight around her neck and pressed
two fingers against her forehead. She flinched at the touch.

"Soldiers? No, never mind. This can wait for another time.
Stay back from the edge, girl. This ledge was ever perilous, but
we will not be here long."

He led her back from the sheer cliff face, and when he
halted she collapsed onto the ground. She heard him speak to
Craw, but she did not understand the words. The battle had
drained her completely. Cassia could hardly believe she still
lived. She shivered with remembered fear and desperation. The
world had contracted to the dirt within arm's reach and she
struggled to keep the warlock in sight.

Fighting against the onrushing dark of unconsciousness,
she watched Malessar take a small pouch from his belt and lay
out a series of objects along the top of the cliff. He spoke to
the dragon again and Craw, transformed once more, shook his
head and gestured in her direction.

It's my fault, she thought. *It must be my fault. I have to tell
them . . .*

But the thread of her thoughts was unravelling so quickly
she could not even remember what was so important. Her
exhausted mind was playing tricks on her, overlaying her
view of Malessar and Craw with a scene conjured from her
imagination . . .

*Two men stand above the Hamiardin Pass, discussing strategy,
dividing up the North between them. Their cloaks are frayed and
weather-worn, crusted with the ice of a hard winter. One man is
thick-set and broad-shouldered, his gloved hands braced against*

his hips. The sharp edges of his armour bulge through his cloak, but his head is bare and the dark ringlets of his hair lie plastered to his skull as he stares down upon Caenthell. His companion is taller, more slender, but his poise speaks of his utter self-confidence and the devastating talents he commands. While he talks, punctuating his calm words with sweeping gestures across the snow-capped mountains, the soldier judges each point with blunt monosyllabic replies.

In the valleys below, the spires of an impregnable castle fly bright pennons in the chill mountain winds. Soon there will be bloodshed – and after that, these men will rule the world. Jedrell and Malessar. And behind them, silent and stoic in the way of all Northmen, a captain named Baum guards his liege lord. The long years of exile have weighed heavy on his shoulders, but now his faith in Jedrell's leadership has been repaid and soon he will return home.

The warlock glances over his shoulder, as if aware that he is being watched. There is a distracted frown upon his face. Although he is far younger here, he still wears the gravitas of a much older man. He says something to Jedrell, but the words are whipped away by the wind. The last High King of the North turns, one hand clasped to the hilt of the greatsword at his side, ready to meet any threat face on. His features – buried for centuries beneath the weight of history – are revealed for the first time.

She gasped, and the vision shattered. *Meredith.*

Craw turned his gaze upon her. His fingers curled and pulled at unseen strings. *The curse affects you, girl. Do not fight this – you must sleep, or your mind will be destroyed.*

Cassia tried to open her mouth to protest, to tell the truth at last, but the words would not come. Her spirit, assailed on all sides by ancient magic, fled into darkness.

Chapter Nineteen

ER DREAMS WERE haunted by visions of Meredith. As a warrior. As a prince. As a lover, bare-chested as he had been in the yard of the Old Soak, hovering uncomfortably close over her. As a king, fierce and remote, casting a shadow the size of a mountain over her life . . .

No, not a mountain. *Two* mountains – and Meredith was framed between them, holding them apart, or else pulling them down upon himself . . .

She woke, so tangled in a blanket that it took her a few moments to unwrap herself and sit upright. That, it turned out, was not a good idea. Her head spun and her stomach heaved rebelliously, as though she was drunk. The fact that both the blanket and her clothes were soaked through with sweat told the remainder of the story.

Cool hands pressed her back down. "Rest," she heard someone say. A familiar voice: soothing, mothering. "Here – drink this."

The water was as sharp as mountain ice. *The mountains . . .*

"Leili . . . ?"

It all rushed back with the force of a blow. The mountains,

the vision of Malessar and Jedrell, Craw and the desperate battle against the mists – everything jumbled into one terrifying blur. *And all of it my fault. It has to be.*

"Leili, I have to speak to him."

"Stop fussing, girl. You're not fit. Drink up and rest." There was an edge of concern in the woman's voice, and her hands pressed more firmly. Cassia did not have the strength to fight back.

"But . . . Baum and Meredith . . . my prince . . . my charm . . ."

Leili clicked her teeth. "The fever's talking now. Whatever it is, it can wait, girl. You sweat it out, eh?"

She closed her eyes again and let her shoulders slump back, but Leili still kept one hand pressed to her chest. The cold of the water had hidden a bittersweet taste that was only now apparent. *A sleeping draught . . . ? But I don't need to sleep! I need . . . I need . . .*

The next time she knew herself to be awake, it was Leili's humming that roused her. The sound echoed through the windows. The shutters were flung wide and dust and insects played in the broad shafts of light. Cassia lay still for a few minutes and watched them, becoming aware of how the light moved in response to the slow passage of time, before she remembered that her room did not have windows like these that opened onto the *dhar's* courtyard.

Shifting around on the cushions, she was able to see that she had been moved into the long room Malessar had originally offered her. It still loomed around her, far too large for her to be comfortable, but she was glad she had not been left to suffer her fever in her own small, darkened room.

Leili was cooking, she thought. That meant everything would be all right.

Except that it won't be. How long have I been asleep?

She began to lever herself out of the bed, but hesitated. Leili would hear the boards creak the moment she stepped upon them. Still, it couldn't be helped. She couldn't lie here all day.

At some point she had been stripped of her clothes and dressed in a plain knee-length shift. The thin cloth was damp and smelled stale; it looked too small to belong to Leili, so it must have been dragged out of storage somewhere. Cassia padded over the floor barefoot, her arms outstretched for balance. She blinked away the sudden rush of dizziness, making for the chests that sat on either side of the door onto the balcony. She was pulling a tunic from the first chest when Leili's shape cast shadows through the windows.

"You shouldn't be up so soon!" the woman tutted. "You're weaker than a newborn lamb!"

"I have to get up," Cassia told her. "It's too important."

Leili shook her head. "And now you sound like the master. You Northerners – you're all as stubborn as each other. You've got three days of meals to catch up on, and I'll be damned if I let you go without them. I'll force them into you one after another if I have to."

Cassia didn't doubt that. Some battles were not worth fighting. Leili hovered attentively over her while she donned a pair of breeches plainly made for a man with much longer legs. The boots, at least, were her own. When she reached for her scabbard, hung on the back of the door, Leili tutted again and Cassia glared at her for a moment before giving in. She took her staff instead, using it to support her as she made her way slowly down the stairs.

"The master," she said between breaths as she descended. "How is he? Is he here?"

"You're as bad as each other," Leili said.

Cassia remembered how Malessar had gone into seclusion after he fought off the storm that chased the *Rabbit* from Hellea. The use of sorcery had weakened him for several days then. How much more of his strength must he have used to

restore Caenthell's curse wards? And how would that incapacitate him?

"But he's here, isn't he?"

"He's in his bed, girl. As you should be."

Cassia's mind moved too fast for her to catch up. She knew
she would have to recover further before she could make the
connections that lurked just out of reach, and that was frustrating enough to bring a curse to her lips. She reached the bottom
of the stairs and paused for breath, taking a firm grip on the
staff to prevent her hands from trembling.

"There's too much at stake, Leili. More than I can say. I
cannot just rest."

The old woman's eyes were filled with sadness. "I said you
sounded like him. Oh, Cassia, you're no girl anymore."

It was a measure of how preoccupied she was that it took
her a full hour to work out what Leili meant.

When one of Leili's cousins arrived at the door to bring
three loaves of tomato bread and to make gossip, Cassia took
advantage of the distraction. She gathered up the clay bowl and
slipped gingerly off the stool, moving as quietly as possible to
the door into the garden. Leili never once turned around.

Cassia had to admit the cook had been right in one respect:
she needed feeding up. The spiced lamb must have slow-
cooked for all the time she had been asleep, it had been so soft.
Nothing she had eaten ever tasted so good.

It sounded as though Narjess was up on the roof; Cassia
wondered if he was repairing the marks in the walls where
Craw had landed. It might cure him of his disbelief in dragons,
although he was so set in his ways that she doubted it. She
walked across the colonnade towards Malessar's private rooms,
glancing up from time to time to be sure Narjess had not seen
her.

Even with her staff to aid her she felt exhausted by the time she reached the far wing of the *dhar*. The garden had never seemed so long before. The clay bowl of stew was warm against her side, and that warmth lent her some degree of strength.

Where the room she had slept in had been thrown open to the daylight, the shutters at this end of the *dhar* were closed tight on both floors, as were the ornately decorated doors. Cassia knew the lower floor held the warlock's library and work areas – she had peered in through the windows once, on a rare occasion when the shutters were open, and seen the dark silhouettes of unfamiliar furnishings there. She had guessed Malessar used the room above as his living quarters. She gritted her teeth against fatigue and took the stairs slowly. Leili's gossiping echoed faintly through the colonnade behind her.

In all her time in Galliarca she had never been in this part of the house. There was no physical wall erected around it, but there might as well have been. Cassia felt the hairs on her arms stir as she stepped onto the balcony. There was sorcery in the air. Of course, she thought. It could not be any other way.

She hesitated and then knocked lightly on the smaller access door that was set into the larger pair. There was no reply from within.

I can leave it. I can leave him. I don't have to do this.

But she did, she knew. Malessar had given her a life – a life she would otherwise never have had. Despite any protestations he might make, that meant she owed him a debt.

Juggling bowl and staff, she lifted the latch. Daylight illuminated a slanted rectangle of rich carpet beyond. "Sir?" she called in a low voice. "Sir, I have food for you."

There was still no answer. She took a deep breath and stepped through, pausing to let her eyes adjust to the gloom. There were cases, hangings and shelves on the walls, alongside alcoves that were darker than the rest of the room, and there were cushions and low tables in the Galliarcan style. At one end of the room another small door must lead through to the warlock's private dressing area. At the other end, curtains had been drawn to hide his bed.

The prickling sensation reached her back, another wave starting at her wrists. Cassia felt the urge to drop both the bowl and her staff and scratch furiously at her skin. "Sir, I'll let some light in," she said.

She left the bowl on a table and used the tip of her staff to flick the upper catches of one of the shutters and push it outwards. Sunlight and colour returned to the room.

Like so much of the *dhar*, Malessar's quarters were a battling confusion of Galliarcan and Northern styles. The carpets were cream, with borders of thorns and trailing ivy. Intricately detailed lanterns hung from the beams high above, Galliarcan to the core. The hangings showed scenes from Galliarcan tales as well as the Age of Talons, while dark figurines of mail-clad soldiers and slender maidens stared up at her from the alcoves and low shelves. Although she thought she had known what to expect, Cassia still found herself distracted and amazed by the variety of decoration.

More to the point, however, was the presence of another two bowls of food, both untouched and congealed, congregated with buzzing flies. Cassia moved the stew she had brought away from that table and covered it with a small mat.

"Sir?"

She brushed one hand against the silken curtain that surrounded the bed. There was nothing for it, she decided. She scooped the curtain aside to see into the divided space.

Malessar lay with his eyes closed, beneath a simple blanket. He looked every inch his nine hundred years or more, his skin pallid and tight against his skull. One hand sat on top of the blanket, the fingers curled like dead worms. Cassia could not conceive of this man as the self-confident, energetic scholar she had met in Hellea. For one terrifying moment she thought he was dead.

His eyes twitched open and he looked up at her, though she wasn't certain he could actually see her. "Aliciana," he breathed. "I could not restore you."

She shook her head. "No, sir. I'm not Aliciana. I'm Cassia. I brought you . . . I brought some food."

The warlock closed his eyes, and for a moment she believed he had fallen asleep again, but when he reopened them they focused upon her more quickly. "Cassia. Of course. Cassia."

There was a long exhalation before he spoke again. "What is it?"

"I brought food, sir. I wanted to . . . to see how you were."

"Tired. Does Leili know you are here?"

Cassia shook her head. Malessar coughed. It could have been a laugh, she thought.

"You have a taste for danger, girl," he said. "Was Caenthell not dangerous enough?"

She managed to smile. "Perhaps Leili could have beaten the mists back with her wooden spoons."

"That would make an excellent story," Malessar said.

Unsure how to proceed, she brought the bowl over and found more cushions to prop underneath him so he could eat without spilling stew all over himself. The warlock tutted and sighed as she worked, but he was evidently too weak to fend her off. The effort exhausted her as well, and she slumped onto the mats by the side of the bed.

"You were fevered," Malessar said. The bowl balanced precariously on his lap. "We believed the curse had ensnared you. You should still be abed."

She could not dispute that. "You . . . Craw . . . you put me in that long room. When I woke up . . ."

"You could not stay there." Malessar smiled. "But not only that."

He was far more observant than he had any right to be in such a weakened condition. "No, sir."

"Questions. We both have questions, for which there are no

easy answers." He stared into the bowl and then dug in with his bare hands.

Cassia sat and waited, uncertain where to start. If she *should* start.

"Sir, are the curse wards secure?"

"Hmm . . ." He chewed and swallowed. "For the moment. I had no idea the energistic power contained behind them had become so . . . overwhelming. So malevolent. I was extremely lucky to counter it with what Artrevia could lend me."

"But how long will that last?"

There was a longer silence. "I have no way of knowing."

"There were ghosts at the fort," Cassia said. "Ghosts of soldiers. They rallied with me and fought back the mists for a while. We kept the fire burning."

"As Craw said. You did well. I felt your assistance." Malessar turned his gaze upon her. "And that is remarkable – again, worthy of a story in itself. Craw has given you his attention. No small feat."

Cassia's skin crawled. The dragon had seen her mind, seen her association with Baum and Meredith, and her place in the plot against the warlock. Craw had seen more besides, yet had not revealed any of it to either Cassia or Malessar. She felt as though she was on the edge of a precipice that she could not see. A step backwards could be safety – or it could plummet her into the void.

Malessar can sense that. I have to tell him.

Mention of the wraith-like soldiers reminded her of how she had almost died at the fort outside Karakhel. The touch of the mists had drained strength from her body. "The mists . . . that was what the wards held back?"

The warlock shook his head. "No. The merest outriders. Harbingers of the twisted revenants in the kingdom beyond."

She shuddered, unable to conceive of anything worse than the numbing, leeching mists. With every minute the dramatic scale of her escape became clearer.

"And if the wards fail . . . ?"

"I shall have more warning," Malessar said. "I was remiss in my duties. I shall not be found wanting again."

"That wasn't quite what I meant, sir."

"No." The warlock sighed. "If the wards fail then those outriders will be the least of anybody's problems. The revenants of Caenthell will burst forth and spread across all of the North. And then into Hellea. And then . . ." He pushed the bowl back towards her, his appetite apparently gone. "Then the world will be ruined."

Cassia soaked up the light the same way basking lizards and flowering plants did. In the early mornings, before the sun rose too high, she worked through her forms on the rooftop, restraining the speed and rhythm of her movements to preserve her strength. At first she managed only a few minutes before fatigue had the better of her, but even over the first week of exercises she noticed a vast improvement. She was still weakened by the effects of the fever and her exertions in the mountains, but she could recover from that. Given time.

Time. The one element she could no longer be certain of.

Leili was happy to feed her as much as she could eat. Sometimes she felt like an over-stuffed doll, bursting at the seams, but she would always be hungry again by the time the next meal was placed in front of her. Malessar, still confined to his chamber, received the same treatment. The prickle of sorcery that she felt emanating from that wing of the *dhar* grew more noticeable with each passing day. The warlock had cast a spell of healing and sustenance upon himself, and as he regained his strength the magic itself became stronger and more powerful, thus hastening the process of recovery. It was a dangerous loop to set in place, but Malessar felt he had no choice. His attention had returned to the problem of the curse wards around Caenthell. They had to be strengthened. Redoubled. Made so tight that humanity would have another thousand years of grace before the spells had to be reinforced once more.

"But what will happen then?" Cassia asked.

The warlock had almost smiled. "That will be my problem, not yours."

But time was not an ally.

Cassia had not broached the subject – she dared not, despite all she knew – but it was obvious Baum could not be allowed to succeed in his quest. The principles he stood for would destroy the North, not rebuild it. Meredith must never come into his inheritance. *And he will hate me for it.*

Wherever they were, they would be drawing closer. Baum was set upon confrontation. He might still listen to her – she could not do anything that would remove herself from Malessar's side.

Does that make me evil, as Malessar was evil, by opposing the resurrection of the North? Surely not. Malessar did wrong for a reason . . .

She stopped abruptly, halfway through one of the forms, and the tip of the staff thumped against the tiles.

I am missing something. Something important. The reason behind all of this.

She was halfway down the stairs before she realised it. The rising heat of the day pressed against her as she emerged onto the balcony by the warlock's rooms. There was a pressure in the air, and it was not related to either the heat, or the spells Malessar had cast. There was not a single cloud in the sky, but a storm was building.

The doors were closed, but some of the shutters had been pushed wide. Cassia ventured a glance through the nearest and saw the curtains drawn around Malessar's bed. It was frustrating. She felt she could not ask the questions she really needed to ask while he was still recovering his strength.

She checked the courtyard to make sure neither Narjess nor Leili were watching, and then entered the room once more.

She wasn't even sure what she was looking for. A journal? From so long ago? It would likely have been worn to dust by the passage of time. But Malessar had surrounded himself with pieces of art from the North. It made sense to Cassia that his private rooms would feature the most meaningful pieces. She had been too tired to study them last time. This time . . .

The most obvious places to start were the alcoves on the far wall. These held the carved figurines, the painted masks that may have been used in worship hundreds of years ago. They all looked far too delicate to touch, their colours dried out and long-faded. Cassia wondered how Malessar had transported them safely across the world.

She was drawn to the alcove closest to the bed-curtains. This contained only one figurine, of a woman seated on a tall throne. She had been carved with a regal bearing, one hand raised in pronouncement, or in greeting. Cassia tilted her head to one side, considered the figurine again, and changed her mind. *In farewell, perhaps.*

The woman's features were characteristically Northern, distinctive across the ages and highlighted by the way the artist had portrayed her with her hair pulled back into a long tail. A young woman, Cassia decided. A princess . . . or a queen.

I feel I should know her.

"You have not been sent to watch over me."

She jumped to her feet, startled by the warlock's sudden appearance behind her. He had come from his private washroom, she realised. He had not been asleep at all.

"No," she admitted. His stare was sharp enough to strip away any deceit. "But . . . I had a question."

The warlock stretched out one hand to touch the figurine gently upon its head. "I see. One of the difficult ones. Well, ask."

"Caenthell," she said. "Why did it happen?"

"Because I was a fool."

For a long moment Malessar said nothing else. Then he sighed. "That is Aliciana. Daughter of Rosmer. Brightest flower of the North. The reason I made alliance with Jedrell."

"You loved her?" Cassia felt the shock rip the breath from her throat.

"Ever since we were children," Malessar said softly. "It would never have been allowed, of course. Not for a princess and the son of a mere half-captain. But for a princess and a mage of the court . . . oh, I bent myself to my future. I disappointed my father, and I apprenticed myself to Damius Scarlet. And I sent letter after letter to Caenthell, to tell Aliciana how I would return for her as the greatest sorcerer the world had ever seen. And she waited for me."

His eyes clouded, lost in remembrance. "This figurine had a twin, once. Aliciana as the Mistress of Blades, caught in mid-form. Graceful and lithe. The sculptor was a genius."

"None of the stories tell of this," Cassia said. She hadn't wanted to interrupt, but that unseen pressure weighed upon her shoulders. She needed to find an answer.

"Of course not. This is *my* story, Cassia. Jedrell was banished from Caenthell for daring to cross Rosmer. He came to me and told me Rosmer had promised his daughter to a Berdellan warchief. I was outraged. I could scarcely believe the High King's temerity. But Jedrell calmed me. He had a plan, he said, a plan to take the throne for himself. And he promised Aliciana would be free to marry me. *I will perform the ceremony myself*, he said, *when my lands are secure*. Of course I believed him. Jedrell was a persuasive man, and I – I was still young and naive."

"I had a vision of you and Jedrell at the Hamiardin Pass," Cassia said. "Just before the end."

Malessar nodded. "The sorcery lingers – for good or for evil, who knows? Jedrell forced Rosmer's hand from the throne of Caenthell, kept Aliciana as a hostage to fortune, as we had agreed, and commenced his rule of the North and his conquest of the lands that eventually became Hellea." He flicked one hand in a dismissive gesture. "History recounts all too much of that. And I, safe in the knowledge that he would not hurt Aliciana, journeyed to Kalakhadze to complete my studies. Time fled, and I buried myself in arcane mysteries. I was afire with the power of the gods. Pyraete illuminated everything that made up the world. Mortal life had no meaning for me, then. I did not notice my beloved's letters had first become infrequent, and then ceased completely."

He stared down at the figurine. "And then I learned the truth. And the gods themselves could not have held me back."

Cassia heard echoes of Baum's version of the story. *He murdered every single man, woman and child inside the castle's walls – burned them or tore them to shreds with his sorcery. His rage consumed the very stones themselves, and he pulled Caenthell down to the ground and left it as a smouldering, ruined grave.*

"She was swayed by Jedrell's honeyed tongue," Malessar said. "That is what I have told myself. I was in distant lands. She must have believed I had abandoned her. And when I returned, filled with the green fires of rage and impotent jealousy – they *smiled* at me. *Be welcome*, they said. *Celebrate the birth of our son.*

"I forswore my oaths and my allegiances – to my king, my home, and my god. What power I still had, I wrested from Pyraete and used against everything and everyone I had ever loved. And I burned them all to death and cursed the land itself. Is that answer enough for you, Cassia?"

But . . . Meredith lives. Jedrell's bloodline. But if I tell him that – what will he do?

Cassia retreated to her own room – or, the long room that she was slowly coming to call her own. Leili had not allowed her to move back downstairs, and she suspected the old storage cupboard would now be firmly locked to keep her out. The weight across her shoulders had not lessened. If anything the pressure had increased, making each step more difficult than the last.

Why have you not told him the truth of who you are?

Craw's words to her. She had still not figured out the dragon's riddles.

Because he does not deserve that kind of betrayal, she thought. *Because he has trusted me. And that's more than Baum did,* she reminded herself bitterly.

But it was not the whole truth. Not according to the dragon.

So what is the truth? How can I tell the truth if I don't know what it is?

Turn your head to the side, girl.

What had Craw seen? There was a small mirror, set into a brass frame with a handle that curled like clinging vines, in one of the chests. Cassia rummaged through her belongings until she found it, and took it to one of the opened windows.

It was odd to think it, but she didn't recognise the girl she had once been. That girl had been brash and dirty, more of a boy in many respects. Now she was tanned, her features more defined, as though she had grown into herself. Still a Northerner, of course, despite her dress . . .

With her free hand she scooped up her hair, pulling it back tight against her scalp. And she almost dropped the mirror in shock.

Aliciana. I look like Aliciana!

For a long moment she could scarcely breathe, so entranced was she by her reflection. By what Craw must have seen.

By what Malessar must see. Because he could not have failed to see the resemblance to the princess he had promised to marry.

She lowered the mirror. Unpleasant thoughts gathered at the edges of her mind. If both Craw and Malessar could see it, then so could Baum and Meredith. And they were the ones who wanted to get to Malessar . . .

Through me. *Oh sweet gods, I must be the stupidest sheep in the bloody field.*

The pieces fell into place before her, a tiled mosaic of conspiracy and naivety. The man who had pointed out Malessar's ship to her . . . was the drunkard, Arca. The man who had directed her to Hellea's great library, where she had initially encountered the warlock . . . was Arca. Arca, who had befriended her on the steps of the temple. Arca, who slept on the benches of the Old Soak – the tavern run by Ultess, who had once been a soldier in a company commanded by . . . Baum.

And the storm that had driven the ship away from Hellea, preventing it from berthing at Corba; could that have been Baum's work? Sorcery intended to keep the warlock baited? To make sure Cassia landed at Galliarca with him?

It was too much to be called coincidence. She could feel the strings attached to her limbs, manipulating her.

He intended to put me in Malessar's path. Because . . . because I resemble Aliciana. Because Baum has trailed him and watched him for hundreds of years. He knows how Malessar thinks, how he acts, how he tries to hold on to his humanity. How he loved Aliciana . . .

But if that was true, then that meant . . . she squeezed her eyes closed against the force of her thoughts. She could not believe how she had been played for a fool. Baum had never been interested in her father at all, or in his skills as a storyteller. It had been her, all along.

And Meredith, too? But – he taught me! Protected me! I loved him!

That's what they wanted me to think.

She became aware that she had collapsed to the floor. The mirror's frame had chipped the bare boards next to her. The air throbbed like the beating of a giant unseen heart, disrupting her sense of balance.

Cassia dragged herself to her bed, fighting against the invisible pressure. This was sorcery too, it could be nothing else. And, suddenly, she knew the source of it.

The stone carving of Pyraete in the mountains had been moved to this room with the rest of her belongings. She had kept it safe beneath her pillow, where it came easily to hand every night and gave her sweet, disturbing dreams of the Heir to the North. Now, even before her hand reached under the pillow, she felt the warmth radiating from it.

She pulled the pillow away and recoiled. The stone carving pulsed, deep red veins within the rock beating as though it was alive. The figure between the mountains no longer resembled Meredith. Now it was aggressively angular, primal, clawing its way out from the peaks towards vengeance.

In that moment she knew it was not a good luck charm. It had not fallen *accidentally* into her possession. It was another part of Baum's grand subterfuge. A signal, she thought. Like a beacon in the night, so they would always know how to find her.

The implication of that reached her an instant later. She scrambled to her feet, her limbs heavy and her senses dulled by the sheer weight of the sorcerous clarion, and grabbed at her sword-belt. There was no time to lose.

Malessar appeared on the balcony at the other end of the *dhar* just as she left her own room, struggling with the belt's buckle. "Cassia! What is that? Something is flooding the air with sorcery!"

"They're coming!" she shouted. "You have to get out!"

"Who? Who is coming? Cassia—"

The house shuddered, and she was almost thrown off her feet. The dull boom echoed between the walls, drowning out Malessar's words. The pressure was so unbearable it hurt to breathe in.

They were *here*.

Chapter Twenty

I T WAS CLOSE to midday, but the sun was not welcome over Malessar's *dhar*. There were no clouds, yet the light had dimmed, hazed and refracted by the two sorcerous powers in dangerously close proximity. The warlock stood firm at his balcony, his hands fast against the rail as though holding it in place, his face devoid of expression. Cassia saw the air around him distorting, tendrils of magic curling up to give him a truly demonic countenance.

She held on to the door frame, staggered to one knee by the force of the quake. Flecks of plaster rained down on her, bouncing from her hair and her shoulders. It was all she could do to keep from screaming, just to be able to hear her own voice and know that she still lived.

"Who dares?" Malessar called out. His voice rang with the authority of a god. "Who dares intrude on my domain?"

For a long moment there was silence, broken only by the gasping that Cassia recognised as her own breath. Then there was the steady click of boot heels against tiles. Someone had come through the entrance hall, and now they stood at the edge of the courtyard, just below her.

"I'm disappointed in you," Baum said. "I thought you might have recognised and welcomed an old friend after so many years."

Malessar's dark eyes narrowed. The rest of the warlock's face was twisted by magic, his brows more prominent and his cheekbones hollowed. The haze made his mouth curl into a violent smile. "I have no friends. You have already outstayed your welcome, whoever you might be. I suggest you leave now, while you are still able."

Baum took two paces to one side. Cassia caught a glimpse of the nimbus that surrounded him, curling as though reaching up for her, and she shoved herself away in the opposite direction.

"I am your past, Malessar. I am your appointed doom, sent by Pyraete to cleanse the memory of the North."

Malessar laughed. "Of course you are. Do you have any idea how many men tried to do that in the *first* hundred years after Caenthell? Did Pyraete tell you *that* when he whispered tender prophecies in your ear?"

Cassia had made it as far as the end of the balcony, where it adjoined the stairwell. If she had considered fleeing downwards, onto the street, the haze of smoke and dust that rose from below dissuaded her. But now she could see Baum, hooded, holding his staff loose in both hands. His stance reminded her of the slaughter of Vescar's men back in the hills. He would not back down.

"You misused god-given sorceries to curse Pyraete's entire land," Baum spat. "Is it any wonder he wanted revenge?"

"What makes you any different to them?" Malessar flicked one hand dismissively. Magic dripped down into the courtyard, shrivelling a cluster of blooms below.

Baum shrugged his hood back. The malevolence in his expression matched that of the warlock. "I survived Caenthell."

That stopped Malessar cold. The sorceries wrapped around him shifted and flickered, as though reflecting his sudden uncertainty. "No man survived Caenthell."

"I am Baum. Captain of Jedrell's guard. Come on, Man of Stone – don't you remember me?"

It was plain Malessar did remember him. "But you were no mage."

"No," Baum agreed. "I was not."

Without warning he lifted his staff and pointed it at the balcony. The air erupted with a deafening deluge of sorcerous energy. The blast drove through the rail and into the wall behind it, shedding splintered wood and chunks of brick and stone in all directions. Cassia dived to the floor and covered her head with her hands as something struck her on the back of her neck.

Another blast answered the first. Power exploded from the courtyard in waves of lethal colours, echoing from the walls like the screams of damned souls. Cassia risked a glance and saw Malessar, balanced upon the upright remains of the rail itself, energy whipping from each outstretched finger. His body was haloed by protective magic. Then the rail crumbled into dust, but the warlock did not fall. Instead he remained in the air, sustained by his own power. Cassia would have named him a god, if she had not known better.

More blasts punctured the balcony behind her, lacerating the frescos that decorated the supporting pillars. The air tasted of stone, sand and nightmares. *I can't stay here. It's not safe.* But she didn't know of anywhere that would be safe. Not while they fought like this.

The ground exploded in waves towards Baum; the waves rebounded from his protective nimbus. Malessar descended beatifically to the ground, spells shattering all around him. The edges of his robes were afire, but he had not noticed. Or he did not care. His attention was fixed upon his opponent.

Cassia fled the length of the balcony, ducking from pillar to pillar, flinching with every piece of sundered masonry that came close to striking her. The backs of her hands were bleeding in several places, although she could not remember receiving those wounds. Her entire body felt energised, blood surging into her extremities and causing her legs to cramp uncomfortably.

They never mentioned this. The heroism, the daring adventures, the noble prince with a blessed sword – but not the terror. Not the foul, sour-fat taste of the air or the feelings of absolute helplessness and mortality. Not the way sorcery sucked at her very soul, trying to tear it out through her skin even though she was not in the direct line of fire.

She skidded to a halt beneath one of the shutters of Malessar's chamber. It hung from a single hinge, the paint bubbling and peeling. The courtyard below was barely visible, awhirl with a cauldron of energy that had taken on a life of its own. She could make out Malessar's silhouette, and one that could be Baum, as they circled each other, but even as she watched the sorcery obscured them both again.

I have to stop this! It's all my fault! I led them here – and I didn't warn him. I didn't do enough. I'm no hero.

I can't stop it. I might as well throw away this sword. I'm not worthy of it.

The balcony she had just crossed exploded violently, the stones illuminated by sickening blood-red shades. Cassia was thrown back against the wall. Breathless, she pulled herself up to her hands and knees again. She was a mouse – a gnat – caught in the open while gods raged about her. Each moment set loose some new terror in her soul.

Caenthell. This is what Malessar did. What Baum lived through. I can't do it.

She was cut off from both sets of stairs now. If she stayed where she was, there was a good chance some random sorcery would find her and turn her inside out. *No. Not like that.* She looked in both directions and judged that the way forward was easier than the way back. The gap in the balcony was smaller outside Malessar's room. She should be able to jump across it.

Cassia checked her belt was secure, and then launched

herself along the balcony before she could give herself time to think about what she was doing. She curled into the air, and saw the courtyard below for a fleeting instant – long enough to *know* she was wrong – and then she landed hard on the other side, all sense driven from her body by the impact. The balcony wobbled underneath her at the impact.

Oh gods, oh Ceresel, oh just let me live!

She scrambled along the wreckage, hugging the wall, until she reached the relative safety of the far stairwell. Her heart thumped against her ribs and her throat was raw.

There was one other thing she had never accounted for. The courtyard rang with a cacophonous howl, layers of sound bursting through her ears and spending themselves through the very bones of her body. Sorcery made a mockery of every natural sound, forcing itself upon the world. The stones of the building seemed to shriek in pain.

A fresh blast of energy shattered the top of the courtyard. Plaster and brick spun down in an arc. Cassia saw it falling, but it was on her before she could force herself to move. Something struck her hard in the ribs. Off-balance, she staggered back – and there was nothing behind her.

The stairs –

She was wedged into a corner. Uncomfortable. Her scabbard jabbed into the underside of her leg, and her shirt was rucked up over her head. She was upside-down, halfway down the stairwell. The iron tang of blood stung her tongue, and her ribs felt sore.

The startling silence was much of a shock as the scale of the violence had been.

Knocked cold – but for how long? A moment? More?

Cassia slid down the last flight of steps on her hands and knees. The air tasted of ground stone and felt as oppressive as the moments before a breaking thunderstorm, but the storm had already been unleashed. Her skin still prickled and strange luminous shapes danced at the edge of her vision, the after-effects of the tumult of sorceries that had engulfed the courtyard.

The garden was all but destroyed: plants withered and burned, the breakfast table twisted and thrown aside like wreckage from a fire. The debris still glowed and bubbled. The pillars around the small yard were chipped and charred and in some places even cracked, gaping fissures that threatened their integrity. One of the beautifully carved doors to Malessar's hall sported a jagged, smouldering gash; its twin had been blown clean out of sight.

A body lay by the far wall, unrecognisably burned, one skeletal arm outstretched and blackened. Narjess. Or Leili. *Oh gods above, no – please, no . . .*

But though the sight of the corpse appalled her, Cassia's attention was drawn away by the other figures in the courtyard.

Incredibly the two sorcerers still stood at either end, facing each other. Splattered with blood and dirt, their robes shredded, neither man had escaped injury. Baum's hair had burned away, his face seared as though by the sun itself. Blood dripped from his fingertips to the scorched stone at his feet. His breath was ragged, his mouth twisted in pain. His shoulders had slumped and, as Cassia watched, he collapsed to his knees, barely catching himself before toppling onto his side.

Malessar had fared no better. His left arm hung mangled by his side and blood stained his face. He held his right hand to his chest to stem the flow from a large wound, and he swayed on his feet, staggering forward to lean against the ruined fountain.

It was a stalemate. Both sorcerers had expended their full strength against each other; now neither man was in any condition to continue. Their struggle for the future of the North would not be resolved here.

She should be moving, she thought remotely. They would need help. Though how could she begin to help a sorcerer?

To tend wounds caused by such awful magic? She felt utterly helpless, and she could not make herself step forward.

Because I have to choose. I have to choose which man to help first. And that choice decides where my loyalties should lie.

Malessar was a murderer. He had twisted history for hundreds of years. He had destroyed the whole kingdom of Caenthell, ruined the world he had known, all because of one terrible fit of impassioned anger. But she thought she had come to understand Malessar much better – even to like him – and she did not believe he was the monstrous tyrant Baum had described with such passion. He had treated her with kindness, had let her through the defences he had constructed over centuries. A proud man, and stubborn too, but principled and fair. A man who regretted everything he had so recklessly done, and who had been brought close to death for those sins.

Baum's obsessive quest for vengeance had almost killed him too, she saw as she turned to look at the old soldier. Even as his body twisted and failed under him, Baum stretched out a burned arm to claw the ground, a pale sorcerous nimbus barely surrounding his fingers. He was so single-minded that he would use the remnants of his powers against his old enemy rather than heal his own wounds.

If he will not help himself then he'll never help anybody else, she thought suddenly, knowing the truth at last.

Malessar coughed and spat blood to clear his mouth. "Enough," he said. His voice had lost its commanding tone, but the word still echoed across the yard. "This has gone on too long."

Baum raised his head. Cassia shuddered at the malice in his eyes. "For once we are in agreement," he snarled.

"There is nothing to be won here," Malessar continued wearily. "Stop this now, before more innocents are hurt or killed by your quarrel with me."

Baum laughed. Red-flecked spittle sprayed from the corners of his mouth. "Spare me your moralising! Did you worry about killing innocent people when you pulled Caenthell down stone by stone around us? Or when you abandoned the defence of Stromondor and left the city to be sacked by the Hordes? I held those gates for two and a half days! Why should you care now?"

The warlock wilted further. "Stromondor," he said, the word heavy with memories and regrets. "I had no idea you were there too."

"Would that have made a difference?" Baum spluttered and shook his head. "You did not care back then, and you do not care now. I'll not fall to honeyed words."

Cassia's attention was attracted by movement. A figure had emerged from the doorway to the main entrance of the *dhar*, and now stood concealed by one of the wide pillars.

Meredith.

Somehow she forgotten about him, and she felt a flash of guilt. He wore a soft Galliarcan shirt, loose over light breeches. His greatsword was belted, as always, over his back. The sight of him squeezed at her heart. She wanted to fling herself into his arms.

But now he was the Heir to the North. Here, that title was his armour, a wall she could not breach. More solid than the mountains, Meredith stared fixedly at the warlock. Cassia could not tell what he was thinking, or what he would do. *His revenge has come. Oh Meredith – please listen . . .*

"Stromondor was my home for over a century," Malessar said, a harder tone entering his voice. "I did not abandon it lightly, nor without reason. You have no right to accuse me of cowardice."

Using his staff to lever himself up, Baum rose to one knee. His only reply was a dismissive grunt.

Malessar drew himself up. "And *your* obsession? Caenthell? You have pursued that lost goal all this time? My death will not return Caenthell to life, nor the people who died within it. Believe me, if you will – if my death could bring anyone back to life I'd have opened my own wrists centuries ago. But that curse can never be lifted, Baum. Not unless you want to damn the whole world to hell. Pyraete's land has spoiled behind the curse wards. To remove them would unleash an unspeakable evil upon the world. I can show you that truth."

Cassia's breath caught as Baum stared steadily into the warlock's eyes and a hard, determined smile spread slowly across his face. She realized with a jolt that he didn't *care* what would emerge from behind the wards. Beating the curse – beating Malessar – was all that mattered to him. She flicked a glance at Meredith and saw with despair that his expression mirrored that resolve.

"You have no choice in this matter," Baum said. "I have not been idle since our paths last crossed. I know the making of curses now; more, I know the *breaking* of curses. This curse, in particular. As much as I wish to, *I* will not kill you."

His head turned and he looked across the yard. Malessar's troubled gaze followed, his brow creased as he tried to grasp Baum's meaning.

Meredith came forward, his stride measured and merciless. Cassia rose to her feet, her heart hammering, indecision suddenly banished from her mind.

The Heir to the North halted a few steps from the ruined fountain. "I am Meredith of Caenthell," he announced.

Malessar stared at him for a long moment. Then he sighed. "You favour your illustrious ancestor, Meredith of Caenthell. A well-designed plan; you would undo me by the terms of my own curse. You have worn me down. I cannot defend myself with sorcery and I am maimed. Very well, so be it. I will not *give* you my sword, however. You must take it from me."

Meredith's reply was the rasp of metal as he drew his sword and settled into a practised two-handed stance. Cassia could think only of the great shrine filled with shieldmen that had frightened her so badly. Meredith resembled one of those constructs, indomitable and implacable. Malessar straightened, stepping gingerly away from the fountain, turning to reduce his profile. The warlock looked exhausted and his sword wavered in his hand. This would be a brief and unworthy fight, Cassia thought.

"Meredith, wait." She moved forward at last, stumbling out from the bottom of the stairwell. "You can't do this. You *mustn't* do this. Malessar's right."

Neither Meredith nor Malessar appeared to have heard her. Their attention remained fixed on each other. Somewhere behind them Baum's low chuckle turned into a hacking cough.

"Meredith, I've been to Caenthell." She tried again, desperately. "Something is waiting there, waiting for the curse to be broken. Can't you see how wrong it would be to do this? Please Meredith, *listen* to me!"

It had no effect. The young prince began to move, inching around to Malessar's left, aiming to slip past his guard. Malessar was forced to react, staggering back a step as he turned.

There was no other way, she thought. It was inevitable. Her story could only end in this manner. Cassia stepped between the pair. "This will not go on," she declared. "If you will not put up your sword, Meredith, you will have to kill *me* first."

Finally his dark eyes locked onto her and she was shocked to see a sad smile settle upon his face. "This fight is my life," he said softly, but his blade never wavered. "This is who I am, why I exist. You do not understand that. It is not my wish to see you hurt in this."

His gaze flickered for a second in Baum's direction and his voice lowered to a whisper. "You may still walk away before this tragedy goes further."

She blinked. He was trying to tell her something, but her mind was so awhirl and battered by the sorcerous battle that she could not comprehend the meaning behind his words. *I have made my decision, for good or for ill. I cannot stand down now.*

Cassia pulled the sword of Pelicos from its sheath. Meredith inclined his head and took a few steps back to give her room.

The sad smile was still upon his lips.

Malessar said something, but Cassia did not hear it. The crushing roar in her head blocked out both his voice and Baum's feeble, croaking laughter. Her arms trembled as adrenaline surged through her body.

Gelis. Pelicos. Lend me your strength, your skill, your luck. She would either be a hero, or else dead.

She stepped forward to close him down, as he had taught her to do. Such a heavy blade needed space to swing and cause damage, while her own sword was more suited to close quarters. It was still nowhere near a fair fight. Meredith was worth ten or more of Yaihl, her last opponent.

Meredith was still in his opening guard stance. Now he sprang aside and his sword came down hard at an angle, a crippling cut aimed at her hip. At the last moment he hauled the blade up again to complete the v-shaped stroke, finishing exactly where Cassia would have been had she stepped inside the blow to attack him. The blade whistled through empty air. Cassia had darted ahead of Meredith's movement, leaving him struggling to catch up as she twisted back and jabbed at his arm, tearing cloth and slicing into his flesh.

A hit! She would have revelled in her success, but this was no practice bout. She had cut him once, now she had to do it again.

Meredith grunted. He brought his sword around in an arc, forcing her back, the notched edge a bare inch from her stomach. Her strike already felt years distant. Meredith had to keep the heavy blade moving to remain a threat, but the weight behind it meant he could finish her off with a single blow. Cassia was painfully aware of her vulnerability.

She glimpsed his face as she sought safer ground. Even though his attention was on her, he seemed distant, withdrawn. He was not using his full strength against her, she thought. That angered her more than she had believed it would.

"Fight me, damn you," she shouted. "Fight me or renounce your claim!"

She remembered how she had fought him in Hellea, using his forms against him. She broke up her own movements, scooping up a handful of dirt to throw at his face. A jab became a kick, in the manner of Galliarcan street fights. Still there was that sad smile on his face as he deflected her attacks and sought his own advantage.

She circled, feinted left, trying to draw him into committing. Meredith was by far the better swordsman. He stepped and swung through forms that never left him unbalanced, never lowering his guard, never taking his eyes from her.

She had scored once. He wouldn't let that happen again.

And she was tiring.

Her ears still rang from the magical battle, and her sight was clouded by white spots she couldn't blink away. Meredith's sword seemed to leave a luminous trail in the air, drawing her attention away from him. Cassia's breath came harder, and her limbs ached with fatigue. She feared dropping her sword every time she met Meredith's own blade.

He pressed in suddenly and his speed overwhelmed her. Cassia was forced back, up against the fountain. She ducked and rolled, hearing the blade slice above her, brick chipping into her face. She slashed with her own sword at his unprotected calves.

But Meredith was not there.

Cassia rolled again, this time with no aim, just a reflexive urge to defend herself. She searched desperately for him as she scrambled across the ground, hearing Malessar's shout of warning far too late.

Meredith's boot landed under her ribs, sending her sprawling. Her blade was knocked from her grasp as the flat of his greatsword smashed against her wrist. She heard bone crack, and her vision flared white for an instant. She tasted blood, and the breath exploded back into her lungs with the pain of defeat.

Meredith stood a pace away, his expression remote. The point of his sword aimed down at her chest. Cassia didn't need the surging pain in her right hand to tell her the fight was done. Her life contracted to the foreshortened steel blade in front of her.

No heroes to save her, no gods to hold fate in abeyance. Just a girl whose story was ended. She had been a fool to think she could ever achieve anything by this.

It's over.

She stared up at the Heir to the North, knowing that his face would be the last thing she'd ever see. There might still be enough time to say –

"Cassia!"

Malessar's voice. She had time for the briefest glance to see him holding his own sword as if about to throw it to her. She raised her uninjured hand to snatch the hilt as it curved through the air. *A chance -*

As her fingers closed around the warm, leather-bound hilt time slowed to a crawl. She felt every stitch of the binding, saw every tiny nick collected upon the blade over the countless centuries. The pain of every wound it had inflicted coursed through her blood.

Her world exploded into violence.

She screamed.

When the light receded, after an eternal second, she gasped. She had to force herself to breathe. Malessar's sword had fallen from her hand and she grasped the bricks around the fountain, hauling herself upright, unable to explain how or why she was still alive.

Something has changed. Something is very wrong.

Baum and Malessar lay in untidy heaps on the ground, puppets thrown carelessly aside by the force of whatever had happened. Neither man was moving.

Meredith was as a statue before her, on one knee, head bowed. His sword lay at his feet. *A vassal making tribute to his liege. Just as Pelicos might have once done.*

"Meredith?" Nothing made any sense to her. Her failing sense of balance made the ground tilt like the deck of Sah Ulma's ship. "Meredith, what's happened?"

The Heir to the North did not reply. Cassia realised with mounting alarm that she could see no sign of him breathing. The wound she had inflicted did not bleed at all. She reached out to touch his cheek with a trembling hand. His skin was cold and unyielding, hard as stone.

Measured, even, emotionless. Words she had always used to describe him. Practised, efficient and unvarying. Not so much cold-blooded as bloodless.

Automaton. Shieldman.

It should have been so obvious.

I taught myself everything that Malessar ever learned. Everything.

But it made no sense. No sense at all. Meredith was Heir to the North . . .

Baum's belaboured gasps penetrated her shocked silence. The soldier still lived, although surely not for much longer. She staggered over to kneel by his battered body, rising anger driving her on through pain and exhaustion.

Baum's gaze fixed on her for a moment then slid away. "It is done. At last. Avenged. Revenged . . ."

"But Meredith—"

"Hah. A tool for the job. No more. I told you. Fooled him—" Baum coughed and fought for words. "Fooled them all."

A tool. No . . .

My flesh and blood is of the mountains, he had said.

Cassia put her hand to her mouth, horror hammering into her heart. The courtyard had become a cold, inhospitable place, despite the heat of the smouldering garden. Again, there was a precipice under her feet – but this time she had already stepped over the edge.

Meredith was no prince. He'd looked and acted the part, but that had been deliberate. Part of the design. In the end he had been nothing more than a decoy, intended to distract Malessar – distract him from . . .

Oh gods, no . . .

"I knew. Knew his temper. Knew he'd return. Save the child – my duty . . . Jedrell taught us both, you see . . ."

Baum reached up suddenly to grasp her shoulder. "Show your enemy what he expects to see, Aliciana."

Cassia pulled away, horrified, and Baum fell back, too weak to help himself any further.

"You bastard." She wept openly now. "You *bastard*. What have you done?" It was all she could do not to kick him as Meredith had kicked her, to finish him off.

Aliciana. I am descended from Aliciana. And from Jedrell. And Malessar passed his sword to me.

"The curse is broken." The truth crashed down around her, powerful as sorcery. "He gave me his sword *freely* . . ."

Baum's eyes had glazed. "Aye," he whispered. "The curse is broken. The High King returns. I can feel him. Aliciana . . ."

Malessar's *dhar* was silent once more.

Cassia stood at last, painfully, and looked around her as she scraped her hair away from her face. She had been played false, played for a fool. Everything she thought she knew was a lie. Baum's quest, Meredith's heritage, Malessar's sorrows – none of them had told her the truth. In her own ignorance she had set in motion this terrible train of events.

Malessar lay unconscious, face down in the dirt. He was breathing, which more than could be said for Baum and Meredith.

She rested her hand on the shieldman's head as she limped past. At the very last, Meredith had tried to stop this happening. He had tried to warn her – he had become almost independent.

He had become a man, and in defending Malessar she had unwittingly taken that away from him. Had he known what would happen? Had his last thought been of her?

She blinked back tears and went to Malessar's side. The least she could do now was to try to take care of the warlock.

And then . . . the High King would return.

The world already felt colder, more hostile. Cassia felt exposed in the courtyard, even with the high walls that enclosed it on all sides.

High above, the sky darkened. Cassia felt the storm gathering in the far distance.

I am the Heir to the North.

This is the end of Heir to the North.
The tale concludes in The High King's Vengeance.

Acknowledgements

There are a lot of people to thank, so let's get to it!

Sammy, Zoë, and Joanne for allowing me into the KI/Grimbold house. And all the friendly folks who live in that house!

Jorge Torres and Ken Dawson for the heroic cover; Joanne Hall (again!) for liberal application of the red pen.

Amanda Rutter, Lee Harris, and Elizabeth Bass were instrumental in encouraging the outward journey. The Incredible Inkbots also deserve a hundred loud huzzahs and your attention – Wes Chu, Laura Lam, JB Rockwell, Emma Maree, John Dixon, Rob Haines, Nate Green, KC Shaw, Josh Vogt, Andrea G Stewart, Lee Collins, Michael Pack, Megan Grey, Vonny McKay, and Michael F Stewart.

The very brilliant Sheffield SFF Writers' Group heard the whole story – most recently, Dave Lee, Dave Kirby, David Sarsfield, Mathew Presley, Chris Joynson, Spleeny, Kathryn Wild, Steven

Harrison, Jo Johnson-Smith, Darren Johnson-Smith, and Sara Smith.

All the excellent folks at Brian Turner's SFF Chronicles – including but not limited to Culhwch, Teresa Edgerton, The Judge, Sue Boulton, Jo Zebedee, Boneman, Harebrain, Pyan, Chrispy, & Panu.

Also big shouts to Alex Bardy, Andrew Reid, Anne-Mhairi Simpson, Alasdair Stuart, Ian Sales, Jo Thomas, Adele Wearing and the Skulk, Alex Davis, Andy Angel, Gary Compton, Richard Webb.

Of course, none of this would have happened if my uncle Andrew Hunt hadn't emigrated to South Africa, leaving behind three fridge-sized boxes crammed full of assorted genre fiction. And it certainly wouldn't have happened if my parents Judith & Ralph Poore hadn't encouraged all of us young 'uns to read above our years. A thousand thanks.

Most importantly, thanks and love to Rachel Rose, first reader and equal in all.

A Selection of Other Titles from Kristell Ink

Cruelty by Ellen Crosháin

Once a year, in the caves deep below the house, the Family gathers to perform a ritual to appease their god. But Faroust only accepts payment in blood.

Eliza MacTir, youngest daughter of a powerful Irish family, was born into fae gentry without the magical gifts that have coursed through the Family's veins for millennia; she was an outcast from her first breath. Desperate for freedom, Eliza's flight from rural Ireland is thwarted by the Family's head of security. The only weapon she has to fight her captor is her own awakening sexuality.

Drawn into the world of magic and gods, Eliza must find a way to break free, even if it means breaking the hearts of those she loves, and letting her own turn to stone.

Cruelty, it runs in the Family.

The Book of Orm by A.J Dalton

This exciting new collection brings together the writing talents of international fantasy author A J Dalton, Nadine West (Bridport Anthology) and Matt White (prize-winning script-writer). Magic, myth and heroic mayhem combine in a world that is eerily familiar yet beautifully liberating.

Fear the Reaper by Tom Lloyd

All Shell has ever wanted was a home, a place to belong. But now an angel of the God has tracked her down, intent on using her to hunt the demon that once saved her. The journey will take her into the dead place beyond the borders of the world, there to face her past and witness the coming of a new age.

A stand-alone novella from the author of *The Twilight Reign* series and *Moon's Artifice*.

CPSIA information can be obtained
at www.ICGtesting.com
Printed in the USA
LVOW12s2353181216
517872LV00002BA/202/P